*Behind*
*The*
*Velvet*
*Curtain*

*Dedication*

*To my son, Edwin, my daughter-in-law, Jennifer,
and our wonderful little granddaughter, Catherine Elanor.*

*Thank you for sharing your talents with me.
Your constructive criticism has been invaluable.
It has always been seasoned with humor and tempered by patience.
Without your help, this book would be quite other than it now is!*

# Behind The Velvet Curtain

*by*
Trudy Harvey Tait

**BRITISH ADDRESS**
Harvey Christian Publishers UK
P.O. Box 510, Cheadle
Stoke-on-Trent, ST10 2NQ
Tel./Fax (01538) 752291
E-mail: jjcook@mac.com

**UNITED STATES ADDRESS**
Harvey Christian Publishers, Inc.
3107 Hwy. 321, Hampton, TN 37658
Tel./Fax (423) 768-2297
E-mail: books@harveycp.com
http://www.harveycp.com

Copyright 2007 by Trudy Harvey Tait

Printed in USA

All rights reserved. No part of this book may be reproduced or transmitted in any form or by any means, electronic or mechanical, including photocopying, recording, or by any information storage and retrieval system without written permission from the copyright owner, except for the inclusion of brief quotations in a review.

Cover design by Malcolm Farrar

ISBN   978-1-932774-70-2

Printed by
Old Paths Tract Society
Shoals, IN

# List of Main Characters from *The Velvet Curtain*

*Esther Popescu:* A beautiful Romanian girl who has been bereaved of both parents and comes to live with her uncle and his family in America in the 80's. Esther has suffered much for her faith in Romania but soon realizes that Christianity in the USA is quite different. She also discovers, that while she has escaped the Iron Curtain, she is gradually becoming enveloped in its Western counterpart—the Velvet Curtain.

*Gabby Popescu:* (Gabriella) Esther's younger sister who eventually joins Esther in America.

*John Popescu:* Esther and Gabby's uncle who immigrated to America in the 60's.

*Mary Popescu:* John's ex-wife and Esther and Gabby's aunt by marriage.

*Ramona Popescu:* Mary and John's elder daughter.

*Rachel Popescu:* Mary and John's younger daughter.

*Aunt Ana:* Esther and Gabby's aunt (adopted sister of Esther's mother) who still lives in Romania.

*Ron Atwood:* Esther's former fiancé.

*Diane Atwood:* Ron's mother who eventually becomes John's second wife.

*Len Atwood:* Ron's cousin and youth pastor of Pine Grove Evangelical Church.

*Keith Cripps:* Pastor of Pine Grove Evangelical Church.

*Betty Cripps:* Keith's wife.

*Margaret Cripps:* Betty and Keith's daughter.

*Hugh Gardner:* The Christian gentleman whom Esther meets while coming over to the States. It is he who warns her of the Velvet Curtain.

*Aaron Gardner:* Hugh's grandson.

# Foreword

In writing my first novel, *The Velvet Curtain*, I fulfilled my long-cherished desire to write something that would help young people, and older ones too, become aware of the dangers which confront Christians who are striving to live out their faith in a materialistic and amoral society. Growing up during the Cold War, I heard frequent testimonies of those who had suffered for their faith in Communist lands. In the twenty-first century, although the Iron Curtain may have indeed fallen, its Western counterpart still makes itself felt in every land where freedom professes to hold sway.

*Behind The Velvet Curtain* continues the saga of Esther and her friends who have insisted that their full story has not quite been told! Exploring the various ways in which Esther seeks to escape the Velvet Curtain has made me retrace my own spiritual pilgrimage. I realize afresh that God often allows suffering into our lives to redirect us into the path of His choosing.

If, as you read this book, you discover that the story takes unpredicted twists and turns, it is because God's marvelous grace produces miracles in the lives of flawed and erring human beings, upsetting the smooth flow of their earthbound existence and giving them an eternal perspective which becomes life-changing.

I wish to express my heartfelt thanks to Beulah Freeman, Margaret Smith, Jean Ward, and Ottie Mearl Stuckenbruck, for their invaluable assistance in proofreading. I am also deeply indebted to my husband, Barry, my son and daughter-in-law, Edwin and Jennifer Woodruff Tait, and to Marie Geisler, for their part in editing the manuscript and for their timely advice and encouragement.

I do trust that *Behind The Velvet Curtain* will not only prove to be a captivating and moving story, but that it will remind all who read it that God's grace knows no boundaries, and if we let it, will make our lives fragrant with His Presence at unexpected times and in unexpected places. It will turn our failures into divine possibilities and lead us in paths of which we have never dreamed. As we close the last page of this book, may we echo the words of Esther and Gabby, Ron and Len, that in the final analysis, it is always and ever, "Only By Grace."

Trudy Harvey Tait
Hampton, Tennessee
October, 2007

## Contents

| Chapter | Page |
|---|---|
| 1 Hurrah for Romania! | 9 |
| 2 Great Aunt Lucy | 17 |
| 3 The Two Sisters | 23 |
| 4 Gabby Goes Home | 33 |
| 5 New Year with Uncle John | 44 |
| 6 Ron and Rachel | 55 |
| 7 Meeting of the Clans | 60 |
| 8 All for the Kingdom? | 71 |
| 9 Len in Shock | 77 |
| 10 Ramona's Wedding | 82 |
| 11 Summer Vacation | 91 |
| 12 Summer at Silver Springs | 102 |
| 13 Caught in the Middle | 115 |
| 14 Outside the Velvet Curtain | 122 |
| 15 Ploieşti Again! | 131 |
| 16 Rachel Gets the Message | 138 |
| 17 Another Proposal | 148 |
| 18 One Last Try | 155 |
| 19 Graduation | 161 |
| 20 Esther Sings Again | 166 |
| 21 The Fourth of July | 173 |
| 22 Len Comes to Tiny Gap | 185 |
| 23 At the Hospital | 194 |
| 24 Esther Awakes | 203 |
| 25 Gabby Gets the News | 207 |
| 26 Gabby's Choice | 212 |
| 27 Under the Bandages | 217 |
| 28 I Want to Die! | 228 |
| 29 Len Takes a Break | 236 |
| 30 The Velvet Curtain Again | 240 |
| 31 In the Looking-Glass | 246 |
| 32 Love or Lunacy? | 249 |
| 33 The Proof of Love | 257 |
| 34 Aunt Lucy Drops a Bombshell! | 266 |
| 35 Duets | 272 |
| 36 Gabby in Shock | 282 |
| 37 Dr. Garrington's Prescription | 294 |
| 38 Wedding of the Century! | 299 |

# Chapter One

## *Hurrah for Romania!*

"Down with Ceaucescu! Up with freedom!" Gabby's voice vibrated through the two-bedroom apartment as she threw a dish towel in the air and pirouetted around the room.

"Keep your voice down, please. You'll waken the neighbors," her cousin warned, as she stepped into the sitting room, coffee cup in hand.

"But Rachel, the Revolution's come at last!" Gabby exploded, seizing Rachel's arm and trying to waltz her around the room.

Rachel pulled herself away and stared in dismay at her half-empty coffee cup. "Now look what you've done! Can't you get a grip on yourself?" she began, and then stopped short. Gaping at the TV screen, she flopped into the nearest chair.

"Down with Communism. We want free elections!" the crowd was yelling wildly. Rachel pinched herself just to make sure it wasn't all a dream. It was the kind of thing you read about in high-school history books. She peered closer.

"Hurrah for Romania!" Gabby began again, grabbing her cousin by the hand and pulling her to her feet. "Can't you get a bit excited about all this? After all, you've got Romanian blood in you, haven't you?"

"You never let me forget that," Rachel grumbled, making for her bedroom. She needed a bit of peace and quiet. "But after all, I was born here in the States and I've never even been to Romania."

"So what?" Gabby chided. "Once Romanian, always Romanian. Oh well," she added with a pout as she released her cousin's hand, "seems like I'm the only one who really cares about what's going on." She eased herself onto the floor, crossed her legs, and stared into the TV.

"Don't be so judgmental," Rachel remonstrated. "I'll celebrate when I'm certain there's something to celebrate about. You don't know what turn all this will take. I'm afraid what the *Securitate* will do now. They won't let this go on. And what chance have the people of Timisoara against them?"

"You're so calculating," Gabby began, and then she stopped suddenly. Her face clouded as she went on more slowly: "But maybe you're right, after all. Come to think of it, a lot of Romanians could be killed before this is all over."

"What has actually been happening this week?" Rachel asked as she pulled up the blinds.

"Well," her cousin began, smoothing out her red and black striped robe as she spoke, "with all our cramming for exams, we haven't been following the news, that's obvious. It seems that a Hungarian pastor from Timisoara has openly criticized the way the Hungarians are being treated. Of course, the government is not going to stand for this sort of thing and has threatened to deport him, but crowds have gathered near the pastor's home in protest." Gabby paused a moment before adding, "I've just got to ring my sister about this. I wonder if she's heard yet."

Gabby reached for the phone as she spoke. She dialed her aunt's number, but it was busy. "Probably trying to phone us," she said with a laugh. "After all, it isn't every day that old Ceaucescu's put in his place."

A few minutes later, the phone rang. It was Esther. She had been up for hours but had waited till she thought the girls would be awake before phoning.

"I still can't believe it," she told Gabby, "and," she went on, changing her tone, "if this revolution succeeds, you know what this might mean for us, don't you?"

"What?"

"It'll mean we can go back home, of course."

Gabby's mouth fell open. She just couldn't picture her meek and decorous sister a part of the noisy mob she had just been seeing on TV. "Sure, I can't wait to visit Romania again and see how this will all work out, but…"

"I don't mean just visit. I mean live there again." Esther's voice was quiet but determined.

"You mean you're going to up and leave here right away?"

Her sister gave one of her low, silvery laughs. "Don't be silly! I've another year and a half to go yet before I finish college. But if this revolution has its way and Ceaucescu goes forever, well then, it'll mean that my dream can come true."

"What dream?"

"To be able to live in Romania again." Esther's voice trembled just a little as she went on, "I'd like to be somewhere where there's no Velvet Curtain."

Gabby frowned. Her sister very rarely talked like this since she had been ill over a year previous. But thoughts like that weren't for today. Today was a day to celebrate, or at least to prepare for the celebrations which seemed sure to come sooner or later. So she only said, "Well, I suppose what's happening today in Timisoara will influence both of us in one way or another. We're still Romanians, you know."

"Of course we are and always will be."

Gabby smiled. Esther might not seem as nationalistic as she was, but when it boiled down to it, she was a loyal Romanian to the core. "By the way, have you phoned Uncle John yet?" Gabby asked.

"Yes. I did it hours ago. He says he's afraid to get his hopes up. But I've not phoned our cousin, Ramona, yet."

"I'll do it now. See you next week." Gabby put the receiver down, feeling just a little confused. She had thought that she would have been the one to run back to Romania at a moment's notice, not Esther. But now she wasn't so sure. America was a great place to live in. Of course, she'd go visit whenever she could afford it. But as for the Velvet Curtain, it was all in her sister's imagination. Maybe she hadn't gotten over that rheumatic fever properly.

Gabby shook herself. This wasn't the time for daydreaming. She grabbed the receiver and dialed her cousin's number. Claude Iliescu, Ramona's boyfriend, answered the phone. Ramona was still sleeping, he told her. Gabby had found out only the week before that Claude and her cousin had just become engaged and that John was really upset about it.

"I've just told Ramona I'd go to Timisoara tomorrow if I could," she heard Claude say. His deep, guttural voice grated on her more than usual that morning. After over twelve years in America, he still spoke with an even thicker accent than she did. "I'm a real good shot," he went on, "and I'd love to have a share in splattering Ceaucescu's blood all over that beautiful palace of his." Gabby shuddered. There was an intensity in his voice which almost frightened her.

She had just pulled on her jeans and sweater and brushed out her thick mop of hair, when the visitors began to arrive. Other students had heard the news and thought they'd drop by. It was lunchtime, however, before Andrea arrived, bringing her brother, Larry, with her. She had met Andrea when they were both acting in *As You Like It* that October. They had taken to each other instantly. Gabby admired everything about her new friend—her red-gold hair, slightly turned up nose, and hazel eyes. She was glad that she would become her roommate after the Christmas vacation.

"This is my brother, Larry, girls. He's a doctoral student at Harvard," Andrea announced, as she shut the door behind her.

Gabby's eyes opened wide. "Wow!" she exclaimed, making no attempt to hide her admiration.

Larry frowned at his sister. He had warned her to omit the word *Harvard* in her introductions, but it was like talking to a brick wall. "Yes," Andrea went on, smiling sweetly, "he's brilliant, and his field is psychology. But he's really cool if you get on the right side of him."

"Then you'd better teach me how to stay on his right side," Gabby said with a merry laugh as she tossed back her thick wavy hair which she had allowed to grow shoulder length for the play. She grinned up at the tall, slim young man and held out her hand. "Hi," she said, fixing her expressive eyes on Larry's face. "I feel as if I sort of know you already. Andrea's always talking about you."

"That's not saying much," Larry retorted. "Andrea's always talking about everyone and everything, though," he added, smiling down on her, "she tells me she's met her match at last."

"I'm afraid she's right," Gabby admitted. "I talk non-stop, don't I, Rachel? By the way, this is my cousin," and she waved her hand in Rachel's direction. "But come on, have lunch with us. I've made enough food to feed a multitude."

Larry caught her gaze and held it for just a moment. Then he gave a short laugh as he ran his hand through his curly auburn hair and dropped into the nearest seat. His smile was very charming, Gabby thought, and everything about him spoke of class. He had blue eyes, too. She was partial to blue eyes, though his, she had to admit, were not sparkling like her cousin Ramona's, or warm and friendly like their friend Ron's. In fact, she could feel those eyes on her as she turned to the stove to finish off the hamburgers. She was quite sure he had analyzed her already.

"Come on guys, eat up," Gabby exclaimed, as she took a plate of tomatoes and lettuce from her cousin and placed it on the table. "You know, this is one of the most exciting days in my whole life! Can you imagine it? Liberty in my country! Just think, there'll soon be lights in the streets, food in the stores, freedom of speech and religion, and…"

"Hold on," Larry interrupted. "It won't happen that fast, even if this revolution is a success."

"Pessimist?" The girl's voice was half playful, half reproachful.

"Realist!" Larry retorted.

"Can realists not be optimists too?"

"Sure can."

"But not usually?" Gabby persisted.

"I think there are realists who are pessimists and realists who are optimists. I've read a fair bit about revolutions and what follows, and based my statement on facts."

"But your personality probably affects your interpretation of history, doesn't it? You can't be objective all the time!" Gabby protested. "Or are you some super historian, someone you read about in books but don't believe they ever exist in real life?"

Larry grinned. Andrea was right, he thought. This girl was going to be great fun to know. "Of course I can't be completely objective," and he gave a short laugh, "but…"

"Oh, come on," Andrea interrupted. "Continue your argument when you're alone. There'll be no peace now," she said, turning to Rachel. "Larry will never rest till he's had the last word."

Gabby rose from her chair. "Well, whatever the future holds for Romania," she told her friends, "the unbelievable has happened today. Excuse me, but I'm going in to see if there's any more news." And she took her plate and slipped into the living room.

Andrea and her brother stayed all afternoon and evening. In between listening to flashes of news about the revolution, they played music, ate cookies and ice cream, and watched a movie. But always the conversation turned back to the momentous events in Romania.

As the clock struck twelve, Andrea and Larry rose to go. "See you next semester," Andrea told her friend as she made for the door. "It'll be great to be roommates. But what are you doing for Christmas?"

"Going to Great Aunt Lucy's with my sister," her friend told her with a slight grimace. "I'm a bit afraid of my ancient relative. They say she's very strict, very opinionated, and very eccentric."

"Good luck!"

"Well, we won't be with her that long," Gabby explained. "We're spending the New Year with my uncle in Velours."

"Why, that's near us," Larry said in surprise.

"Yes, we live in Indianapolis," added Andrea. "Let's get together while you're up there. Here's our phone number," and she slipped her friend a piece of paper.

"Thanks. And a very merry Christmas to you both!" Gabby told them as she followed them into the hallway.

"Happy Holidays and take care!" Andrea said over her shoulder as she took her brother's arm and made for the stairs.

"Have you met Gabby's family?" Larry asked, as they stepped out into the frosty December night.

"No. I haven't met them. I've seen pictures, though. Her sister's a real beauty."

"Gabby's not bad looking herself."

"Not bad at all. In fact, she's pretty attractive, or so most of the guys at college seem to think. And she's bright too. She has most of the professors on their toes—never stops asking questions. I'm glad you've met her at last."

"So am I."

"She's great fun even though she is a bit odd at times."

"Meaning?"

Andrea gave a short laugh. "You'll soon find out if you hang out with her long enough. But," and her face darkened a little, "I hope you won't change her too much. It's her *old world* charm that makes her so fascinating. And I want her to stay that way. Better remember that, Mr. Larry Porter!"

"As if I'd try to change anyone!"

"Oh yes?" Andrea laughed. "You maybe don't know it, Larry, but you've a very strong personality."

"Me?" Larry exclaimed, as he swung the car onto the highway. "Well, that friend of yours seems to know her own mind. I wouldn't think she's very easily influenced. But then, I hardly know the girl."

Andrea was silent. She hoped it had been a wise thing to introduce her friend to her smart and sophisticated brother. Then she smiled into the darkness. She didn't need to worry. Gabby was one of a kind and she didn't think anyone in the whole world could ever *unGabby* her.

Gabby didn't sleep much that night and could hardly wait until it was time for the morning news. It seemed that, at last, orders had been given to subdue the protestors in Timisoara. The Securitate had moved in with tanks and helicopter gun-ships and had opened fire on the crowds. There were several hundred casualties reported in this first clash.

As a new week dawned, it seemed that the people of Romania were proving more than a match for the Secret Police. By the time the two cousins reached their home in Tiny Gap that Wednesday, it was announced on the evening news that the demonstrations were spreading to other cities. "Look," shouted Gabby gleefully, "the crowd is turning on Ceaucescu, at least some of them are."

"Yes, but they're being fired on," and Esther hid her face in her hands. "I can't bear to look. Our friends might be among them." A government sponsored rally had been staged in Bucharest, but it had obviously not turned out as the organizers had planned.

At last the news was over and they all gathered round the table for supper. Mary was like a clucking hen, delighted to have all of her brood under her wings again. After her ex-husband had remarried over a year ago, she had moved from Indiana to the mountains of Tennessee and had found a rented house in Tiny Gap where she had opened her doors and her arms to her two orphaned nieces.

"It's happening at last and it's spreading," Gabby exclaimed, as she took a second helping of chicken casserole.

"I know," Esther replied. "I just can't believe it." She glanced at her sister from across the table and thought how she had matured over the past months. A year before, Gabby had enrolled at the University of Tennessee where Rachel was already studying, but Esther had preferred to stay close home and commute to a Christian school about thirty minutes away. At first, the sisters had seen each other every second weekend or so, but after the first semester, Gabby had announced that she couldn't come home that often. Esther had wondered at that. If Rachel could make it to Tiny Gap every few weeks, then surely her Gabby could too.

Gabby sensed Esther's eyes upon her. She flushed a little as she pushed aside her plate and leaned back in her chair. "I wonder where it will all end," she exclaimed, looking round the table.

"In a free Romania," suggested Rachel.

"I sure hope so," Gabby's eyes sparkled as she spoke. "Romania—the land of the free. Sounds strange."

"I wonder what'll happen when freedom does come there," Esther remarked thoughtfully.

"Our friends will be able to live in peace and quietness at last and do absolutely anything they like for a change," Gabby answered quickly.

"But if freedom does come to Romania, do you think the Velvet Curtain will eventually spread there too?" Rachel asked suddenly. Her two cousins stared at her in surprise. "Of course not," Esther replied decidedly. "At least, it won't make much headway if it does. I mean, how could it? With all that Christians have suffered over there..." She stopped abruptly as she saw Rachel's expression and guessed what she was thinking.

"Oh, I know I suffered too and that didn't seem to help me escape it," she went on quickly, "but then, I was here in America; that was the problem."

Aunt Mary changed the subject quickly. "Come, girls. You're all tired, I think, and have seen enough of revolutions for one day. How about a game of Scrabble?"

"Great idea, Aunt. Do you know that I can actually beat your daughter now?"

"Once, Gabby Popescu, only once!" Rachel laughed. "Be honest!"

"Yes, but it was the last time we played, so watch out, Miss Champion!"

And so, for several hours at least, the Revolution was forgotten at Tiny Gap. In a few days, the two sisters would head off for the unknown. "Christmas with Great Aunt Lucy!" Gabby repeated to herself as she jumped into bed. And two whole weeks with her sister after being so long apart!

"*Noapte bună,*" she heard Esther saying from the next bed.

"*Noapte bună, dragă* (Good night, dear)," she answered back, her voice muffled by the blankets. She almost wished her sister wouldn't speak Romanian to her so often. It reminded her of the world she had left behind eighteen long months before. For right now, she was experiencing the American dream and wasn't about to let anything spoil it, not even her precious, wonderful sister.

## Chapter Two

### *Great Aunt Lucy*

Lucy Farthington drew back the frilly lace curtains and stared in dismay at the falling snow. She could see from the accumulation on the garage roof that about three inches had fallen already. She glanced uneasily at the clock on the mantelpiece and shook her head. More snow was forecast for that evening. Why on earth those great nieces of hers hadn't already arrived she had no idea. It was only a two hours' drive from Tiny Gap, and they were to have left right after lunch. Lucy didn't really approve of young girls gallivanting all over the country by themselves. It was dangerous, especially in the winter.

"Everything's ready, Miss Lucy," called a voice from the kitchen. "The beds are made up, and I've put out clean towels for each of the girls. The closet's emptied ready for them and the dresser, too."

"Good, Rita!" Lucy shouted back.

"Thought you'd be relieved to know all's in apple pie order," Rita went on. "And supper is nearly ready. The roast is just about cooked and all the veggies are peeled and in the pot. I just have to pop the biscuits in the oven and whip some cream for the pie."

"Great!" was the response. "We just need those girls to arrive, and then everything will be complete."

"They're probably stuck in a snow drift somewhere between Tiny Gap and here," Rita commented cheerfully as she entered the sitting room, wiping her hands on her checkered apron and heaving her three hundred pounds into the rocking chair by the window.

"Nonsense," Lucy said sharply. "There's not enough snow to get stuck in, at least not yet, though I suppose youngsters nowadays could get stuck in anything."

"I can't wait to see your great nieces," Rita bubbled, rubbing her hands together in excitement. "It was just a wonderful idea to invite them here for Christmas."

"Well," the old lady began slowly, "I thought I'd better get to know them before it was too late. I should have done it before, but somehow or other, I couldn't feel the time was ripe. There is a time for everything, you know. We mustn't run ahead of the Lord or lag behind Him."

"No, we mustn't," echoed Rita, leaning back in her chair.

Lucy said nothing. She did sometimes wish Rita would have the courage once in a while to differ with her. It was rather boring having your sentiments repeated back to you a hundred times a day. But then, that was certainly better than being contradicted all the time. So on the whole, it really suited her to have Rita about the place. At ninety, she couldn't live alone any more in her four bedroom, two-storey house, set back from the road amongst the pine trees. And so when Malcolm Morgan, the pastor of the small independent church just one mile up the road, had suggested Rita as a companion, it had seemed most providential.

"What do the girls look like?" Rita began again.

"I've no idea. I didn't want to see photos of them. First impressions are so important. I want my first glimpse of them to be in real life, not in photos." Miss Lucy tightened her lips and half closed her eyes. Rita knew better than to continue the conversation.

A whole half-hour passed by. There was no sound in the room but the ticking of the clock and the squeaking of the springs in Rita's chair as she slowly rocked back and forth, her eyes fixed on the old lady's immobile features.

Then, suddenly, the phone rang. Rita began to ease herself out of the chair. "I'll get it," Lucy told her as she rose to her feet. The phone had given eight rings by the time she finally reached it. The girlish voice at the other end of the line was clear as a bell. Miss Lucy listened a few moments in silence, one thin, wrinkled hand grasping the nearby table for support. Then she gave a gasp of dismay. "What? You've gone into the ditch? The car's been damaged?" Her voice was shrill and tense. "Well then, you need help," she went on. "Don't worry, I know someone down the road who can come and fetch you."

Lucy paused, her eyes narrowing as she listened. "What? Who? Aaron Gardner? Yes, I suppose it will have to be OK. Come when you can. Supper will be waiting. See you in no more than two hours, that is, if you don't go and get stuck again."

Lucy shook her head as she put down the receiver. "Those careless girls have gone into the ditch and their car's been damaged. So they've asked some man from Tiny Gap to drive them here. And they say he will probably need to stay the night. You'd better get the other spare room ready and air the bed. Oh dear, I do hope one of my nieces hasn't gone and gotten herself a boyfriend. They're both far too young for that."

"Just how old are they exactly?" Rita asked timidly.

"Oh, I'm not sure, maybe twenty and twenty-two."

Rita thought privately that it would be very surprising if the oldest one, at least, did not have a boyfriend. She did wish sometimes that Lucy Farthington wouldn't live in such an isolated world.

"I'm afraid I'm in for a load of trouble inviting these girls." Lucy gave a long sigh. She had known that this invitation of hers would greatly inconvenience her and shatter the very regular routine of her life. But she had done it for her brother's sake and now she must make the best of it.

Night had fallen and Rita had read two whole chapters of *Foxe's Book of Martyrs* to the old lady before they heard the sound of an engine chugging up their long driveway. Miss Lucy's pale face was unusually flushed as she opened the front door to welcome the weary travelers.

"Great Aunt Lucy!" a voice exclaimed in the darkness, and before she knew it, she found herself enfolded in her niece's arms.

"All right, all right," the old lady managed to say as she disentangled herself. "You don't need to smother me to death."

"Oh, I'm so sorry," the girl apologized, stepping back and pushing her sister forward as she did so. "It's just that I've been longing to meet you for ages now. We've so few living, flesh-and-blood relatives that meeting one of them is the event of the year. By the way, I'm Gabriella Maria Popescu, but please call me Gabby, and this is my older sister, Esther Lydia Popescu."

Miss Lucy gave them both a peck on the cheek and then she stopped. Looking over her shoulder, she caught sight of a figure shivering on the doorstep.

"Well, why don't you introduce me to your chauffeur, girls? Come in, young man, come in. You'll get your death of cold standing there."

"I'm sorry," Gabby apologized. "This is Aaron Gardner. Aaron, this is our Great Aunt Lucy."

The young man in the doorway shook the snow off his boots and stepped inside. "Pleased to meet you, Mrs. Farthington," he said, his lips chattering with cold. "I'm sorry to intrude like this, but someone had to come to the rescue of these maidens in distress."

"I suppose you weren't sorry to be their Good Samaritan, were you? Come in and shut the door. There, that's better." Miss Lucy held out her hand. "Thanks for bringing the girls. They need someone to keep any eye on them in this weather, that's obvious."

It was only when they were all sitting around the table in the large, old-fashioned kitchen that Miss Lucy had time to study her nieces. She had already summed up the youngest as a headstrong, impetuous girl, who needed a lot of restraint to keep her in check. But the other one had hardly said a word and looked very weary. She peered at her over her spectacles. "Hmm, very pretty indeed," she commented to herself. "Far too pretty I'm afraid." Her ninety years had taught her that beauty was often synonymous with vanity. And the girl seemed very reserved. That could mean deceit. Maybe the younger of the two would prove the safest after all.

Lucy turned her attention to the young man sitting opposite her at the far end of the table. "Aaron, are you any relation to Hugh Gardner of Tiny Gap?" she asked, peering at him over her spectacles.

Aaron smiled. "Yes. He's my grandfather. Do you know him?"

"I know *of* him. But then, who doesn't in these parts."

Aaron grinned. "Yes, Granddad is pretty notorious."

"Notorious?" Miss Lucy repeated with a frown.

Aaron reddened. "Well yes, in a good way, I mean. He's quite an individual," he explained, half apologetically.

"Yes. Must be from what I've heard. You are very fortunate to have a grandfather like that, you know."

Aaron nodded and eyed his plate. Sometimes having a wonderful relative like Hugh Gardner proved a mixed blessing. He looked up and caught Gabby's eye. She seemed to be reading his thoughts. He flushed a little and then said with a slight laugh, "Well, I think you must be quite an individual yourself, Miss Lucy. I've been scanning your books since I came. Quite a collection!"

The old lady raised her eyebrows. "You haven't had time to scan my books. You're flattering me."

Aaron took the bowl of vegetables from Gabby and spooned some onto his plate before replying: "I'm not flattering you. It's just that I'm always drawn to books. And I had more time than you think. The girls took at least ten minutes to get ready for supper, and you can notice a lot of books in ten minutes."

Miss Lucy nodded and decided that she rather liked this young man even though he was a bit eccentric. But then she was eccentric too, very! And they both loved books; that was common ground for a start. She hoped she'd get on as well with her two great nieces.

Lucy glanced over to where Gabby was sitting, quiet for once, and obviously enjoying her meal. She frowned a little. The girl's hair was too flyaway, and she had on pants. That was against her right away. But she had a bright, open face and was very attractive, too, in her own peculiar way. Her aunt looked again. Yes, she could see her dear brother in those grey-green eyes. The girl didn't look a bit Romanian.

Then her gaze fell on the older sister, her thick, dark, wavy hair tied back in a very respectable manner, and her long plaid skirt reaching nearly down to her ankles. Lucy wondered, as she motioned to Rita to bring in the dessert, why couldn't God have combined Gabriella's looks with Esther's subdued spirit? But then, who was she to dictate to God? And for once, she just might not be able to rely on first impressions.

It was nearly eleven before Gabby and Esther found themselves alone in their bedroom. Their aunt had insisted that Aaron read a chapter from the Bible and then had prayed almost round the world before finally kissing them goodnight.

"Great Aunt Lucy's quite a character," exclaimed Gabby as she took out her pajamas from her bag.

"Yes," agreed Esther with a smile. "She's much like I expected, though."

"Is she? No, I thought she would be short and plump and not as solemn. But she's still good looking even at ninety and very dignified. Her features look so very spiritual," Gabby said dreamily. Then she gave one of her chuckles. "But she certainly gave us both the once over. I'd give anything to know what she really thought of us. She seemed to quite like Aaron. His noticing her books did the trick."

"Yes, but I'm sure he didn't say it just to get on her good side," Esther commented as she hung up her skirt on a hanger.

"No, he seems to be a very decent sort of guy, from what I've seen of him at any rate, and that's not much."

Esther nodded. "You know," she said confidentially, "I've always thought that the two of you would get on great together if you really knew each other."

Gabby frowned. "I don't know about that, Esther. He's not my type at all."

"But why not? When you first came to Tiny Gap, I thought you liked him a lot."

Gabby gave her thick hair several vigorous strokes of her brush. "Oh, maybe," she said rather airily. "I was young and inexperienced then. Now…" she paused a moment, "well, my tastes have changed a bit, I suppose."

Esther bit her lip as she knelt down by the bed for her usual nightly devotions. Maybe spending this week together would give her a clue as to what was going on in Gabby's life.

Gabby grimaced. Her sister's piety sometimes made her feel like a heathen. Not that she had ever been very religious, but now she hardly ever knelt to pray. Why should she? It would just be hypocritical.

She reached for the book she had placed on the table by her bed and turned the pages slowly. It was about an American student who traveled to India and became greatly attracted to Hinduism. Gabby had always been rather curious about Eastern religions and talking to some Indian students at college had whetted her appetite to know more.

After a few moments' perusal, she put down the book and snuggled between the warm, fleecy blankets. She was tired, and there was no heat in the large, high-ceilinged room. She soon discovered, however, that Rita had thoughtfully turned on the electric blanket. Gabby gave a long, contented sigh as she closed her eyes and settled down for a good night's sleep.

Their adventure in the snow had been rather exhausting, and by the time the clock struck twelve, both sisters were already fast asleep. But in her room downstairs, Great Aunt Lucy was wide awake. This was a momentous event in her life—her brother Graham's grandchildren under her own roof! What purpose did the Lord have in this she wondered as she finally turned off the light? Only He knew that. She felt pretty certain, deep inside, that something would come of it, and those interior feelings of hers, she told herself as she turned to face the wall, had rarely ever let her down.

## Chapter Three

### *The Two Sisters*

"Esther, Esther, come quick. You'll never believe it. He's gone! It's all over! Three Cheers!" Gabby put her coffee cup on the table with a clatter and ran to the foot of the stairs.

"Gabriella, please, quiet now. We're not used to such noise in this house." Aunt Lucy's voice was stern as she put her bony hand on her great niece's shoulder.

"Oh but Aunt Lucy," the girl began, "don't you understand what's happened? He's gone! Ceaucescu's gone, and his wife too, the old hag!"

"Gabriella, do you need to use such words? And please calm down. Esther," she turned to her older niece who had just entered the kitchen, "please do something with your sister. She's beside herself."

"But listen, both of you, listen!" pleaded Gabby, pointing to the radio sitting on the table.

Esther walked over to the radio and sat down near it, bending closely to catch what the newscaster was saying. The reception wasn't very good.

"The turmoil of the past week has culminated in a final coup by the people of Romania," came the announcement.

"They've done it at last!" Gabby said in a loud whisper.

"Shhh!" Esther frowned, and leaned closer to the radio. "The dictator Ceaucescu and his wife have been captured as they were attempting to leave from the roof of the party headquarters by helicopter," the announcer continued, sounding very much as if dictators were captured every day from the top of buildings. "The people of Bucharest are going wild with joy. In fact, all over the country there are celebrations."

Gabby grabbed Esther and pulled her to her feet. She swirled her round the kitchen, stepping on her aunt's toes in the process.

"Gabriella," began Miss Lucy but it was no use. Her niece was transported to the seventh heaven.

"It has happened at last," Gabby panted, as she released Esther's hands and tried to regain her breath. "Please, Aunt Lucy, isn't there a TV in the house that we could watch? Right now? Please!" Gabby's voice was pleading, urgent.

Aunt Lucy drew herself to her full height and replied icily, "Gabriella, I never ever watch the TV except on very momentous occasions."

Gabby's eyes flashed dangerously though her voice was calm. "Aunt Lucy, if this isn't a momentous occasion, then what is?"

"Look, Gabriella," her aunt's voice was raised a little now, "if I got out the television every time there was a revolution somewhere on this globe, it would become a permanent fixture in my living room. And that's just what I won't have. It lets the world into our homes and poisons our thinking."

Gabby grabbed the old lady's hands in hers as she exclaimed excitedly, "But you do have one after all! And this isn't just any revolution. It's *our* revolution. And it's not happening just somewhere in the world. It's taking place in *our* land—the land your brother chose to spend his last days in. And *our* family, *our* friends might be involved in one way or other. Please, can't we see what's going on, just for the next few days?"

"I've told you, Gabriella," Lucy began and then she stopped. Something in Gabby's expressive face and the pleading in Esther's beautiful eyes made her bite her tongue. She remembered that these girls had lived most of their lives in Romania and had probably suffered indescribable hardships under their tyrannical leader.

"I'll have to pray about it," she told them. "Meanwhile, get your breakfast, both of you, and listen to the radio all you like."

Rita watched the old lady leave the room in amazement. If Miss Lucy yielded on this, then those great nieces of hers had some power of persuasion that no one else had.

Half an hour later and when Gabby was nearly beside herself with impatience, her aunt returned to the kitchen, a smile on her thin lips. "Well, Gabriella, I've just received the assurance that the Lord won't mind our bringing out the old TV that belonged to my son Donald, just for the next few days, that is."

Gabby put down her knife and fork with a clatter and ran over to her aunt. "Oh, thank you, Aunt Lucy. Now, can we help you set it up?"

Lucy frowned. The girl was so impetuous. "It's a bit heavy. Aaron can help. Have you forgotten about him in all this excitement?"

"I suppose we have." Gabby gave a short laugh. "After all, he wasn't at breakfast. I thought maybe he'd gone home."

"No, he's been up for hours. He's very kindly offered to dig out my driveway. It's covered in snow." Esther pushed back the frilly curtains. Sure enough, there was their chauffeur, shovel in hand, pausing in his work to survey nature's fairyland.

"He's eaten hours ago," Aunt Lucy continued. "And he's been into my books again. Strange boy. I'll call him in."

Half an hour later, Miss Lucy surveyed the ancient TV, hands on hips. "We'll put this away the moment the revolution's over," she announced.

"Romanian revolutions sometimes last for years, Aunt Lucy," Gabby said mischievously. Aaron turned his head away so the old lady couldn't see his smile.

"This is not a joking business, Gabriella," Miss Lucy chided.

"I agree." Gabby's face was sober now. "It's deadly serious. So do you mind if I put the TV on?" she asked, her finger on the knob.

Her aunt turned abruptly to face them. "Mind? No, I don't suppose so. But I'll just go to my room. I'd like to be alone a while. And remember, don't look at anything else, girls. Only the Revolution."

Esther reassured the old lady that they would certainly remember. Not that they could have watched much else, Gabby commented some time later. It had taken Aaron ten minutes to place the aerial in such a way that the images on the screen were at least semi-discernible.

"This TV's as old as Aunt Lucy," she remarked crossly, as she threw herself into Rita's rocking chair.

"Not quite, Gabby," the young man told her with a laugh. "Television hadn't even been invented when your great aunt was growing up. But look, at least you can see enough to know what's going on."

"But it's only black and white," she complained, pointing to the TV with a groan.

"What did you expect? Anyway, you asked for it," Esther went on in a tone her sister did not appreciate, "and that's what you've gotten. Personally, I'd rather listen to the radio."

"Go ahead then," Gabby said with a pout. "But now that the TV is here, I'll make the best of it." She felt out of sorts. She'd pretty much forced her aunt to go against her conscience and all for the privilege of straining her eyes at some vague images flitting about the screen.

By lunch time, Gabby had had enough. "We can put away the TV, Aunt," she declared, as she dished out the *ciorba*. Her sister had offered to make lunch and treated them all to a dish of good Romanian soup.

"After all that!" Lucy exclaimed. "Well I never!"

"Sorry, Aunt, but the reception's so bad we're only straining our eyes to watch it." Lucy's thin lips broke into a smile, but she said nothing.

"When do you have to go home, Aaron?" Gabby asked abruptly.

"Pretty soon. It looks as if there's more snow in the offing."

"Yes, young man," Miss Lucy told him. "I think there is, so you'd better be off when you've finished your dessert. But thanks so much for digging out my driveway. I really appreciated it."

"I enjoyed the exercise. I'm with books so much of my time, so work like this does me a world of good."

"So you're a regular bookworm?"

"My grandfather calls me a *bookaholic*."

Gabby's eyes widened. "That's a new word. Am I one too?"

Her sister looked at her fondly. "Sometimes; not always."

Aaron rose from the table. "By the way, a word about your car before I go. It needs to have the front fender straightened, the back right hand door won't open, and two of the tires are ruined."

Esther's face clouded. "Oh dear! And we planned to stay here till the 28$^{th}$."

"Don't worry," Aaron assured her. "We'll get it fixed for you, if that's OK, that is."

She shot him a grateful glance from under her long eyelashes. He reddened a little. "Not that I'm much good with cars," he said with a laugh, "but Granddad has a good mechanic who will see that it's back in working order by the time you're ready to come home. I thought," he cleared his throat as he caught Miss Lucy's eye, "that I could come back for you. I don't know any other way, though it means you won't have a car to use while you're here."

"Oh yes they will," said the old lady proudly. "I have one though I never drive it. But they probably won't need it. Malcolm, the pastor down the road, will drive them anywhere they need to go. In fact, I think he would gladly drive them back to Tiny Gap."

Esther's expression made Aaron say hastily, "It's all right. I'll come for them. Anyway, we'll keep in touch by phone. I've got to go now. Bye, girls; bye, Miss Lucy. Thanks for your hospitality."

Esther followed him out to his car. "Thanks a lot, Aaron. I don't know what we would have done without your help."

Aaron grinned. "I enjoyed it. Couldn't you tell?" He turned to get in the car then asked abruptly. "Is anything wrong with your sister?"

Esther stared at him. It seemed an odd question to ask out of the blue. "Well, she does seem a bit out of sorts today," she admitted thoughtfully.

"Yes, she does. Something seems to be bothering her."

"Maybe. Or maybe it's just one of her many mood swings."

"Oh, I see." Aaron sounded unconvinced but then, he didn't really know Gabby very well.

By the time the girls had returned from a long walk in the snow, Gabby had regained her spirits. The clouds had gone, and the snow-laden trees stood out in stark contrast to the blue of the sky above. "It's like a fairyland, Esther. It's so beautiful," and Gabby let out a long sigh of satisfaction as they turned into their Aunt's driveway. "I suppose that all this beauty does prove that there must be a Higher Mind somewhere Who designed it all."

"Prove it? I don't see how anyone can doubt the existence of God."

"No?"

Esther raised her eyebrows. "But *you've* never doubted it, have you?" she asked.

Gabby reddened as she answered slowly, "Not everyone thinks like you do. I know a lot of good people who aren't quite as sure about God as you are."

"It's not how I think that is important. It's what the Bible says."

"That's what I'm always told." Gabby's voice was petulant now.

"Because it's the truth." Esther was trying hard to be patient. She had never had a conversation like this before and didn't know how to handle it.

They had reached the house much to Gabby's relief. Their great aunt met them at the doorway. "I've invited Malcolm Morgan for supper," she announced, as the girls took off their coats. "He's the pastor, or overseer I think they call it, of the little church up the road. They live about five miles from here. He's a widower and has two little girls. His sister is coming too, if they can find someone to take care of the children. I thought you'd like to meet them."

Esther fell in love with Marion Morgan at first sight. Aunt Lucy had said she was at least twenty-eight, but she didn't look it. She looked Scandinavian and had a complexion any girl would envy. She would be a stunner, Gabby thought, if she didn't pull back her long silky, blonde hair so tightly, or hide her shapely figure under her ankle-length, dark blue dress.

Malcolm was much quieter than his sister and hardly spoke during the meal. He seemed a bit awed in the presence of so many women. But he did find courage to invite the girls to his church on Sunday, though he warned them that there would be no special Christmas service.

"But why not?" Gabby blurted out before she could help it.

Malcolm wiped his short, auburn beard with his napkin before replying in his slow, deliberate way: "Well, we don't celebrate Christmas. It's a heathen custom."

Esther flashed her sister a warning look from her dark eyes, but it did no good. "A heathen custom?" the girl spluttered. "Well, that's a new one! So celebrating Christ's birth has heathen origins, Mr. Malcolm? But that's impossible. The heathen don't even believe in Christ, do they?"

Malcolm turned to Marion in desperation. She flushed and brushed the crumbs from her lap before replying slowly, "It's not Christ's birth we don't believe in, Gabriella. But the celebration of Christmas has so many heathen origins—the Christmas tree for example. And we don't even know exactly when Christ was born, do we?" She paused and fidgeted in her chair under Gabby's stare.

"In our day, Christmas has become commercialized," Aunt Lucy broke in. "The Christ of Christmas has nearly been forgotten."

"So you don't celebrate it either, Aunt?" Gabby asked, turning her gaze to the old lady who was sitting bolt upright in her chair, lips pursed.

Lucy gave a grim smile. "Well, I read the Christmas story and play some carols, but I don't give gifts and don't expect any either."

The sisters exchanged glances. "I don't know of any Christian in Romania who doesn't celebrate Christmas," Gabby exclaimed. "And even here in America, I've never heard of anyone who doesn't believe in Christmas."

"There are many families in America who are coming to think like we do," Marion began defensively. Then she saw the expression on Esther's face and her tone softened. "All this must seem strange to you, and even a bit shocking," she went on. "But we find other ways to remember the Incarnation. And we do sing carols together, but not just on December 25th. We do it all year round, so we really don't miss Christmas."

"Not miss Christmas?" Gabby gasped in astonishment. "Well, I suppose America does allow for freedom of expression."

"And it's a good idea to remember Christ's birth for twelve months instead of one," Esther put in.

Malcolm turned to her and smiled for the first time that evening. "So you do understand us, Miss Esther, at least a little? That's good, and you will come to church this Sunday?"

Esther didn't have a chance to reply. "Yes, of course they will, Malcolm," Aunt Lucy assured him, wiping her lips with her starched white napkin. "You have the best church around. Most Biblical, that is."

"And you'll be there too? I'll come and get you, of course."

Miss Lucy frowned. Although it was true that she considered the Bible Church the best around, it was still a long shot from what she thought a church ought to be. It rather bothered her to go there and anyway, it was a real effort to get out with her arthritis troubling her as it did, especially in the cold weather.

"I don't think I'll make it this year, Malcolm, but my great nieces will be glad to go, won't you, girls?"

Esther nodded, but Gabby remained silent for a few moments. She wasn't used to having decisions like this taken out of her own hands. It had been months since she had darkened a church door, and though she had decided it would be good to go just once at Christmas, she wanted it to be a church with a tree and lights and candles and all the trimmings.

"I'm not sure, Aunt. I'll have to think about it," she said finally, making it very clear that she did not want to continue the conversation.

Gabby was still thinking about it an hour later when the company had gone and she had made a quick exit upstairs. When Esther entered the room half and hour later, she found her sister lying face down on her bed. She said nothing for a few moments and then went over and began gently stroking her thick, wavy hair.

Gabby brushed her hand aside and sat bolt upright. "It's no use. I just don't fit in here. I've upset everyone and I know I'll never last a whole week with Aunt Lucy."

Esther tried to say something comforting but the words stuck in her throat. "If I had the car here," Gabby went on, "I'd go home right away, Esther. But I can't. I'll have to stick it out. Oh, don't try to say anything. You can't understand. You always get on with everyone."

"Not everyone," Esther protested. "Who was the most popular at high school? Remember?"

"I was, I suppose," Gabby admitted reluctantly. "But that was because you were more up front with your religion than I was."

Esther nodded. "Yes, I remember being bothered by that."

Gabby smiled a little in spite of herself. "You need to admit to yourself that I'm not pious or holy like you, never have been. I've always gotten on well with people you thought weren't good Christians." She paused and looked straight into Esther's dark eyes as she added slowly, "It's even more like that now."

"Why?" Esther asked tentatively. She wasn't sure she wanted an answer to her own question.

"Because I never was a real Christian. I told you that when I first came to America, didn't I? Well, that's how I still feel, only worse. I mean, it's so confusing here. I've lots of doubts about piles of things."

"Doubts?"

"Yes. Don't look at me like that. Don't you have any doubts, ever?" Gabby sat up and leaned towards her sister as she spoke.

"Well," Esther said slowly, wanting to be truthful, "it depends what you mean."

"Oh, I mean about the Bible, and the life to come, and even," her voice got lower now, "about God Himself. He seems so far away that sometimes, when I see all the mess our world is in, I wonder if He even exists. If He is there somewhere, then why does He allow all the suffering in the world to go on without interfering?"

"How can you talk like that!" Esther's tone was sharp now.

"Well, it's a whole lot better to come out with it than to bottle it up inside, isn't it?" Gabby asked defensively.

"I suppose. But I'm a bit shocked. I mean, the way we've been brought up…"

"Oh, stop it, will you," Gabby almost shouted now. "Don't keep throwing that back at me. The way we were brought up made you into a saint and me into a…" She stopped abruptly.

"Into a what?" Esther demanded. She had to know what was going on inside her sister.

"Oh, I don't know, but it certainly didn't make me into a Christian, that's for sure."

Esther rose and came over to where Gabby was sitting and grabbed her by both hands. "Look, you've got to put all this kind of thing out of your mind. I suppose it's college that's doing it." She let go of her sister's hands and went over to the window.

"Well, so what?" Gabby's tone had defiance in it now. "I'm learning that there're a lot more points of view than the one we've been taught or that Mom and Dad believed. I know they were wonderful, but I'm me, Gabby Popescu. I live in a different generation and am my own person. So give me space, please. I need to sort a lot of things out."

"You'd better shut the door on all these questions," Esther warned. "It's dangerous to question God like that."

"Well, if you think that I'll just blindly believe, then you'd better think again." Gabby was going to leave the room when she thought better of it. She turned, her hand on the doorknob. "If only you could see inside me, Esther, and know how I really feel! I keep waiting, thinking God will speak to me somehow, some way. I keep hoping that He will reassure me that He *is* all Love after all, but He never does. No, don't interrupt," she told her sister. "I have to get it all out of my system. What kind of a God is He to let Dad ruin his health in prison when he had been put there because of his faith? Why didn't He intervene if He is as powerful as the Bible makes out? And why did this God of yours leave us fatherless when we were still so young and so very vulnerable?"

Gabby paused a moment for breath. "And what about Mom?" she went on. "She loved God just as much as Dad, didn't she? Then why was she allowed to die such a horrible death?" Gabby hid her face in her hands as she spoke. She would never ever forget that awful Saturday morning, the day after the earthquake struck Bucharest. She and Esther had spent the weekend with their Aunt Ana in Ploieşti or they, too, would probably have lain side by side with their beautiful mother, three mangled corpses, under the ruins of their apartment building.

Gabby raised her head slowly, her large, grey-green eyes meeting her sister's dark brown ones. For a moment, it seemed that they were plumbing the depths of each other's souls. Then Gabby broke the silence. "What on earth have we done to deserve being orphans, when both our parents were more devoted to God than anyone else I know? And," she went on, her voice changing a little, "there's all that about Ron. Why did God let him fall in love with you and then nearly let you die before you got the message that you should break it all off because he wasn't your type of Christian? And yet Ron was about the nicest guy I've met since coming to the States, and he adored you."

"It's a bit late to tell me that now, isn't it?" Esther exploded. She was thoroughly angry now. "Who came over and told me I was completely changed, and who told Ron he wasn't a *Romanian Christian* and that he'd drag me down if we married?"

Gabby hung her head. Her anger had evaporated and the tears were trickling down her flushed face. "I'll never forgive myself for my part in it all. I never should have stuck my nose into your affairs. You and Ron were made for each other."

Esther rose from the bed and walked over to the window. "No, we weren't," she said, trying to keep her voice from shaking. "You helped save me from making the mistake of my life. We wouldn't have been happy together. We were worlds apart."

"But you were the happiest I've ever seen you and the most beautiful," Gabby wailed. "Oh, I know," she added hastily as she saw the expression on her sister's face, "I accused you of being wrapped up in your own world and not loving me any more. I was just a selfish beast, that's all, thinking of myself all the time. I've helped spoil your life. Now you're sad most of the time."

"Me, sad?"

"Well, call it pensive if you like. You're so quiet and almost mournful, as if you'd lost something precious."

Esther stared at her. Was that the impression she was giving everyone? "Well," she said defensively, "since my illness, I've discovered that life is serious. And, Gabby, it breaks my heart to think that you doubt God and aren't even sure you're a Christian."

"For goodness' sake, Esther," Gabby spluttered, "lighten up a bit. You're talking like a preacher. I really can't stand it!" She saw her sister's face and went on hastily, "I know you don't mean to come across like you do. You're doing your best to help me, but I've got to try some things for myself. And you're not going to stop me. I'm over eighteen, you know." And she grabbed her night clothes and disappeared into the bathroom.

Esther put on her pajamas and then knelt by her bed as usual, but no words would come. She felt wretched and tired and cold. She pulled back the comforter and slipped into bed.

Soon afterwards, she heard her sister's bare feet on the wooden floor. Esther turned her face to the wall. "Oh God," she breathed under the blankets, "is this the Velvet Curtain again? And if it is, what do I do?"

# Chapter Four

## *Gabby Goes Home*

"Try some of my apple butter, Esther. I made it myself."

Esther dipped her spoon into the jar. "You seem to make a lot of things, Marion," she said with a smile. "Your clothes, your food, and who knows what else!" The nearly three-hour service had ended, and it was time for refreshments.

"What did you think of the service?" Marion asked curiously.

"It reminded me of our church back in Romania," Esther found herself saying. She was glad Marion had phrased her question like that. When she had first entered the hall, she could have almost believed herself back in Romania—the men were on one side, the women on the other; all the ladies wore head-coverings, and the singing was beautiful, just as in her church back home, though without accompaniment. Then there was more than one preacher; that, too, was like home. Maybe, she told herself, it was because she had gotten used to short services that she found it hard to stay awake.

Marion saw Esther's thoughts were miles away. "I'm glad your sister came after all," she ventured after a few moments of silence.

Esther's face brightened. "Me, too!" She glanced at the far corner of the meeting-room and smiled. Gabby was in the middle of a group of children, obviously telling them one of her stories.

"Gabby isn't a bit like you," Marion commented. "I mean, I'd hardly believe you two were sisters, you're so different."

Esther nodded. "We're different all right, but," her face fell as she went on, "now there's a gap between us that never existed before. She's changed a lot, Marion. Please pray for her. College hasn't seemed to do her any good."

"Seldom does," Marion said decidedly. "Too much learning can be dangerous, you know, especially for a woman."

Esther stared in astonishment but made no comment. "Yes," Marion went on, "the Bible clearly teaches that a woman's place is in the home. So, after graduating from high school, we concentrate on domestic training, and even long before we graduate," she added with a laugh. "I wasn't very old when I began to learn how to cook, and sew, and garden, and prepare myself to be a good wife and mother or to be a missionary." She had blushed as she uttered the word wife, Esther noticed. She had been wondering how such a beautiful girl as Marion, probably the prettiest in the church, could reach twenty-eight and remain unmarried.

Marion seemed to read her thoughts. She lent forward and said in a low tone, "I don't know why, but I feel as if I've known you for ages. That's why I'm going to tell you something." She paused, and her face took on a wistful expression as she said softly, "You're wondering why I haven't married, aren't you? Most of the girls around here get married very young as you've probably noticed. Well, I was engaged when I was twenty-three. I had known my fiancé since we were children, but I wanted to wait till I really knew my mind. But," here her voice faltered, "at last the date was settled, and then he suddenly broke it off four weeks before our wedding and married my best friend within six months. I've never gotten over it."

Esther put her arm on her friend's shoulder. "I'm sorry," she said. "I know what a broken engagement feels like. It's pretty tough."

Marion looked at her curiously. "You're very young to have gone through that."

"That was part of the problem. I got into it too quickly. I mean, my fiancé wasn't a real Christian, so we finally agreed to break it off."

It was Marion's turn to sympathize. She seemed to have a lot in common with this young Romanian. She was such a beautiful girl, like no one she had ever met, but troubled, it seemed, and sad.

"But it's all over now," Esther went on. "And I don't think I went through half as much as you did by the sound of it."

"I'm not sure of that. Anyway," Marion went on brightly, "don't feel sorry for me. I'm very happy."

Esther looked at her intently. From the first moment she had set eyes on her, she had been struck with Marion's serenity. Peace seemed to emanate from her eyes, from her smile, and through her soft, sweet voice.

"Yes," Marion went on, "after a nervous breakdown and trying to cope with many other problems, I finally found peace of mind and heart at last."

"How?"

"Well, I stopped fighting against God's will for my life and realized that He wanted me to take a vow that I would never marry."

"Never marry?" Esther repeated. "But God would never ask you to do that, would He?"

"I know it sounds awfully strange, but yes, that's exactly what He did ask me to do," Marion's voice was low but firm, "and I've never regretted my vow."

"But you're still young," Esther protested. "What if you meet someone who really loves you and is worthy of you and whom you love too?"

"God will take care of that," Marion said calmly. "If He has asked me to do something, then He will see me through. He won't put me in a position I can't face."

"Sorry to interrupt," Malcolm's voice broke into their conversation. "But we have to go now, Marion."

"Come home with us," Marion suggested as she gathered up the leftover food.

"I don't think I can," Gabby put in, coming up from behind them. "I promised Aunt Lucy I'd read to her after church."

Esther stared at her in surprise, then caught the look in her sister's eyes. "But I can drive home myself if one of you will bring my sister later," Gabby continued brightly.

"I'll be glad to drive her home," Malcolm put in quickly, and before Esther could comment further, her sister had given her a peck on the cheek, reached into her pocket for the car keys, and tripped lightly down the steps.

Esther sighed as she put the last dirty plate into the cardboard box Malcolm was holding. "Please excuse Gabby," she told him, tucking in a stray strand of hair beneath her head covering. "She's not herself these days."

Ten minutes later, they pulled up in front of a double-wide trailer, set in the middle of a large field. Marion's two little nieces ran forward to meet their father who swung them up in his arms and carried them inside.

"My brother dotes on them," Marion said fondly. "Before I came to stay with him a year ago, he had to be both father and mother. It was really hard on him."

Esther followed Malcolm up the steps. The trailer was simply furnished, even rather bare. There was no TV or radio that she could see. As they sat and chatted over a cup of mint tea, she learned that Malcolm had been interested in Romania for years, and now that freedom had come, he had made up his mind to go there as a missionary. And Marion was thinking of going with him, to act as mother to the children and generally take care of her brother.

"This makes you sort of special for us," Marion told her friend as she made for the door. "We're always interested in anything to do with Romania."

Esther smiled. "Actually, I want to go back there when I've finished college," she told her friend. "I don't fit in to America very well."

Marion nodded. "I'm not surprised. Well, maybe we'll see you over there one day."

"Maybe," Esther replied. "Who knows?"

"I'm ready to drive you home any time?" she heard Malcolm asking from the doorway. "Only don't let me rush you."

"I'd better get back now," Esther told him. She turned to go and then turned back, "Marion, can I see you again before I go back to Tiny Gap? You seem a more mature Christian than I am. I know you could teach me a lot."

Marion shook her head. "I don't know about that. But why don't you and your sister come for supper on Tuesday?"

"I'd love to, but I can't answer for Gabby. She's got a mind of her own, especially these days."

When Esther got back to her aunt's that afternoon, she discovered that Gabby had just come in from a walk and was taking off her coat in the hallway. She frowned when she heard of the invitation. "I don't want to go back to those people," she said decidedly.

"You don't want to do anything I do," her sister began, then bit her lip. She must be patient. Marion would never speak like that.

"It isn't that, really it isn't. Marion is too holy and saintly for me. She makes me feel the biggest sinner."

Esther's eyes flashed. "She's one of the most wonderful girls I have ever met. And can you believe it? She and her brother want to go over to Romania?"

"Whatever for?"

"As missionaries!"

Gabby's lip curled. "Yes. I'm not surprised. There will probably soon be a bunch of their kind of missionaries flocking into the country, trying to convert the Romanian heathen."

Esther's patience gave way. "Gabby, will you stop it! You're sarcastic and spiteful. College is ruining you."

"Agreed," Aunt Lucy put in. She had heard the girls' voices and sensed they were having another disagreement.

Esther looked up in surprise. "Yes," the old lady went on, "your sister has no appreciation of spiritual things. She refused to read out of *Foxe's Book of Martyrs* this afternoon. In fact, I wonder if she's even a Christian."

"Actually, I'm not," Gabby blurted out, her face reddening as she spoke.

"Not a Christian?" Lucy collapsed into a chair by the window and fanned herself with the edge of her shawl.

"No, I respect your beliefs, Aunt, but I can't share them. I think that Christianity is great for some people, but it isn't the only way to God." Two pairs of eyes stared at her in shocked silence, then Gabby turned on her heel and left the room.

Upstairs, she flopped on the bed. How on earth would she stick it out till the 28$^{th}$? She reached for her library book. She found herself fascinated with the story of the girl who had become disillusioned with Christianity, traveled to India, and eventually converted to Hinduism.

When Aunt Lucy called her down for supper, she found her niece in another world. Gabby was wondering what it would be like to be a Hindu, or Buddhist, or anything other than the type of Christian her sister expected her to be.

That evening, the old lady, much to their surprise, agreed to play a game of Scrabble with them. She was a good player but took an age to figure out her moves. Gabby slipped upstairs for her book. She often did this at home when the game dragged on and on.

It took her aunt some time to notice that her younger niece was not fully focused on the board. She glanced at the book in the girl's hands, raised her eyebrows, but said nothing. It was only at the end of the game when Esther was taking an unusually long time to move that Lucy became curious to know exactly what Gabby was reading.

"Must be a good book," she commented. "It certainly holds your attention."

Gabby looked up with a smile. "Yes, it's fascinating, Aunt Lucy," she said quickly and then caught the look on her sister's face. She put it down hastily and turned her attention to the board.

The old lady leaned forward and reached for the book. "Hmm," she commented, as she adjusted her glasses. "Let's see. Seems like it's about India. Interesting. My grandparents were missionaries in India."

Esther groaned inwardly. She had picked up the book the day before and been rather surprised at its contents but she had said nothing to her Gabby. They had had enough arguments already without adding another to the list.

Both girls watched apprehensively as their aunt scanned the foreword. "Not exactly a missionary book, Gabriella," Lucy commented, after a few moment's perusal. "Looks like it's the reverse, if you ask me anything." She closed the book in disgust.

"Now what on earth do you find fascinating in the story of a girl who finds fulfillment in a heathen religion?" she asked sharply.

Gabby reddened. "Any search for truth is fascinating, Aunt Lucy," she said defensively, "even if it doesn't coincide with my search or with yours."

"Maybe it fascinates you, Gabriella, but I'll not have a heathen book like that in my house."

Her great niece stared at her. Even her father wouldn't have been as strict as this. "But it's a library book, Aunt," she explained.

"Well," Lucy's voice was calmer now, "as long as you don't read it again while you're here."

"I can't promise that, Aunt. After all, we are in America, aren't we?" she asked slyly. Miss Lucy glanced at Esther who was concentrating on the letters on the board.

"I mean, that's the beauty of this country, isn't it?" Gabby went on. "Freedom of speech, freedom of conscience. The first amendment and all that?" Esther gave her a warning look, but her sister would not be stopped. "I'd really like to know, Aunt Lucy, what harm it is doing you for me to read that book?"

"More than you'll ever know, young lady," Lucy retorted. "It'll lead you far from the faith of your fathers. And while you're with me, I'll not aid and abet any such waywardness. You'll promise not to read it while you're here, or you'll go home first thing tomorrow."

Esther pushed aside the Scrabble board. "Come on, Gabby," she pleaded. "It won't hurt you to put the book aside just for a week or so, now will it?" Her dark eyes were filling with tears.

Gabby tossed her hair out of her face and muttered, "OK, I give in, but I think it's awfully unfair." And with that she got up from her chair and left the room.

*Gabby Goes Home* 39

Upstairs Gabby did a lot of thinking. She had complied with her aunt's wishes, but she knew that it wouldn't work to stay on in the house. There'd only be constant trouble. She'd leave the next day if she could get home somehow.

A few moments later she was telling her aunt what she had decided. "Look, I'm spoiling things for all of you here," Gabby told her, keeping her eyes fixed on the carpet. "I don't fit in here. You're all too religious and expect me to be the same as you are. Well, I just can't right now. I know that it'll be best for all of us that I go as soon as I can." And with that, she turned on her heel and left the room. Esther rose to follow her.

"No, don't go after her," Aunt Lucy remonstrated. "Stay and have a prayer with me for your sister." Her voice softened a little. "I'm sorry it's turned out this way, but I feel responsible for her while she's with me. I had to protest. She's reading dangerous stuff."

Esther flopped back into her chair and turned her face so her aunt couldn't see the large teardrops that rolled down her pale cheeks and plopped onto her lap. Why, oh, why had things to go so wrong, and at Christmas, too?

"You know why my sister refused to read *Foxe's Book of Martyrs*, don't you, Aunt Lucy?" she asked after a few moments of complete silence. Aunt Lucy reddened a little but said nothing. "She was thinking of Dad and how he was really a martyr," Esther went on, her dark eyes fixed on her aunt's face. "She has always had a problem with his death."

The old lady coughed a little. She was embarrassed. Maybe she had been over-conscientious. But no, the girl was on the wrong track, that was evident, and she couldn't sit by and watch her without a protest. "It is her decision to leave, not mine," she told her niece. "And she's right. There will only be constant trouble between us if she stays much longer."

Esther felt a draught of icy air filtering in through a chink in the window and shivered. There was nothing left for it. They would have to phone Mary to come and get them.

"Where are you going?" Lucy demanded as her niece made for the kitchen.

"To phone Aunt Mary to come and get us," she said slowly.

"You're not going as well, are you?" her aunt asked in surprise. "I mean, this has nothing to do with you."

Esther smiled weakly. "I suppose it hasn't," she agreed, "but if Gabby goes then I suppose I'll go too. I mean it is Christmas and…" She paused as she saw the hurt in the old lady's eyes.

Lucy put a thin hand on the girl's arm. "I'm lonely," she said softly. "And I was looking forward to spending a week with my long lost relatives. But if you must go, then you must."

Esther thought for a moment. "I'll think about it," she said slowly as she disappeared into the kitchen and was soon dialing Mary's number. It didn't take long before her aunt had grasped the situation.

"And are you coming home too?" she asked.

Her niece hesitated. "I'm not sure, Aunt Mary. I need time to pray about it."

"Fine, only think of your great aunt, Esther. She might seem like a tyrant, but I'm sure she has a soft side. Besides, she must be awfully lonely."

"She is," Esther answered briefly. "Very."

That night, neither girl spoke much, and each heard the other tossing and turning till well past midnight. The next morning, Gabby was up first for a change. She had to pack and be ready to leave right after breakfast. The smell of fried eggs and bacon wafted upstairs as she closed her bag and made for the door. Her eyes filled. She had so looked forward to this vacation and now it had all been spoiled.

"I'm not going with you," Esther told her sister when they were ready to go downstairs. "I've promised Marion to visit her and besides, Aunt Lucy seemed disappointed at the thought of spending Christmas alone."

Gabby said nothing and Esther went on, "At her age, this might be the last time I'll have a chance like this, while, hopefully we'll have a lot more Christmases to spend together."

"No need for explanations," her sister told her curtly. "The problem is between Aunt Lucy and me. You are her favorite, of course. You couldn't disappoint her." Gabby bent down, grabbed her bag and made for the door.

They had just finished breakfast when, to their surprise, Aaron Gardner arrived. "Mary had a bit of a cold," he explained cheerfully. "So I told her I'd go instead. Hope it's OK?"

"Of course it is," Esther reassured him. "And by the way, I'm not going. Please tell Aunt Mary that. She'll understand."

Gabby glanced at her sister but said nothing. She wasn't sure she liked this turn of affairs. But then, in her present mood, nothing pleased her. It didn't make her feel any better when Rita told them that Aunt Lucy had taken to her bed. She had not slept a wink and was exhausted, so she wouldn't be able to see her great niece off. "But I'm to say goodbye for her," Rita announced cheerfully as she gave Gabby a peck on the cheek.

"That's very kind of you," muttered the girl sarcastically as she kissed Esther and made for the door.

Rita's plump face crumpled into a frown. How could two sisters be so different, she wondered?

"Drive carefully!" Esther shouted after them as they got in the car.

"I will," Aaron reassured her. "Have a blessed Christmas!"

"A blessed Christmas?" echoed Gabby, as she settled into her seat.

"Yes, of course."

"It won't be blessed for me, now," she grumbled.

Aaron gave her pitying glance. "You and your great aunt haven't hit it off, is that it?"

Gabby nodded. "Yes, but it's more than that. Esther and I have had more arguments this week than we've ever had in all the past years put together."

"Esther doesn't look as if she could keep up an argument for long."

"No, she doesn't usually. But I've really upset her this time."

Aaron gave the girl beside him another compassionate glance as he edged the car onto the main road. "Look, you don't need to tell me about it if you don't want to."

Gabby gave a short laugh. "If you promise not to be shocked, I'll tell you."

"I don't think you'll shock me very much."

"Oh, you don't?"

"Try me!"

Gabby cleared her throat. "Well, I told my sister that I didn't think I was a Christian any more and that I had doubts about a lot of things, even about God's existence."

"So?"

She stared at him. He didn't seem shocked at all. She went on more slowly, "Well, that gave Esther a big scare, and made her angry, too. She didn't understand how I could say such a thing after the way we've been brought up."

Aaron stared at the road ahead and said nothing.

"But I didn't even tell Aunt Lucy everything," Gabby continued. "I mean all that about doubting if there was a God. But I did tell her I wasn't a Christian any more."

"That would be shock enough."

"It sure was, and that wasn't all. I refused to read out of *Foxe's Book of Martyrs*, though I did read to her for two hours from *Wesley's Sermons*. Then I told her that I thought that Christianity wasn't the only way to God, and that I couldn't agree that non-Christians like Hindus, Buddhists and others will go to hell."

Gabby paused for breath. "Then," she went on, "the crisis came when she caught me reading a book about a girl who went to India and became Hindu. She made me promise not to read it in her house. I finally agreed, just to please Esther, but it was no use. After thinking about it, I knew that my aunt and I would never survive a week together in the same house. Actually," she gave a chuckle in spite of herself, "Aunt Lucy didn't know, but I had at least three other books she'd have disapproved of in my duffle bag. I knew I couldn't be a hypocrite so I decided to leave." Gabby let out a long sigh and settled back into her seat. She had been sitting bolt upright as she had catalogued her offenses.

"Is that all?" Aaron asked calmly.

"So you're not shocked?"

"Not really. I mean, it was sort of what I expected."

Gabby smiled in spite of herself. She felt more relaxed already and they had only been traveling about fifteen minutes. "You'd have been very surprised if my sister had said all this, right?"

"Probably."

"But I'm not Esther."

"That's more than obvious." Gabby frowned and wondered what he meant by that. There was another long silence before Aaron began slowly, "Look, the reason I'm not shocked is that I've had thoughts just like yours."

"What?"

Aaron laughed. "It's you who's shocked now. Yes, I went through the whole gamut—wondering if there was a God, worrying about the justice of there being a hell, feeling that there must be other ways to God besides the Christian way, etc."

"And?"

"Well, it's hard to get away from your upbringing."

"I don't think so," Gabby countered.

"And then there were my friends," he went, ignoring her last comment.

"Your friends?"

Aaron swerved to avoid a parked car. "Yes," he said with a slight smile. "I had a few close friends who were pretty blunt with me and showed me by example as well as by words that I was being very foolish and immature."

Still the girl made no comment. Aaron went on as if half talking to himself. "I'm not saying that college didn't change me. It did. I still have a lot of things to think through and a lot more leaps of faith to take. And some of my ideas still shock my granddad at times and worry him, too. But I am saying that I've come out at the other end with my own firm belief that God does exist, that Jesus did die for us, that we can know Him personally, and that He is full of love and mercy for us sinners."

Gabby closed her eyes for a few moments. She could see her father's face, hear his voice, almost feel his arms round her. She tried to stifle a low sob, and after what seemed an age to Aaron, he heard Gabby say in a faltering voice, "But you didn't have a father who died for his faith or a mother who was killed when you were only very young, did you?"

"No, I didn't," was all Aaron could say. He wanted to tell her that life hadn't been all sunshine for him either, that he had often fought against frequent bouts of depression and resentment over the fact that he had been separated from his missionary parents for eight, long years. He could tell her, too, that he and his granddad had had some terrible disagreements and that he even stopped coming home for several years. But when he opened his lips to speak, no words would come out.

Gabby made a cushion of her thick, wooly, scarf and laid her head back on it. Soon her eyes were closed, and Aaron thought she might even be asleep. Half way home they stopped for a hamburger and a drink, but long before they reached their destination, weather conditions had worsened and it was all he could do to concentrate on the road. Aaron was glad when he pulled up at Mary Popescu's white board house and saw his young charge safe in the arms of her aunt.

Gabby said goodbye to her chauffeur, drank a steaming cup of hot chocolate, and went straight upstairs to take a hot shower. Her aunt asked no questions, much to her relief. And while Christmas day was not the same without Esther, Gabby found Mary's presence a great comfort. And, of course, Rachel was also there to share her joys and sorrows. Then the news of Ceaucescu's trial and subsequent death temporarily put her own troubles into the shade.

## Chapter Five

### *New Year with Uncle John*

"Esther, it's so good to see you again!" John Popescu exclaimed, as he gave his niece a bear hug. Marion and her brother had just dropped her off on their way to Indianapolis. They were spending a week with their parents and had offered to drive her to her uncle's.

For a moment, Esther imagined that she was the young, innocent nineteen-year-old girl, in her faded skirt and heavy black shoes, tramping up the path to her uncle's house, Ramona standing in the doorway, welcoming her cousin into her new life and her new home.

John smiled as he watched her step into the hallway and slip off her shoes. "Still Romanian, eh?" Her uncle's deep, bass voice reminded her so of her father.

"In some ways." Esther smiled as she took off the white fur jacket he had given her as a present several years before and hung it on a peg.

His niece was as beautiful as ever, John thought as he followed her into the lounge, but not at all like the glamorous young woman who became a star overnight. Hair tied back in a bow and dressed in a long grey skirt and blue blouse, she looked more like the young girl who had first wrapped herself round his heartstrings, but not quite. Something was missing now, he thought, something intangible but very real nonetheless.

Esther glanced around the spacious living room. Her uncle's new wife hadn't made many changes, she noted. It felt strange to be back in Velours again. She had seen her uncle the Christmas before when he had taken a trip up to the mountains, but it had only been for a few hours. This year, she had accepted his invitation to spend New Year with him, knowing that Ron would be away at his father's for the holidays.

"Well, Esther," John exclaimed when they were both seated, "what have you been doing with yourself all these months?"

"Doing? Oh, going to college, helping Aunt Mary around the house, and of course, cooking *ciorba* and *sarmale* when I have time," she added with a short laugh, "to say nothing of keeping an eye on the girls when they come home for a visit."

"And are they behaving themselves?"

"Well, I'm not with them that much," Esther admitted. "Actually, I see a lot more of Rachel than Gabby."

"How's that?"

"Well, Rachel comes home more often."

"Seems like Gabby's causing her big sister a few problems," John commented. He was joking, but Esther did not smile this time.

"Not too much so far, Uncle, but I am worried about her."

"Oh, she's a great kid. Don't keep too many tabs on her, or you'll regret it. That's my advice for what it's worth."

Esther frowned a little. "But I've always felt responsible for her since our parents died, that's the problem. I can't get out of the habit, I suppose. But that's enough about us, Uncle. How about you?"

"Oh, life goes on much the same. Diane takes very good care of me. The business is prospering, but at times I miss you girls terribly, I must say."

"But Ramona's only in Terre Haute."

John's face darkened. "She might be hundreds of miles away for the little I see her. It's that Claude guy. They're engaged. You know that, I suppose?"

"Yes," Esther answered briefly. She noticed her uncle's expression and thought the less she said on the subject the better, but John wasn't finished.

"I've wanted a word with you about it."

"Me? But I hardly see Ramona these days."

"No, but you know her pretty well. What do you really think has made her go and do this?"

Esther's eyes opened wide. "Love, I suppose," she replied, almost without thinking.

"Do you really think she loves Claude Iliescu? Now be honest."

His niece shifted uneasily in her chair. "Well, I haven't seen them together much, Uncle, so…"

John leaned forward in his chair. "Stop beating round the bush. You know as well as I do that Claude isn't Ramona's type. Then why has she gone and done this?"

Esther looked down at her lap. "Tastes differ, Uncle John, you know that," she said slowly.

"She seems fascinated by him but it's not what I'd call love. Claude has some power over her," he persisted. No one spoke for a few moments then he began again. "Tell you what, they're coming for New Year's dinner. I may ask you the same question after you've seen them together. It's not that I'm trying to snoop, but I am concerned. After all, she is my daughter, my own blue-eyed little idol." He stared out the window as he spoke. "Trouble is, I've spoiled her. Couldn't say no. Now, it may be too late to put my foot down. But I'm just afraid that Claude can never make her happy, never."

Esther let out a long sigh. "Now I've made you morbid," John said remorsefully, "and it's easy to see you don't need that."

"Oh, I'm OK, Uncle," Esther said, lightly laying her hand on his as she spoke. "And I'll never forget how you and Ramona took that odd-looking little Romanian waif and stray into your home and hearts. Maybe some day I can repay you both in some way."

Tears filled John's eyes. "You have already repaid me," he said quietly. Then his tone changed. "Well, you've been here at least half an hour and I've not offered you a drink. Diane's gone to the hairdresser, so I'll act as host." He rose and soon returned with hot tea and homemade cookies.

Diane returned home an hour later with two large pizzas. She came over to where Esther was sitting and gave her a kiss. "I'm glad you could come," she said quietly, and her smile made the girl feel quite at home. "You look as pretty as ever, but pale and tired. Now come and eat. You've driven a long way and must be ravenous."

Esther followed her hostess into the kitchen. She was glad that Ron's mom was doing her best to put the past behind her. She must do the same. They had just begun to eat when Gabby and Rachel arrived from Tiny Gap. She noticed that Rachel was still ill at ease with her step-mom. Only Gabby seemed truly at home.

Esther shed some tears that night as she climbed into her old bed by the window, and it was hours before she could get to sleep. Everything reminded her of those memorable ten months she had spent in Velours when so much had happened so quickly. She glanced over at Gabby's sleeping form in the next bed. In the brief time she had seen her sister that evening, she had sensed that those five or six days with Aunt Mary seemed to have done her a world of good.

The next morning, however, she was disappointed when neither Gabby nor Rachel showed any inclination to go with her to church. So she drove alone to Pine Grove Evangelical and was greeted by the youth pastor in the vestibule.

"Great to see you again," Len greeted her warmly. "Will you favor us with a song this morning?"

Esther flushed. "I haven't sung since I've been ill," she replied uneasily.

"No? That's a pity. Well, when you decide to sing again, let me know," he said, with one of his charming smiles.

Esther enjoyed the service. It was so good to hear Pastor Cripps pour his heart out as he always did, good to hear the choir sing, to listen to Margaret's solo, to feel the warm handshake of young and old as they welcomed her back. And, of course, she was invited to dinner by rosy-cheeked Betty Cripps, just as in the old days. Len was there too, a trifle more subdued than usual, Esther noticed, but still very much Len.

"He's been a bit quieter ever since his mother took ill," Margaret told her later. "Not quite as effervescent."

"His mother is ill?"

"Yes, with leukemia. She hasn't got long, the doctor says. His father has taken a church in Cincinnati so Len sees a lot more of them than he used to. And then, Mom's words or warning to him may have given him something to think about."

"Really?" Esther was curious now.

"Yes," Margaret said with a wry smile. "Believe it or not, last Sunday noon at lunch she made my dad quite embarrassed. She told Len flat out that she had been worried for some time about his attitude to the girls in the church. She kept hoping he would grow up, as she put it, but so far, that hadn't happened. She also pointed out that the youth group had shrunk considerably over the past months and hinted that his behavior might have had something to do with it. Of course, that hit him between the eyes."

Esther was silent for a few moments. She remembered how Len had once supposedly converted her cousin Ramona and how it had all ended. She couldn't help thinking that the young youth pastor deserved every bit of criticism he got. "I'm glad your mother tackled him," she told Margaret. "He needed it."

Her friend nodded. "Yes, he did. Knowing how eternally buoyant the guy is, I wasn't sure if what Mom said sunk in, but seeing him today makes me realize that at least something made him think."

"Well, I hope it stops him playing on girls' emotions as if they were a musical instrument."

"So do I," Margaret agreed, "though I'm not sure I'd want Len completely different."

"That's hard to visualize," Esther said with a smile. "He is quieter but still the charmer. Still, maybe a reformation is on the way."

"Maybe, though it'll take a lot to change Len Atwood. Some changes, however, are not for the best."

"Meaning?" Esther raised her eyebrows.

"Meaning that I don't like the change I see in you. You hardly say a word, look as if the wind would blow you away, and your eyes have a mournful look that goes right to my heart. No, don't laugh. It's true. I have to admit, though, that it kind of suits you. You look sort of mystical—as if you were mostly all spirit. It certainly makes you seem more like an angel than ever, but we don't want you being wafted away to Heaven just yet."

Margaret noticed that tears had filled Esther's dark eyes. She decided it was time to change the subject. "I've got something to ask you," she said mysteriously. She stepped closer and whispered in her friend's ear: "I want you to be one of my bridesmaids." Margaret laughed as she saw Esther's expression of bewildered surprise. "Please, for my sake," she pleaded. "I've made up my mind even though I know very well you'll dazzle everyone as you always do and put me quite in the shade."

Esther blushed. "Oh, Margaret, that's nonsense. You'll be the center of attraction, of course."

"The radiant bride and all that? Well, my fiancé tells me he can't wait to see me in my long white gown, and I couldn't really care less if no one else looks at me as long as my Robert does." Margaret's eyes shone as she spoke. Then she paused, struck again by the sadness in her friend's face. "Your day will come, too. And then maybe you can have me for your maid of honor."

Esther turned her head away. "I'm not ready to talk about marriage, Margaret. In fact, I've been thinking lately that God might want me never to marry."

Margaret took Esther by the shoulder and made her look her full in the face. "Listen to me a moment. Maybe you don't realize it, but you're just not the spinster kind. You're the kind of woman who needs a good man to protect you from the world, and from other men," she added, lowering her voice. "You're too beautiful to go alone in life, believe me."

Esther turned a deep red. She could never forget she was beautiful. Wherever she went, eyes followed her. Even when she tried to look as plain and unassuming as she could, it still happened; she couldn't hide her looks. And, anyway, did she really want to?

"Penny for your thoughts," interrupted Margaret. "But think about what I've asked and give me your answer by the end of the month." She sighed as she waved her friend off that evening. Those very long skirts and somber looks couldn't hide the girl's beauty, but it all didn't add up. She wished another Ron Atwood, a Christian version of course, would come along to bring out the real Esther. Len had told her that his cousin was burying himself in his career, or so it seemed, and never ever darkened a church door as far as he knew. Why was life so sad for some people when she had been so blessed?

New Year's Dinner at Uncle John's was a huge success. Diane was a superb cook and a marvelous hostess. Esther glanced across the table at Ramona and Claude. Her cousin seemed much like the Ramona of old, except that she would give what seemed rather furtive glances at her fiancé from time to time and seemed over-anxious to please him. As for Claude, he said little, ate a lot, and gazed at his sweetheart most of the time. He had eyes for no one else. Esther couldn't help thinking that they seemed a rather unlikely pair, and fervently hoped her cousin wasn't making the mistake of her life but, as she told her uncle later that night, she still had no tangible answer to his question.

"The only thing I can think of," she concluded thoughtfully, "is that Ramona wants someone who worships the very ground she walks on. And maybe," she flushed as she spoke, "she's hungry for the love he showers on her and is willing to pay any price to keep it." Her uncle gave her a long, searching glance from under his bushy black eyebrows but said nothing.

By the time Tuesday arrived, Esther was anxious to head for the mountains. John was worried about his niece returning to Tiny Gap alone, but she assured him she was an old hand now at driving and would be fine. Rachel and Gabby planned to stay a week longer and then go back to college with Andrea, who lived in Indianapolis and had agreed to give them a ride back to Knoxville.

The morning after Esther left, Gabby and Rachel were eating a late breakfast when Ron arrived. "Good morning, girls," he exclaimed, as he took a stool beside Gabby. "It's been ages since I've seen you, though, come to think of it, I did see you last Christmas, Rachel, but Gabby, I can't think when I saw you last."

Rachel, sitting opposite, studied Ron's face as he chatted and laughed with them. He still looked the same handsome, gallant, young man who had fallen head over heels in love with her beautiful cousin, except that he was thinner and older looking, she thought, and his eyes had a wistful expression that she had never seen there before.

Just then the phone rang. When Rachel had slipped into the hallway to answer it, Ron leaned towards Gabby and asked in a low voice, the smile all out of his face now, "Your sister was here with you over New Year?"

"Yes, she left yesterday morning."

"How is she?"

Gabby weighed her words carefully before replying, "She's beautiful as ever, of course."

"Of course," Ron repeated.

"But..." Gabby hesitated.

"So there is a *but*?"

Gabby's eyes met his. The intensity in them almost frightened her. She didn't know how to go on. "Here's Rachel," she spluttered, "she's better with words than me."

"What? No way, Gabby." Rachel laughed and then saw they were having a very serious conversation and her face sobered instantly.

"Ron is wanting to know how Esther is."

Rachel swallowed hard. "Well, Ron," she began very deliberately, "it seems like she's trying to turn the clock back a few years and forget everything in between."

"She's not the only one," Ron muttered under his breath.

Rachel ignored his comment and went on, "And, if you saw her, you'd probably think at first that she'd succeeded, but..." It was too much. Ron's eyes were off-putting. They said what his tongue couldn't say.

"It's all right, Rachel. You've said enough. I get the picture." He got up abruptly and left the kitchen.

The two girls looked at each other and shook their heads. Then Rachel remembered she hadn't mentioned the phone call. "It was Andrea," she told Gabby. "She's had a brainwave, as she calls it." Gabby smiled. That was nothing new.

"And?"

"Well, she suggests that, instead of coming for us next Monday as planned and going straight to college, we go for a skiing weekend together and leave on Thursday. There's a bunch of them going."

"What did you say to her?" Gabby asked anxiously.

"I said nothing definite till we'd had a chance to talk it over."

"Wise girl." Gabby ran her hand through her hair as she got up from her stool. "But what do you think about her idea?"

"Well, you can count me out. I'm no skier. I wouldn't enjoy it a bit."

Gabby put her dishes in the sink and rinsed them off before she answered slowly, "I couldn't say that. I love skiing. Dad used to take Esther and me when we were young. And then I went with the school a few times. But I'm not sure I want to go without you." A shade came over the girl's face as she spoke.

Rachel said nothing. She had a feeling that Gabby wanted her to go, but why should she? She'd be perfectly miserable the whole time and spoil it for the others. And anyway, her cousin was old enough to take care of herself. Then she remembered something else. "I forgot to mention that Andrea said she and Larry were going to Terre Haute today," she told her cousin, "and wondered if they could drop by and take us out for a meal. I told them Ron was here, and they said to bring him too."

Gabby brightened. "Good idea. He and Larry should be fun together. We'll have some good discussions."

"Arguments, you mean," and Rachel grinned. "Larry can't talk long to anyone without getting into some argument or other."

The girls had soon cleared away the rest of the dishes. Neither of them saw Ron again until their friends arrived. Introductions were made and Ron was invited to lunch. He hesitated a moment, took one look at Gabby's face, and then said, "OK, I'll come. It's good of you to invite me."

"Not at all! Any friend of Gabby and Rachel is our friend, too," Andrea assured him with a disarming smile.

Ron said little during the meal. With Andrea and Gabby in the party, there was no fear of the conversation dragging. It wasn't long before the subject of their skiing weekend came up. Rachel was adamant that she was not going.

"But you'll come, Gabby, won't you?" Andrea pleaded. "It won't be the same without you. Come on, be a sport. It'll do you good.

Wipe away the cobwebs that have gathered during the vacation," Andrea joked.

"I don't think Gabby lets many cobwebs gather in her brain," Ron put in with a smile.

"No? But then you probably don't know her family," Andrea continued. "I'm not speaking of Rachel, of course. I mean her sister and aunt."

"Well, actually, I do know them a bit." Ron's voice was cool, and there was a glint in his eyes that Rachel hadn't seen there before. She tried to give the girl a warning look but it was no good.

"Oh? Then you'll understand what I'm talking about," the irrepressible Andrea went on. "They take their religion far too seriously. Her great aunt's even worse, from what I've heard, so poor Gabby probably needs livening up a bit after spending her days in church and reading the Bible every morning. She's not half as much fun as she was two weeks ago."

Larry gave a short laugh. "Gabby doesn't seem to me the type to spend her days in church," he remarked airily, "but I suppose she has to cater to her family when she's with them, just to keep the peace." He gave a little laugh as he wiped his mustache.

Gabby threw a furtive glance at Ron. He had put down his knife and fork and leaned back in his chair. Toying with his napkin he asked quietly, "Have your friends ever met your sister and aunt, Gabby?"

Gabby blushed to the roots of her hair. "No, Ron. Not yet."

"Oh, I thought…"

"Gabby's told me plenty," Andrea put in with a laugh.

"I didn't think you could have met them," Ron told her, his blue eyes colder than normal and his voice edgy. "Actually, Gabby's sister is the most charming girl I have ever met. She's beautiful, gorgeous in fact, and has the voice of an angel. And she's very intelligent. And so is her aunt. I don't think they'd let many cobwebs linger in Gabby's head even though you're right, they are very religious."

Larry raised his eyebrows. "Most charming girl you've met? That's saying a lot." Ron's face flushed a deep red. "But to change the subject, would you like to come with us for our weekend?" Larry continued, not giving him time to comment.

Ron thought a moment. "Actually, I love to ski, but I promised my aunt that I'd spend the weekend with her. She's quite ill, and this may be one of my last chances to see her."

Larry didn't seem particularly disappointed at this news. "But you're coming, aren't you, Gabby?" he asked, fixing his eyes on her face.

Gabby flushed a little and glanced at Ron. "Oh, I guess I'll come," she said at last. "As you say, it'll probably liven me up a bit."

"Sure will," Andrea put in. "There'll be a dozen of us going—mostly girls and guys from college. I think you know most of them."

And so it was all settled, or so Rachel thought to herself that evening as she cleared away the dishes. That was why she was completely taken aback when she heard Ron's voice behind her. "So you're not going with them this weekend, Rachel?" he asked abruptly.

She whirled round to face him, dish cloth in hand. "No, of course I'm not," she answered quickly. Then she gave a short laugh. "Did you think I'd enjoy a skiing weekend?"

"No, not really," Ron admitted, as he took a seat on a bar stool. "But I thought you might go for Gabby's sake."

Rachel's eyes flashed fire as she raised her eyes to his. "For Gabby's sake? So you expect me to be her chaperone, do you? Well then, why don't you go yourself if you think my cousin needs protection that badly?"

Ron cleared his throat and wondered why he had ever tackled the girl. He ought to have known better. "Like I said, I can't, Rachel," he replied with a sigh. "Len's mother is dying. It's my one chance to spend some time with her. But you can go, can't you?"

"Of course I can go if I want to," the girl snapped back, "but why on earth should I? Gabby's over eighteen, isn't she, and Andrea and her brother aren't exactly the criminal type, are they?"

Ron gave a rather nervous laugh. "No, not exactly. But neither are they Gabby's type of friends, or yours either, for that matter."

"Well, that's our business, isn't it?" Rachel exploded, glaring at Ron. She had barely managed to quiet her conscience, and now he was stirring everything up again. Then she reddened. After all, she didn't want to get into Ron Atwood's bad books. She respected him too much for that. "Well, actually," she explained slowly, "I've only met Larry once before, and Gabby's just known Andrea since October and I know her even less. But Andrea seems really nice."

"Well, I'm not at all impressed with either of them," Ron told her firmly, "especially that Larry guy. Andrea wouldn't be so bad on her own." Ron's eyes searched hers for a moment. Then he gave a short laugh. "Come on, Rachel, surely an intelligent girl like you can't be all that naïve." His tone was edged with sarcasm. "Don't you know what these weekends are really like?"

"I've never been to one, but I can guess. But maybe this one will be different. I don't think Andrea and Larry would be involved in anything really disgraceful."

"Don't you?" Ron got up from his chair and took a few steps towards her. His eyes were blazing now and he was clearly angry. "So you'll hide away in your little cocoon and not lift a finger to help your cousin when she needs you most?"

Now it was Rachel's turn to be upset. She tossed back her long, dark hair and fixed her great black eyes on his blue ones. "Maybe you've forgotten that Gabby's actually older than I am, and besides, she's terribly independent with a will like iron. What on earth can I do to stop her from going?"

Ron's voice was gentler now. "You can go with her, Rachel."

Rachel gave a gasp. He was actually asking her to do that? "Gabby may be older than you," Ron went on, "but she's very naïve. She's not been brought up in America like you have. And she hasn't a clue about many things."

Rachel lowered her eyes. He was too much for her. And he was right, of course. "So, you're asking me to go with them, Ron?" she faltered.

Ron looked at her steadily. "I'm suggesting that you do," he replied.

Rachel looked him full in the eyes. "It's all about Esther, isn't it?" she asked pointedly. "You want to be sure her little sister is kept safe, for her sake, isn't that right?"

"Yes, Rachel," Ron muttered as he made for the door, "you've found me out. Of course it's for…" his voice faltered, "for her sake."

Rachel went to reply, but he was gone. "Why should I do what he wants for Esther's sake," she muttered angrily to herself as she made her way upstairs. "Why can't Esther go herself to protect her baby sister?" But a few moments later as she glanced at the bed by the window and heard her cousin's even breathing, she knew what she would do. And it wouldn't be for Esther's sake, or for Ron's. It would be because she had grown very, very fond of her cousin, with her infectious laugh, and eyes that revealed her soul, and because she wanted her to stay that way for as long as ever she could.

# Chapter Six

## *Ron and Rachel*

"Tell me honestly, Rachel, how did the skiing weekend go?"
They had placed their order and were waiting for the food to arrive. Rachel had returned from her vacation to find a message from Ron on her answering machine, suggesting that she meet him at a Shoney's restaurant not far from the university. He'd be in Knoxville the next day, he said, and wanted to see her. If she couldn't make it, it was fine. He would understand.

But she had made it, and there they were, sitting opposite each other, just as if they dined together every day. The old, bitter smile had played on her mouth as she had made her way to Shoney's. No eligible bachelor like Ron would get pleasure from her company, that was for sure. So when he asked about their weekend, she smiled again to herself. She had been right. He had wanted information from her, that was all. And of course, it was all for Esther's sake.

"That weekend was a bit of an eye-opener," she told him abruptly.
"Meaning?"
Rachel hesitated. If it had been anyone other than Ron Atwood, she would have deeply resented this sort of questioning.

Her dark eyes looked into his. "Meaning," she began slowly, "that I realized that I'd lived in my own little world for the past two semesters, and that weekend brought me brutally back to reality. And it was a shock."

Ron said nothing. He was waiting for her to go on. Rachel toyed nervously with her fork. "It wasn't that anyone tried to force either of us to do anything we didn't want to do." She hesitated. This wasn't easy, but maybe she needed to get it out of her system. "But no one seemed shocked at anything anyone else did. You could sleep with a different guy each night, and it was thought quite normal. I mean, some of the girls talked about it openly. That's what was scary. Of course, I knew this sort of stuff went on during these weekend parties, but I thought that at least there would be some raised eyebrows, or stares, or r other. But there was none, apart from me, of course. ed what I was thinking on my face."

't Gabby shocked as well?"

₁﹎ckered her brow before replying, "I'm sure she must have been, but she didn't say anything. That's what bothered me. But then," she went on thoughtfully, "she wasn't really involved with anyone except Andrea and her brother, and they didn't do anything shocking. They stuck by us and were great company. And we had some good discussions together. Larry, especially, seemed eager to get my cousin talking about everything—her family, her background, her beliefs or lack of them," Rachel added with a short laugh. "And you know Gabby. She's as open as the day is long and hid very little.

"Then, the last night we were there, there were interviews on TV with several Romanians who spoke out freely about life under Ceaucescu's dictatorship. When it was over, Gabby ran up into her room and wouldn't come down for a long time. When she did, it was obvious she had been crying. Andrea soon got it out of her that she had been reliving the whole trauma of her mother's death and her father's sickness and imprisonment and all that went with it. She poured it out for nearly an hour—how her faith had been shattered and how she had been bitter against God for allowing it all to happen."

Rachel paused and tears welled up in her eyes. Ron was listening intently. "We all tried to comfort her. Larry ended up telling her that she needed release from the feeling of guilt she was carrying. The conversation was interrupted at that point, and I'm not sure if they continued it later or not. But something in Larry's attitude bothered me. Yet thing is, it seemed that his words comforted Gabby more than mine did."

Rachel's face flushed a little. "I'm sorry to have gone on like this, but I've bottled it up for a week or so, and now it's come out."

"I'm glad you shared it with me," Ron told her quietly. He pushed back his plate as he studied the girl opposite. He had never noticed before how intelligent she looked. Her eyes seemed to be trying to comprehend the whole universe.

"And then, of course, there was the skiing," she went on. "Gabby's such good fun, you know."

Ron nodded. "I mean," Rachel said with a smile, "she could ski like the best of them. So she was very popular with everyone. As you've probably guessed already, I can't ski at all, so I was out of it most of the time."

"Didn't Larry try to teach you?"

"Teach me?" Rachel gave a short laugh. "Of course not! He'd have been wasting his time."

"It's a pity I wasn't there. I'd have taught you," Ron assured her. "I've got the patience of Job, didn't you know?"

"You obviously have no idea how bad I am at sports," she exclaimed. "Ask Gabby. She'll tell you."

"You'll have to prove that to me—how bad you are, I mean," Ron joked. "And I'll have to prove to you one day what a wonderful teacher I am! That's a date, right?"

Rachel blushed a little and then laughed outright. She looked quite pretty when she lightened up, Ron thought. "I think that's the joke of the year," she told him lightly, "but maybe I'll keep you to your promise one day. Seriously though," she went on, "I got the impression that I was really in the way a lot of the time, tagging on behind the others. Once, Larry cornered me and asked if you had badgered me into going."

Ron grinned. "What did you say?"

"What could I say but tell him the truth?"

Ron grinned again. "You don't mince words, do you?"

"So I'm told," she replied, laughing again. "I explained to Larry," she went on, "that you were an old friend of our family and that you had suggested that it would be a good idea if I went along too. That was all I said. It was all I needed to say."

"I'm so sorry if I've caused problems," Ron apologized.

Rachel gave him a look that reminded him very much of Esther. "Well, you did stir up things a bit, but I'm rather glad."

"Glad?"

"Yes. It made me see the direction both Gabby and I were heading." Rachel drained her glass and then put her elbows on the table and cupped her chin in her hands. "On the way to the mountains," she went on, "Larry and Andrea drove us by their home. Their dad's a doctor—a real charmer. He seemed to really take to Gabby. He's living with a woman—has been for five years or so. She's much younger than Dr. Porter and she was charming too, and very hospitable. Gabby was surprised that such nice, intelligent people could do something she had always been taught was wrong and not blink an eye about it. Andrea asked her what harm they were doing. Their family accepts it, and no one seems hurt by it, so why was it wrong? Larry saw Gabby's reaction and said sarcastically that he knew the Bible condemned this kind of thing, but that no one really intelligent took it seriously any more."

"And Andrea is going to live with you two next semester?"

"Yes." Rachel looked at Ron steadily for a moment. "Gabby's awfully fond of her. Personally, I'm still not sure about Andrea. I mean, I kind of like her. I tend to blame her family for her way of thinking. But her brother's not really like her." She frowned. "He's cold, somehow, but scary bright and knows how to get his point across. I'm just glad he's not studying at UT, that's all."

"Does Esther know about Gabby's friends?" Ron looked down at his plate as he spoke.

"Well, she's never met them."

"Maybe she ought to be warned."

"Maybe, but I'm not sure it would be a good idea. Esther tends to scold Gabby for nearly everything these days, and so they end up arguing. It's because she's worried about her, and that's only natural." Rachel shifted awkwardly in her seat, paused a moment, and then added slowly, "America seems to have a tendency to polarize families."

"Polarize?"

"Yes, especially immigrants. I watched it happen in Claude Iliescu's family. You might as well know the truth, Ron. Esther and Gabby are each going in directly opposite directions. Gabby's very close to being an agnostic now and is interested in every religion under the sun, while Esther still seems to be trying to escape her Velvet Curtain as she calls it." She saw Ron's face and knew she had slipped up.

"I mean," she went on hastily, saying the first thing that came into her head, "she never sings, hardly ever plays the piano, avoids men like the plague, and is talking of being a missionary. She's friends now with a girl and her brother who…"

Ron stopped her short. "I thought you said she avoids men's company?"

"She does, at least she has done up till now. The girl does have a brother, a widower with two kids. But it's the sister that she's friendly with. She only got to know her this Christmas while at her Great Aunt Lucy's."

Ron cut his steak with such vigor that a piece flew off his plate and landed on the floor. "Sorry," he muttered.

Rachel couldn't help smiling in spite of herself. "Ron, I don't think Esther's ready to become a step mum, if that's what you're afraid of. I wouldn't think that's at all in her line at the moment."

Ron had recovered his composure and looked steadily at his companion. "Come on, Rachel, let's not fool ourselves. Esther's eventually going to find a wonderful Christian guy. It's bound to happen. So I'm trying to prepare myself, but I haven't done a very good job so far."

Rachel's dark eyes filled with tears. "But you've got your life in front of you, Ron. You'll have to forget Esther if you can."

"Forget her? You wouldn't say that if you'd ever really been in love," he exclaimed heatedly.

Rachel blushed scarlet but said nothing. Ron could see she was embarrassed and what was more, deeply hurt. There was a long awkward silence and then he reached forward and patted her hand gently. "Sorry for that one. It was rude of me to put it like that. But when I start on to the subject of Esther, I get pretty much out of control."

Rachel said nothing and kept her eyes focused on her plate. "But I *have* tried to forget her," Ron went on. "I even went out on a date a month or so ago, but it was no good. Problem was, I immediately started to compare the girl with *her,* and that was the beginning of the end."

Rachel looked up at last. "I know you can't forget her," she told him gently. "I shouldn't even have mentioned it."

Ron looked at her in surprise. It seemed that he had never really known the real Rachel Popescu. Somehow, it seemed that this girl really did understand him, at least more than most of his friends did.

There was silence between them for a while. Rachel had nothing more to say. She couldn't tell Ron she'd pray for him. She didn't really know how to pray. So she just sat there, her heart welling up with pity as she watched him struggling for control.

The rest of the meal they talked little. When it was time to go, Ron held out his hand. "Thanks for putting up with me," he said with one of his charming smiles. "I'm not much company any more."

Rachel smiled back. "I'm not good company either. Never have been. So thanks for putting up with me."

"It's done me good. I never get to talk it all out with anyone and you..." he faltered, "you seem to understand. Thank you!" He turned on his heels and was gone.

The girl stared after him. "Life takes some strange twists and turns," she thought to herself as she made her way back to her apartment. "A few years ago I thought *he* wasn't good enough for Esther. Now I think *she's* not quite good enough for *him!*"

# Chapter Seven

## *Meeting of the Clans*

"Esther, why don't you play something for me tonight? It's been so long since I heard you play. Let's have a Romanian melody. I love those minors." Aunt Mary pulled out the piano stool and motioned for her niece to take a seat.

Esther shook her head. "No, Aunt. I don't play anymore."

"So I've noticed," Mary replied, a little sadly, "but why ever not?"

"Can't you guess?"

"Not really. It used to do you so much good. I can remember the evenings you would come over to my apartment and play and sing for hours on end."

"But those days are over, Aunt."

"Well, all I can say is that I can't imagine why you would keep such gifts bottled up inside. It'll do you harm eventually. What about the man who hid his talent in the ground?"

Esther's face darkened. "I tried to use mine, Aunt, and see what happened?"

Mary came to where her niece was sitting by the window and laid her hand on her shoulder. "I saw what happened when you allowed yourself to be manipulated and forced into a mold that wasn't meant for you. But that doesn't mean that there isn't a way to use your voice, a way that's just *you*. And you'll never find that out if you don't at least give it another try."

"I know you mean well, Aunt Mary, but I don't trust myself any more, especially here in America," Esther said sadly. "The Velvet Curtain's too much for me. I can't let it touch me any more, after all I've been through."

"But don't you realize that it touches you, all the time?" Mary sat down beside her niece and went on in a gentler tone, "This Curtain, as you call it, is all around us. The only way to avoid it completely would be, I suppose, to become a hermit. And then what good would we do for God, isolated like that? And, anyway, most of us couldn't take that kind of life."

"You might be strong enough to cope with this culture, Aunt, but I'm not. I've proved that all right." Esther's large eyes filled with tears. "I don't intend to be a hermit exactly, but I can do my best to keep myself from what would tempt me and, in the end, ruin me."

"But you're retreating into your own little world just when your sister needs you. Think at least of her."

Esther gazed out of the window for a few moments then laid her head back in the chair and gave a long sigh. "She doesn't want me right now. She's going a different path from me, Aunt Mary. You know that."

"Yes. I know that all right," Mary said grimly. Gabby and Rachel had just been back for mid-term break and she had noticed that the sisters had had little to say to each other and when they did, it usually ended in disagreement.

"Maybe you don't know what Gabby thinks now, Aunt," Esther's voice was defensive. "She never goes to church, never reads her Bible or prays, she's researching into all sorts of religions, watches R rated films, and I don't know what she does when I'm not around. I need to ask Rachel what is going on down there in Knoxville."

"No, don't make Rachel your spy," Mary's voice was sharp now. "Leave her out of it. She's stumbling around in the dark herself. And if Gabby is on the wrong track, I'd have thought that she needs you more than ever. For goodness' sake, can't you be less selfish?"

Esther's face flushed and she fidgeted uneasily in her seat. Her aunt had never talked like this to her before. And anyway, Mary was older and should take some responsibility for her wayward little niece. She was involved in so many other things—playing the organ at church, working overtime at school, helping tutor backward children, filling in for Marjorie at the Christian guest house up the road. Esther opened her mouth to say, "And she needs you too, Aunt, but you're always too busy," but no words would come out. Mary had been so kind to her. Esther could not hurt her for the world.

"Sorry I was a bit sharp," Mary apologized before her niece could think of something else to say.

"It's OK, Aunt," Esther told her. "And I suppose I am selfish at times without realizing it. But is it selfish to try to keep myself unspotted from the world? After all, I can't win Rachel or Gabby by going their way. That wouldn't work, would it?"

"Did I ask you to do that?"

"No, not exactly, but…"

"Esther, you've not been yourself since you spent Christmas with Aunt Lucy at Silver Springs. What exactly went on there?"

"I've told you, or Gabby has, I'm sure."

"I'm not talking about your quarrel with Gabby. I'm talking about yourself. You've altered since you came back home."

"Well, in the first place, I realized that I'd utterly failed with Gabby since she joined me in the States. When she first came, I was so occupied with myself and my own happiness that I miserably failed to help her adjust to life in this Western culture. But, as Aunt Lucy warned me, I'll never help her by compromising with her sin. I have to show her another path."

"I see."

"Yes, so naturally that affected me. And then, I met the most wonderful girl I've ever seen while I was there." Esther's eyes shone as she spoke and she looked a little more like the Esther of old. "She's absolutely beautiful and has a peace and serenity I desperately need."

"Did she tell you her secret?"

"Not exactly, but she lives it out."

Aunt Mary raised her eyebrows. "How?"

"She's the kindest and most thoughtful person I've ever met," Esther said enthusiastically. "She never gets ruffled, and she's always so gentle with her brother's kids. She's had a real tragedy in her life but she's overcome it. She told me she's made a vow to God never to marry and she's only in her late twenties."

Mary's blue eyes widened. "So that's her secret?"

"She didn't put it like that, but it could well be." Esther looked dreamily into the log fire that was burning in the grate. Her aunt studied her intently.

"So you think that celibacy is the way to peace?"

"I didn't say that." The girl's tone was reproachful now. "And Marion never advised me to copy her. She told me that she had discovered God's will for her life, and I had to find out His will for mine. But you know, Aunt Mary, I really think she has discovered a way to escape the Velvet Curtain; at least, that's what it seems like to me."

"Oh?" Her aunt tried hard not to sound too skeptical. "I really must meet this wonderful girl. Invite her down here for a weekend."

"I don't think she'd come, Aunt. She looks after her brother's kids and besides, she doesn't travel much."

"Then we'll take a run up to see her, and stop in at your Great Aunt Lucy's on the way. How about next Saturday? Phone your aunt and see if we can drop in. We won't stay the night but if we set off early, we'll be back before midnight at least."

Esther said nothing. Her animation seemed to have evaporated like the dew on a hot summer's day.

"You don't seem pleased at the idea?" Mary asked, her eyes narrowing.

"Well, of course I want to see Marion again, and Aunt Lucy, but…"

"You're afraid that they won't approve of me, right?"

Esther blushed scarlet. She wouldn't have put it like that but her aunt, as usual, had hit the nail on the head. Rachel was just like her in that.

"Esther," Mary went on, changing the subject, "have you talked all this out with Mr. Hugh? Does he know about Gabby's doubts, about Marion, and about your not playing or singing any more?"

Esther shook her head. "I haven't been up to his place since Christmas. He doesn't seem himself lately and hasn't been down here in a long while."

"That's true," her aunt mused.

Esther rose from her chair. She had had enough conversation for one evening. "Excuse me, but I need to get to bed. It's ten already," and she grabbed her sweater and slipped out of the room.

Her aunt sighed as the door closed behind her. She felt so unable to deal with either of her nieces, or her daughter for that matter. At that particular moment, Rachel seemed the least problematic of all the girls, except that she had not yet found her way to God, and that, in itself, was worry enough.

That night, Mary stayed on her knees longer than usual. Her conversation with Esther had deeply troubled her. Maybe she had been too busy to really understand her problem, and Gabby's too. Then she remembered how little she really knew what her own daughter, Rachel, was thinking. As for Ramona, she had seen so little of her for some years now, ever since she had walked out on her father, that memorable

Saturday afternoon, three and a half years before. Kneeling in the quiet of her bedroom, Mary felt so utterly helpless. All she could do was to bring each girl to the Lord, one by one. This done, she crawled into bed, exhausted but feeling, somehow, that her prayers had been heard.

She slept soundly and awoke the next morning feeling more relieved than she had felt for many a long day. It was Saturday morning. Mary remembered that Gabby was bringing Andrea and her brother for lunch. Rachel would be with them, too. Andrea wanted a ride into the mountains and so suggested that they combine it with a visit to Tiny Gap.

Mary had just set the house in order when the phone rang. It was Esther's friend, Marion, wanting to stop by for a brief visit. They were on their way to visit relatives in Virginia and had just reached a turnoff for Tiny Gap. If it was OK, they would be there within the hour. Ever hospitable, Mary invited them to stay to lunch. She smiled to herself. No visitors for weeks and then two carloads of them! And what a combination!

"The chicken casserole I've just put in the oven will never go round everyone," Esther exclaimed, as her aunt put down the receiver. "I'll go and fetch some Kentucky Fried Chicken from town."

Marion and her brother and his two children had been introduced and had just made themselves comfortable in the living-room when Esther returned, two large cartons of chicken in her hand. Marion's serious face blossomed into a welcoming smile.

Mary studied the girl intently. Her niece had been right. She was indeed a beautiful young woman who looked as if never a cloud shaded her angelic features. She glanced from her to her niece—equally beautiful, maybe even more so, but in a different, more earthy way.

"What well-behaved children you have, Mr. Morgan," Mary commented while the girls were chatting together.

Malcolm glanced fondly at his two daughters; the youngest was perched on his knee, and the other standing demurely at his side. "Marion spends a lot of time with them," he explained in his slow, deliberate way. "That's the secret." He glanced fondly at his sister as he spoke. "She's like a mother, you know. My wife died when the youngest was only six months old."

Mary had no time to reply. She heard a car door bang and hurried to the kitchen door to welcome the newcomers.

"We're here, Aunt Mary," Gabby shouted, as she sprang up the steps and flung her arms round her aunt's neck. She stopped short. "Oh, you've already got guests."

"Yes, Gabby. Esther's friends, Marion Morgan and her brother, have popped in for a visit."

"Of all things!" she exclaimed, as she turned to introduce Andrea and her brother.

"Now, you all make yourselves at home while I get the table set in the other room," Mary told them as she led the way into the lounge. "No, wait, there're too many of us for that. Let's have a buffet lunch."

"Good idea," Gabby agreed. "Here, let me help you, Aunt Mary."

"No, you stay and entertain your visitors, and you, too, Esther. Rachel and I will have everything done in no time."

Mary had just announced that all was ready when the doorbell rang. It was Aaron. "Talk about the gathering of the clans," Gabby said with a laugh as she introduced him to Andrea and Larry. "And those are Esther's friends," she added, as she pointed out Marion and her brother at the other end of the room.

"Stay for lunch, Aaron," Mary invited. "One more to feed won't make a difference."

Aaron took a seat beside Larry. "You're also a doctoral student, I hear," Larry said with a grin, as he made room for him on the sofa.

"Sure am."

"But you don't look a day more than eighteen."

"Looks are deceiving."

"Sometimes," agreed Larry. "What's your field?"

"Church History, sixteenth and seventeenth centuries; and yours?"

"Psychology."

"Really? I've never been too interested in that area of study, though it must be fascinating for those who have an inclination in that direction."

Larry stroked his goatee. "Yes, it is fascinating. Each man to his own taste, I suppose."

"Exactly! I thought I'd stick to English," Aaron said with a smile, "but I'm glad I didn't. It has been really helpful to study my heritage."

Larry's lips curled. Gabby leaned forward to hear what Aaron would say. They were the two smartest guys she had ever met, or just about.

"You're referring to America's heritage?" Larry asked.

"I'm referring to my heritage as a Christian," Aaron replied quietly.

"So you consider yourself a Christian, of course?"

Aaron looked thoughtful. "There's no of course about it," he said. "I think if you get through grad school with a firm belief in Christ, it's a sort of miracle nowadays."

"Not just grad school," Gabby chimed in.

Andrea looked at her sharply. "But Gabby," she protested, "you didn't consider yourself a Christian when you started college, now did you? At least, that's what you told me."

Gabby flushed. The room was quiet now and all eyes seemed to be focused on her. "Not the sort of Christian my parents were, or Esther was," she said slowly.

"*Was*?" Andrea repeated.

Gabby flushed again. "Well, I mean…" she stammered.

"I'm sure there aren't many nowadays who are the sort of Christian your parents were, Gabby," Aaron told her, feeling he had to come to her rescue. "I certainly know I'm not."

"Come on, let's eat," Mary interrupted. "The chicken will not be fit for anything if we don't tuck in right away."

Aaron found himself standing beside Malcolm and his sister as they waited in line. He studied them for a moment or two. He had always thought that Esther Popescu had something of the angel in her, but this young woman looked as if she had just stepped straight out of paradise.

Just then, Malcolm turned around. Aaron reddened and introduced himself. He found neither brother nor sister was very talkative, but they did tell him that they planned to go to Romania as missionaries.

"Both of you?" Aaron asked.

"Yes. For a while that is. At least till I get married. Marion's bound for Africa eventually. That's where she feels called to labor for God."

"So you plan to get married soon?"

"Well, everything hasn't been settled yet," Malcolm told him, flushing scarlet. "But I'm sure God will work it out in His time." He closed his mouth tight as if to say, "And that's all I'm telling you."

Aaron had reached the table by then and was piling his plate high with food. He took it back to the sofa. This time, he found himself sitting by Larry's sister.

"So you really are a Jesus guy, then?" Andrea wasn't going to let that subject pass.

"That's one way of putting it, I suppose," Aaron replied, frowning a little as he put down his plate on the coffee table.

"Seems a bit odd that you're that bright and yet believe all this stuff."

"Odd? I don't see anything odd in that. Scholars much more brilliant than I'll ever be have been *Jesus guys*, as you call it."

"But you said it was a miracle that kept your faith. What kept you on the straight and narrow?" persisted Andrea.

"For one thing, I never could forget my upbringing."

"You couldn't or you daren't?" Larry chimed in as he took a seat on the other side of Aaron.

"Both," Aaron replied promptly.

Larry raised his eyebrows. "I think any belief based on fear won't stand the test of life," he said, his voice tinged with sarcasm. "We have to be liberated from fear in order to become our true self."

"That's true," agreed Aaron thoughtfully. "But then, is anyone fully liberated in this life?"

"So you think that there is a life to come?"

"Yes, I do. In spite of our doubts, there seems to be something immortal within us which hints, at least, that death does not end it all."

"I think that it's rather foolish to speculate on a life hereafter and neglect the life that exists in the here and now."

"And by neglect you mean…?" Aaron raised his eyebrows.

"Failing to develop our potential to the fullest."

"But who really does that?" Aaron sounded rather skeptical. "And, anyway," he went on, "I don't think it's either/or, Larry. I mean, living truly up to one's potential is surely the best preparation for the life to come."

Larry was about to make a quick retort when a voice from the other end of the room, deep and sonorous, broke into their conversation. "Let's have a prayer for the food." It was Malcolm. He had risen, cap in hand and had already closed his eyes. Andrea stared in astonishment while her brother leaned back on the sofa and shut his eyes, out of resignation rather than reverence, Gabby supposed.

Malcolm's voice soon filled the room. Mary wondered how such a quiet man could suddenly become so loud and voluble. He prayed for God to have mercy on them all, to lead the erring into truth, the unbelieving into faith, the sinful into holiness, and the fearful into rest and peace. And then, of course, he thanked God for the food, said "Amen," and sat down. For a while, there wasn't much conversation in the room. Everyone seemed intent on their food. At last, Malcolm put down his plate and rose from his chair.

"We have to go now," he said in his slow, deliberate way.

"So soon?" Mary queried.

"I'm afraid so. We are already later than we had planned. Thanks for the food, Mrs. Popescu. And God bless you all." He made for the door with a nod at everyone. Esther followed Marion and the children to the car.

"Talk about pretty girls!" Larry exclaimed under his breath. "That blonde would be a real stunner, if she wouldn't hide so much of herself in her long clothes. And as for your sister, Gabby, she's simply fabulous."

Gabby grinned. "Wait till I show you a picture of her taken a few years ago," she whispered as she put down her plate. "I'll see if I can find it upstairs. Esther's hidden it somewhere."

Her sister was still outside with her friends when Gabby returned with a large studio photo of a slim, tanned girl in a long and rather revealing golden gown, a radiant smile on her beautiful face.

Larry studied it closely. "Wow!" he whistled. "Talk about a beauty queen! She's simply fabulous. Wish I'd known her then!"

"Here comes Esther," Gabby whispered hurriedly. "Put it away, please."

"She shouldn't be ashamed of a photo like that," Andrea commented. "She looks like a model."

"That's exactly the problem," Gabby muttered.

"Look, I've got to go now," Aaron interrupted. "It's been good to meet you. Bye, Gabby. Bye, Mary. Thanks for the meal."

"Strange guy," Larry muttered when Aaron had gone.

"He's a sort of genius," Gabby explained, flushing, "and geniuses are strange. You ought to know that, Larry!"

"You both have more brains than are good for you," Andrea interposed, as she rose from her chair and looked at her watch. "Gabby, you said there's a rather spectacular waterfall near here. Can you take us to see it?"

"Great idea," Gabby agreed. Then she turned to her sister who had just entered the room. "Esther, are you coming with us?"

Esther was about to refuse when she caught her aunt's eye. "If Aunt Mary doesn't need me to clear up here," she replied.

"I'll stay and help Mom," Rachel reassured them.

Esther was glad later that she had gone to the waterfall. By the time they had walked the two mile trail there and back, she had had plenty of opportunity to observe Gabby's friends. Andrea chattered incessantly about parties and holidays on the beach, about various movies she had seen recently, and, of course, about boys, moving from one subject to another at such speed it left the others little time to respond in any sensible way. Esther marveled at first that her sister had chosen this girl for her best friend, but by the time they had made it back to the car, she had to admit that there was something rather naïve and charming in Andrea that was very attractive.

Larry, however, was a different matter. His condescending air grated on her. Most of the time, he said little, his eyes roving from Gabby to herself, like some farmer, assessing prize cattle at an auction. This was unpleasant enough, but what was much more disconcerting was the uneasy sense that Larry Porter's gaze went far deeper than her face or her body. It probed her soul, as if trying to unearth secrets that she wanted no one but God to know.

"Your sister needs limbering up," Larry told Gabby as they drove back to Knoxville that evening. "She's so prim and proper."

"She's gone more that way lately," Gabby told him. She turned her head to look out the window. For some reason, she didn't want to discuss Esther just then.

"But she's got it all— figure, eyes, lips, hair! I'm afraid I couldn't keep my eyes off her."

"That was rather obvious," his sister commented dryly.

"Really?" Larry reddened.

"Really!"

"Well, what are beautiful girls for if not to be stared at?"

Gabby laughed. "You're not the only one that thinks like that, Larry."

"Jealous?" Andrea prodded.

Gabby flushed. "If I am, can you blame me?"

"You've no reason to be jealous," her friend reassured her, patting her on the shoulder affectionately. "Your personality makes up for everything. Why, your sister would bore me to death if I was alone with her five minutes, but you're great fun. Isn't that right, Larry? And I noticed that Esther wasn't the only one you were eyeing." Larry flashed Gabby one of his most captivating smiles but said nothing.

"And Marion Morgan looks like an angel," Andrea went on, turning to her friend who was toying with her watch strap and looking anything but comfortable. "But her brother was something else! I had the greatest job to keep from bursting out laughing in the middle of his prayer."

"He reminds me of a clown," Larry commented with a laugh, "only I guess he performs in church instead of a circus."

Andrea chuckled. "Great way to put it, Larry," she commented. Gabby frowned a little. She didn't like the way they were making fun of Esther's friends. Not that she was particularly fond of them herself, but there was no need to speak like that about anyone.

For the rest of the journey Gabby was unusually silent. "She's always like that after she's been home," Andrea told her brother later when they were alone.

"Why not invite her down to our place for the summer?" Larry suggested. "A change of environment will do her a world of good. She's looking for a job, isn't she? What about working in Sally's nursery, or maybe with Uncle Simon?"

"What a brilliant idea," Andrea told him. "Did you notice how Dad took to her when we stopped by the other day?"

"Yes, he sure did. But then, who wouldn't take to her?"

"You'd better watch out, Larry," Andrea warned. "Gabby's not interested in guys, especially American ones."

"That's what she's told you?"

"Sure has, more than once."

Larry grinned. "Maybe she'll change her mind before next summer is over. I think she needs liberating. And I think she really wants that. She's chafing at the bit right now."

"Never thought of it that way, but I suppose you're right."

"I'm always right," her brother replied with a grin. "At least when it comes to summing up girls, I am."

"I'm glad you like each other, you and Gabby, I mean," Andrea said dreamily. "Most girls find you intimidating, but I don't think Gabby does."

"No, I don't think the girl is intimidated by me," Larry agreed. "But she's not completely at ease with me yet either."

"Give her time, Larry."

"Sure will," he said with a laugh. "All summer."

# Chapter Eight

## *All for the Kingdom?*

"Keith, we've just got to do something about our youth pastor."

Keith Cripps stared at his wife thoughtfully for a few moments but said nothing.

"Are you listening? We've got to do something," Betty repeated.

"But you've already spoken to him, haven't you?"

"A little. I suggested that his behavior with girls might just have something to do with why the youth group is dwindling so steadily. It's only been the last week or so that I've had definite complaints, something concrete to make me feel that I was right all along."

"Well, whatever you said seems to have sobered him up a bit, hasn't it?"

"Maybe a little, either that or his mother's illness, or both combined," conceded Betty. "But the damage has been done already. Let's take Connie Frith, for example. She poured her heart out to me yesterday. She's been so hurt. No wonder she's not been in church for an age."

Her husband caught her gaze and held it. "Just what are you trying to say, Betty?"

Betty cleared her throat before replying, "I'm saying that things can't go on as they are, can they?" She got up from her chair and began pacing the room.

"Wait a minute," her husband interrupted. "Exactly how did Len hurt her? What did he do? I can't think that it was something terribly disgraceful, or I'd have heard about it before now." He looked up at his wife as he spoke, his eyes searching hers.

"He hasn't gone to bed with her or with any other girl in our church, if that's what you mean by disgraceful," Betty began, ignoring her husband's shocked expression. "No, it's not like that. It's more subtle."

"Len, subtle?"

Betty groaned. "I know you're fond of your talented youth pastor, and so am I, but let's face reality. You've been so busy preparing sermons, visiting the sick, marrying and burying, that you've been pretty oblivious to what's going on among the young people."

"What has been going on?" Keith was growing impatient now.

"Your colleague, your partner in the ministry, has been playing on the emotions of the girls he was supposedly winning to Christ." Betty's eyes flashed fire as she went on heatedly: "It seems as if he thought the end justified the means. I mean, he did seem to have quite a few converts at one point. Interestingly enough, they were nearly all girls, and pretty attractive ones too, and all under twenty." Betty couldn't keep the sarcasm out of her voice. "I've had complaints from more than just Connie. It seems that each girl tells the same story. He would begin by showing a personal interest in them—a meal out, a walk in the park, always accompanied by a Scripture reading when he would show them the way of salvation, or how to walk with the Lord. He always would pray with them too, very moving prayers, I'm told." Betty's tone was definitely sarcastic now. "Of course, he gained quite a few girl converts, but you can imagine the rest." She paused a moment for breath.

Her husband said nothing but motioned for her to go on. "Maybe Len didn't realize the full impact of his charm," his wife continued with a wry smile, "but Connie told me that when he would look deep into her eyes and tell her she was very special to the Lord and to him, she really thought he cared for her. And he would often accompany his words with an arm round the shoulder, or a squeeze of the hand, so you can imagine what kind of a message he was giving. Connie said he even gave her a goodnight kiss once or twice and she said he did it with others, too."

Keith's eyes opened wide. "He actually kissed them? You mean he had one girlfriend after another?"

Betty shook her head. "No, that was part of the problem. The girls would have understood that kind of behavior better. But it wasn't like that. In Len's eyes, none of them was his girlfriend in the usual sense of the word. To him, they were all potential converts who needed winning to Christ and then discipling. When he figured they could stand on their own two feet, he would move on to the next potential convert.

This caused jealousy among the girls, and provoked some of the guys into the bargain."

"That's bad," Keith exclaimed, now thoroughly roused. "And kissing them! Well…"

"Now it was just a big brotherly kiss on the forehead," Betty put in, "or so Len has called it, but you know young teenage girls. Any physical contact with a charmer like Len, a flattering word, those dark eyes staring into theirs, and they're a goner."

Keith Cripps frowned. "It's more serious than I thought. And I suppose Len deceived himself into thinking he was doing it all for God's glory. He certainly seemed successful for a while—we had the biggest youth group in the city, or almost."

"We don't any more," Betty assured him. "And what's worse, just think of our testimony. Connie's mom, for one, is thoroughly disgusted with our church. As I said before, Keith, we've simply got to do something."

Her husband leaned back in his chair and stared at the ceiling for a few moments. "All this has come at a very bad time," he said slowly. "Len's trying to cope with his mother's terminal illness and he seems distracted. He's a lot more subdued lately. I can't think that these complaints have anything to do with his recent behavior."

"No, they don't," Betty agreed. "But the damage has been done. And besides, I'm not sure how permanent Len's change is. I don't think he realizes what harm he has done. Personally, I don't think he's cut out for a youth pastor, but we'll have to watch our step." Betty's eyes filled with tears as she went on: "We don't want to knock him when he's down and yet we can't go on like this. I think a good long break from any sort of ministry is what he needs right now."

Keith nodded. "I hate to do this, but yes, I think you're right. Let's call him today and meanwhile, we'd better do a lot of praying."

In the days that followed, both husband and wife came to the conclusion that Len must be held accountable for what he had done. And so one Friday afternoon, a very nervous Betty Cripps ushered Len into her husband's study, brought him a glass of his favorite homemade lemonade, and then shut the door softly behind her. She had refused to be present at the interview. She had confronted him once, she told Keith, and that was enough.

Keith cleared his throat and began: "You probably know why I wanted to speak to you," he told his colleague sadly when they were alone. Len kept his eyes focused on his shoes and said nothing.

"Betty has already broached the subject," Keith went on awkwardly, "so it won't come as a surprise when I tell you that there have been quite a few complaints about your conduct." Silence again. Len was certainly not making it easy for him.

"I'm going to have to enumerate these complaints," the older man said slowly. "It's not easy for me, but it has to be done."

Len raised his dark eyes to Keith's. "I'm sorry," was all he said.

Pastor Cripps toyed with his pen for a few moments; then, very deliberately and painstakingly, he repeated what his wife had told him, point by point. "What do you say to all this?" he asked Len when he had finished, hoping wildly that his colleague would stand up and denounce the whole thing as a trumped up case against him.

"I'm guilty on every point," Len said abruptly when Keith had finished. The pastor's heart sank. "My only excuse would be that I thought I was doing it *all for the Kingdom,"* Len added half-apologetically.

Keith groaned. "I thought you might say that," he said sadly.

"But I do want to make something very clear." Len's tone was defensive now. "I always made quite sure that I did not transgress what I considered to be a moral boundary. I mean…"

"Moral boundary!" Keith exploded. "So playing with one girl's affections after another is not transgressing a moral boundary?"

Len stared at his friend in dismay. Keith's words shook him to the core. "Playing with a girl's affections," he repeated to himself. So that's what he'd done, was it? Put like that, it didn't sound good at all. In fact, it sounded utterly despicable.

Len buried his head in his hands and sat crumpled in his chair. Keith came over to where the young man was sitting, and placed a hand on his shoulder. His anger had gone now, leaving only pity in its place. "There, there, Len, don't take it so hard," he said gently.

Len shook off his hand and rose to his feet. "You hit me over the head with accusations," he began angrily, "and then you tell me not to take it so hard? My whole career is ruined. With a reputation like I have now, I'll never get a decent job. No, don't pity me! Just give me space and time to think it all over. Excuse me, but I can't take any more right now."

Len stalked to the door, opened it and then let it bang behind him. Keith stared after him in dismay. He had never seen Len like this before. He was usually so charming, so suave, so self-possessed.

Keith ate little for supper that evening. Betty had cleared away the dishes when the doorbell rang. It was Len Atwood, back to apologize. He was ashamed of himself, thoroughly ashamed, he told Keith and Betty, as he stood facing them in the hallway. His face was bathed in tears and his voice trembled as he spoke.

"I'm handing in my resignation," he spluttered, ignoring their invitation to take a seat. "You may be too polite to fire me, but you and I both know that the only solution is for me to go."

Husband and wife exchanged glances but said nothing. "How blind I've been," Len was speaking so hurriedly that Keith had to bend forward to catch his words as he went on: "I thought I did it *all for the Kingdom*, when I did it mostly for me, the wonderful youth pastor, who had more in his youth group than any church around. Connie's mother has every right to be mad. I may have damaged her daughter for life. And Ramona Popescu, Esther's cousin, saw right through me when she had the courage to tell me straight out that I mixed flirtation with religion and that it was dangerous and wouldn't work. And as for Esther," he choked back another sob, "I saw myself transforming this simple Romanian into a glamorous singer who would live to credit me with her rise to fame. How could I be such a conceited fool!" Len wailed.

"Please ask Connie to forgive me, Betty," he begged between sobs. "I can't do anything more than that, except to leave the church. If I leave, she'll come back again."

"Of course I'll ask her, Len," Betty reassured him, fighting back the tears.

Len turned towards the door. "Let's pray," he heard the pastor saying behind him and his voice seemed a long way off. He let himself be led into the lounge and over to the sofa where he knelt by the man with whom he had worked for five whole years. He listened while his friend poured his heart out to God, but was scarcely conscious of what he was saying.

"I can't pray yet," he muttered, when Pastor Cripps had finished.
"No? That's not surprising. You are still in shock."

"Yes, I am, but I need to ask more than Connie's forgiveness," Len muttered under his breath. "I need yours, and Esther's, and Ron's, and Ramona's, and all the other girls in the youth group and most of all, I need God's. I've made a mockery of my profession."

"But you can change, Len. Repentance brings transformation, you know." The pastor's voice was comforting. "Oh, there's the phone. Just a moment."

He picked up the receiver. "What? Oh I'm sorry. I'll tell him to come immediately. Where? OK, I've got it. I'll pass on the message."

Len looked up, face ashen. "It's my mother, isn't it?"

"It is." Keith's face was full of sympathy. "Poor Len, it never rains but it pours."

"She has been very ill for so long, I was expecting this. She's been unconscious for weeks now. I was reluctant to leave her but Dad told me I needed a break. She's been taken to the hospital?"

"Yes." Keith handed the younger man a slip of paper with the room number written in his clear, bold hand.

"Our prayers will be with you," Keith told him softly.

What was God trying to say to him? Len asked himself as he sped down the interstate towards Cincinnati. He gripped the wheel tightly. "God," he breathed in an agony of desperation, "I need You as never before. Forgive me. I know I've been a very unworthy servant and now Mom's dying. Oh God, I need You! I need You!"

Len heard no answering Voice, felt no reassuring hand on his shoulder, saw no blinding light. But as he stared at the road ahead, even it seemed more real, and the street lights, and the road signs. And even his tears—they were real tears for once, yet it felt as if each drop seemed to leave him weaker, as if he were crying his life blood away.

# Chapter Nine

## *Len in Shock*

"So she's gone," was all Len could say, as he stood gazing at his mother's lifeless form. He had arrived just half an hour too late.

"Yes, she's gone," his father repeated with a choking sob. "She was asking for you right up to the end."

Len came and knelt by his mother's bed. He took her hand in his and buried his face in the bedclothes. His father left the room to make several phone calls and came back to find his son in the same position. He let him stay there for at least an hour and then, stooping over the grief-stricken young man, he tapped him lightly on the shoulder.

"We have to go now," he told him gently. "The funeral home is taking over. We'll have a chance to see her tomorrow and stay as long as we like."

"But she'll be artificial tomorrow—all painted and made up to look like she isn't," Len sobbed. "This is the way I want to remember her—emaciated, ravaged by disease, but still Mom."

Steve Atwood took his hand away and tiptoed out of the room. It was past midnight when, at last, tearstained and weary, Len rose from his knees and joined his father in the waiting-room.

He would never forget that evening. It was his first close-up brush with death and it devastated him. He had arrived at the hospital shattered but determined to face his past and remedy it if he could. But he had not realized the effect his mother's lifeless form would have on him. And now, wandering through the spacious house that had been her *home*, he felt as if he were searching for something—some token of something eternal—something that would defy death and the grave. Oh, he knew all about the Christian doctrine of immortality, and so had his mom. But now, with death stalking their home and ravaging their lives, what did he have to cling to?

He picked up his mother's Bible lying on the table and opened it. He knew she read it regularly, along with her women's magazines, and several catalogues that lay strewn over the room. He remembered how she had been determined, during those last months, to always look her best—colorful clothes, nails manicured, hair styled just as she liked it—anything to hide the deadly cancer that was eating her life away.

It was true that he had read the Scriptures to her whenever he was home, and it did bring some comfort. And he knew that his mother had an assurance that she would meet her Lord and Master and live with Him forever. But it was a hope that seemed to have had little relevance to her present-day living.

Len sighed. Is this how it would be one day with him? Would his son, if he ever had one, be wandering around the home that had once been his, groping for some vestige of assurance that his father had truly lived for things eternal, not just preached about them?

He slumped into a chair and covered his face with his hands. He must have dozed a little for when he woke, Steve Atwood was sitting opposite him, an envelope in his hands.

"Len," he whispered hoarsely, his face grey and drawn, "your mom wanted me to give this to you if you arrived after she…" He couldn't go on.

Len reached for the envelope and broke open the seal. "If you don't mind, I'll let you read it alone," his dad told him. "That's the way *she* wanted it."

Len began to read the two-page letter, written in his father's clear, bold hand. His mother had obviously dictated it to her husband. She had not had strength to write clearly for some weeks.

"Dear Len," he began to read, his hope soaring a little. Maybe this letter would have some exhortation, some legacy of faith, some advice, anything above and beyond what he could see and touch.

"What I am now going to tell you should have been told years ago." Len gave a start and then forced his eyes back to the page. "But somehow, I reasoned that it was better for you not to know. Steve has been urging me for years to tell you the truth. I kept putting it off until now. I couldn't face the God above without confessing to you that I'd lived a lie all these years."

Len's hands were trembling now as he read on: "I have to tell you, Len, that the man you have called father all these years is not your real dad." Len stared at the words in front of him in disbelief. He simply could not believe what he was reading. It was utterly impossible. And yet would a dying woman tell an untruth to her only son? No, it must be true. He tried to focus once more. "Your real father," the letter went on, "was a good friend of Steve's; in fact, he was the song leader of the first church he ever pastored. I have no excuse to give for my sin except that I was, or I thought myself to be, a victim of circumstances. Young and beautiful and talented, or so they all told me, I found, soon after our marriage, that I had little in common with my down-to-earth husband who hardly ever paid me a compliment or seemed to recognize my consuming ambition to do something with my life. I was merely *Pastor Atwood's wife*—young and beautiful but full of whims and impractical notions that nobody paid any attention to.

"Then Steve was always so busy that I felt quite neglected and so became more and more open to the marked attentions that this other man gave me. He was brilliant, outgoing, and strikingly handsome. He recognized my talents, listened to my ideas, and told me that God had poured His gifts into my lap and that I should use them for His glory. I happened to be the pianist at our church which threw us constantly together. We began to confide in each other, and I soon discovered that his wife did not understand him any more than Steve understood me.

"At last, we both became convinced that we were madly in love with each other. I struggled against my feelings for a while and even begged Steve to leave the church and get another pastorate. Not knowing the real reason behind my request, he thought it was just another whim of mine, and told me that it was utterly impossible.

"Then, one September while at a choir retreat in the mountains, neither of us could control our passion any longer. It was not long before rumors reached Steve's ears which roused his suspicions. I was utterly ashamed at what I'd done and resigned my position as pianist and tried to be the perfect wife. But it was too late. I soon found out I was pregnant and in panic, I confessed everything to Steve. At first, he was terribly angry and threatened to divorce me, but when he saw I was truly sorry and didn't want anything more to do with the song-leader, he forgave me. It was then that I discovered he really and truly loved me.

"Before the baby was born, Steve asked for a transfer. Because you looked so like me, we seemed to get away with our secret. And we tried to justify our deceit by saying that, if the church knew the truth, God's Name would be discredited. And, after all, I had repented, hadn't I? I had been forgiven?

"God might have forgiven me, but I could not forgive myself. I tried to forget my sin and my shame by making sure I looked attractive, dressed in the latest fashion, and was always smiling and upbeat. Nearly everyone held me up as the model pastor's wife. But I think my brother-in-law, Ron's dad, guessed the truth. It was the way he looked at me when he remarked that you were not a bit like an Atwood. I could be wrong, but I think this is probably why he would never listen when I used to urge him to become a Christian. He seemed to sense that my witnessing was a cover-up for what I really was—an attempt to redeem my past.

"Steve and I never could have a child. This is why I idolized you and utterly spoiled you. As you grew, I saw more and more of your real dad in you. And you and Steve never had much in common. You never could understand each other.

"I want to tell you all this the next time you come home, but if I never see you again, I have asked Steve to give you this letter. What can I say, Len, but that I'm terribly sorry that I kept this from you all these years. You had a right to know long before this. Please, please forgive me.

"If you ever wish to look up your real dad, Steve can give you his name. I can't bring myself to do it right now. I don't really want you to meet him. He's somewhere in Australia, I believe.

"I'm too weak to go on now. Goodnight, Len. See you in the morning, Mom."

Len read through the letter at least three times before he finally put it back in its white, scented envelope. He was thoroughly stunned. In one day he had received three blows, any one of which would have been enough to send him into a month's depression: he had been pretty much forced to resign from his pastorate; the one person in the world whom he truly loved had been snatched from him just when he needed her the most; and now, before he could even bury his mom, he had discovered that he was her bastard son, and what was worse, that she had lied to him for all these years.

Len's world collapsed around him as he sat staring into space for what must have been hours. Shock turned to a deep, fierce anger that threatened to consume every vestige of love and hope that he had ever cherished. Then, before morning dawned, his anger turned into self-pity. It swept over him in waves. What had he done to deserve this? So it wasn't his fault, after all, that he had made a mess at Pine Grove Evangelical Church! It was his father's fault—his real dad's fault. And his mom's.

Len shut himself in his room the next morning for hours. Always emotional, it now seemed that every emotion there was took its turn to engulf him, every negative one, that is. Joy and hope and peace seemed as inaccessible as the North Pole. Then, at noon, he heard Steve's knock on his bedroom door. "Len, please, we need to plan the funeral," the older man pleaded.

Len stood stock still in the middle of the room. "Plan it yourself," he muttered.

Steve knocked again. "Len," he begged. "Please, please come out. I..." There was a sob as the voice stammered, "I need you."

Len stared at the locked door. Was he hearing correctly? The competent, self assured Steve Atwood needed *him*—the failed preacher, the illegitimate son? Len turned the key, and threw open the door. The next moment, the two men were in each other's arms.

"We've got to stand together," Steve muttered. "It's only you and I now."

"But... but... I'm not..." Len couldn't finish the sentence.

"Please forgive us, Len, for hiding this from you. It wasn't right. But for today, and tomorrow, and the next, can you put this aside? Your mom's dead. There are relatives to be phoned, the funeral service to arrange, and I just can't cope alone." Steve looked up and met Len's gaze. "I loved her, Len," he sobbed, "and she's gone."

Suddenly, Len realized who Steve Atwood really was. He had been faithful to a woman who had cheated on him; he had fathered someone else's son. And even though he had never understood Len or shown him much outward affection, he had supported him through college, had come to his graduation, had never spoken harshly to him or abused him in any way. And, best of all, he had truly loved his wife, put up with her whims, supplied her with all she wanted, and nursed her as tenderly as any woman during her long illness.

Len grasped Steve's hand in his. "Dad," he began, his voice faltering, "can I still call you that? You are the only dad I've known and as you said, right now we sure need each other."

Steve's grip tightened as he whispered, "You are the only son I'll ever have, Len," he murmured brokenly. "And you're all that I've left of *her*."

## Chapter Ten

### *Ramona's Wedding*

"I never thought Rachel and Esther were so alike," Gabby whispered.

"The first time I met your sister, I saw the similarity," Mary told her niece. She shaded her eyes as she scrutinized the wedding party. "And dressed all alike as bridesmaids," she added, "they certainly could be taken for sisters."

Gabby laughed. "Nothing could make *me* look very much like Esther."

Mary thought she detected just a trace of bitterness in her niece's voice and tried to change the subject. "They say you're a lot like your dad."

"In looks, maybe, but that's about all." Gabby adjusted her sunglasses as she spoke. "I sometimes feel the odd one out in my family."

Her aunt shook her head at her. "You're just Gabby Popescu, that's all," she said lightly. "You're unique and always will be. And I love you just as you are."

"You're sure?" The girl's voice was wistful now.

"Positive!" Mary put her arm round her niece as she spoke.

"But you wish I'd be more religious, don't you?"

"I wouldn't put it like that, Gabby," Mary replied quietly. "But I worry that you seem to think you can get on in life without the Lord. I..."

"Here's Uncle John coming our way," Gabby interrupted. "I'll go and see him. It'll save you having to say much."

Mary glanced over her shoulder. "I've said hi already, and that's about all I can take right now." A shadow flitted over her expressive features. "I'll go and have a word with Ron. He's alone over there."

"Gabby, you look great today!" John told his niece as he gave her a hug. "Green sure suits you. But you seem a bit serious for a wedding. Hope you don't feel left out. I wanted you to be a bridesmaid too, you know."

Gabby flashed him one of her special smiles as she took his arm. "Me feel left out?" she asked with a short laugh. "Why should I? After all, Ramona hardly knows me. And Marci and Kelly are her best friends. I'm just glad she asked Esther. Doesn't she look fabulous today?"

"When doesn't she?" John asked with a smile. "Ramona had a job to persuade her to be a bridesmaid," he went on, "but she eventually gave in."

"I suppose it seemed a bit much for her, two weddings in two months. I mean, she was a bridesmaid at her friend Margaret's wedding not long ago."

"So I heard," John answered absentmindedly. He was thinking how young Mary looked in her sky blue two-piece outfit. No one would guess that she was nearing fifty. He wondered again why everything had happened as it had. No, he must not give in to that kind of thinking. Diane was his wife now and he was comparatively happy. They were really very well suited, he told himself. They took good care of each other and had quite a lot in common. What more could a man of fifty wish for?

John turned his gaze to the wedding party and let his eyes feast on his pretty daughter. Her golden curls peeked out from under her veil, and her blue eyes were dancing. She was the blooming bride all right, though her fond father couldn't help wondering if, deep down, she was truly as happy as she appeared.

John had spared nothing for her wedding, even though he secretly wished that the groom were someone other then Claude Iliescu. But he and Claude's parents were old friends; they had assured him that while their son certainly didn't wear his virtues on his sleeve, they were sure that he would prove a very faithful and loyal husband. The boy might seem strange at times, they told John, but he was a good lad at heart and had doted on Ramona for years. He'd never looked at any other girl, as far as they knew.

John had thought over the matter and ended up giving in. Perhaps he knew it was no use to refuse. Claude and Ramona would have gotten married anyway, and why cause them to do it clandestinely? No, this was by far the best way, he had told himself, as he heard his daughter take her vows. Tears filled his eyes. He wished he'd been a better father. He wished he and Mary had made a go of it. He wished... He came to with a jolt. What use was it recriminating himself like that at his daughter's wedding?

Then his gaze turned to Esther. He knew she had dreaded this wedding. She had known that Ron would be there and she would have to meet him for the first time since her illness. Then, even at the distance John was standing, he could see a deep blush spread over her face. He looked around. Ron was standing a few paces away, his eyes riveted on the dark-haired beauty. His mother watched him and her face clouded.

"Can't you forget her?" she whispered in his ear.

"No. It's impossible," Ron answered without shifting his gaze.

"Esther's a picture today, I admit. She's really the beauty of the show."

"Even outshines the bride," Ron said, a curious smile playing on his lips.

"Depends if you prefer raven-haired maidens to blondes, which you certainly seem to do." His mother laid her gloved hand on his shoulder. "Ron, if Esther lost her beauty, would you still love her?" she asked gently.

"Of course," Ron did not hesitate.

"But, if her fabulous looks were demolished, would there be anything else left for you to love?"

Ron was about to give his mother an angry retort but he bit his lip. He knew she was trying to help. She was worried that he'd die a bachelor, in love with a shadow till the end of his days.

Ron didn't get a chance to speak to Esther till after the reception. It had been held in a large tent that John had erected on their spacious lawn. The tables had now been cleared away and the dancing was beginning. He saw her make her exit and slipped out after her.

"Esther!"

She turned round and blushed scarlet. "Ron!" She held out her hand. He took it and held it just for a moment before releasing it with a smothered sigh.

"You look gorgeous." His voice seemed strange even to himself.

"Thanks." She dropped her eyes.

"John thought you hadn't regained your health fully when he saw you at the New Year, but today you look a picture of…" He paused. "Words can't describe what I think you look like."

Esther's heart beat fast as she let him lead her back to the house. "Let's sit down a moment on the porch," Ron suggested as they both took a seat. "Now, tell me all about yourself."

"Oh, there's not much to tell. I'm commuting to college. I have one more year and then I hope to go as a missionary to Romania."

"Really?" Ron had known that already but he rather hated to hear it from her own lips.

"And what about you?"

"I have one more year also and then I'll be a full-fledged lawyer, I suppose," and his voice held no animation in it. They chatted on for a while about everything in general and nothing in particular. Then Ron turned to the girl at his side and said in a low voice, "I saw you catch the bouquet this afternoon."

Esther flushed scarlet. "It came right to me," she began. "I thought of letting it drop but…"

"Oh, don't make excuses," Ron told her with a wry smile. "Everyone knows that you're the most eligible girl in this whole place. You must see how all the guys look at you. Only…" He got up from his chair. "Sorry, but I just can't take it, Esther. When you get married, I'll have to be oceans away."

"I don't intend to ever get married, Ron." He stared at her for a few moments. "I mean," she went on, avoiding his eyes, "I think God might be asking me to be single all my life."

Ron laughed, and his laugh was hard and brittle. "That's joke number one," he told her, and his voice sounded strange to Esther. She couldn't bear to think of Ron Atwood growing into a cynical old bachelor. She let out a smothered sob.

Ron looked at her in concern and saw the tears trickling down her cheeks. He took out his handkerchief and handed it to her. "Sorry, Esther. I'm awfully sorry. But sometimes I feel as if I almost hate God for what He did to us. Oh, I know I shouldn't talk like this, but I've got to be truthful. And I'd never mean to hurt you, never."

"I know that," she told him looking up at him with those eyes that he could never ever forget, those eyes that always totally unmanned him. Before he could stop himself, he had bent down and kissed her, long and passionately.

Esther pulled away. "No, Ron, please," she began, as she reached for her purse. She must get away. He was too much for her.

"Sorry again. It just won't do for me to see you, Esther," he muttered, helping her out of the chair as he spoke.

"I think I'll get on home now," she said in a low voice. "I'm staying with Margaret's family in Terre Haute and I want to get back before it's too late."

"I'll see you to your car." He's always the perfect gentleman, Esther thought as he held the car door open for her. "I wish you all the best," he told her, as he watched her put the key in the ignition. "And remember, I still love you." Esther dropped her eyes. "I know it's all over between us—you a missionary, me an avaricious lawyer," he went on. Esther hated to hear that bitterness in his tone again.

He saw tears making wet patches on her dark pink dress. He gritted his teeth. But he had to say just one thing more. "You will always be my angel, Esther," he murmured, taking her hand and giving it a gentle squeeze. "And I hope, I really hope, that some miracle happens and I'll see you with all the other angels, one day."

He closed the door and turned away. Esther put her foot on the accelerator and then braked. Rolling down the window she called, "Ron?"

He stopped in an instant and looked round. "There's just one thing more. It's Gabby."

Ron smothered his frustration. He didn't want to talk about Gabby right then. He'd tried to do his best for the girl, more than Esther knew, but right then he just wanted to be alone. That one kiss had upset him terribly. For two whole years he had tried to forget and now he seemed to be reliving all the pain and anguish of that fateful summer.

Esther sensed his annoyance. "Sorry," she faltered, "but I'm worried about Gabby tonight."

"Worried?" His voice was gentler now.

"Yes. Aunt Mary's left already and, well, my sister's already had a few glasses of wine, so I wondered if you could please keep an eye on her for the rest of the evening?"

Ron glanced towards the tent that had been set up on the lawn. The music was getting louder. He hoped the neighbors would be tolerant, just for one evening.

Then he looked down into Esther's worried face. "I'll do my best," he said softly. "Not that my best amounts to very much these days." He knew he shouldn't have added those words as soon as they were out of his mouth.

"Thanks a lot, Ron," Esther murmured, her face clouding. She revved up the engine. Ron watched as she edged the car onto the road. He clenched his fists as he turned away once more. Life had no right to continue like it did, an endless succession of waking and sleeping, of working and eating, of talking and laughing, of trying to constantly throttle this indestructible love of his for a girl he would never ever hold in his arms again. It was just his luck to have God for a rival. He might as well give up. He'd never win, never.

"Getting a bit raucous in there, Ron. Just thought I'd better warn you." He gave a start as he peered through the gathering shadows. He saw Rachel coming up the path towards the house, arm in arm with Gabby. He could just make them out in the twilight. "We're going to bed," Rachel announced. "We've had enough."

"Speak for yourself," Gabby muttered thickly.

"Very wise girls," Ron told them, ignoring Gabby's comment. Esther was right, that sister of hers did need a bit of watching, but it seemed that her cousin was managing pretty well without his help. He turned on his heel. "Think I'll turn in myself for the night. I'm not one for partying much these days. Good night."

"Good night, Ron," Rachel's voice echoed in the darkness. Ron stared after them. Rachel was certainly showing a sense of responsibility to that wayward little cousin of hers. And that relieved him of his promise to Esther.

He gritted his teeth as he slid open the patio door. He'd have to make it his life's work to forget that girl. He just hoped he was at the other side of the world when she married, as he knew she would in spite of all her protests. He flopped into the nearest chair. He could hear the girls in the kitchen. Rachel was probably making her cousin a strong cup of coffee.

"Ron, do you mind if I join you?"

He started. John had come into the room and was standing by the bookcase. Company was the last thing Ron wanted at that moment, but he had come to have considerable respect for the man his mother had married, and it looked as if he had something rather important on his mind.

John set down his glass of wine on the table and took a seat. "I've wanted to have a talk with you for a long time but never dared. I didn't think I knew you well enough. But seeing you at the wedding today and noticing how you looked at my niece, I thought the time had come."

Ron said nothing as he leaned back and crossed his long legs, waiting for whatever lecture might be coming.

"What I'm going to say isn't easy for me, Ron, but it might just do you good some day in the future, even if you're not ready to hear it today." He paused, and Ron waited in silence.

"I'm not sure if Esther ever told you, but I was in love with her mother." Ron nodded. He had heard the story before, or part of it at least.

"But she chose my brother because he was a Christian. I couldn't really blame her, but her choice broke my heart. I had to leave the country. So I came here, married on the rebound, and you know the rest. Maybe what you don't realize, though, is that until very recently, I kept Lydia Popescu in my heart and compared every other woman, including my own wife, with her. It ruined my first marriage. I saw it would do the same for my second, so I finally got rid of her picture from my room and, I hope, from my heart. At least, I don't think of her daily, or dream about her at night any more though, of course, she was my first and..." he paused. He was gong to say his only true love. But he couldn't say that, even if it were true, not to Diane's son.

Ron stared at his shoes. He had more in common with this man than he had thought. "So what has this to do with you, you are asking?" John paused, waiting for an answer.

Ron gave a short laugh. "There's no need to ask, is there?"

"Yes, it is pretty obvious, isn't it? So, don't you go and be the fool I was. Try to put Esther out of your heart forever. But," he paused and looked the young man straight in the eyes, "if you can't do that, then don't marry anyone else. It's not fair to the woman you will call your wife."

Ron got up from his chair. He couldn't speak. "Thanks, I'll remember what you've said," he muttered, and fled from the room.

Ron was still remembering John's words as he drove down to Cincinnati with his mother two days later. His aunt had died just before the wedding. He had not seen Len since his visit to Cincinnati in January. Neither had he seen his father, Len's uncle, since Christmas. He would be at the funeral, he was nearly certain.

Ron was right. As he entered the church with his mother, he noticed his dad, sitting in a pew at the very back. He had evidently chosen not to be included with the chief mourners at the front even though it was his sister-in-law's funeral. He looked thin and worn and sad, and was obviously still battling with his old enemy—alcohol. If Ron's mother noticed him too, she gave no indication. Ron's heart ached for them both, and he vowed again that he would rather be a bachelor all his life than marry the wrong woman.

From where he was sitting, Ron could see that Len's dad, usually so self-contained, was completely overcome with emotion during the service. And later, at the graveside, it was very evident that Len and his father were much closer than they used to be. But then, Ron figured, death often brings many changes to a family. Maybe this was one of them.

After the reception given in the basement of the mammoth church where Steve Atwood was senior pastor, Len waylaid his cousin and suggested they go somewhere quiet for a cup of coffee. "I want a few words alone with you, Ron," he whispered as he pushed open the large, swinging doors.

Ron was very surprised. Len had never gone out of his way to talk to him for as long as he could remember. They had never hit it off together, so why his cousin should want a private talk, he had no idea.

"You'll be wondering why on earth I asked to talk to you," Len said with a wry smile as they set their coffee mugs down on the round, wooden table of the little café just round the corner from the church.

"Yes. It's not often we get to chat together."

"No. And that's been my fault."

"Yours?"

"Yes." Len cleared his throat. "I might as well get to the point right away. It's no use beating about the bush. I want to apologize, Ron, for the way I've treated you over the years. I was always preaching at you as if you were the biggest sinner out there."

"Well, maybe I am, at least in your estimation," Ron suggested with a grin.

"I didn't exactly consider you a saint, that's for sure." Len laughed nervously, as he drained his coffee cup. "But I've been through a lot lately, and it's made me think hard about my life." Ron nodded.

"I don't just mean my mother's death," Len continued. "It's other things too. I'm having to leave Pine Grove Church." Len thought of his mother's letter, but couldn't bring himself to talk about its contents to anyone, at least not yet.

Ron stared at his cousin, open mouthed. Len's face was white and drawn. "Having to leave Pine Grove?" he repeated.

"Yes. I made a fool of myself, and what is worse, I hurt others, especially girls, through my ego trips," he added, keeping his eyes on his coffee cup.

Ron kept silent. He was stunned that Len was making this admission, especially to him of all people.

"And," Len continued, tears welling up in his dark eyes, "I need to apologize for what I did to Esther and to you." Ron winced. He wished Len would keep Esther out of it, but his cousin seemed determined to have his say.

"I don't want to stir up painful memories, Ron, but I need to say that my confounded arrogance made me push Esther into that singing business and encourage her to become like all the other stars, so that I would get the credit and the gratification of being instrumental in her transformation. I did a lot of damage, I know."

Ron couldn't speak. Len wasn't acting in character right now. He felt confused. "And, there's more," his cousin went on. "I was jealous of your love for her. I was just used to having my way with every girl I met, and Esther's preference for you piqued me, so I once let out a hint about your past."

"She told me," Ron said grimly. He wasn't sure he could forgive Len for that.

"Well, I'm very sorry, very. I know I've hurt you, more than once. Please forgive me, Ron."

Ron was silent for just a moment. This was all happening too quickly. Len had always been a good actor, so how did he know that he was for real? Then he was reminded that it must have taken a lot of courage for his cousin to come to him like this. He stretched out his hand slowly across the table. "I forgive you," he said, as Len gripped his hand. "And as for Esther, it would have all happened as it did even if you had had nothing to do with it. We were in two different worlds, still are. I'll never be able to enter the world she's in. I…" but he couldn't go on.

"I'm not sure about that, Ron. The two of you seem so suited in so many ways. Maybe it'll still work out," Len added hopefully.

Ron shook his head mournfully but said nothing. "I've got to get back to the church," Len went on, rising from his chair. "Maybe we can keep in touch."

"Yes, let's," Ron agreed. "After all, we are cousins so we'd better begin to act like cousins," Ron remarked.

"But we're not related at all," Len wanted to say, but he bit his lip. It had only been a few days since he had read that letter. One day he'd probably tell his cousin the truth, one day when he'd gotten used to it himself.

When Ron told his mother later that night the gist of what had passed between them, she shook her head in wonder. "Maybe there *is* something to religion after all, Ron," she exclaimed with a slight smile. "For an Atwood to apologize like that took some power from somewhere to make him do it. For the first time in my life, I can honestly say that I admire your cousin, and that's something, coming from me."

Ron smiled down at his mother. "Yes, Mom, it sure is."

"God knows we've all got a lot to apologize for, if we'd only be honest."

"That's true. But being honest isn't always easy." Ron stopped. He was speaking into thin air, for his mother had left the room.

# Chapter Eleven

## *Summer Vacation*

"Excuse me, miss, but could you tell me what flowers would be good for a border round my lawn?"

Gabby was bending over some plants with a watering can. She started when she heard a voice at her elbow. She straightened her aching back and turned round to face the speaker.

"Why, Aaron Gardner!" she exclaimed in surprise. Aaron thought she sounded rather glad to see him. "What on earth are you doing in Indianapolis this time of year?"

"The same as you, I suppose. Trying to drum up enough money to survive next semester," Aaron retorted with a grin.

"Who told you I was here?"

"I mentioned to your aunt that I was going to spend the summer up in Indianapolis, and she said that was a real coincidence, as you would be there, too. She didn't have your address handy at the time but told me the name of this garden center. I had a bit of time to spare this afternoon, so here I am." Aaron didn't tell her all that Mary had said. He figured that wouldn't be wise.

"Where are you working?" Gabby asked, putting down her watering can. "Not in a nursery, I hope?"

"No one would hire me. I just don't have a green thumb. I'm afraid I'm not much good for anything but teaching and maybe writing. Actually, I'm tutoring the nephew of one of my professors. He's been out of school for ages. And," he lowered his voice, "he's got leukemia. But he's very bright. I'm tutoring him in Latin and French, and throwing some history into the bargain."

Gabby's face softened. She was extremely fond of children. "Sounds like you're doing someone some good which is more than I seem to be doing. I never knew plants could be so ornery."

Aaron gave one of his hearty laughs. Gabby joined in. She hadn't laughed like that for a whole week, she reckoned.

"So where are your friends? You are working for Andrea's father, aren't you?"

"Well, for his w… I mean his lady-friend." Her face flushed as she spoke. "But they left for Alaska the day after I arrived. They'll be away another week."

"So you stay all alone here?"

"No, I'm rooming with a girl who also works here. We live over there," and she pointed to a doublewide trailer just over the nursery fence.

"You sure must feel lonely at times."

Gabby nodded. "You're right there! My roommate's unbearably quiet and out a lot of the time. But I expect I'll have plenty of company when the others get back. And," her eyes brightened, "one main reason why I came down here to work instead of staying near home or working on campus was that Dr. Porter's brother is an artist, and hopefully he's going to give me some lessons now and then, or at least let me potter around his studio."

"Exactly what kind of man is he?" Aaron quizzed.

"Now don't start being like Aunt Mary and Esther," Gabby grumbled. "I'm twenty now and quite able to take care of myself. Any relative of Andrea and Larry should be at least semi-respectable."

"You think so?" Aaron couldn't hide the skepticism he felt inside. But seeing the girl's expression he hastily changed the subject. "By the way, when do you get off work today?"

She looked at her watch. "In half an hour."

"How about having supper together somewhere? I feel a bit lonely here, too. I don't know anyone much in the city. Have you ever visited the Botanical Gardens?"

"I've been nowhere since I've come here. It's not much fun going anywhere alone. I've kept pretty much to myself the past week."

"We can go there after we've eaten, if you're not sick of plants, that is."

"I'd go almost anywhere to get out of this place for a while."

"I'll be back by five. I'll head off to the library for a bit. I noticed there's one just up the road."

Gabby nodded and turned back to her flowers. But she found herself humming a tune. She felt happier than she'd been in a long time.

That evening, she forgot that she had been a bit wary of Aaron Gardner. She soon discovered that he was good company. They talked a lot, laughed a lot, walked a lot, and ate a lot. It was ten when she let herself in the door of the trailer. Her roommate was watching a movie and looked up when Gabby came in the door. "Been out for a date?" she asked inquisitively.

"No, not really. Just met an old friend from where I live. We were both lonely so we went out for a meal together."

"Boyfriend or not, looks as if you've enjoyed yourself."

"Yep, sure did. Aaron's great fun when you get to know him."

Sue said nothing. She rarely spoke unless she had to. She had worked in the nursery nearly three years, ever since she had graduated from high school and she didn't intend to go on to college, she said. She had had a baby, but had given him up for adoption. Gabby had found out that much about her, but little else.

The next morning, Gabby was just turning over for another snooze when the doorbell rang. She jumped out of bed, grabbed her dressing gown, and ran to the door. Dr. Porter had warned her not to open to anyone she didn't know. She looked through the peephole and there, large as life, stood Aaron Gardner. She couldn't believe her eyes. What was he doing there at that unearthly hour? She slid back the upper bolt, turned the key, and opened the door a little.

"Sorry for disturbing you, Gabby, but it's Sunday in case you've forgotten, and I've come to take you to church. We don't need to leave for an hour yet. Service starts at eleven. So..."

"And who gave you the idea that I'd be going to church this morning? I'm sure I didn't."

Aaron had never seen Gabby look so cross. Not that he could really blame her, coming on her like that. "Well, I saw in the paper that Dr. Sandelescu from Bucharest is speaking at the First Baptist Church in the city this morning. He's going to tell about..."

"I don't want to hear him, and I don't appreciate you pouncing on me like this and acting all friendly yesterday just so you could drag me back to church. Bye!"

Aaron had already put his foot in the door, much to Gabby's exasperation, so it wouldn't close. "I don't plan on dragging you anywhere, so calm down, please," he told her, trying hard not to sound annoyed. "But I thought you would be interested in hearing a Romanian speak."

"You just might be wrong for once," the girl grumbled, glaring at him. "When did you find out about this guy?"

"Last night, after I left you. The man I'm working for showed it to me in the paper."

"Why didn't you phone and ask me to go?"

Aaron grinned. "Knew you'd refuse if I did that."

"I'll refuse anyway."

"OK. If that's how you want it. Just thought I'd give you the chance to go and hear him. Tell you what, I'll be back at ten, and sit in my car. I won't even come to the door, but I'll be here just in case you change your mind." He turned to go. Gabby gave a sigh of relief. "Oh, by the way," Aaron called over his shoulder, "this Dr. Sandelescu, he knew your father."

She opened the door wide and called after his retreating figure, "How do you know that?"

Gabby decided to take a shower; it was no use going back to bed. Aaron had wakened her up good and proper. She reached for her jeans and then hesitated. It was Sunday after all. She'd put on a skirt and blouse for once. She'd brought them along just in case she'd have to dress up for something or other.

Just as she was making herself some coffee and toast, Sue tottered into the kitchen. "What are you doing all dressed up like that? You must be going to church with that guy who disturbed our peace this morning."

Gabby reddened a little. "I'm awfully sorry, Sue. I had no idea he was coming. He never said so last night."

"But you are going?"

"No. I don't think so."

"Then why on earth have you put on a skirt and blouse?"

Gabby was silent. The words "he knew your father," rang through her head as she stirred her coffee.

"OK, you don't need to tell me. It's none of my business, only I think your driver's waiting out there for you." And Sue disappeared into the bathroom.

Gabby glanced out the window. Sure enough, there parked by the side of the road, was Aaron's cream Ford Escort station wagon. The clock on the wall opposite said five minutes to ten. She gulped down her toast, and coffee, went back into her bedroom and adjusted her collar in the mirror and flicked the comb once more through her thick wavy hair. Then she picked up her shiny black purse and went to the window. It was five minutes past ten. She'd keep him waiting a while; she couldn't let him think she'd capitulated that easily.

Gabby sat down on the chair and flicked through a magazine that was lying on the coffee table. Five minutes later, she heard the engine start up. She ran to the door and opened it. Aaron didn't look round. He was beginning to pull away.

"He knew your father," resounded for the umpteenth time in her confused brain. She dashed out the door. "Wait, I'm coming," she shouted. Aaron didn't seem to either see her or hear her. She slowly turned round and made her way indoors.

Gabby changed back into her jeans. She felt an utter fool. And she was secretly disappointed. She had missed a chance to meet someone from the old country—someone who actually had known her beloved father. Her pride had kept her from going out to that car at ten as Aaron had said. After all, he had waited till ten past. Had she wanted him to come back and beg her to go with him? Probably, she told herself, as she flipped on the TV.

That afternoon about two, the phone rang. "Sorry to bother you again, but Dr. Sandelescu really wants to meet you." Gabby heard Aaron's voice saying. He sounded apologetic. "He was very fond of your dad," he went on, "and I think has actually met you or your sister when you were very young."

Gabby held the receiver tighter. Conflicting emotions fought for supremacy. She didn't really know how to answer this persistent guy who wouldn't leave her alone.

"You still there?" Aaron's voice was asking.

"Yes. I'm here."

"There's something else. Dr. Sandelescu's interpreter was a complete flop this morning. I wished I had known Romanian well enough to take over, but I thought it was too big a risk to take. I..."

"You know Romanian?" Gabby interrupted.

"Yes. I've been learning it with Granddad's help and by reading from the Romanian Bible every morning. But listen, Dr. Sandelescu was wondering if you would interpret for him tonight?"

"Me?" Gabby was almost shouting. "You can't mean me?"

"Actually, I do mean you."

"I can't do it, Aaron. I really can't. You know what I feel about religion."

"I told the man that. I thought he should know that a girl who doubted God's existence might not be the best interpreter for him."

Gabby gasped. "And?"

"He just smiled and said that if God used a donkey in the Bible to get across his message, God could use someone like you." Actually, those hadn't been the exact words. He had really said, "Well then, surely

God can use a poor, young girl who thinks she knows better than her good father."

Gabby didn't know whether to laugh or be offended. "I just don't know, Aaron."

"Please, Gabby."

"All right. I'll do it this once."

"Thanks. It'll mean an awful lot to Dr. Sandelescu, it really will."

Sue opened the door when Aaron called for Gabby a few hours later. "Why did you go off like that this morning?" she asked with a grin. "Gabby tried to run after you. Didn't you see her?"

Aaron's mouth fell open. "No, I didn't. I guess I was too annoyed with her to think of looking round when I was driving away." He caught Gabby's eye and bit his lip. She had come up behind Sue and was standing all dressed up and ready to go. "Let's go," was all he said.

Gabby was very nervous in the car and talked in monosyllables. Aaron had never seen her like that before. Maybe, he thought, he had made a mistake to interfere like he had. But when he saw the girl's eyes fill with tears as she heard the doctor's deep voice saying, "Gabriella *dragă*, how like Andrei you are," he threw his misgivings to the wind. It would all work out for the best, he felt sure.

"We haven't time to chat now," Dr. Sandelescu told Gabby in Romanian, "but maybe Aaron can take us somewhere after the service. Now, let me show you the Bible passage I've chosen. Most of what I'm going to say will be my testimony." Then the good man prayed his heart out in Romanian. Gabby's tears fell freely. It seemed as if her father's presence was with them in the little room.

As the service began, Gabby grew extremely nervous. She usually took things pretty much in her stride, but this was different. To be up there, sitting beside her new friend and in full view of several hundred people, was an ordeal in itself; but the growing conviction that she was acting the hypocrite was even worse. Here she was, not even sure if God existed at all, and yet giving the impression that she and the man she was interpreting for shared the same faith. But Aaron had told him all about her. At least she was not lying to her father's friend. That was one comfort.

At first, she was rather hesitant. Gabby was glad she had really mastered English during the last eighteen months. Esther had told her that her vocabulary was even richer than her own now, though her accent was still much stronger than her sister's. And then to interpret a testimony was easier than interpreting a sermon. The language was familiar—smuggling Bibles, holding unauthorized religious services for young people, writing religious propaganda as the Communists called it, and it all resulting in several terms of imprisonment. Gabby had heard it all before. But then the Doctor was saying something that struck her as rather strange:

"The Romanian church is now entering perhaps the most dangerous period in her history. Freedom has come at last. Everyone is glad. Preachers come from the West. We go to the West. There is an interchange of ideas now; equipment is pouring in; churches are being built all over the country; container loads of aid are standing in the docks waiting to be unloaded. But will the Romanian Christians be able to stand a new test? Only time will tell. Brothers and sisters, we still need your prayers. In fact we need them more than ever." And with that the speaker sat down.

"Well done, Gabby," Dr. Sandelescu whispered as the last hymn was being sung. "I sensed you were doing a good job."

"There was no comparison with this morning," Aaron commented, as they waited for their friend in the vestibule. "But you look exhausted."

"I am. It's not only the mental exercise," Gabby confided, "but it was a very emotional experience. I couldn't do that every day."

"You won't have to, though I think he has a few more services in this area before he moves on. He may want you to interpret for him again in the next week or two."

Gabby gave no reply, but when half an hour later the doctor put the question to her at a small restaurant near the Church, she could do nothing but agree. After all, she was being pretty well paid for her services.

They chatted pleasantly for a while over their milkshakes and then Aaron excused himself. "I'll leave you two alone," he suggested. "I'll be back in half an hour." He knew that Gabby wasn't at peace with herself, and figured that, if she were left alone with her father's old friend, she just might open up to him.

"He speaks Romanian like a native," commented Dr. Sandelescu as he watched Aaron leave the restaurant. "And what a thoughtful boy!"

"I had no idea he spoke so fluently. Maybe my sister knew. He knows her much better than he does me."

"Esther?"

"Yes. Do you know her?"

"I remember her very well. One night your father brought one of his daughters to my house. She was much darker than you and looked very much like her mother."

"You knew my mother?"

"A little. She was a beautiful woman and a good one. But you're just like your father. What wonderful parents you had!"

She bent her head lower over her milk shake. Her friend noticed that the tears were falling into the glass. He leaned forward and asked gently, "You miss them very much, don't you?"

Gabby nodded. Then she raised her large, grey-green eyes to the doctor's and said very slowly, "I don't understand why God, if there is one at all, could do a thing like He did—taking them from us, I mean." Her words were jumbled but her companion understood what she was trying to say. Then she looked up, the old defiant look on her face once more. "After Dad died, nothing was the same for me any more. In the beginning, I just felt I could never trust myself to a God Who had acted like He had. It seemed so very unfair. And then, gradually, I wondered if it might not be more charitable to God to doubt His existence than brand Him as a cruel, heartless, all-powerful deity. That would make more sense." She didn't realize that those had been Larry's exact words to her a few months before when she had poured out her troubles to him and Andrea at the ski retreat.

"I don't think God needs charity like that, Gabriella." Dr. Sandelescu's voice was just a little stern now. "And anyway, surely you knew your father well enough to realize he wouldn't give up everything for some fantasy? His faith was founded on something solid and genuine."

Gabby softened a little. "Yes, he was sincere all right. But many wonderful people have been sincerely wrong." The doctor's kindly face looked very troubled. "And besides," she went on, "Dad would want me to base my life on my own faith, not on his."

"Yes, but it's better to base it on his faith than on no faith at all."

"Is it?"

"Of course." Dr. Sandelescu saw that the girl seemed unconvinced, but felt he had said enough.

When they had dropped Gabby off at her trailer and arranged to pick her up the next Wednesday evening, the doctor turned to Aaron. "Are you very close to Gabriella? She says that you know her sister better than you do her."

Aaron nodded. "That's right. I'm only just getting to know the girl. She's changed quite a bit since coming over here, Esther says. And her friends at college haven't helped. But I can't judge her too harshly. I went through a very difficult period when I first left home."

"Well then, you can help her, I'm sure."

"If she'll let me. But she's stubborn and already very influenced by her other friends' philosophy of life."

Dr. Sandelescu studied the young man for a moment. "Stick by her if you possibly can," he advised. "I'm sure her parents' prayers will win out in the end. But it's going to be tough. America's not doing her much good."

"Granddad would call it the Velvet Curtain."

His friend thought a moment. "Instead of the Iron Curtain?"

"Yes."

"Very apt." Then Aaron told him what he knew about Esther's encounter with the fateful curtain. The Doctor looked sad. "That's why I won't live here," he explained.

"You mean you could?"

"Yes. I've just received a teaching position in a Baptist seminary in Texas somewhere."

"But you think that you would be susceptible to the dangers of our culture?" Aaron was shocked. "I mean, you've withstood so much."

"Yes, but that's why I'm so susceptible. This aging body of mine would love comfort, an easy job, nice clothes, a decent car. I mean who wouldn't? And the fact I've been deprived of all these things for so long makes me want them even more."

Aaron looked thoughtful but said nothing. His companion changed the subject. "I think you're part Romanian, aren't you?" he asked with a smile.

"Yes. My grandmother was a native Romanian, and I've got some relatives over there."

"If ever you get over to my country, look me up."

Aaron smiled. "I certainly will."

That Wednesday Gabby felt much more at ease in her role as translator. By her third attempt, the last Sunday morning that Dr. Sandelescu was in the city, she was actually enjoying her role as interpreter. And she was becoming very fond of the doctor. He was due to leave for New York the next evening. It was a rather sad parting for them both.

"I suppose there'll be no excuse to take you to church next week?" Aaron asked a little tentatively as he dropped her off at the door of the trailer.

"Maybe you don't need an excuse," Gabby found herself saying. Then she bit her lip. She'd have to be careful. "Oh, I don't know," she said rather airily. "I'll have to think about it."

"I'll give you a ring in a few days."

"OK, but my friends are coming back from Alaska this weekend."

"So?"

Gabby seized her bag and opened the car door. Then she turned her head and looked the young man full in the face. Her expressive eyes had an intensity in them that almost frightened Aaron. And there was definitely anguish in those eyes searching his. She opened her mouth to say something and then closed it abruptly.

"Bye," she told him, holding out her hand. "Thanks for cheering me up these weeks and for introducing me to Dad's old friend." And she was gone. It seemed like some final farewell, Aaron thought, as he did a three point turn. He looked in the rear vision mirror. The girl was standing at the door watching him drive away. He gave a wave as he straightened the car and drove up the dirt path. Gabby put up her hand, and disappeared into the trailer.

"Andrea left a note for you," Sue called after her as she went into the bedroom to change her clothes. "She was here this morning and seemed a bit upset that you'd gone off to church."

Gabby unfolded the paper Sue had handed her. If Andrea had been upset, the note certainly didn't show it. It invited her to supper with them that evening.

"Been lonely?" Dr. Porter asked her when they were all seated round a sumptuous meal in their spacious dining-room.

"At first. I had to get used to being here, Dr. Porter."

"Call me Ken, please," the doctor told her. "We know each other well enough for that now, or soon will," and he gave her a wink. "But I worried about leaving you like we did. Sue's OK, but not your type. What did you do with yourself?"

Gabby threw a quick glance at Andrea who was concentrating on cutting her steak. She gulped a little and then began slowly, for it wasn't in her nature to be devious or to beat about the bush: "About a week after you left, Aaron Gardner, a friend of the family who lives near us in Tiny Gap, appeared on the scene. He's working in the city this summer. We went to the Botanical Gardens together and a few other places and then it turned out that my father's old friend was here from Romania so I spent some time translating for him in a few churches. I did it mainly for Dad's sake."

"Of course," Ken replied. His tone was very matter-of-fact. "I'm glad you weren't quite alone. But now we'll see to it that you get plenty of company. I've arranged for you to meet my brother in his studio tomorrow afternoon. In fact, he said that he thinks he can employ you for the rest of the summer. He has a store as well as a studio and it seems he's in need of a temporary assistant. The girl who was helping him is having a baby so will be off work for a while."

"But what about the nursery?"

"You'd prefer working there?"

Gabby shook her head decidedly. "Oh no. But…" and she looked at Sally as she spoke.

Sally smiled. "It's OK; we'll manage."

"And you can sleep in the basement here," Dr. Porter went on. "We've plenty of room and it's far more comfortable than in the trailer."

"That's very kind of you, but I hate to leave Sue alone," Gabby told him. "We're just getting used to each other. She seems so sad and lonely."

Ken Porter's face was a perfect study as he leaned back in his chair, folded his arms over his napkin, and said quietly, "That's fine if that's how you want it. But you're eating the night meal with us and remember, you can come and go here as if you were at home."

"Thanks very much," muttered Gabby, and that evening as she opened the door to her rather shabby living quarters, she wondered why she had refused the doctor's invitation.

"What on earth are you doing here?" Sue asked when she came in some minutes later.

"What do you think?" Gabby asked laughing. "This is my home now, isn't it? Or have you decided to throw me out?"

Sue gave her a long look. "Of course not, but I would have thought that the Porters would have invited you to stay up there with them now."

"They did."

"And you refused?"

"Yes."

Two very large tears trickled down Sue's face. Then she got up and made for her bedroom door, muttering in a voice so low Gabby had to strain to hear, "So some people have a heart, after all."

# Chapter Twelve

## *Summer at Silver Springs*

When Aunt Lucy had invited her to spend the summer at Silver Springs, Esther had hesitated. She had become quite fond of her great aunt, but she wasn't sure that even she could cope with three whole months of reading *Foxe's Book of Martyrs* every evening, listening to long harangues about the state of the church, and being reminded that beauty was a snare and pretty clothes utter vanity. But when Marion had mentioned that a family who went to her church and who had recently opened a country store was looking for a shop assistant during the summer months, Esther decided that getting away from Tiny Gap for a few months might not be a bad idea.

The pay at Mercer's, her friend warned her, wasn't all that great, just minimum wage, but then there were other perks: she would have free room and board with her aunt, be a stone's throw away from Marion, and get to see "the simple life" as her friend had put it, first hand. There was just one thing—the Mercers had asked that she would dress like one of them while she was working there. She already had long hair. That had been their chief requirement, so it seemed, and it had to be tied back, always. But that didn't bother her. She hardly ever let it hang loose now anyway. As for the long cotton dresses, aprons, and black stockings and shoes, Esther was quite willing to put them on for a few months at least.

"My, but anything suits you," Aunt Lucy had commented when her great niece had come down to breakfast, dressed in her new clothes. And the admiring glances she received from her customers from time to time echoed her aunt's sentiments. As she had studied herself in the long mirror in her bedroom that first morning, Esther thought that her face looked more peaceful already, more like Marion's. She smiled contentedly. Maybe she was going to find the secret of true spiritual living that summer. Maybe she would beat the Velvet Curtain once and for all.

As the weeks slipped by, Aunt Lucy grew very fond of her great niece. They would sit together on the verandah in the long summer evenings and Esther would read by the hour in her clear, bell-like voice; it soothed the old lady and not infrequently lulled her to sleep. At first, Rita seemed not a little put out that a girl half her age should usurp her place. But gradually she came to appreciate the hours of free time which she had never had before, and by the end of the summer, she was nearly as fond of the Romanian girl as was Aunt Lucy herself.

Esther, however, never stopped missing Mary and Rachel and, of course, her sister. She worried about her constantly, but had breathed a sigh of relief when Aaron had told her he would be spending the summer in Indianapolis, and would look Gabby up. He had even taken the trouble to phone her and tell her about Dr. Sandelescu.

She was thinking about her sister one hot, steamy day in late June, and wishing, just for a few brief moments, that she was anywhere but in Mercer's Country Store. She had never realized until then, how much she had grown dependent on air-conditioning.

She mopped her forehead as she readjusted the fan behind the counter. The oldest Mercer girl had gone away for the day and had left Esther in charge. "You know the ropes pretty well now," she had said as she left that morning. "And if you need help, just phone the Morgans. They said they would help you out if business got too brisk."

Esther looked at her watch. It was nearly two o'clock and she had held out so far. She smoothed her starched apron, and tucked in a few stray strands of hair that had escaped her cap.

"You're new here, aren't you?"

Esther looked up from the till. The lady in the very skimpy shorts who had been in the store at least forty minutes had finally finished her shopping. Her teenage daughter was emptying the shopping cart onto the worn, wooden counter.

"Yes," Esther replied. "I'm just here for the summer."

"A student?"

"Yes. And my great aunt lives near here, so I'm staying with her."

"Thought you weren't from round here. You don't look quite like the Mercers and their crew."

"Yes, she does, Mom," the little boy of eight or so put in, as he stared at Esther with big brown eyes. "She looks exactly like them."

Esther blushed as she handed the woman her change. The teenage girl was gazing at her very strangely as her mother tucked a shopping bag under each arm and made for the door.

"I've seen you before, somewhere," she exclaimed, pausing at the counter for a moment. "I think it was on TV."

"Don't be so stupid, Sadie," her mother shouted over her shoulder.

"I'm not being stupid, Mom. It's all come back to me." She turned to Esther, her eyes blazing with excitement. "You were singing at the Christian concert in Indianapolis about two years ago. You're from Romania, right?"

Esther stared at the girl in amazement. "Yes, I am." Then she smiled. "You certainly have a great memory."

"So I am right?"

"Yes."

The girl ran up to her mother and pulled at her elbow excitedly. "It's her, Mom. It's Esther Popescu. I've got a picture of her in my bedroom in her gold dress. She was fabulous."

Her mother put down her bags on the floor and came back to the counter. "So you're the singer that turned my daughter's head and made her want to take to the stage. I thought you had glamour hidden somewhere under your long clothes and black shoes."

Before Esther could answer, the door opened and a tall figure dressed in well-worn overalls entered the store. "Did you know you've hired a famous singer to work in your store?" the girl bubbled as she nearly collided with Malcolm Morgan at the door. Esther wished she could drop through the floor.

"It's obvious from the way you've shocked him that you've kept your singing career a secret," the older woman said rather sarcastically.

"But, Mom, I want Esther's autograph," her daughter insisted. "And I want to know why she's not answering fan mail and why she never sings any more. I've written her at least twice and got no answer."

Esther never heard the mother's reply, for the woman had obviously no interest in prolonging the conversation and was already putting her groceries into the trunk of her old Mercedes car. The girl stood for a moment at the door and then slipped back to the counter.

"Please write me," she said. "Here's my address. I think you're really cool, you know. I want to be like you when I grow up." She stuck a crumpled piece of paper into Esther's hands, gave her one last long admiring look, and was gone.

Malcolm had slipped behind the counter and collapsed into an old worn sofa that sat in the corner. He crossed his long legs, folded his arms, and began in his slow, even voice, "Now, Miss Esther, what was all that about?"

Esther turned to face him. This was the first time he had come into the store and it had taken her by surprise. She was blushing furiously though she didn't quite know why. "I suppose you never knew that I sang a few times on stage as a Christian singer," she stammered. "But that's all in the past. That was before I took ill, about two years ago now."

"I see." Malcolm sounded relieved. "But you've never told us about your singing career."

"No," Esther said a bit defensively. "I didn't see why I needed to. It was very short, only a few months, and it's all over now."

"For good?"

"Yes. For good."

Malcolm got up from the sofa. "Look, I've come to relieve you."

"But I'm not due off till five. It's only two-thirty now."

"I know. But it's awfully hot and you're probably used to air-conditioning. I'm free for a few hours, so thought maybe you'd like to get home early today."

Esther wiped her forehead with her handkerchief. "Thanks, Malcolm," she told him gratefully. "It has been pretty busy." She grabbed her purse and made for the door.

"Take it easy," he called after her.

"I will, don't worry," she called back.

"In this weather, I don't need any encouragement to take it easy," she muttered to herself as she drove home to her Aunt Lucy's. Working as a store clerk wasn't exactly her sort of job and she had been surprised at the number of customers who found their way to Mercer's Country Store, fifteen miles from the interstate and on a road that seemed to lead to nowhere.

Five minutes later, Esther braked in front of her aunt's stately, two-storied house. She was glad that the old lady had decided to install air conditioning the previous summer. Miss Lucy met her at the door.

"You're early today!"

"Yes. Malcolm came to relieve me."

"Very considerate of him I must say." Aunt Lucy sounded a bit grim. Her niece frowned. "And I've heard from a few mothers around here that their sons are suddenly very keen to go shopping in Mercer's Store," the old lady went on.

Esther blushed scarlet, but her aunt wasn't finished. "And I've had at least three phone calls this week from prospective preacher boys who need to borrow a book from my library."

Esther pushed past her aunt into the cool of the hallway. Lucy followed her into the kitchen. "It's rather curious that I've never had such interest shown in my books all the years I've been at Silver Springs. Any explanation?"

Esther was tired and hot and not in a mood to take her aunt's teasing especially when it had an edge to it as it often did. She grabbed a glass of water and flopped into a chair by the window. "Look, Aunt Lucy," she began heatedly, "I know what you're getting at. But I can't help it, can I? And if you don't like it, then why did you invite me to stay with you this summer?"

Aunt Lucy adjusted her spectacles and took a seat opposite her niece. "I didn't say I didn't like it, did I? I'm human enough to be proud to have a beauty for a great niece. But I'm also wise enough to know the dangers."

Esther rose from her chair and made for the door. "Look, Aunt, I need to lie down for a while. I'm sorry, but if God made me this way, then maybe you should address your complaints and fears to the Almighty, not to me."

"Esther!" she heard her aunt exclaiming reproachfully, as she climbed the steep stairs to her attic bedroom. She threw herself on her bed and stared up at the whitewashed ceiling. It was pleasant, she had to admit, to be admired by nearly every man she met. After a few moments of day-dreaming, she got up from the bed and stood in front of the mirror. She often did that, just to see, she told herself, what it was that made her so admired. And then she would kneel down again and ask for forgiveness for her indomitable vanity. But what more could she do? She had put aside her makeup, her jewelry, her pants, her alluring dresses; she had refused invitation after invitation to sing, had turned down contracts, had torn up old fan mail, and had determined when she got home to destroy her engagement photograph. But instead of eliminating her cursed vanity, it seemed, in a sense, to only augment it. Now she was considered holy as well as beautiful. She still had admirers, only of a different sort than in Velours. She sensed that not a few girls in Marion's church were eaten up with envy when they saw heads turn as she slipped in, as unobtrusively as possible, and took her usual seat beside Marion on the fourth row from the front.

On rare occasions, when she felt the hopelessness of ever getting the better of herself, she almost felt like getting out her pen and paper and writing Ron Atwood. After all, what had she gained by refusing him?

Yes, he had spoiled her, but right now, she told herself as she adjusted the fan which stood in the corner behind her, she could do with a bit of spoiling. Then she remembered her illness and how near to death she had been and how far from God she had felt. She shuddered. No, she hadn't gone far enough in her devotion to God, that was the problem. For someone like herself, maybe only a really drastic step would make her safe for ever from the snares of the Velvet Curtain.

All this and more swept like waves over her as she gazed at her image in the glass. She thought of her meeting with the young girl in the store. She remembered how much she could earn in one single concert and gave a long sigh. She had to talk it all out to someone. So when the supper dishes had been cleared away that evening, she told her aunt she was going over to Marion's for a chat and would be home by ten. Aunt Lucy frowned and then remembered that her niece needed to have some time to herself.

As the sun set behind the distant mountains, Esther sipped homemade lemonade and shared her fears and her frustration with Marion. They were sitting on the back porch, watching the children play in the yard below.

"So, Marion," Esther concluded, taking a deep sigh and smoothing out her white pinafore, "I've given up all my ambitions. I've deliberately stopped my career as a singer. I've…"

"Yes," interrupted her friend, "Malcolm told me about the incident in the store today."

"Did he? Well, I didn't mean to hide my past from you. I've just tried to put it behind me and start all over again. But that's not all. I've refused one of the best men I ever knew, and yet I still fight with my inner desires and ambitions, and most of all, with my vanity. How on earth did you find such complete peace of mind and soul?"

"It all lies in accepting God's will for your life," Marion had replied quietly.

"Yes, but what is God's will for me?"

"That's for *you* to find out." Marion's words were slow and deliberate. "And first of all, you must begin by making sure you are obeying God's will as far as you see it outlined in Scripture. Then, eventually, God will show you how to apply it to your own life. The Bible says: 'In His light, we see light.'"

"Give me an example, please."

"For one thing, He demands that we keep ourselves separate from the world."

Esther gazed down at her black stockings. "That's what I'm trying to do." Marion thought that her friend sounded just a little petulant.

"I know, I know," she said soothingly. "But you can't go just halfway, Esther."

"What do you mean?"

"I mean that it has to be all or nothing. At least it was that way with me."

"You mean taking your vow?"

Marion smiled. "Yes, but for you it might entail a different kind of vow."

"Like what?"

Marion smoothed her apron as she talked. "Wedding vows." She smiled at her friend's very evident discomposure. "I mean," she went on, "being willing to marry the man God has chosen for you and being subject to him instead of going by your own whims and fancies all your life."

Esther raised her large dark eyes to Marion's clear, blue ones. "Well, I think I'd be willing for that, Marion, though as I feel right now, I'd rather never marry at all."

"That's what I mean. There has to be a cross in your life, if you follow the Master."

"You mean that my marriage would be my cross?"

Marion frowned a little. "I'm not saying that, exactly. I really don't know. I'm sure God would want you to love the man you married, or at least He would put a love for him in your heart eventually when you got to know him, but at first you might have to take a step of faith. Marry first and fall in love later. Many have done that."

"I know, but I don't like that idea at all. That's not what happened to my parents, that's for sure."

"But God works differently in every life." Marion shifted uneasily in her chair. She didn't like taking on the role of preacher and counselor. She cleared her throat as she went on: "You're used to having your own way in a lot of things, aren't you? Marriage would alter that, you know. And besides, you need to be married." Something in Marion's tone made Esther look at her sharply.

"I've seen the way men look at you, Esther," her friend went on. "You need the protection of a husband, that's more than obvious. But look, here's Malcolm. We need to go in and have supper."

After that, Esther and Marion became closer than ever. One evening as they were sitting in the twilight, listening to the crickets chirp and the owls hoot, Marion turned to her friend. "Esther, when are you going back to Romania?"

"When I get my degree. That'll be next May. I'll go as soon as I can after that."

"Any idea of what you'll do when you get there, apart from visiting your family?"

"I'd like to teach. I'll have my diploma in English and French and my teacher's certificate. I could also do some interpreting. I hear the churches are really short of interpreters, now that a lot of Westerners are going over. Although," and she made a wry smile, "I'm sure they prefer men to do that job."

"We're going too, you know." Marion announced, ignoring Esther's last comment.

"I heard something about that," Esther replied. "When are you going?"

"It depends when things are ready. Our church is connected with a mission society which is planning to build an orphanage, a farm, and a school, probably in the north of Romania, in Moldova I think they call it."

Esther sat bolt upright. "Really? How fabulous! And you and Malcolm are going to stay there or just visit?"

Marion looked dreamily out the window. "He's going for good, and I'll be with him as long as he needs me but, I don't know if I've told you this, I feel a call to Africa."

"Africa?"

"Yes. So I told him I'd go with him and stay till he got married." Esther stared at her friend. "So he's planning to get married?"

Marion nodded. "Of course. I mean, he needs to find a good mother for the girls. I can't stay with them always, you know."

"No, I'm sure you can't. But that's just wonderful," Esther exclaimed. She felt immensely relieved for some reason or other. "I'm sure he deserves a very good woman, though after you, Marion, the kids will find it hard to have as good a mother as you've been to them."

"I'm not worried on that score."

"So you know his future wife?"

Marion beamed at her friend. "Oh yes. Sure I do, but I'm not free to tell you her name just yet. I'll let Malcolm do that when the right time comes."

Esther thought this a bit strange. Malcolm didn't tell her anything, so why would he tell her this?

"But to get back to our immediate plans," Marion's sweet voice broke into her reverie. "We're going over to Romania at Christmas to scout around. The children will stay with our parents."

"That's great." Esther looked wistful. "Wish I were coming with you."

"But you can."

Esther's mouth fell open. "What are you saying, Marion? Of course I can't. I don't have the money and you wouldn't want me tagging on behind you."

"Oh, yes, we would. We've talked it over together and thought you might like to see where we'll be living and maybe even consider eventually teaching in the school that will be built there."

Esther's eyes shone like stars. "What a wonderful idea!" Then her face fell, "I don't have the money. I mean, if I go at Christmas, I'll use money I'm saving for my final fare when I've finished college."

"We'll pay your way."

"You can't."

"Yes, we can. We've discussed it together. If you'll give us a few lessons in Romanian before we go and then interpret for us while we're there, that'll be a fair bargain. We'll need to negotiate, maybe buy land, etc., and we'll have to have someone we can trust to translate for us."

Esther nodded. "Yes, you would need an interpreter. But my fare over? That's paying me a lot."

"Not for three weeks of work. Not by modern pay. Anyway, pray about it and give us your answer by September."

Esther certainly did pray about it, though she thought she knew God's will right from the start. She'd discuss it with her aunt, maybe, when she returned to Tiny Gap on July 4th—that was only a week away.

The week soon passed, and Esther found herself back in the old two-storied white board house among the trees. She found that Rachel had already gone to Velours to spend the holiday with her father. On the evening of the Fourth, Aaron turned up and offered to take the two ladies to Gallanton, the nearest town, to see the fireworks display. His grandfather, for once, had agreed to go with them. Esther noticed that Hugh was much quieter than of old and looked worn and rather sad. But she was glad to have his company. He had played such an important role in her life.

"How's Gabby?" Mary asked Aaron on the journey home.
"I haven't seen her for weeks, actually."
"No?"
"No," Aaron repeated rather abruptly. "Since her friends got back, she's either out or not available when I call or stop by. So I've stopped trying. After all, I don't want to push myself on her."
"She'll be with Uncle John today, won't she?" asked Esther.
"I think so. At least that was her plan."
"Oh God," Hugh prayed that night. "You know what a failure I feel I am these days—how I helped young Esther to escape one temptation but seem unable to prevent her from falling prey to another. And then there's Gabby, not even sure she believes in You any longer. I feel so helpless, so old, so lacking in strength and wisdom, but i can bring them to you and place these dear ones in Your loving arms. Oh, and Rachel too, and her aunt, and my dear grandson." Hugh let out a long sob then he quieted. God's peace filled the room. He was weak, yes, very, but His strength would be perfected in his weakness if he would only let it. He smiled into the shadows, turned over on his right side as he always did when he wanted to sleep, and not long afterwards, Aaron heard him snoring loudly.

"Granddad sleeps like a baby," he said to himself as he climbed into bed, "but not quite, for babies don't snore like that."

A few days later, Rachel returned from Velours. "Here's a letter for you," she told her cousin after she had deposited her bags upstairs and changed her clothes.

"Good, but tell me first, how is everyone?"

"Dad's fine, and Diane, and Ramona. I stayed with her for a night or two." Rachel puckered her brow. "I still don't like Claude, though. He's got a good job as a mechanic, and Ramona's got one more year to go at college. Oh, you know that already, I know." Rachel helped herself to an ice cold drink from the refrigerator as she spoke. "But what you probably don't know is that they're planning to go to Romania and live there when she has graduated."

Esther couldn't believe her ears. Ramona in Romania? "Whose idea is this, Rachel?" she wanted to know.

Rachel puckered her forehead. "I really don't know. Probably Claude's."

"And what does your Dad think about it?"

"He thinks it's crazy—says she won't last a month. He finally got them to promise to go for a visit first before they plan to settle there for good."

"Wise idea," Esther commented. "And how's Gabby?"

Rachel pointed to the letter. "That'll probably tell you what you want to know." She told her cousin rather abruptly.

Esther opened the envelope and began reading,

"Dear Esther and Aunt Mary,

"I'm keeping very well. It's hot here and in general, I prefer the mountains. But it's not every day I get the chance to work in an art studio. Simon, Andrea's uncle, is kindly giving me art lessons from time to time as partial payment for my work, though he pays me pretty liberally in addition. I enjoy every moment of my work. I'm so glad I didn't need to work in the nursery all vacation.

"I'm still staying in the trailer with Sue. I've gotten very fond of her and she's come out of her shell a lot. I'd like to invite her home some time. I think she needs mothering, Aunt, and you're good at that.

"I eat supper with the Porters and then we go out together somewhere, or I spend the evening reading. Dr. Porter has given me the run of his library. Sometimes, I go back to the studio and have an art lesson. Simon says I'm making real progress.

"I'll be home for a few days before college begins. Don't worry about me. I'm well and behaving myself but I miss you all.

"Love, Gabby."

"She and Andrea certainly get on well together," Rachel commented, as she watched her cousin fold up the letter and put it back in the envelope.

"But Andrea's father? He's not married to the woman he lives with, is he?"

Rachel shook her head. "No, he's not and yet they seem really happy together."

"But it's not exactly the best atmosphere for Gabby right now, I'm afraid," Mary said sadly.

"What bothers me," Rachel put in, "is that she doesn't seem to want to be home much these days. By the way, our family spent the Fourth at the Porters'. They have a gorgeous house. I must say they made us very welcome. Ramona and Claude came with us. Andrea's brother and Gabby seem to have a lot in common. They're always deep in some discussion or other."

Rachel got up from her chair. "It's a gorgeous evening. I'm going to sit a while on the back porch and read," she told her cousin.

Esther put the letter in her pocket. So Gabby wasn't even coming home this vacation, at least, not for more than a day or two at the very end.

She stared dreamily out the window. Only one more year of college and then she'd have her degree in English and French. And Romania for Christmas! That was too good to be true. She hadn't told anyone yet as it hadn't quite been settled. Maybe she should consult her aunt, but why? She was of age and nothing or no one on earth would keep her back from going to her beloved land. She'd see Aunt Ana again and spend Christmas in church with all her old friends. She'd be away from this cursed Curtain for at least a few weeks. And maybe she'd get a promise of a future job into the bargain. She did wish Malcolm weren't coming along. She and Marion weren't as free together when he was around. But she supposed he was vital to their trip. After all, he was the missionary to Romania, not Marion. She was set for Africa some day. Then she stopped.

"I wonder who he's marrying?" she asked herself. "Strange they don't tell me, though it's none of my business, but I do hope the woman has tons of patience." Esther smiled as she thought of the Romanian lessons together she had given them both. Marion learned three times faster than her brother did.

"I'm not sure he'll even be able to say *Bună Ziua* (Good day or Hello) when he arrives," she told Rachel the next day. "He's so slow."

"You're teaching him Romanian?"

"Yes."

"Whatever for?"

"He's going to be a missionary in Romania."

"Oh yes? Well, that's very handy."

Esther frowned at her cousin. "I think I know what you're thinking, but it's not true. Marion said he's been interested in Romania long before he met me. And anyway, he's going to get married."

Rachel looked very relieved. "Who's the lucky woman?"

"Marion didn't say."

Rachel studied her cousin. "Esther, you look very happy about something. What is it?"

Esther came up close and whispered something in Rachel's ear. "Now don't tell anyone. It's not settled yet."

Rachel took a step back and studied her cousin intently. "Sounds great! But they're paying your way? Aren't there some strings attached?"

"None, only my teaching them both Romanian and acting as translator for them once we get there. Those were the only conditions."

"I certainly hope you're right."

"At the moment I couldn't really care what price I paid if I only get back to Romania."

"You must be very eager to get away from here to say a wild thing like that!"

Esther dropped her eyes. "I love you all so very much and Tiny Gap is a wonderful place, but I don't fit into this American culture. And when I did try, look what happened. No, I've had enough of Velvet Curtains. My life is cut out for me in Romania."

"You deserve the best, Esther, the very best," Rachel whispered, giving her cousin a hug. "I only hope the price you pay for your trip to Romania isn't more than you can afford, and I'm not talking about money either. And," she paused as their eyes met, "I also hope you don't find the Velvet Curtain over there too!"

"Don't be so ridiculous, Rachel. As if there could be! You don't understand Romania, that's obvious, to suggest such a thing. And you've no idea how much I love my country, either. I mean, the very idea of going there so soon makes me nearly crazy with joy." Esther grabbed her cousin's hands and twirled her round as she spoke. Then she skipped towards the door, chanting to herself, "Romania, here I come. Christmas in Ploieşti! I can't believe it!"

Rachel stared after her as she left the kitchen. It was ages since Esther had acted like that. But no Velvet Curtain in Romania? The girl shook her head in disbelief. "Where there's liberty there'll be the Curtain," she muttered as she emptied the dishwasher, "unless I'm very much mistaken."

# Chapter Thirteen

## *Caught in the Middle*

"What's wrong, Gabby? You haven't been the same since we came back from Alaska." Andrea came over to where her friend was sitting. It was a sultry July evening; Ken and Sally were preparing a barbecue on the verandah.

"I guess I feel caught in the middle," Gabby replied truthfully, as she looked up into her friend's questioning eyes.

"In the middle of what?"

"I mean, I feel trapped." She laid her head back on the chair and stared up at the cloudless blue sky above.

"Trapped?" Andrea looked completely nonplussed.

"She means that she feels caught between her old life and the life she wants to live." Gabby gave a start and looked up to see Larry standing just behind her, in his white shorts and T-shirt. He had just been out playing tennis with some friends.

"You seem to be a mind reader," she told him archly.

"I sure have trouble reading yours at times."

"At times?"

"Yes. At others you are very transparent, as you are now."

"Really?" Gabby dropped her eyes.

"Really! It's quite easy to see that you've been upset ever since that preacher guy from Romania turned up."

"He's a very good person, Larry," her voice was defensive now.

"Maybe, but sometimes good people can prove very troublesome, you know."

"Think so? Anyway, I'll have to decide one thing or another. I'm caught between two worlds and it seems at the moment that I'm in neither and that feels awful."

Andrea grabbed her friend by the arm. "For right now, you're in our world, thank goodness. We're going to have a barbecue and then go to the movies. And tomorrow's my birthday, remember? Dad's planned a surprise. It'll be great fun. We won't let you have time to mope about past and future and all that stuff."

Simon and his friend Gilbert were there that evening, plus a few other friends of the family. Andrea remarked that Sally had cooked enough meat to feed the whole neighborhood. When everyone had eaten their fill, the doctor suggested a game of croquet. He was an old hand at the game and had already taught Gabby to play. She was fast becoming an expert herself. She had finished a game and was standing with Simon discussing a new picture he had just finished painting, when Gilbert came up to where they were standing.

"Gabby, meet my partner, Gilbert," Simon said casually. "We've lived together for six years now and I couldn't do without him. Gilbert, here is my little prodigy, the girl I'm always talking about."

Gabby forgot her manners for once and stood staring at Simon's friend as if she had seen a ghost. She soon recollected herself, however, but not before Gilbert had seen her shocked expression. He dropped the hand he was holding out to her and turned away. The girl blushed a deep scarlet and opened her mouth to say something, anything to ease the tension. But what could she say?

"What on earth's wrong?" she heard Andrea's cheery voice behind her. "You look as if you'd been to a funeral."

"I'm awfully sorry, Andrea," she apologized, turning round to face her friend. "I've offended your uncle and probably Gilbert as well, but I didn't mean to." Andrea looked over to where her uncle was standing. She could tell that he was very upset.

"Don't be cross, Andrea. I'll apologize, I really will," Gabby told her pleadingly. "Only he introduced his friend as his partner. I mean, I had no idea…"

Andrea took her friend's arm and led her to a bench in the rose garden. "I should have warned you, but I'm not used to having to warn my friends about such things."

"But is this normal?" Gabby felt she couldn't take all the blame for what had happened.

Andrea opened her eyes wide in amazement. "Of course it's normal!" she exclaimed emphatically. "Where have you been all your life?"

Gabby heard the sarcasm in her friend's voice. Her eyes filled with tears. Andrea had never talked to her like that before. "I'll apologize for my rudeness," she said hastily, "even though I didn't say anything, you know."

"I bet you didn't need to. Your face probably said it all," Andrea grinned a little in spite of herself. "I'll go and have a word with my uncle and explain for you. Then when you meet him next, just act as if nothing has happened."

There was no more time for conversation. Sally had called Andrea to help her clear away the dishes. "I'm going home," Gabby whispered as she made for the garden gate. "I can't face anyone tonight."

Back in the solitude of her tiny bedroom, she had more time to think over what had just taken place. She felt embarrassed, hurt, confused, and a little angry. Why should she be the one to apologize? She knew that she ought to, for she had been rude. But didn't the Porters realize that not everyone looked at life like they did?

She had just finished showering and had barely dressed when she heard the doorbell ring. She straightened her shirt, flicked a comb through her hair, and made for the door. It was Andrea and her brother. Sue was out, so she invited them in and told them to take a seat.

Andrea was the first to speak. "We knew you'd be upset, and we didn't want you to spend the whole evening by yourself."

Gabby gave her friend a mournful smile and nodded her thanks.

"First of all," Andrea went on, "I talked to Uncle Simon and he understands. He said to forget the whole incident."

"Thanks," Gabby said shortly. She still felt, deep down, that maybe he should have done some apologizing too.

"I know that this is hard for you, Gabriella," Larry said in a tone unusually gentle for him. "It goes against all the norms you've been taught."

"It certainly does," Gabby told him emphatically. "But I know it's wrong to shun people because they are different and I don't intend to do that, but to accept their life style as normal, I mean, it's…"

"Against the Bible?" Larry's voice wasn't so gentle now.

"Well, yes."

"And you still believe in the Bible?"

Gabby looked down at the carpet but said nothing. "It all depends on how you look at things," Larry continued. His voice was calm and soothing now. "If my uncle and his partner are harming you, or their family, or anyone else, then they are doing wrong. But if they're perfectly happy together and living a quiet life, helping others when they can, then it seems that to any *intelligent thinker*," Gabby noticed he laid special emphasis on those last two words, "they should not be condemned as evil, or shunned like lepers, or looked upon as perverts." The inference that she might just not be intelligent or a thinker stabbed Gabby like a knife.

"And," Larry went on, "it seems to me that the greater sin is to condemn and to judge our fellowman. This isn't love, is it? And Jesus Himself told His disciples to love their neighbors as themselves."

"I'm sorry," Gabby burst out. "But I need time and space to think all this out."

"Of course you need time," Andrea reassured her, coming over to her friend and putting her arms round her. "But right now I think a bit of distraction is what you need more. Did you forget that the movie starts at eight and it's nearly that now?"

"That's right," Larry agreed looking at his watch. "Come on, Gabby, a good, exhilarating film is the best thing to blow some of these old cobwebs that are gathering again in that intricate brain of yours. Get changed into something snazzy, and let's paint the town red."

Gabby stared at him for a moment. Had she heard correctly? Then her face broke into a broad smile. "Just give me a minute," she told him as she disappeared into her room.

Ten minutes later a transformed Gabriella announced, "I'm ready." She waltzed round the room and came to a halt in front of where they were sitting. She made a mock curtsey. "Now, will I do?" She had put on an outfit Andrea had persuaded her to buy the week before—a rather revealing bright pink top, and a daringly short white mini skirt.

"What I'd give for your figure and especially your legs. They're something else. And you've got such a wonderful tan!" Andrea told her friend admiringly. "She looks pretty fabulous, doesn't she?" she asked her brother.

"You bet!" Larry replied, letting his eyes feast on Gabby's slim, lithe figure. Gabby blushed a vivid red. Conflicting emotions surged through her. Larry stood up and held out his arm.

Gabby took it without a word and made for the door. Then she flashed her escort one of her most captivating smiles. "I'm ready to go," she said. Her words were bold and brave but, Larry thought he detected just the slightest catch in her voice.

"She's not quite as ready as she thinks," he said to his sister when they had dropped Gabby off at the trailer late that evening, "but she will be one day, and when she is, I, for one, sure want to be around. She'll be one great, fun gal."

Gabby was ready to jump into bed when she heard Sue call from the next room. "Bye the way, Aaron Gardner called again tonight. You know he's called time after time, and you've not been in."

"I know." Gabby sounded cross.

"I told him you'd phone him back."

"Well, it's too late tonight. It's past midnight."

"Then you'd better call him tomorrow."

"I never asked him to call," Gabby snapped. "He's so persistent, and I know it's only because Esther or Aunt Mary have asked him to keep an eye on me."

"I'm not so sure. I think he likes you a lot."

"What if he does? Maybe I don't like him that much." Gabby wished Sue would mind her own business.

By this time Sue had slipped out of bed and was standing in the doorway. "Gabby, I know I shouldn't interfere in your personal life, but maybe I should just say one more thing."

Gabby gave her hair one last vigorous brush. "Go ahead. I'm listening, though it is a bit late for a lecture."

"If you ditch Aaron now, you might be making a huge mistake. And really, he's a lot more your type than…"

"Larry Porter?" Gabby interrupted, eyes blazing. "Mind your own business, will you. I'll decide who's my type, not you." She was very upset now. "And anyway, it's Andrea I'm close to, not her brother."

"Oh, come on, don't get angry again. You flare up so easily. Look, you've been kind to me. I like you and I'm going to miss you when you go. But," Sue paused a moment, "you sure are gullible."

"Me, gullible?"

"Yes, very. You don't know the world like I do. I'm not as clever as you are and I'm not as pretty, though I was once. Look at this." She took Gabby's arm and led her into her bedroom. On the dresser by the bed, stood a small, colored photograph. "That was me two years ago."

Gabby studied the picture closely for a few moments and then glanced from it to the girl at her side. Sue's face was much thinner now, and hopeless resignation was etched on every feature. The thick, glossy brown hair had blonde streaks through it and hung lank and lifeless. But the almond shaped black eyes were the same though lacking in luster, and the rosebud mouth was easily recognizable.

"You were a stunner," Gabby told her.

"Yes. I won a few beauty contests," Sue said proudly. Then her face grew dark. "But I had a child at eighteen; the father deserted me; my mother couldn't care less, and my dad was married to some other woman and hardly saw me."

Gabby put her arms round the girl. "Come up with me for a few days to Tiny Gap. My aunt and sister would love to see you. They'd do you some good. I'm not religious like they are, but they'd pray with you."

"I'll come and see you some time if I can get away, but I want *you* to pray with me, not your relatives. I don't know them."

"I don't pray any more."

"But yet you think *I* need prayer?"

"Well, maybe," Gabby admitted reluctantly.

"But *you* don't need it, right?"

"Oh, Sue, don't quiz me any more. I'm tired and confused. Life's so complicated. I think I've got it sorted out and then it gets all jumbled again. I'm going to bed. Good night." Gabby made for the door.

"But Gabby?" Sue called after her.

"Yes?"

"I don't know why you think *you* can do without God and yet you think *I* need Him. Seems to me you're kind of running away from Him. I've done it too, and it never works, never!"

"Running away from God," Gabby repeated to herself as she undressed a few minutes later. "How can I run away from a God Who probably doesn't exist?"

"But," a little voice inside suggested, "if there is a God like your Dad and Mom and Esther and Aunt Mary and Mr. Hugh and…" Gabby jumped into bed and pulled the bedclothes over her head but it was no use. The voice continued persistently, "and Aaron and Aunt Ana, and Dr. Sandelescu and Granny Sandelescu, and…"

Gabby could stand it no longer. She sat bolt upright in bed. "But if there isn't a God like Andrea and Larry and Dr. Porter," she argued, "and Sally, and Simon Porter and…"

"Yourself?" the inner voice suggested.

"No, I didn't say that." Gabby thumped the bedcovers with her fist. "I never said I didn't believe there was a God only that there might not be." She let out a sob and stuffed the corner of the pillowcase in her mouth. She didn't want Sue to hear her.

"It's no use. Tonight's my losing night," she thought sadly. "Oh God," she began automatically.

"Prayer's a crutch for the weak." She could see Larry's mouth curl as he said these words.

"Prayer is real," she heard her father say. "It works."

"But prayer is all in the mind," Larry was telling her.

"I've literally lived by prayer, Gabby," her father's voice was insistent.

"You can't be bound by your upbringing," Andrea was reminding her.

"My upbringing helped me through my doubts," Aaron's voice chimed in.

Gabby slipped out of bed, tiptoed into the living room, and switched on the TV. Soon the late night movie was the only voice she was hearing. Shooting and love-scenes didn't leave much room for arguments about religion. Maybe it was a poor medicine, she told herself as she crept into bed two hours later, but better than ending up in a psychiatric ward any day, wasn't it?

## Chapter Fourteen

### *Outside the Velvet Curtain*

"What's in your luggage?" The unsmiling customs' officer pointed to one of Marion's bulging cases. Marion strained to catch his broken English.

"Mainly shoes and clothes to give away," Esther hastily explained in Romanian.

"You speak good Romanian, Miss." The face of the official softened a little.

"I ought to; I'm from Romania." Esther drew herself up rather proudly as she said this.

"Oh? Then tell your friend here that if she's bringing aid into this country she needs a letter of donation."

"A what?" Esther was shocked. Hadn't the revolution done away with all this red tape? But she wisely said nothing.

"A letter of donation," the man repeated firmly.

"But we haven't brought a container load of aid with us, only a few suitcases," she protested.

"Doesn't matter," the man's face was grim now. "The law's the law. I'll have to confiscate the luggage containing humanitarian aid if you don't produce a letter."

Esther looked at her friends in dismay as she relayed to them what the official had said. "If there are any fees, I can pay," offered Malcolm, taking out his wallet.

Esther tried to signal him to put it away immediately, but it was too late. The customs officer had seen it. "Have you declared your money?" he asked suspiciously.

"No. We don't have that much," Esther put in quickly.

"How much?"

The three weary travelers put their heads together and came up with the sum of five thousand dollars in all. Malcolm had brought sufficient money to purchase some land, or at least secure it with a down-payment.

"Not that much?" the man repeated with a sneer. "You must be awfully rich if you think five thousand's not much."

"I didn't know how much the others had. I only knew that I didn't have much on me," Esther faltered. This was far worse than she had expected.

"Well, you can't take more than one thousand dollars per person into the country." The man leaned back against the wall of his booth folded his arms, and gave her a rather impudent stare. Esther put up a quick prayer. Her two companions were gazing helplessly at her, trusting her to get them out of the mess they had so innocently gotten themselves into.

She thought hard and fast. What would she have had to do in the old days, the days of Ceaucescu? Give him some money, of course. Why hadn't she thought of it sooner? Esther took a step closer. She strongly suspected that the man was interpreting the new laws to his own advantage. "How much do you want?" she asked quietly.

"Want?" The man acted surprised and then added in a whisper, "Well, between you and me, and I wouldn't do this for anyone but a pretty girl like you, if you'll hand me over fifty dollars, I'll make it a deal. But," and he made a motion as if he were zipping up his lips, "it's just between us, isn't it?"

Esther regarded him coldly. "Fifty? That's far too much. After all, we didn't know what the laws are now, did we? We'll know next time."

"Forty?" The man grinned.

"Thirty," countered Esther.

"Thirty-five," the man said firmly. "That's the lowest I'll come."

Esther turned to her companions. "He says that he'll let us through if we give him thirty-five dollars."

"Bribery," muttered Malcolm. "Esther, you know we can't give bribes. We're Christians and the Bible forbids it."

"Call it a gift then," Esther whispered back.

"No, it's a bribe. I'm surprised at you, Esther."

Esther felt like stamping her foot. They couldn't dissect the Scriptures standing there in the cold customs' shed. She shivered and pulled her red fleecy jacket close about her. Slipping her hand into her purse she brought out her wallet. She only had two hundred dollars on her, as all her expenses were to be paid by the others, and she had wanted so much to give most of that as a gift to her aunt. But if Malcolm was going to be so stubborn, then she'd have to pay the official herself or bribe him as Malcolm had put it. She put down the notes on the counter. The official took the money almost before she had let go of it. Putting his fingers to his lips and looking furtively around, he motioned them to go.

Esther saw Malcolm's frown and deliberately avoided his eye. She noticed, too, that Marion's sweet face looked troubled, but this was no time for explanations. "I'll take the blame," she told her friends as she grabbed her suitcase. She looked round for a luggage cart, but soon found that she needed Romanian money to pay for it. She told the others to wait while she changed some dollars.

At last the luggage was piled high on the cart and they were ready to go. Malcolm grabbed the handle and began to wheel it towards the *Exit* sign. Clutching their purses tightly, the two girls pushed open the heavy metal doors. Esther heard her friends gasp in astonishment as they saw, jammed into an unbelievably small place, what seemed to be hundreds of people, all pushing and shoving to get a good view of the passengers of flight 303 from Chicago. Someone from Good News Missions was supposed to be waiting for them, Malcolm had told the girls.

"Taxi? Taxi?" The taxi drivers were descending on them like vultures on their prey.

"No," Marion shook her head, for the man was addressing her. "Thank you, but we don't want a taxi," she told him in her soft southern accent.

The man paid no attention whatsoever to her gentle protest. Marion stared in dismay. He had taken the cart from Malcolm, who had been totally unprepared for such a move, and was making off with their luggage.

Esther saw what was happening but had been unable to reach the man in time. Pushing past her friends, she shoved her way through the crowds and finally caught up with the taxi cab driver.

"We told you we didn't want a taxi," she said rather crossly in Romanian, grabbing the cart.

The man seemed surprised that she spoke his language so fluently. "I didn't understand your friend," he muttered, relinquishing the handle very reluctantly.

Esther grabbed the cart and pushed it to the edge of the crowd. She stared in wonder at the sea of humanity, surging around her. Her friends seemed helpless in its ebb and flow. After what felt like an eternity, she could distinguish Malcolm's tall figure pushing through the crowds. He was holding his sister's arm firmly in his.

"You didn't tell us it was this bad," Malcolm told her, panting for breath as he came up to where she was standing.

"I didn't know it was like this," Esther said defensively. "I've never been back here since the revolution."

Just then Marion caught sight of a large placard. "There's our man," she told her brother. "Over there."

Esther breathed a sigh of relief. Soon they were introducing themselves to Glen Thompson, the missionary from Good News Missions who had invited Malcolm to stay with him for a few nights before they headed north. Not many minutes later they found themselves being squeezed into the back of a dilapidated 1970's Land Rover. The driver, who was called Radu, tied four of the suitcases to the top with rope and then heaved the other two into the rear and banged the door shut.

"You'll have to take your hand luggage on your knees," Glen told them. Malcolm's large frame left the girls little room in the back seat, but Esther didn't care. Romanian signs loomed at her from all directions and she smiled happily to herself. She was home at last!

They paid the parking fee and edged onto the busy highway. They were soon racing along at a breakneck speed. The two girls held each other tightly. It seemed that their driver felt it his duty to pass nearly every vehicle on the road and he timed his passes down to the second. Once they braked so fiercely that Marion, who was sitting in the middle, was flung forwards between the two front seats.

Esther grabbed her friend's arm and pulled her back. "You're in Romania now. Be prepared for anything," she warned her. She was having to tell herself the same thing over and over again as they jolted along the highway towards Bucharest. It was far from a smooth ride. As they neared the city, Radu made several abrupt swerves to avoid the deep potholes that loomed up suddenly in their pathway.

"Sorry the roads are so bad," he apologized in Romanian. "There's no money to fix them right now. They keep promising, but we've given up believing much in what any politician tells us."

Esther translated for her friends. "So things aren't better since the Revolution?" Malcolm asked curiously.

"I wouldn't say that," Glen told him with a smile. "You wouldn't be here right now if Ceaucescu were still in power."

Radu grinned a little. His English was good enough to understand what was being said but he didn't have the nerve to speak it. Then his face sobered. "But in some ways we're even worse off now," he told them.

Esther stared in surprise. "How's that?" she wanted to know.

"Before, we were at least all in the same boat," he commented as he turned the steering wheel abruptly to the left to avoid a gaping hole. "Now a lot of former communists have grabbed the best jobs and are getting rich quick, while the poor are becoming poorer."

Glen gave a wry smile. "That's true enough, but I still think some of my friends are forgetting just how bad it was a year ago. They're expecting a utopia overnight."

Just then, they pulled up to a traffic light. Two scruffy looking urchins descended on them from nowhere, holding up a brush and cloth. Radu wound down his window and told them that his windscreen didn't need washing. He had just had it done on the way to the airport.

"Let them do it again," Glen pleaded. A few moments later, the boys had finished. The missionary slipped some coins into two grimy palms thrust in the open window. The boys grinned their thanks, the lights changed, and they were off again.

Esther noticed tears in Marion's eyes. Her friend would need plenty of Kleenex during the next few weeks, she thought to herself. Her own eyes were moist, too. She had not thought much about this side of Romania lately. She had forgotten how small the cars were, how run down the houses looked as they whizzed past them, and how sad her fellow countrymen seemed compared with Americans. Not many in the crowds that crossed the pedestrian crossings, or thronged both sides of the streets, looked relaxed or happy. Head down, bags in hand, they plodded onwards, probably rushing to get home, or to the stores before they closed. Survival had top priority in this land, just as before. Nothing seemed to have changed that much outwardly she noted, as they wove their way through the city streets, except, as their friend had reminded them, the simple fact that they were there, a miracle in itself, without police surveillance or harassment, so far at least. She hoped there were no hidden cameras now in hotel rooms, or secret police dogging their footsteps, or neighbors spying from bedroom windows. Surely one year of liberty had done away with all that!

Finally, after what seemed an age, they arrived at the missionary's home—two rooms on the eighth story of an apartment building south of the city center.

"Where will we sleep?" whispered Marion, when their host had ushered them into the small, plainly furnished living-room. "There only seems to be one bedroom."

"Don't know yet. On this sofa maybe," Esther whispered back.

"Malcolm will stay here," Glen informed them after he had introduced his wife, a frail little lady of about sixty years old whose smile warmed Esther's heart immediately. "And the girls will sleep at Radu's house." He nodded towards the driver who stood, cap in hand in his sock feet at the door. "We don't have room for you all, I'm afraid," he apologized, "and though Radu knows little English, Esther can interpret for her friend."

"Have a meal first," Tina Thompson invited them.

"Roxana has prepared food for the ladies," her husband reminded her. "She's been at it all day. She'd be awfully disappointed if they didn't eat with them."

Tina nodded understandingly. "Romanian hospitality is hard to beat. You'll soon find that out."

Radu lived only a block away. It was a three-roomed apartment their host told them proudly. "That means two bedrooms," Esther explained to her friend as they dragged their cases into the lift. Radu pressed the button. Nothing happened.

"Seems like it's not working today," he told them in Romanian as he backed out into the hallway. The girls followed, glad that their host lived on the third floor and not on the ninth. Esther had not realized that she had become such a weakling. She paused on the first floor, utterly exhausted. She had never been quite the same since her illness those two and a half years previously. The doctor had told her that the rheumatic fever had probably affected her heart for life.

"I'll take your friend's case up and come back for yours," Radu told her. "Both of you stay there till I come back."

Esther threw him a grateful glance. She felt thoroughly done in. She stared at the dirty walls, grimy stone steps, and pinched herself. She, Esther Popescu, was back in her native land. Her dream had come true at last! She closed her eyes for a moment then opened them quickly. Two drunk men were stumbling up the first flight of stairs.

"You need help," the older man said thickly, as he reached for her case.

"*Eşti foarte frumoasă, domnişoară* (you are very beautiful, miss)," the other muttered as he lunged at Marion. "Here, give me a kiss."

Marion put up one hand to keep him away and looked at her friend appealingly. Esther stepped in between them.

The man leered into Esther's face. "*Tu eşti şi mai frumoasă* (you are even more beautiful)," he slurred. She was more than relieved to hear Radu's voice shouting from the second floor. "Get away from the girls, Claudiu. They don't need your help."

He ran down the steps and grabbed the suitcase. A few minutes later, Esther collapsed onto a worn green sofa. Radu's wife soon had a cup of strong coffee in her hand. "Drink that, dear, and you'll feel better," she urged the exhausted girl in her sweet, musical voice.

The coffee was thick and strong and sweet. Esther hadn't tasted anything like it for over three years. As she sipped her coffee, she noticed Marion staring at the spotless, starched, white tablecloth and sparkling silverware. There were even crystal glasses laid out for them and beautiful hand-painted bowls. Then her friend's gaze turned from the well-set table to the antique china cabinet in the corner, the polished oak book case, and the rich tapestry hanging on the wall. Esther guessed what Marion was thinking. If these people were so poor, then how could they afford to own such things? She knew the probable answer. They were most likely heirlooms handed down from one generation to another. The silverware and crystal had been taken out for this special occasion. As for the furniture, it doubtless had been bought when such items had cost little.

"Do they have children?" whispered Marion as they took their seats.

"I think Radu said they had six," Esther whispered back. "They're probably eating in the kitchen." She was right. The youngest, a round-faced toddler, peeked in at them while they were finishing their *ciorba* and the eldest, a pale, slender girl of about thirteen, brought in more bread and filled up their glasses with Coca Cola.

"Don't eat too much soup," Esther cautioned Marion. "There'll be several courses yet."

Marion's blue eyes opened wide. She had expected to eat crusts of dry bread, a little salami maybe, and a bit of cheese now and then. But this feast was more than she could fathom.

"That's far too much," she protested, as the girl put down a heaping plate of mashed potatoes, a large piece of fried chicken breast, and a small bowl of salad especially for her.

"Eat what you can," Radu told her.

"Don't worry," Esther reassured her under her breath. "It won't go to waste."

Marion was speechless. Their hosts' kindness overwhelmed her. It would take a while, Esther told her, to get used to the Romanian way of life.

When they had eaten apple tart and cookies, their hostess led them to the sofa. She had unfolded it into a bed and put one large snowy white pillow at either end.

"There, sit with your feet up while we chat a while before bed," she told them.

Radu had gone over to the missionary's house to discuss the plans for the next day, so Roxana settled in a chair opposite and eyed the two girls curiously. They were both very pretty, she thought, and modest too. She hadn't expected that from Americans.

It wasn't long before Roxana had found out all about them and their families. Marion wondered at first at such personal questions, but saw that Esther was taking them in her stride. At one point, however, her friend blushed beet red and no translation seemed forthcoming.

"What's she saying, Esther?" Marion asked curiously.

Esther gulped and then replied, "She's asking which of us is Malcolm's wife. I told her neither; what else could I say?"

Marion was silent. Yes, what else could Esther say? "But then I said you were his sister and that made everything OK," Esther went on. She didn't translate all the woman had said. She didn't need to, she figured. After all, it was very nosy of Roxana to ask if she were engaged to Malcolm. Esther sighed. She would probably be asked that more than once before this trip was over. Maybe she shouldn't have come with them after all. It might be very embarrassing. She heard the children whispering in the kitchen. Were they discussing their guests, she wondered?

Her eyes rested on the large family Bible lying on the small table by the window, then roved from it to the neat stacks of schoolbooks on the dresser. The bookshelves were obviously full to capacity. She noticed Roxana's well-worn hands, her mended socks, and her patched house shoes. It all seemed so very familiar. Right at that moment, it seemed very hard to believe that she had ever lived anywhere else than in Romania.

Just then, Esther caught her hostess' eye and smiled. Roxana had told them she had just turned forty but she looked much older. She was wearing a white T-shirt with *The Sunshine State* emblazoned on it in large red letters. The girl looked closer. Roxana's skirt seemed almost identical to an Alfred Dunner that her Aunt Mary had bought at a sale a few months ago. Their hostess had probably worn it in their honor.

She leaned back on the pillow and gave a sigh of satisfaction. Romania was still a land of enigmas but it was her country. These were her people. This was where she belonged. After all, once Romanian always Romanian—that was what Gabby was always saying, or at least, Esther frowned a little, that was what she used to say.

The clock in the corner chimed eleven. Roxana kissed them both and bade them good night. Soon the lights had been turned out and they were in bed. Esther had told Marion it would be best to sleep head to toe—give them more breathing space. They hadn't had evening devotions but she thought God would understand. She felt so utterly weary.

It was two o'clock before Esther got to sleep. It was hard to find a comfortable position between the broken springs in the old sofa. She thought again how soft she had become. What had Rachel said about the Velvet Curtain coming to Romania? She almost laughed out loud at the thought. She wished her cousin could be with her and see for herself what it was really like over here. She tried to shut out the chiming of the clock and the maudlin tones of a drunk man singing on his way up to the floor above them. The smell of moth balls on the starched sheets tickled her nose, and Marion's feet seemed awfully close to her face.

A wish, very faint but very real, stole into her heart at that moment, that she could be back with her aunt in her own bed with its orthopedic mattress and soft pink comforter. She wrinkled her brow in disgust. A few hours in Romania and she felt like this? She only hoped three weeks would harden her up a bit. If she were going to live here once more, she really would have to be tough, like she had been in the old days before the Velvet Curtain had spoiled her.

## Chapter Fifteen

*Ploieşti Again!*

"Esther, can I have a word with you, please?" The girls had eaten breakfast and gone over to Glen and Tina Thompson's for some prayer together. The others had gone into the living room and Malcolm, to Esther's surprise, waylaid her as she was taking off her shoes in the hall.

She looked up at him inquiringly. His face was very serious and his voice unusually solemn. "As we are to travel a bit together these next few weeks," he began slowly, "I want to warn you that I'm not going to let you give bribes any more. It wasn't right."

Esther flushed as she put on her house shoes and stood up to face him. His grey eyes were looking right at her. "It happened so suddenly, Malcolm," she explained. "And it was the only thing to do under the circumstances. If I hadn't *bribed* the man as you call it, we would have had to give up some of our money and a few of our cases, too."

"I'm sure there would have been another way out of it. God always makes a way of escape, Esther," Malcolm protested.

Esther grimaced a little. "Well, maybe I was His way of escape this time."

"Don't joke about it." Esther had never heard Malcolm sound so stern. "I'm in dead earnest."

Esther looked up pleadingly into his face. "It's a way of life here," she told him, her large eyes searching his. "And everyone is so poor that I consider that I'm really putting bread on their table when I'm forced to do this."

Malcolm dropped his eyes. He couldn't think with the girl staring at him like that. "I've prayed over it and talked it over with Glen," he muttered. "He agrees with me. It's wrong to give in to such pressure. You must never, never do it again when you're with me. Promise?"

"When I'm with you? OK, I promise, if you'll take the responsibility for what happens, that is."

"Of course I'll be responsible."

"But when I'm alone, it's a different matter. After all, I have a right to do what I like with my own property, don't I?"

Malcolm stroked his beard thoughtfully. "Esther, I feel very sorry for you." The girl flushed and tossed her head. She wasn't sure she wanted his pity.

"You have no one to guide you," he went on in the same tone, "and every woman ought to be under a man's protection. You seem a law unto yourself. You need to be married." He gave her another long look and went in to join the others.

Esther leaned against the faded wallpaper and gasped in disbelief. He had never spoken to her like that before. What was it all about? She had no time for further reflection for Marion had come in search of her. "Get out your headscarf, Esther," she advised. "We're going to pray together."

Esther drew her dainty, pink scarf from her purse and tied it on her head. Then she fished out a small mirror from her bag, loosened her hair just a little so that it peeked out from under her head-covering. Then she checked that she had put the scarf on straight. Marion sighed impatiently. Her friend was so fastidious, at times, she thought, and maybe just a little vain.

Esther wondered why Marion looked at her as she did as they entered the living room, but understood later when Glen and his wife had gone out to the market and left them to discuss their plans for that day. The girls sat waiting for Malcolm to speak. His eyes were fixed on Esther's pink scarf. He cleared his throat and then began, "Esther, seeing that you are really in our employ these weeks, when you are with us, we would like you to wear more subdued colors."

Esther fidgeted in her chair. What could she do but acquiesce? "OK. If you both think it best."

"Yes, we do. And there's that bright red jacket you wear. Sister Tina has a dark blue coat with a hood which will fit you, she thinks. While you travel with us, please, we'd like you to wear it. Red is gaudy and draws attention to you, and," he paused and reddened a little, "even in your plain clothes, you draw attention enough." He averted his eyes as he said this and coughed nervously.

Esther turned to Marion. "But why didn't you tell me before we left? I could have brought different clothes."

"We never thought. We always saw you dressed like we were, Esther, and forgot, I suppose that you didn't dress like that when you were away from our community."

"Well, I thought I'd dress pretty much like I did when I lived here," Esther explained, feeling thoroughly mortified. "Though I should have thought about the red jacket, I suppose. It was a bit bright. I'm sorry. But," and she looked at Malcolm as she spoke, "I didn't bring any long dresses like Marion wears, if that's how you want me to dress, though mine aren't short by any means."

"Tina has some warm ones, just your size, Esther. She has a daughter your age."

Esther's heart sank, she didn't fully know why. It had been one thing to dress like Marion in Mercer's store but here, in front of her church in Ploieşti?

"Thanks," she muttered. "But I can't promise I'll dress like that when I'm on my own here."

"On your own? But you won't be on your own much, will you?"

Esther stared at him. She remembered that she was a paid translator and would have to devote most of the next few weeks to her task. "I don't suppose I will," she mumbled. "Though maybe I could have a few days with my aunt—a weekend maybe?"

"Well, we want to meet your aunt, Esther, and your church. So we'll all go there together," Malcolm told her.

Esther hid her disappointment. Rachel had been right after all. There were more strings attached to this arrangement than she had realized. She oughtn't to have been so naïve.

Marion told her later that Glen had thought that all three of them belonged to the same church and had been surprised to see Esther in her red jacket, her long, thick hair tied back with a clasp, and not done up like Marion's.

"They don't know you like we do, Esther," her friend had whispered as she put her arm round her.

"But Malcolm seems different, Marion, sterner and more exacting. Has Glen had a hand in this too?"

Marion's face clouded but just for a moment. "I don't think he's that different, Esther. He doesn't want you to be under any sort of reproach, so he's being careful. He's very fond of you."

It had slipped out before she could stop it. Marion put a hand to her mouth and gasped. "I didn't mean to say that, but you might as well know it now as later. He really likes you, Esther."

Esther turned away her head. Two large teardrops trickled down her cheeks. Were there going to be complications here on this trip, the trip she had so looked forward to for months? Then she squared her chin and turned back to face her friend. She wasn't going to let something like this spoil her time in Romania.

"Well, he'd better like me if we have to travel together for three weeks," she said lightly. "Now for my transformation." She slipped into the bathroom and changed into a long navy blue serge dress with a simple white collar and long sleeves. Then she pulled back her thick waves and put them in a bun on the top of her head.

At lunch, she noticed Malcolm's approving glances. Esther kept her eyes on her plate most of the time. Marion gazed admiringly at her friend across the table. She would look like a queen even in sackcloth and ashes, she thought privately.

The next day, while the men were busy planning and discussing and praying, Marion and Esther set out on their journey to Ploieşti. Aunt Ana knew her niece was in the country, but having no phone, had not been able to get in touch with her. It was a Saturday so Esther was sure her aunt would be at home.

As they pushed through the crowds in the metro station, clambered in and out of rickety trams and buses, and went up and down what seemed countless escalators, Esther felt very happy. She was home again. She noticed that, if anything, the trains were a bit dirtier than of old. The beggars were still there: old men with no legs; women with children on their hips; teenage girls, ragged, and blue with cold, and small boys, who sang carols in the train compartments and then held out grimy hands for tips.

Marion gave until she had no change left. Her flaxen hair, bright rosy cheeks, clear blue eyes, and winning smile made her an easy mark. It was all too obvious that she was not a Romanian lady. The gypsies followed her, hands outstretched. Taxi cab drivers mobbed her shouting, "Taxi, madam?" Esther groaned inwardly. She wished for once that her friend was not so sweet and gullible.

But at last they were on their way to Ploieşti. The carriage was crowded—eight of them, sitting four to a side like sardines in a can. It was only an hour's ride, and Esther's heart beat faster as she glimpsed the tall, dark towers emitting flames into the dull grey winter's sky. Her city was one of the most polluted in Europe, or so it was said. Students came there from all over the world to learn about oil refining.

*Ploieşti Again!* 135

At last they pulled into the Gara de Sud. "Quick, Marion. The train only stops for three minutes," she told her friend as they grabbed their bags. The narrow corridor was crowded, and the train had ground to a halt by the time they reached the door.

Esther wished their dresses weren't quite so long as they jumped down onto the platform. A few moments later and they were seated on tram 101. The seats were broken, the floors filthy, and the doors let in drafts of icy air. But she was back in Ploieşti and her heart sang like a lark.

Marion noticed her friend's shining eyes and the smile that came and went much more often than it had done in Mercer's store or in Aunt Lucy's fine sitting room. Half an hour later, when Aunt Ana had thrown her arms round her niece and held her as if she would never let her go again, Marion had to wipe the tears that would come in spite of all her efforts to stop them.

Her aunt finally released Esther and turned to welcome her niece's friend. Soon they were sipping hot mint tea with lemon and sugar in it. Esther licked her lips. "It's delicious, Aunt Ana. Oh, just think, I'm back home again. I can't believe it! It's wonderful! But you look paler and thinner than you used to be. Are you all right?"

Aunt Ana put her bony hand on Esther's shoulder and bent down to give her another kiss. "Never mind about me. You're prettier than ever, a lot prettier, *Estera dragă*. And more mature too. And so modest!"

"You're surprised, aren't you? Did you see a picture of me in my yellow dress, singing at the concert?"

"I did. I think Gabby sent it—a clipping from the newspaper. I couldn't see the color of the dress but I saw its shape. It certainly didn't hide much." Aunt Ana's eyes narrowed as she spoke, then she smiled again as she went on quickly, "But you're not a bit like that now, are you?"

"Not outside, at least," Esther said, a shadow on her face. "But let's talk about you. Did you lose your job after all? I haven't heard anything about you for ages."

Aunt Ana looked down at her patched apron. "I did lose my job after Gabby left. You probably can guess why. But I work for some missionaries now who have come to town. I clean house and cook but have the weekends to myself. And they pay me well, Esther."

Her niece's face glowed. "So liberty has come here after all. I was beginning to doubt it when I first arrived."

"Yes, Esther, liberty has come." Ana didn't sound overly happy about it. "But it has brought a lot of problems with it. You'll soon see for yourself."

Esther translated for Marion and smiled a little as her friend's blue eyes opened wide in disbelief. But she couldn't blame her. She even found it hard to believe that liberty could have its dark side here in her beloved land.

The two hours they had to spend with Aunt Ana seemed like ten minutes. "I'm going to come to church tomorrow evening with Marion and her brother," Esther whispered as she gave her aunt a goodbye hug. "So I'll be seeing you soon. We girls could sleep here with you for a night or two, and maybe you can find a place for Marion's brother?" Her aunt nodded. It wasn't hard to find hospitable people in Romania, and by the time they arrived the next evening, it had all been arranged.

As Esther turned into the familiar road that Sunday evening, she thought that nothing had changed during the last three years. It was still the same—hundreds packed into the three or four rooms which had been transformed into one large hall. And the singing was as heavenly as ever, Esther thought, and the praying, and the preaching!

The youth choir presented their program just as they used to do. Quite a few of her former schoolmates were there, though there were also many faces among them which she did not recognize. Some read verses from the Bible, some recited a poem in between songs. When they had finished, Malcolm was invited to speak. A young student whom Esther knew tried to translate but couldn't make out the speaker's strong southern drawl. Malcolm whispered to the chief elder for a moment and then motioned to Esther to come to the front.

She saw smiles on many faces as she began to translate. Granny Sandelescu was sitting on the front row, holding a bunch of roses, ready to give them to any visitor who might stray into church that night. The old lady beamed up at her, her face more lined than ever, but her smile just as bright as it had been three years previously. Esther found it fairly easy to interpret for Malcolm; he spoke slowly and without emotion as was his wont, but she could sense that the people liked him.

When he had finished, Brother Luca, who was the chief elder of the church, motioned to Esther to stay on the platform. "We are pleased to welcome back our dear sister, Estera Popescu, as well as her two friends from America," he told the congregation. "You will probably want to hear Estera sing as she used to do when she was with us. I'm sure she hasn't lost her song."

Esther should have been prepared for this but she wasn't. She stood for a moment transfixed. She had been determined not to accept invitations to sing but this was different. She wasn't behind the Velvet Curtain any more. She was in her own dear Romania. So she nodded to Brother Luca, went up to the organist, whispered something to him, and then took her stand at the mike. She saw Marion's mouth fall open. Her friends had never heard her sing before.

Soon the strains of *Numai Harul* were filling the packed room. "She's not forgotten Romanian," Granny Sandelescu whispered to her neighbor.

"She sings better than ever," a lady sitting by Marion said, but of course Marion couldn't understand her.

Esther tried hard to push out images of her uncle and Ron as she sang. She had been afraid she would be so out of practice that her voice would break, but instead, it seemed to soar upon angels' wings. Even the men were wiping their eyes. She didn't look at Malcolm, but Marion could see that he was absolutely transfixed.

Esther couldn't get away that evening. Everyone wanted to speak to her. She was exhausted but very happy as she dropped into bed that night. Her aunt's old sofa wasn't any more comfortable than the one at Roxana's house, but her dreams were sweeter. Spiritually, she felt cleaner than she had for months, maybe years.

Her aunt came in at midnight to have a look at her sleeping niece. "She's like an angel," she whispered to herself as she bent over her. "America's not spoiled her in the slightest. But Gabby, my dear, headstrong Gabby!" Aunt Ana let out a long sigh. Esther had told her a little of Gabby's troubles and of her own. But Aunt Ana couldn't understand much about the Velvet Curtain and how it had nearly smothered Esther. She only saw that her precious niece looked the same as always, or nearly. But Gabby—with doubts and dubious friends and headstrong ways? She turned from the bed where the girls were sleeping so peacefully and dropped on her knees by her old green chair.

She clasped her gnarled, knotted hands tighter and lifted her wan face heavenwards. "Oh our Father," she breathed, "please bring my wayward lamb back into the fold. And thank you for bringing Estera home to me. Thank You, Oh thank You!"

## Chapter Sixteen

### *Rachel Gets the Message*

"Don't they make a pretty picture, Sally?" Dr. Porter remarked to his companion as they lounged on the beach one warm December afternoon. They had come to Florida the week before, bringing Gabby with them.

Sally followed his glance and nodded. Gabby was in a deck chair, reading aloud to Larry, her eyes flashing, her hands moving animatedly, while he lay at her feet, gazing up intently into her face. "Gabby's one of a kind," Sally mused. "I've never known a girl so brimming full of life. Everything about her is vibrant."

Ken Porter smiled. "You're right," he agreed. "She's remarkable. The girl sure has come out of herself this vacation."

"They make an extraordinary pair, those two," Sally commented thoughtfully.

"Yes. They seem to have such a lot in common." Dr. Porter gave a smug smile.

"Think so?" Sally sounded a little worried.

Ken looked at her intently. "Well, isn't that good?" he wanted to know.

"I hope so," Sally hedged. Then she let out a long sigh.

Her companion raised his eyebrows. "Why the sigh?"

"I was just thinking that it's refreshing to meet someone different in our secular society. Problem is, that we often have some perverse desire to change the person we most admire and then we discard them like a used-up plaything once we've obtained our objective."

"Maybe you missed your calling," Ken Porter commented with a grin. "You should have taken up psychology like my son!"

"You're forgetting that I did major in psychiatry, Ken," Sally retorted. "I haven't always worked with plants, remember?"

Ken Porter leaned over and kissed her. "How could I ever forget how we first met!" he told her tenderly.

Sally blushed. She could still vividly recall that day five years ago when, exhausted and depressed, she had been sitting alone on a bench outside the hospital where she was doing her internship. She had already completed four years of med school and her goal to become a psychiatrist seemed just within her grasp. Then, quite suddenly, her world had fallen apart. A failed marriage, a mother who was dying, the pressure of exams—it had all been too much. Sitting on the bench that morning in early September, she felt she was swinging over a deep abyss at the end of a long rope. Her hands were slipping. She could hold on no longer.

Then, looking up, her eyes had met those of Dr. Ken Porter, the tall, handsome gynecologist. It had been love at first sight, they both told each other later. Her new friend not only saw to it that she received professional help, but took her under his wing. It seemed that they spent every spare moment together. And when Sally's mother died a few months later, it was the handsome doctor, nearly twice her age, to whom she looked for comfort.

Ken's wife had left him two years earlier, so it wasn't long before he persuaded Sally to move in with him. She temporarily gave up her studies, always intending to finish them one day. When the nursery near their home came up for sale, Ken had bought it and put Sally in charge. It had turned out such an astounding success that she was still running it five years later.

Sally always felt that Ken Porter had come along just at the right moment. He had done so much for her. She would be eternally grateful. And she really did love him. Only, sometimes she did wish they could get married. She often remembered her mother's teaching about the sanctity of marriage, and couldn't always fight back the guilt that would sweep over her. But when she mentioned her feelings to Ken, he had kissed her gently and told her that in God's sight they were already married. Then he had changed the subject abruptly and that had been an end of it.

Now, sitting on the beach in the Florida sun, Sally told herself that being Ken's mistress might be all right for her, she had long since abandoned her mother's religion, but she would hate to see the young and naïve Gabriella follow her example. She shifted uneasily in her deckchair. "Ken," she began hesitatingly, "do you seriously think that Larry will try to change Gabby? I mean…"

"You mean will he discard her like a used-up plaything once he's obtained his objective, as you put it a moment ago?" Ken interrupted, his frown matching his companion's as he added, "Do you really think Larry would do that with the girl?"

"Consciously no, but…" Sally paused, not knowing how to voice her fears.

The doctor's frown deepened. He didn't appreciate Sally's inferences about his son. His eyes fell on Gabby once more and his face brightened. "Whatever influence he is having on the girl, it certainly isn't negative. Just look at her! She's acting as if she's been truly set free at last."

Sally studied Gabby for a moment. What Ken had said seemed true. Her face relaxed into a smile. Everything would be all right.

Gabby had told herself the same thing that very morning. Life seemed burgeoning with promise, beckoning her to explore its secrets and experience its pleasures. She felt as if she were in another world from the one she was used to—a carefree, uninhibited world where it was not considered a sin to enjoy yourself. She knew Esther would call it the Velvet Curtain closing in, but she really didn't care any more. If Velvet Curtains felt like this, then they were more than welcome in her life.

"Where's Andrea?" Ken asked suddenly, as he glanced around.

"With Mark as usual," Sally told him archly. "They're never apart now."

When Larry had joined them on Christmas Eve, he had brought along a college friend, Mark Gifford, whom none of the family had ever met before. Tanned and handsome as well as being good at every sport imaginable and with a smile that could melt the hardest of hearts, Mark had soon become a favorite with everyone.

"I thought he preferred Gabby," Ken remarked.

"He did, at first. But I think he soon discovered that the charming Gabriella Popescu was not like most other girls."

"Meaning?"

"Oh, just that she held him at bay more than he liked. It's just obvious that the girl's not used to guys like Mark," Sally said with a knowing smile. "And anyway, she much prefers your son."

"That's true. And I think Andrea can hold her own with any guy," Ken commented smugly, as he rose from his chair and made his way over to where Gabby was sitting. "Enjoying yourself?" he asked. The girl gave a start and looked up from her book.

"You crept up on us like a ghost, Dad." Larry sat bolt upright and gave his father a reproachful look.

"Sorry!"

"Oh that's OK," Gabby said reassuringly. "I'd about finished the chapter. Your son keeps me busy, Dr. Porter."

"I've told you to call me Ken," he reminded her, chucking her under the chin. "But I hope Larry isn't working you too hard."

"Oh, no! He's great fun," Gabby exclaimed. "He gets my mind so full of ideas that sometimes I think my head will burst."

"Well, just remember it is vacation," he said good-naturedly.

"But we can't swim all the time, you know," Gabby told him smiling. "And it's great to talk with someone like Larry."

"We're on the same wavelength, Dad," Larry commented quietly. Gabby flushed bright red. That was the greatest compliment he could have given her.

"That's the first time he's ever said that about any of his girlfriends," Ken commented, giving the girl a knowing wink.

Gabby blushed scarlet. "I'm not…" she began, then broke off abruptly.

"She's not just any girlfriend." Larry finished the sentence for her. "She's…" he paused, giving his companion a meaningful look as he went on, "I've discovered these weeks that she's also my soul mate."

Gabby rose from her seat. "Excuse me, but I need to go into the condo a moment," she stammered.

The two men watched her as she made her way along the beach. "You embarrassed her no end," Ken told his son.

"Oh did I?" Larry didn't sound at all concerned. "Well, embarrassment suits her, is all I can say. Isn't she great?"

"She sure is, Larry, in more ways than one. But please, go easy with her."

Larry got up from the sand and turned to face his dad. "Go easy?" his voice was edgy now. "I'm not sure that's what Gabby needs now or even what she wants. Don't worry, I'll take it just as easy as is good for her. I know the girl pretty well by now."

"You seem to," Ken shrugged.

"But I'll know her a lot better before this vacation is over."

"Good luck," his father told him with a pat on the shoulder. "You may need a lot of it before you're finished."

The last week of the Christmas vacation sped by. The next day but one and they would all pack up and head north. Rachel, who was staying a few days with her dad and Diane in Orlando, was to come and get Gabby the next day, stay overnight and then take her back to Tiny Gap.

Gabby wanted to be back home before Esther returned from Romania. The others would stay on in Florida a little longer.

That evening, Gabby remarked to herself, everyone seemed to be doing their own thing. Simon and his friend were at a country club up the road; Ken and Sally were visiting some friends in Tampa, some thirty minutes away by car, and Mark and Andrea had gone off to a bar in town for a drink. She and Larry had just had a sumptuous meal in a local restaurant.

"What'll we do tonight, Gabby?" Larry asked as he paid the bill and followed her to the door. "Let's make it something memorable."

"Like what?"

"You suggest something for a change."

Gabby's eyes sparkled. She had come to enjoy every moment she spent with Larry. She had often pondered his words to his father that afternoon on the beach. She wasn't quite sure what he had meant by them and it wasn't really that important. Nothing had changed between them, except that they spent more and more time alone together, sitting side by side on a favorite rock in a secluded part of the beach. And their discussions had grown more personal. Gabby found it a great comfort to be able to bare her soul to someone who never chided her for her doubts, her anger, or her frustration and, what was more, seemed to actually understand why she felt this way.

"Let's go barefoot for a walk on the beach," Gabby suggested, as they sped along the highway.

"And?"

"Oh, sit on our favorite rock as we always do."

"And?"

"And talk of course."

"And?"

Gabby laughed merrily. "You think up something else, then. I've run out of ideas."

"I sure haven't," Larry said with a grin, wondering at the girl's utter naivety.

"I guess I'm not very imaginative tonight," Gabby replied. "So it's over to you."

Larry gave a whistle. "Sure you realize what you're doing, giving me a *carte blanche* like that?"

Gabby stared at him, realizing suddenly what he was thinking. "I'm not very romantic, Larry," she stammered, turning scarlet. "You know that by now!"

Larry laughed. "You not romantic? No, I don't know that!"

"Well," Gabby stammered, "I mean I'm not romantic like other girls you probably know."

Larry raised his eyebrows. "Really? Well, maybe after tonight I'll be able to tell you whether I agree with you or not," he said with a grin, as he brought his car to a halt outside their condo. "Anyway, what exactly does romance mean nowadays?" he went on, as they made their way to the beach.

"Sex!" Gabby blurted out before she could think better of it.

Larry laughed. "Sex?" he repeated. "Well that's certainly part of it. Always has been since Adam and Eve. But come on, Gabby, you and I don't need to worry about definitions, at least, not tonight! Whatever will be will be!"

Gabby blushed as she kicked off her shoes and felt the soft warm sand between her toes. Next thing, he had taken her hand and they were off like the wind, Gabby's hair streaming behind her as she ran.

"Slow down, Larry," she panted at last. "I suggested a walk, not a run."

"Tired? I'm surprised," he commented as they slowed to walking pace. "Nothing usually tires you, Gabriella. But isn't it a perfect night?" He gazed out to sea. The sun would set within the hour. Already they could see the crescent moon beginning to appear above them.

When they reached their favorite rock, Gabby let go Larry's hand and sat down. She stared out to sea as she began slowly, "You know, I feel bad sometimes about not spending more time at home. I know I'm hurting my sister and aunt. But I don't feel at home with them now like I do with you. I take a guilt trip every time I'm with them."

Larry frowned. "I know you do. Just thank your lucky stars that you've come as far as you have towards achieving the freedom of spirit you're aiming for. But let's not talk about your family. Tonight, I feel as if you and I were all alone in the universe."

Gabby nodded. "It's a perfect evening," she breathed. She sat stock still for a while, gazing at the ocean.

"Even nature is celebrating," Larry said, as he drew a little closer. "Let's enjoy this last night together. We've gotten to know each other pretty well these past weeks and there's not much we haven't shared together. Maybe it's time to make our sharing complete." He put his arms round her and drew her closer. "Lean your head on my shoulder. There, that's better."

Gabby seemed to have no power to pull away even if she had wanted to. "Look at those stars coming out and that moon," he went on, "and smell the sea." He looked deep into her eyes, flecked with green and grey, and thought he had never seen eyes like them.

"I'm not ready for this kind of romance," Gabby meant to tell him, but she couldn't get the words out, couldn't because she wasn't sure she meant them, not just then at any rate.

"From now on, Gabriella," he murmured, "when we're together, every moment will be a wonderful surprise." He put his hand on hers as he spoke. "Let's not worry about the past or future. The present is ours to enjoy to the full."

He felt her relax in his arms. Her eyes were dreamy and there was a half smile on her lips. She seemed in a sort of trance. This was the very first time she had sat like this with any boy. She gazed up at the night sky. The stars were truly beautiful. She remembered reading *The Voyage of the Dawn Treader* and wondered if her father could be one of those stars C. S. Lewis had pictured so graphically, looking down on them.

The thought of her father brought her to her senses. What was she doing, sitting very close to a young man with her head on his shoulder while he caressed her hair? That wasn't much, surely; nothing to be ashamed of. Dad and Mum must have sat like this many a time. But what was she really doing? She imagined that she saw a tear trickle down her father's face. Then she remembered the clubs she had visited in Tampa during the past few weeks, the wine she had drunk, the movies she had seen, and the young man whose arms were wrapped very tightly around her now—a young man who didn't believe in her father's God and was not ashamed of it either.

Larry felt a tremor go through the girl's frame. "You're shivering," he said. "It's getting too chilly to stay here any longer. Come on," and he pulled her to her feet. "Let's go back to the condo. The night's young, and no one will be home for a few hours."

Gabby glimpsed something in his eyes she had never seen before and was seized by an overwhelming sense of fear. She saw the light from the condo shining in the distance and pulled her hand away. Before Larry could stop her she was off like a hare, speeding into the darkness.

Larry hesitated a moment and then sped after her. She had almost reached the condo when he caught up with her. "Afraid, Gabby?" he asked reproachfully, turning her around to face him. "But not of me! I wouldn't hurt you for the world. You're afraid of yourself, aren't you?"

She nodded, a large tear trickling down her cheek. Larry saw it glistening in the moonlight and took his finger to wipe it away. "Trust your feelings, for once, Gabby," he whispered. "You were created for moments like this. It's not sinful for us to enjoy each other, is it? Relax, there, now, that's better."

Gabby felt the tension drain out of her body. She had been so free the past few weeks. She mustn't become shackled again by fear and restraints. Her father would never want her to be miserable. She looked up at Larry and smiled. And then, before she knew what was happening, they were locked in each others arms. He had just kissed her for the third time when Gabby gave a start and pulled away.

"Someone's on the porch," she whispered. Larry peered into the shadows.

"It's just me," Rachel's clear, girlish voice called out.

Gabby and Larry stood still and looked at one another in dismay. Larry took her hand firmly in his and led her towards the porch steps.

Rachel got up from her chair. "Sorry to intrude," she said in her matter-of-fact tone. "I did try to call before I left, but no one was in. Dr. Porter had originally invited me to stay a week, so I figured that if I came one day early no one would mind."

Gabby flopped into the nearest seat and buried her head in her hands. Then, she couldn't help it, she began to cry. She saw her father's face again just as she had seen it while sitting out on the rock. She heard her mother's sweet voice singing lullabies and reading Bible stories. She visualized Esther, delirious, begging Ron to "lift the curtain."

"There, there," Larry soothed as if talking to a child. He stooped and whispered in her ear, "Don't let your cousin's coming spoil our last night together. She had no right to come in on us like that. It was rude to say the least."

Gabby leaned her head on his arm for a few moments. Maybe he was right. Then she became conscious of Rachel's eyes fixed on her. She got up from her chair and made for the stairs. "Look, you two, I'm very tired. Think I'll get an early night. Thanks for a wonderful evening, Larry." She avoided his eyes as she spoke.

"But it's only nine. The night's young."

"I know, but I've got a headache. So please excuse me. Rachel will entertain you."

Larry turned on his heel and made for the car. "Think I'll go for a drink or two," he muttered as he disappeared into the darkness.

When he had gone, Gabby turned on her cousin, her eyes flaming. "Now look what you've done. You've made Larry mad. And no wonder. You've spoiled our last night together."

Rachel said nothing. She couldn't really justify her actions. She didn't even understand them herself.

"I'm sorry," Gabby exclaimed suddenly. "I shouldn't have said that. Come on, let me show you our room. You'll have to share my bed for tonight."

The girls mounted the stairs in silence. Gabby opened her bedroom door and then, suddenly threw herself face downwards on the bed, and lay there for what must have been a good half hour, not moving a muscle or so it seemed to the watching Rachel who sat in a chair by the window. She remembered so clearly how that afternoon, as she was sitting with her father and Diane on their porch in Orlando, she had suddenly felt that she must go immediately to her cousin in Tampa. She didn't usually go by impressions, but this had been different, very different!

Then, at last, Gabby turned over and sat up. Very mechanically, she began to get undressed. Rachel decided it was about time to break the silence. "Look," she began, "I should really apologize for coming in on you like this. I know Larry's hopping mad and you're not exactly pleased."

"No, I'm not," Gabby replied shortly. "It wasn't like you."

"No, it wasn't," her cousin admitted slowly. "I just felt that I must come, and come right away."

"But you don't usually go by impressions."

"No," Rachel agreed. "I don't. But this was different. It was more a compulsion than an impression and it was totally overwhelming. I couldn't seem to do anything but obey it."

Gabby's eyes opened wide in astonishment. Then she jumped up from the bed and ran over to where Rachel was sitting. She flung her arms around her cousin and began to sob uncontrollably.

Rachel had never pictured herself doing very well in the role of comforter, but that night not even her own mother could have done better. After some minutes, she led Gabby back to her bed and sat down beside her. "Want to tell me about it, or shall we leave it for tonight?" she asked gently.

Gabby shook her head. "I feel as if I'll explode if I don't get it out of my system," she muttered. Then she began to tell Rachel all that had happened, not just about that evening or about the last few weeks.

She shared how she had never been the same since her father's death, how she had struggled with doubts and then finally succumbed to them that summer in Indianapolis. She couldn't stand being torn apart. And so she had decided to make Andrea and Larry's world her own. This decision had seemed to bring her the peace and freedom she had been yearning for.

"But that guy has some sort of control over you," Rachel interrupted. "He's too much for you."

Gabby looked confused. "I don't know. We've gotten very close during this vacation. We understand each other. And, anyway, he didn't do anything shocking tonight. I mean, he put his arm round me and we were sitting pretty close. Then I got frightened and ran away from him."

"You didn't look very frightened when I saw you."

Gabby's cheeks were flaming now. It seemed as if she had only just realized the implication of the evening's events. Then she tossed back her hair a little defiantly as she met Rachel's searching gaze.

"Well, what if he did kiss me? So what?"

"And you think it would have ended with those kisses?" Rachel asked pointedly. She couldn't keep the sarcasm out of her tone. She had seen the two of them on the beach and could hardly believe that her cousin was as naïve as her words implied.

Gabby stared at her for a few moments and then hung her head. "It all happened so fast," she muttered. "I felt all sorts of emotions I've never felt before. But Rachel," her voice sounded piteous now, "I'm not sure what is right and what is wrong any more. Union of body, soul, and spirit with someone who has become your soul mate seems very noble to me. And yet, I thought I saw Dad looking down from Heaven. I actually saw him twice, and I know he was worried about me."

Gabby paused a moment and then put her hands to her head. "I've got a thumping headache. I'm going to bed," she announced abruptly. Another mood swing, Rachel thought as she slipped into bed.

Eventually, Rachel could tell by her cousin's even breathing that she had fallen asleep. She was very fond of Gabby. She smiled into the darkness. She had beaten Larry in his game for that one evening, at least. And maybe, just maybe, it had proved that she, Rachel Joanna Popescu, was of some worth after all in this world.

## Chapter Seventeen

### *Another Proposal*

"Bye, Marion, I sure will miss you!" Esther put down her bag and gave her friend another hug. "Thanks for having me."

"Thanks for coming with us. You were such a help."

"I'm glad."

"We'll keep in touch. Oh, by the way, Malcolm wanted me to give you this."

Esther stared blankly at the envelope in Marion's hand. It couldn't be money. They had paid all her expenses. And why had Marion kept it till they were saying goodbye before giving it to her?

Her friend put a hand on her shoulder. "Esther," she whispered, "Malcolm told me not to give it to you till we arrived in America. And he also said to read it privately and that you don't need to write back." Marion gave her a peculiar smile. "You can tell him your answer when he comes in a month's time."

Just then, Rachel approached the bench where they were sitting and took the luggage cart from her cousin. "Mom's got the car over there." She pointed to Mary's cream Honda.

"You're sure you'll be OK, Marion?" Esther turned to her friend one last time.

"Positive. My dad will be here any moment."

"Bye, then!" Esther shouted over her shoulder.

"Bye!"

Rachel heaved her cousin's suitcase into the trunk of her aunt's car. Esther opened the front passenger door. Mary was at the wheel. She leaned over and gave her niece a quick hug. Somehow Esther felt strangely glad to be back. Velvet Curtain or not, America had its blessings, not the least being her aunt's warm presence. Then she felt Rachel's hand on her shoulder and heard her serious voice saying, "It's just great to have you back. I was afraid you'd stay in Romania."

"You can't get rid of me just yet," Esther said with a laugh. "One day I'll be off for good, but one day isn't today. How's it been at Tiny

Gap, and how's Gabby? I thought she might have been with you today. College doesn't start till Tuesday, does it?"

"No," Rachel told her, "but Gabby has come down with the flu. She picked it up in Florida."

"Florida?"

"Yes. She spent three weeks there with the Porter family." Rachel remembered that Gabby had not disclosed her plans for the Christmas vacation until Esther had left for Romania.

Esther sat back in her seat and stared out the window. Everything seemed so massive—the cars, the houses, and even the people. "So that explains it," she exclaimed suddenly.

"Explains what?" Rachel wanted to know.

Esther turned around in her seat so she could see Rachel's face. "It explains why I've been terribly worried about her though I didn't know she was down there with Andrea and the others. But let's see, it would be last Thursday evening at midnight…" She paused. She saw Rachel's eyes blaze with excitement as she twisted a stray strand of dark brown hair round and round her finger.

"What's wrong, Rachel?" Esther queried. "Why are you looking at me like that?"

"I'll tell you in a minute. Please, go on."

"I had gone to bed at eleven and had just dosed off when I woke suddenly. There was no dream, no nightmare, just a terrible sense of impending danger for my sister. The room seemed charged with it. I crept out of bed and knelt down. Marion was sleeping soundly. I could hear her regular breathing. The clock in the hallway was chiming midnight when I poured it out to God. I told Him to please protect my sister from whatever danger she might be in."

Esther stopped abruptly, noticing the expression on her cousin's face. "You look as if you'd seen a ghost!" she exclaimed.

"Do I?" Rachel sounded self-conscious. She wasn't used to sharing her heart with anyone. "It's just…" she stammered. She didn't really want to talk about it, and yet maybe the others needed to know. She took a gulp and then slowly and deliberately began to tell them how she had felt a strong urge to go to Gabby that afternoon. She was careful not to relay much of what her cousin had confided in her so that left Esther and Mary to piece together Gabby's part of the story as best they could.

"You're right not to repeat everything," Mary said, catching her daughter's eye through the rear view mirror.

Esther gave a long sigh. "Gabby doesn't confide in me much any more. She's so stubborn these days. She won't listen to me. I'm afraid only sad experience will teach her the lessons she very much needs to learn."

Rachel did wish Esther didn't sound so preachy at times. No wonder it grated on her sister. "I think an extra bit of love and understanding right now is what she needs," Rachel said slowly. "Don't be too hard on her, Esther."

"Hard?" Esther bristled. Then her voice changed. "Sorry, I'm tired. I've been traveling almost twenty-four hours. But can't you tell us how it all ended, even if you don't feel free to repeat Gabby's words?"

"There isn't much more to tell," Rachel replied. "That night Andrea came in late and was still sleeping when Gabby and I rose early the next morning. Gabby wanted to leave immediately instead of staying over another night as planned. She had to have space and time to think over everything. She left a note for the Porters, but Larry must have seen us leaving. He came out to the car just as we were about to drive off.

"Gabby was all jitters as she said goodbye. Larry told her how glad he was that she had been with them that vacation and he hoped they'd be together in the summer. Gabby thanked him, and then she said, and these were her words pretty much, 'I'm going to back off from everything for a while, Larry. I've got to finally decide where I'm going and what my life's going to be all about. Please tell Andrea "bye" for me. I'll be seeing her soon at college.' He stared at her for a moment then nodded, and that was that."

"You know, Rachel, it's more than just Andrea and Larry. It's the Velvet Curtain again!" Esther said decidedly. "We need to get my sister to Romania."

Rachel gave a short laugh. "So you didn't find the Curtain there then?"

"Not a trace of it," Esther said emphatically. "I found dirt, and poverty, and bribery, and a lot of unpleasant things, but not the Velvet Curtain. I told you it wouldn't be there, didn't I?"

Rachel bit her lip and said nothing. For a long while, no one spoke. At last she said softly, in a voice very unlike her own, "I've been thinking that what happened last week in Florida almost convinces me that there really is a God Who is interested in us individually."

Mary couldn't believe her ears. She felt like stopping the car right there and then and giving her daughter a bear hug.

Esther was very quiet the rest of the journey. Gabby was in bed when she got home and fast asleep. She was sharing Rachel's room that evening so that her sister could unpack and get settled in without disturbing her.

After a cup of hot chocolate that tasted extra good, Esther made her way upstairs. She had never thought she would feel so glad to be back. She still was far too fond of creature comforts; she had soon found that out on this trip. Then she gave a start. That letter! She hadn't read it yet.

Esther changed quickly into her nightclothes, jumped in between the sheets thinking how wonderfully soft they seemed, switched on her reading lamp and tore open the envelope.

"Dear Esther," the letter began, "You will be miles away from me when you read this. But you will be still in my heart and mind. You have been there ever since I first saw you in your great aunt's kitchen at Silver Springs. And that night after meeting you, while saying my prayers, God spoke to me definitely. He said, 'Malcolm, Esther Popescu is the woman you are to take for your wife.'"

Esther dropped the letter on the bed and put her face in her hands. Did this have to happen? Then she picked up the notepaper and read on:

"I have tried to hide my feelings though probably not very successfully. But now I have to speak out. I am at a crisis. Marion can't look after my children indefinitely. She has her own life and her own calling to take into account. So, dear Esther, will you be my wife? You need protection, I've seen that. You are very vulnerable. And I've also seen you are willing to adapt to the ways of us simple folk.

"Please take time to think this over. And give me an answer when I return in one month. Till then, may the Lord bless you and give you guidance. You are precious to Him as well as to me. With all my love and prayers, Malcolm."

Esther placed the letter on the bedside table and leaned back on the pillow. All was so peaceful, she thought. No drunks shouting outside her window, no brawling neighbors, and a whole bed and bedroom to herself. She thought of the letter she had just read. It was like the man who wrote it—simple, unaffected, and sincere. He was a good man, she knew that, and he had a wonderful sister. But love? Did it not matter that she didn't love him in the way a wife should? And what had they in common except their faith? Maybe that was enough. With Ron, it had seemed that they had everything in common except their faith, and that hadn't been enough. Did men really love her as they said they did? Would they love her just the same if she became disfigured, or maimed in some way? She shuddered at the thought. What man could she really believe? Had Ron really loved her for what she really was inside? Had he even known who she was inside? Was her beauty her curse? But God had made her that way. Well, the real point was, how should she answer Malcolm Morgan—yes or no?

The next morning, Gabby was feeling some better. She seemed glad enough to see her sister but was not nearly as talkative as normal.

"Everyone's asking about you, Gabby," Esther began, as she slipped on her dressing-gown.

"So you told me in your letter."

"And it was so great to be back in Ploieşti. Aunt Ana's got a good job with some missionaries now."

"I'm glad."

"Your friend Anca is married to David, the boy who plays the organ."

"Is she?"

"Yes. She seems real happy."

"I'm glad."

Esther frowned. It seemed nothing she said really interested her sister. She let out a frustrated sigh and tried again. "And what sort of vacation did you have?"

"Interesting," Gabby said, flushing a little. Then she turned to face her sister. "Now don't pretend that Rachel's not told you the whole story in the car. I'm not going to repeat it all, if that's what you're wanting." Gabby grabbed her towel and disappeared into the bathroom.

Downstairs, Esther found her aunt alone in the kitchen. "Here, read this, Aunt Mary. I really do need advice."

Her Aunt unfolded the notepaper and read Malcolm's letter. "I thought as much," her aunt said with a grim smile when she had finished reading it.

"You did?"

"It was as plain as the nose on your face! He needs a wife to mother his kids and help him in Romania. A beautiful girl with a face like an angel turns up at the right moment. She's Romanian into the bargain. So?"

"Don't be so skeptical, Aunt. You don't think then, that he really heard from God about me?"

"It's not for me to say. You need to ask yourself if the two of you are really suited to each other. And what is more important, do you love him? And if not," her aunt was serious now, "it's no kindness to marry where you don't really love. Your uncle John did that and you see where it took us all as a family. So my advice is, if you love him, consider it at least, but if you don't, then run from this proposal as you would the plague."

"Yes, Aunt," Esther replied meekly. And there it would have been left—a straight-forward but polite letter saying "no" written after a week or two. She knew she had a month to think it over and that she didn't really need to write. Malcolm wanted a verbal response, but that was something Esther couldn't face. No, she'd write after a bit and that would be the end of it.

But life is never as simple as you'd like it to be. After Rachel and Gabby left for Knoxville, Marion arrived one day, unexpectedly, at Tiny Gap and had a long talk with her friend. She pointed out her brother's sincerity, God's word to him, his call to Romania, Esther's own future in that country, and how providence seemed to be bringing them together. Then Marion suggested with a gentle smile that maybe this was the step which would bring Esther the peace she had been seeking.

"But love, Marion, love! Doesn't it come into the picture at all?"

"What is love?" Marion asked, cupping Esther's chin in her hand. "Look at me, dear Esther, and tell me. You do respect my brother, don't you?" Her clear blue eyes searched her friend's for an answer.

"Yes, very much."

"You think he's a good man?"

"Yes, very."

"Well then, aren't respect, a mutual love for God, and a host of providences the best foundation for a successful marriage?"

"I suppose so." Esther didn't sound terribly convinced.

"Some of the best marriages have been arranged," her friend went on. "This sort of passionate, romantic love is made far too much of in movies and novels."

It was Esther's turn to look deep into Marion's eyes. "So your experience of love hadn't much to do with passion and romance?" The question was out before she could stop it. Her friend blushed a deep crimson and her blue eyes flashed fire. Esther had never seen her so upset before. Then she turned her head away to brush a tear that was trickling down her cheek.

"Sorry, Marion," Esther apologized. "I shouldn't have asked you that. It's none of my business."

Marion turned to face her friend once more. "It's maybe because I've had so much experience with that kind of love that I'm wary about it. You see what's come of it, don't you? But to get back to you and Malcolm. Do you think God would speak to my brother so definitely, only to have you refuse him right off the cuff?"

Esther had never seen the calm, collected Marion Morgan so much in earnest before. She hated to disappoint her, but then it wasn't Marion she would be marrying.

Marion left soon after that. Esther went upstairs and flopped on her bed. It was a mess, an utter mess. She had hurt her best friend, worried her aunt, and now was about to terribly disappoint a simple-hearted Christian man. Confusion and more confusion! Finally, after a few days of inner turmoil, Esther wrote a polite but definite "no." But she did not mail it. She wanted to be sure she wasn't missing the chance of a lifetime to escape the Velvet Curtain once and for all. So the little white envelope lay in her top drawer day after day.

At last, unable to concentrate on her studies and feeling very unhappy, Esther tore up her letter and wrote another—a postponement letter. She had received no light from God, she told Malcolm, to say yes or no. She'd have to wait till she finished her studies and had time to think. She'd take the summer to seek God's will.

She signed it, mailed it, and felt relieved. Malcolm wrote back that he was content to wait patiently till August would come and with it a final answer from the girl he felt almost sure would one day be his wife.

## Chapter Eighteen

### *One Last Try*

"Are you mad at me, Gabby?" Andrea leaned across the table and looked into her friend's eyes. They had just finished their lunch at a pizza inn on their first day back at school.

"Mad?" Gabby sounded surprised. "No, of course not! Why should I be?"

Andrea laughed. "I don't really know why, except that you're not the same anymore."

Gabby's face reddened a little. "I'm embarrassed rather than mad," she confessed.

"Embarrassed? You've no need to be!"

Gabby gave a short laugh. "Oh, come on, Andrea. You know very well what happened that last night at the beach."

"You're coming to the wrong conclusion, Gabby," Andrea said with a frown. "All I really know is that, for some reason or other, you took off that morning without even saying goodbye to me or to Dad and Sally."

"Was Dr. Porter upset?"

"At first. But Larry said that Rachel had come to get you earlier than planned—that there probably was some sort of emergency at home. Dad seemed satisfied with that explanation. But it didn't fool me."

"I am sorry," Gabby apologized. "It was rude to run off like that. Actually, I told your father and Sally that in a letter I wrote them last night. I also wanted to thank them for a wonderful vacation." Gabby paused a moment and then went on. "So you're saying that your brother didn't tell you what happened that night?"

"Absolutely not. He didn't want to talk about it and got quite cross when I tried to find out more."

Gabby stared at her friend. She was lost for words. "Of course," Andrea went on with a smile, "I've guessed at what made you run away

155

like that. And I blame Rachel for it all, I'm afraid. Seems to me she stuck her nose in where she shouldn't have."

Gabby said nothing. She still had very mixed emotions about what had happened that night. "I'm so confused, Andrea," she said rather piteously.

"Spill it all out then, Gabby, and let me *unconfuse* you. You never confide in me any more," she added with a pout.

"Give me a chance!" Gabby laughed. "We've not been together twenty-four hours yet. Look, we've got to get back to college now, but we need to have a good long talk together sometime soon."

"OK. Whenever you like," Andrea told her as they walked out to the car together.

That night while Rachel was in the library, they sat on the sofa together in their little living room and had their talk. Gabby told her friend all that had happened that night in Florida. When she had finished, Andrea sat silent, toying with her bracelet and avoiding her friend's eyes. She seemed completely lost for words for once in her life. Then she said slowly, raising her eyes to Gabby's as she spoke, "I really think you owe my brother an apology, Gabby. He seemed very hurt and wasn't the same for days after you left."

Gabby hung her head and muttered. "You just don't understand. I've just not been brought up like you."

"You never let me forget it either."

Gabby's eyes flashed as she replied, "No? Well then, maybe we're just too different to be close friends anymore. And anyway, Andrea, maybe you should take some responsibility for what happened. That last week at the beach you hadn't much time for me."

"Jealous, eh?"

Gabby looked annoyed. "Of course not. Mark wasn't my type at all. You saw that."

It was Andrea's turn to be upset. "I saw that all right. You were downright rude to him, so he told me."

"Rude? Well if putting him in his place was rude, then I suppose I was. But seriously, Andrea, if you hadn't left me alone with your brother so often, it would have all turned out differently."

Andrea raised her eyebrows. "You really think so? Well, I don't. But to get back to Mark," she persisted. "I partly went off with him because I thought you needed to grow up a little. I couldn't chaperone you forever."

"So having sex with a guy is growing up?" Gabby rose from the sofa and began pacing the floor.

"Part of it."

"But I thought..." Gabby began in consternation.

"You thought I was a little, innocent blue-eyed doll," Andrea said with a laugh. "Well, I wasn't. And what girl is at my age?" She saw Gabby's expression and went on hurriedly, "It's not that I agree with having sex with any one and everyone. You have to be careful, of course, for your own good. But when you really like a guy and he's respectable like Mark or Larry, well then, sex is part of getting to know each other."

Gabby stared down at her friend for a very long time. She couldn't take it in. This girl whom she had trusted as she would her own sister, was, after all, just like all the others. Her ideal had collapsed, vanished into thin air. She felt utterly let down.

That night, as she tried in vain to sleep, Andrea's words rang in her ears, "You're in 1991 now, Gabby, not in the Victorian age. Stop living in the past. It's time you got with it and grow up a bit. You're so immature."

The next day she told Andrea that she had to find out, once and for all, if the life style her family had chosen was feasible for her or not.

"Be patient with me, Andrea," she pled. "I've got to give it another try. If I do turn my back on my upbringing, it'll only be because I'm convinced it just isn't for me."

In the weeks that followed, the strain between the two friends sometimes grew so acute that Andrea would threaten to move out. Rachel, for her part, was conscious that both girls held her somewhat responsible for what was happening. She watched helplessly, as her cousin struggled to find her way, caught more than ever between two worlds.

One night, Andrea poured out her frustration in a letter to her brother. She told him that she didn't like the new Gabby that was emerging—one who went to church every Sunday, tried to read her Bible, stopped her late night movies, and refused to go to parties. "Hang in there," he wrote back. "This won't last forever."

At last, midterm break arrived. Gabby was glad to be back in Tiny Gap once more. For several nights in a row, she and Esther talked for hours, and in the end, Gabby even knelt down and prayed, telling God she was sorry for her past attitude and promising to be different in the future.

She felt more at peace for a while, but as the days slipped by, something in Esther's attitude irked her. She knew her sister did not understand her struggles. She had never questioned things like she had, so how could she? Gabby longed to talk to someone who could listen to her without being shocked at every second sentence she uttered. She found it much easier to confide in Rachel, but her cousin couldn't help her past a certain point. After all, she didn't even know what she believed herself.

Gabby had a feeling that maybe Aaron Gardner would understand her struggles better than anyone else in Tiny Gap, but both he and his granddad were with Aaron's missionary parents who were on furlough and had rented a cottage on the coast for six months. And, she admitted to herself, after the way she had treated him in Indianapolis, she wasn't at all sure that she would have either the nerve or the humility to approach him with her troubles.

Aunt Mary, she figured, was the only hope left to her. Her religion seemed more down to earth than her sister's. The night before she was to return to college, Gabby had a long talk with her aunt. Gabby listened intently while Mary told of her own journey into faith.

"But you had to try out the world first, Aunt," she protested when her aunt had finished.

"Yes, I did. And in the process, I broke many hearts. And I wasted precious years. It's just not worth it, Gabby. Please, don't follow my example." Gabby let her aunt pray with her, but Mary knew deep down in her heart that her headstrong niece was not convinced.

Maybe it was because Gabby slept so badly that night and woke feeling totally out of sorts that she blew it all the next morning. "Please keep my sister from evil," Esther prayed just before she left for school, "and make her truly repentant for her attitude to You; help her to see how serious it was to doubt Your existence."

## One Last Try 159

Gabby could take it no longer. She jumped to her feet and turned to face her sister. "So you think I'm not truly repentant?" she asked, eyes blazing.

Esther rose from her knees and sat on the bed. "I don't know, Gabby," she said solemnly. "I just want to be sure, that's all, because otherwise, you can't really receive God's forgiveness."

"It's you, not God who won't forgive me. It's you. You think I'm a disgrace to you."

"Gabby stop, please."

"Stop? I can't stop. I've got to get it out of my system. Just being with you makes me feel guilty. You haven't a clue what I've gone through. You're quite cozy in your little cocoon of your own beliefs. I've tried to fit in here, God knows I've tried, ever since Christmas—I've gone to church, read my Bible, stopped looking at R rated movies, stopped partying. And I'm more miserable than ever. I've treated Andrea and her brother disgracefully which seemed to please you all right. Well from now on, they're going to be my friends. I'm much happier when I'm with them than when I'm with you, much happier. You're always scolding and reproaching me. And really, Esther," Gabby concluded with a toss of her head, "your religion has no appeal for me. I want to go where I can enjoy life without feeling guilty all the time."

"OK then, go your own way." Esther's dark eyes flashed dangerously. She was far too hurt to notice that her sister's cheeks were wet with tears and her chest heaving. "Have your own friends," she told her as she rose and went over to the dressing-table. "And," she added, turning round to face Gabby, "when you're pregnant and friendless, don't say I didn't warn you."

Gabby stared at her sister in total disbelief. Then she exploded: "So that's what you expect of me, is it? Maybe I'll just live up to your expectations, then," and Gabby turned on her heel and made for the door.

Esther realized, too late, what her words had done. She grabbed Gabby's arm and swung her round. As they stood in silence, each looking into the other's eyes, their anger ebbed away. Esther saw a deep anguish in her sister's expressive eyes that she would never forget.

"Forgive me for speaking like that, Gabby." Esther felt thoroughly ashamed of herself now. "I know I hurt you."

It was a few moments before Gabby could reply. "I can't really blame you, Esther," she began slowly. "Truth is, I just have to know what the world is all about and I'm too stubborn to go by others' advice. I've got to find out for myself. Goodbye, Esther." She leaned forward and gave her sister a light kiss on the cheek. "And I'm sorry, too, that I spoke like I did just then. You've been a good sister to me. But you're so holy and pure, how can I expect you to understand the struggles of a sinner like me? Maybe some day, I'll find your God, but now…?" She couldn't go on and left the room sobbing.

Gabby did not see Esther again before she left for Knoxville with Rachel. Her aunt had tried to speak to her over breakfast, but Gabby was in no mood for confidences.

Andrea was already there when she and Rachel reached the apartment that afternoon. As soon as Gabby entered the kitchen, her friend knew the barrier that had been between them since the beginning of the semester had melted like snow in the summer's sun.

"Dear Larry," Andrea wrote later that night, "Good news! Gabby came back from mid-term break her old lovable and exuberant self. Now it's Rachel who's the odd one out. Well, she'll know now what I went through for weeks. You were right to tell me to hang on. Gabby's already agreed to spending the summer with us. She can't be at home much any more, she says. She's seen the light at last. Drop in and see us when you can. If you can't, look forward to a wonderful summer—Paris, Rome, Venice, and maybe Romania! But best of all look forward to a liberated Gabby. And I think that even you may be in for a big surprise. When Gabby does something, she does it right!!

"Good Night. I'm so happy. Andrea."

# Chapter Nineteen

## *Graduation*

Mary wiped the tears that would come into her eyes as she watched her daughter receive her diploma. Rachel had graduated valedictorian and had already been accepted at medical school. She had wavered between law and medicine but finally decided on the latter. She would stay on at UT for she wanted to be near her mother.

"It's your turn tomorrow," Rachel told Esther as they sped homewards.

"And mine next year," put in Gabby thoughtfully, "if I can finish in time, though it might be a year from Christmas now that I've changed majors." She had decided she wanted to be a social worker. Her aunt and sister had been glad that she had given up her dream of being an actress, though Rachel just wasn't sure what lay behind Gabby's change of majors. She still took drama and art as minors and was involved in nearly every student activity that was on the agenda.

"I'll be graduating two years from now," Andrea put in. She had been invited to spend a week with Gabby in Tiny Gap. Since midterm break, the two girls had become thicker than ever. In fact, they were almost inseparable and now they were looking forward to spending the summer together.

Larry had visited them once at midterm break and everything had seemed almost normal. Almost, Rachel noticed, but not quite. At times, her cousin still seemed confused in his presence: one minute she seemed wary of him and on her guard; the next she was drinking in his words as if her life depended on it. Larry, for his part, acted as casual and self-contained as ever.

It was late before they reached Tiny Gap that evening. Esther found it hard to sleep. Tomorrow would be her big day!

The next morning, as Mary watched the graduates process down the aisle, it seemed that even in her black cap and gown, Esther stood out from everyone else. "You're now a fully qualified teacher," she told her niece as they met on the lawn after the service. "Congratulations!"

"Thanks! And now I'm all set for Romania." Esther's dark eyes sparkled in anticipation.

Her aunt frowned a little. "Gabby will feel very alone without you," she told Esther.

"But you'll be here, Aunt Mary," Esther reminded her. "You're like a mother to her. She'll confide in you as much as she does in me. And there's Rachel. She's closer to Gabby than I am these days. And besides, it looks like she won't be home much for a long while to come."

Mary hated to hear the coldness in Esther's voice. "But you're the closest," she remonstrated.

"God will take care of Gabby, if I do His will, Aunt," Esther replied. "And after all, my prayers will be more effectual than anything I can say. But I *must* go to Romania."

"Must?"

"Yes. I know it's God's will and besides, I've had enough of this Velvet Curtain."

"What exactly are your plans?"

Esther had blushed a little before replying. "I'm not absolutely sure. I've got a few alternatives."

"Such as?"

Esther took a deep breath. "One is marriage; the other is to go as a translator with some mission or other, and the third is to teach English."

"What's all this about, Esther?" Esther gave a start and turned around. Gabby and Andrea were standing just behind her.

"I'm thinking of going to Romania."

"That's hardly a surprise," Gabby said with a laugh. "You've been talking about it for years. But when are you actually going and what are you going to do there?"

"I hope to go this fall, if I can. As for what I'm going to do, I've not settled yet."

"I suppose you'll go and help those friends of yours," her sister said with a pout.

"Maybe. Or maybe I'll translate for some mission."

"Well, whatever you do, good luck! I'm glad for you, Esther. I want you to be happy." Gabby leaned forward and gave her sister a hug.

"Congratulations!" said a deep voice in her ear. Malcolm Morgan and his sister had edged their way through the crowd and were waiting to shake hands with the new graduate.

## Graduation 163

Esther gave Marion a hug and turned to shake hands with Malcolm. Rachel noticed he was looking very solemn as if he partially disapproved of the whole graduation procedure. She also noticed her cousin's blushes and wondered what it meant. Surely she wasn't interested in a man like that? Mary thought it polite to invite them to their little party at Marjorie's, but they declined.

Esther walked with them to their car. As Malcolm got behind the wheel, he put his head out the window and motioned her to come closer. She took a few steps forward, half dreading what might be coming next.

"Have you an answer for me yet?" he asked in his slow, deliberate manner.

Esther blushed furiously. "I still don't know my answer," she replied in a low voice.

"I can wait a bit longer, but not till August," Malcolm said quietly. "I have to be in Romania by September 1$^{st.}$ If we get married," (he spoke so calmly, Esther felt almost sure he was expecting her to say *yes*,) "we would need some time for you to get to know the children better, and myself, too, of course, before we set off for another land." He smiled slightly. "So please tell me by the beginning of July. After all, you've had weeks to think about it."

Esther nodded as he started up the engine. Marion gave her a knowing smile and waved as they pulled away. "I've only six more weeks," she told herself, as she stared after their Jeep Cherokee. "Oh God, you must show me what I should do."

Mary noticed that her niece seemed lost in her own thoughts when she rejoined the others on the lawn. She did hope Esther would do nothing foolish, thinking that she was making a choice that would please God.

That afternoon, Marjorie Porteous who owned the guest house in Tiny Gap, threw a party in her large dining room in honor of both graduates. She had been away in Texas for nearly two years looking after her aged mother and had just returned to the area, much to everyone's delight.

It was a merry get-together. Gabby seemed her old jovial self. She was determined not to let personal feelings spoil this special day. Andrea was there, too, feeling very awkward most of the time, though Mary, especially, did all she could to make the girl feel welcome. Hugh joined them for an hour or so. He seemed in better spirits than they had seen him for a long time. Aaron had not yet returned from grad school.

Mary missed his pleasant face and lively comments. She had grown very fond of Hugh's grandson during the past few years.

Rachel had invited her father, but he had declined to come, saying that it would only make things awkward. She missed his presence at times like this. He had made it to her graduation at UT the day before and had taken all the girls out for a sumptuous meal afterwards.

Aaron arrived a few days before Gabby left for Indianapolis. He was going to Germany almost immediately, where he would spend the summer doing research for his doctoral dissertation. Gabby avoided him like the plague much to his annoyance and frustration. But on his last evening in Tiny Gap, Hugh invited Mary and the girls up for a barbecue. And while the others were preparing the food, Aaron managed to get a few words with Gabby.

"How are things?" he asked casually.

"Fine. Just fine." It was quite obvious that Gabby didn't want to talk.

"Now just a minute," Aaron turned and faced her. "What's going on? You treat me as if I had some contagious disease. I think that's hardly fair, Gabriella."

Gabby tossed her head. "You were a bit overpowering last summer. I felt you were dogging my footsteps and I resented it."

"Oh, you did, did you?" Aaron hadn't meant to lose his cool but he found her attitude intolerable. "Well, I'll make it the business of my life not to do that again. Only," his voice changed, "I never thought you could be rude. Stubborn, yes, but plain rude?"

Gabby stared at him. "I'm sorry. I've really nothing personal against you. Only I hate to be shadowed and controlled. I'm trying to find my own place in life and it's not easy."

Aaron nodded and figured that maybe he had been too hard on the girl. "I want to be your friend, not your enemy," he told her with a warm smile. "I can't stand having enemies. So let's shake." He held out his hand.

Gabby smiled and put out hers. "No one can be mad at you for long, Aaron Gardner."

"You've been mad with me for twelve months, by the look of it."

Gabby reddened. "Sorry! I'll try never to be mad at you again."

"I'll hold you to that."

"OK, but you must try not to provoke me, then."

"I probably won't see enough of you to provoke you," Aaron said a little wistfully.

Gabby reddened. "How long will you be in Germany?" she asked, changing the subject.

"Most of the summer, but I'm going to sandwich a quick trip to Romania and try to look up some relatives and improve my Romanian."

"Really? I'll be in Europe for a month later in the summer."

"Oh? Then maybe we'll run into each other."

"Oh, sure! Probably in some night club in Paris. Or a bar in Rome," Gabby said sarcastically. Then she bit her lip.

Aaron said nothing but his eyes showed pain. It seemed that this girl had some perverse delight in showing him her worst side.

Gabby saw his reaction and said quickly, "If you do get to Romania, I'm sure Aunt Ana would love to see you if you're in Ploieşti. Wait a moment and I'll write out her address for you."

Aaron's face brightened as he watched her fish out a piece of paper from her purse. "Thanks," he told her as she handed him the address. "I'll look her up if I get over there." Just then, Hugh announced that the barbecue was ready, so they had no time for further conversation.

The day soon arrived when Gabby had to leave for Indianapolis. Esther had tried several times during the past week to get closer to her sister. But she always seemed to rub Gabby up the wrong way. And Andrea was nearly always nearby which made private conversation practically impossible. But now, Esther felt Gabby's tears on her cheek as she said goodbye. The sisters clung to each other for a few moments and Andrea watching, wondered if her brother hadn't made a mistake, after all, when he had commented after their Christmas vacation: "Get the girl away from her family for a while, and you'll see a totally new Gabriella." But then, Andrea figured, Larry didn't really know Gabby's sister or her aunt. A week at Tiny Gap had taught her that while Mary and Esther and all their friends were certainly misguided and dreadfully bound by their religious beliefs, their sincerity shone through every aspect of their lives. She understood better why Gabby found it so difficult to break away from her upbringing.

As the car whizzed northwards, however, Andrea noticed a marked change in her friend. By the time they had drawn up in front of the stately, tri-level brick house in the suburbs of Indianapolis, Gabby was the same laughing, high-spirited girl who had wormed her way into all their hearts just twelve months before.

## Chapter Twenty

*Esther Sings Again*

At first, Esther was almost inconsolable after her sister's departure. Gabby wrote occasionally, but said nothing of any importance, and this did little to alleviate her concern. But as the weeks sped by, she found that she had other things to worry about. Every day she would ask God for some sign which would indicate how she should answer Malcolm Morgan. She was quite aware that she did not love him, but, as Marion had reminded her, "Marry first and fall in love later," had certainly worked for some young women, then why not for her?

Esther had been invited to work in Mercer's Country Store again, and Aunt Lucy had practically expected her to spend another summer with her. But she couldn't face Marion and her brother when she was still in such an indecisive state of mind. Instead, she helped Marjorie Porteous in her guest house and spent the long evenings with her aunt on their porch overlooking the mountains. This would probably be her last summer in America and she wanted to spend it in Tiny Gap.

Esther was sitting on the porch one afternoon in late June when a Lexus rolled up the driveway and came to a halt a few yards from the front door.

"Miss Esther Popescu?" a well dressed gentleman asked as he got out of his car.

Esther rose from her chair. "Yes, I'm Esther Popescu," she told the stranger, tucking in a stray strand of hair that had escaped her clasp.

"And I'm Justice Hannigan. I don't think you remember me!" Esther looked more closely at the man. He did look vaguely familiar.

"I was the gentleman who asked you to stand in for us in the concert in Indianapolis about three years ago," the stranger continued. "You remember?"

Esther's heart beat furiously under her pale pink blouse. "Yes, I remember the concert," she replied as calmly as she could. How could she ever forget?

"Well, we're in desperate need once more, Esther. Only this time, it's at Knoxville, not very far from you really. I finally traced you down through Ron Atwood."

Esther blushed scarlet but waited to hear what was coming. "I tried to get Len to give me your address but he refused. He's changed a lot, you know."

Esther stared at the man. "Yes," he went on with a short laugh, "he sort of hibernates now. When I talked about you he shut up like a clam. He said he wasn't having anything to do with encouraging you to sing in my concert. But Ron was a little more cooperative, though not much. So here I am. I was passing nearby and thought it better to see you in person than to speak over the phone."

"Won't you come in?" Esther asked.

"All right. I suppose we can talk better inside."

Esther ushered him into the sitting room, brought him a drink of Sprite, and sat down in the chair opposite. She did hope he wouldn't stay long, for she was the only one home that afternoon.

Justice Hannigan cleared his throat. "I heard you had been very ill a few years back and that you stopped your singing career. Is that right?"

Esther nodded. "We are in desperate need of someone to fill in for us in about ten days' time," the man continued. "Short notice, I know," he apologized, seeing her consternation, "but you did it before so beautifully that I'm sure you can do it again."

"No, Mr. Hannigan," the girl's voice was firm. "I can't. I haven't sung in a concert for several years and I'm quite out of practice."

Justice Hannigan sat back in his chair, crossed his long legs and studied the young woman opposite. She was dressed atrociously, he thought, but she was as pretty as ever. And her voice, even when she spoke, made you think of a skylark, or nightingale.

"Just this once, please," he pleaded.

Esther blushed and shook her head. "You might not understand this, but I promised God I wouldn't sing in concerts anymore," she explained.

"I see," Justice commented thoughtfully. Then he smiled. "Maybe your promise didn't cover an emergency like this," he told her. "This is just a one-time offer, and it'll pay well and bring blessing to many, I'm sure of that. And," he leaned forward and spoke more confidentially, "this time we won't force you to wear a dress you disapprove of. And you can sing in your own style as you did that first evening. So relax and think it over. Here's my card. Let me know tomorrow night."

As the car pulled away, Esther gave a long drawn-out sigh. She had prayed for some sign. Was this it? But if so, in which direction did it point? Was God saying she should sing again? Or was it a sign she should flee from what might be a temptation of the devil?

By the time Mary had returned, Esther was in a state of utter confusion. She told her aunt of the offer. Mary raised her eyebrows but said little.

"Well, what do you think, Aunt?"

"It's too great a responsibility for me to advise you, dear. But you need to pray about it and not just refuse it off the cuff."

Esther did pray about it, for hours, but came no nearer the solution. So she went over to Mr. Hugh's, hoping to receive some advice from her old friend, but he was away and wouldn't be home for a week. The worst of it was, she really wanted to accept Justice's offer but was terrified to do so.

"Will you come with me if I do sing, Aunt Mary?" she asked that evening when the supper dishes had been cleared away.

"Yes. Of course I will."

"Then I'll give it one more try."

Mary smiled as she saw her niece go to the grand piano. She hadn't touched it for several years. Soon her beautiful voice was filling the house. Justice had said he didn't care what she sang—she could throw in a few Romanian songs if she liked. And it was only for one evening, that was all. They were so desperate, he said, that they'd grab at anyone, but she was by far their first choice. And he had promised a thousand dollars as payment. Esther could see the money in her hand. She desperately needed funds if she were to go back to Romania that fall.

After more than an hour at the piano, Esther went to the phone and dialed Justice's number. He was overjoyed when he heard her answer. He would come and get her, he said. She assured him that would not be necessary.

A week later, Esther was in the dressing room of the large auditorium in Knoxville. She had brought her white gown to wear, the one she had bought with Betty Cripps, and, if the truth were known, the one she really liked best of all. It was simple yet elegant and made her look like an angel. She thought Justice raised his eyebrows a little when he saw her in the familiar gown, but he said nothing.

Esther eyed herself in the full-length mirror. She had decided to wear her hair up as she used to do and allowed the girl who was helping her dress to place one white rose in her dark wavy locks. As she gazed at the image in the glass, mixed emotions flooded over her. She could visualize Ron's admiring gaze, the applause of the crowd, and the warm feeling of being loved and adored. She knew she had lost none of her beauty and at the same time was still simple Esther Popescu. Or was she?

She wondered exactly who she was when she stepped on stage. The crowds broke into thunderous applause and for half an hour she was carried into another world. She heard her voice, rich and full, swelling the auditorium. She saw some in her audience wiping tears from their eyes; she noticed others were sitting entranced, eyes riveted on her face.

In the intermission, she was asked to say a few words. She told her audience of her illness those years ago, of how, since then, she had refused to sing in concerts, of her call to her native land. This would be her last concert in America, she felt sure.

As she began to sing again, Esther felt free, liberated, just herself, a simple girl with a talent sent straight from God. She sang of God's grace, of His love for sinners, and of His liberating power. When the last note had died away, you could hear a pin drop in the large auditorium. Justice had given no appeal so he was surprised and deeply moved to see a young woman rise and make her way to the front where she knelt down and began sobbing her heart out. Others followed her, maybe about twenty, and throughout the audience, you could hear muffled sobs. This, Esther thought to herself as she slipped quietly backstage, was far better than encores and curtain calls.

Justice met her at the door of the dressing room. He slipped an envelope into her hand. "I've added five hundred for Romania," he whispered. "God bless you, Esther, and reward you for coming tonight, though I think you have already had your reward."

Esther nodded, unable to speak. "And," he went on, "if ever it doesn't work out to go to Romania, remember, you're needed right here in this land. If you can keep your head, which I'm afraid not many young budding stars can do, when suddenly pushed into the limelight, you'll become a Christian singer with a difference."

Esther shook her head. "But it spoiled me before, that's why…"

"That's why you're running away from it, you mean," Justice said in his straightforward manner.

Esther opened her eyes wide and stared at him. "Just be sure you're in God's will," he told her as he turned to go. "Be very sure. Good night, Esther, and Goodbye."

Esther seemed in a daze as she made her way outside. She couldn't face any fans that evening, or offers to sign contracts, or any of the trimmings that usually had accompanied her concerts. Not that there would be anyone offering to sponsor her after that performance, she thought with a wry smile. Justice had utterly surprised her by his reaction. Maybe it had just been an emotional response to her singing. But he didn't seem a man governed by emotions. She had summed him up as a hard-headed business man, who happened to be religious. But it seemed that she had been wrong.

Mary saw that her niece was exhausted and said little on her way home. She also noted the contented expression in her beautiful face. Her eyes were closed and there was a faint smile on her lips as she lay back in her seat.

It was past midnight when they reached Tiny Gap. They had just poured themselves a cold drink when the phone rang. "It's for you, Esther," her aunt told her as she handed her the receiver.

"Esther, I won't trouble you, but I saw you on TV," said a musical voice at the other end of the line. She had quite expected to hear Ron's and was just a little disappointed. It took her a moment before she realized that it was his cousin Len who was speaking. "I want to say that I watched you tonight," the voice went on. "I hadn't meant to. I refused to give Justice your phone number. He probably told you that. I did it because I felt i had pushed you into Christian show biz for my own ends. I wanted to make you into a star and then receive a lot of the credit for it. It was awful, Esther. Please forgive me."

Esther stared at the receiver in her hand, speechless. She could not find her voice. "But," Len went on, "I saw and heard you tonight. You were just yourself and, well, all I can say is, God used you more than you'll ever know."

There was a choke in his voice. Was this another play act, Esther wondered? She didn't really think so, this time. "I certainly forgive you, Len," she told him quietly, "and thanks for calling tonight."

"And, Esther, please do ask God about your…" He stopped abruptly. He had been about to repeat what his friend Justice had already said. But what right had he to advise anyone? "It's OK; I've said enough," he concluded abruptly. "Good night and God bless you."

It was not Len but his cousin who was on Esther's mind as she tried in vain to sleep that evening. Her singing had seemed to unleash the past upon her once again. And Ron, three hundred miles away, was also reliving those eventful months when he and his beautiful Romanian girl had spent so much time together.

Len had not been the only one who had watched the young Romanian performer that evening. Against his better judgment, Ron had found himself glued to the TV, admiring, as always, the startling beauty and grace of the singer and the angelic sweetness of her voice. Maybe, he thought to himself, Esther was finding her niche after all. And if she didn't go to Romania, then perhaps he still had a chance!

Yet watching her had been bitter-sweet. He had been reminded more forcibly than ever that the same gulf still yawned between them. She knew God and loved Him. He didn't. He had tried, Heaven only knew how he had tried, but it had been no use. He was still stumbling in the dark, still unconvinced deep in his heart that he really needed God except to enable him to win Esther as his wife. And that thought was beneath him. He despised himself for even thinking of it for a moment. And if he called her that evening, it would only rub salt into his wounds and maybe into hers too.

Esther of course, knew nothing of all this. She only knew that Ron Atwood had not phoned her, and that it was really best that way. She glanced at the clock. It was three in the morning. She gave a long sigh. There was another reason for her sleeplessness. It was already the first week in July and Malcolm Morgan would be waiting for an answer.

Her eyes fell on her dresser by her bed. She switched on the lamp above and sat up. Pulling out the top left hand drawer, she reached for a small, white envelope. There it lay, stamped and ready—a simple "no" which would settle everything. But would it? She had asked for a sign. Had God answered her through that invitation to sing at the concert? But even if He had, in which direction did the sign point—towards a singing career once more, or towards life in her beloved Romania, doing some good in the world by taking care of two motherless children and a man who obviously loved and served God with all of his heart?

Esther turned over the envelope in her hand. Why did she want to go back to Romania so badly, she asked herself? To flee the Velvet Curtain, of course. She wasn't blind to the queenly figure who had stared back at her from the dressing-room mirror. She hadn't failed to notice the admiring glances of Justice and his team. And the applause when she had come on stage had been nearly deafening. God had kept her that one evening from herself, but her vanity, she felt sure, would win out in the end.

She grabbed the envelope and tore it in two. Then getting out her note paper she began to write. She had only written, "Dear Malcolm," when she laid down her pen and shook her head. She reached for the light switch. She could wait just a little longer, couldn't she, just to be sure? Then a vision of Marion's tranquil face rose before her. She wanted that same peace her friend had and would pretty much pay any price to get it. She gave a start. What was she saying? Any price?

She stared up at the ceiling. She wished she could hear God's audible voice as Samuel had done. But He had promised to guide His children unerringly, she knew that. She grabbed the pen again. "Oh Lord," she breathed as she began to write once more, "I'm so afraid of missing Your will whichever decision I make. If You don't want me to marry this man, if I'm misguided in thinking it will be the final step which will burn my bridges behind me and seal me as Your servant forever, then stop this letter, somehow, from reaching its destination."

Her fingers tightened on the pen as she breathed "Amen" into the stillness of the mid-summer's morning. The dawn chorus was beginning outside. Another day had come. She would write now or she would never do it. She began again, and in ten minutes it was done. A simple "yes." That was all. There was no "I love you"; she couldn't say that. She could only say that God had seemed to indicate through providence that she should accept his proposal.

Esther finally snatched a few hours sleep before the light streaming in the window at the foot of her bed made her sit up and rub her eyes. Then suddenly, she remembered her letter. She dressed quickly, grabbed the sealed envelope, slipped downstairs, and ran to the mailbox. She pushed the letter inside, put up the red flag, and turned away. Her fate was sealed. As Mrs. Esther Morgan she would never have the opportunity to sing in such a concert again—she would never wear such beautiful dresses again, but, she would be safe within the four walls of her own little home; she would have someone by her side, day and night, to shield her from danger and temptation. Then she let out a choking sob. She would be a wife, a stepmother, under a man's protection, yes, but knowing Malcolm Morgan, also under his control, loving control she hoped, but control nevertheless. She would never again be Esther Popescu, free to do what she wanted.

She paused a moment on the doorstep and gazed at the distant hills. Then she thrust out her chin as she pushed open the front door. As Mrs. Morgan, she would never be vain again in her long, dark dresses, black shoes, and pulled back hair. Wouldn't that strike a blow to her vanity forever? And peace and serenity, like Marion's! She'd give anything for that! It was done, once and for all. She would take up her cross and follow, come what may.

# Chapter Twenty-One

## *The Fourth of July*

"Have you forgotten that it's the Fourth of July today, Esther?"

"I don't think I can celebrate, Aunt," her niece replied disconsolately. They were eating breakfast together, just the two of them. Rachel had gone to spend the Fourth with her father. Gabby would be on her way to Europe. She was, in fact, to leave that very day.

"Not celebrate?" Mary sounded surprised.

Esther couldn't tell her aunt, at least not just yet, that her food was sticking in her throat and that all she could think about was her acceptance letter which would be speeding on its way by now. She knew she felt as no prospective bride should ever feel, but it was too late. She couldn't and wouldn't draw back. She had already broken one engagement and caused a good man to suffer. She would never do it again, never.

"Aaron's not here to take us to a fireworks' display this year, but we could go up and visit Mr. Hugh tonight, couldn't we?"

"I don't feel like it, Aunt."

Mary said no more. She thought something besides Gabby's absence was depressing her niece. Maybe it was the concert. Pity, because God seemed to have been in that concert last night.

"Esther, why is the flag up?" her aunt asked suddenly as she peered out the window. "Have you forgotten there's no mail today?"

"No mail?" Esther gasped. She put down her spoon with a clatter, and pushed back her chair. Mary stared in surprise. What had gotten into the girl this morning?

Esther flung open the door and ran into the yard. The mailbox had never seemed so far away, but at last she reached it and stood panting for a few moments, hands on hips. Then she opened the box slowly and stared inside. There lay her letter just as she had left it a few hours earlier. It was not speeding towards Silver Springs after all. She grabbed the envelope and flew back indoors.

The look on her aunt's face made her laugh. She felt like jumping, like shouting. She had asked God to intervene and He had. But wait, was this God saving her just in time or was He simply testing her? After all, He hadn't really intervened, had He? She had just been a fool and forgotten it was the Fourth, that was all. Her face fell as she slumped into a chair. Mary was just about to ask her what it was all about when the phone rang. It was Malcolm Morgan.

"Esther, I need to talk to you personally," he began in his low, measured voice. "Have you written me your answer?"

Esther glanced down at the envelope in her hand. Had she or hadn't she? She tried to speak, but no words would come.

"I take it you haven't written yet," Malcolm went on. "Maybe it's just as well. We need to talk some things over personally, and it needs to be very soon."

Esther was puzzled. His tone was different somehow—colder and more distant. What had she done and why couldn't he speak to her over the phone? Then a thought struck her. Mary had wanted to meet her Aunt Lucy. Why not take a surprise run over to Silver Springs and kill two birds with one stone.

"OK, Malcolm, I'll be over," she told him. "I'll be there about three this afternoon, if that suits you?"

"Yes. That's fine. We'll make it three, then."

"Are you upset that you haven't received your answer yet?" Esther was determined to find what lay behind his wanting to see her so suddenly.

"No, it's not that," he told her. "Actually, it's just as well you haven't given your final answer. It's very important that we have a long talk first."

"But you sound upset, Malcolm. What have I done?"

"Don't you know?"

"Haven't got a clue." She paused. Visions of herself in her long white gown, hair piled up high and that one little rosebud nestled in her dark waves, floated before her.

"Is it...?" she stammered.

"It's that concert," Malcolm finished her sentence for her. "A neighbor was watching some program on TV and called me. He said he was sure that the girl who had worked in Mercer's Store last summer was the main singer in a Christian concert. Well, we thought he must surely be mistaken, so he invited us over to see for ourselves. He was right. It was you, Esther. Both Marion and I were shocked. We thought you had truly left all that sort of life behind you forever. But it seems you haven't. That's why I need to talk to you."

"See you this afternoon then," Esther said, trying hard to keep the joy out of her voice. Maybe God was supplying her with a way of escape that she'd never dreamed of.

A word with Mary, a phone call to Great Aunt Lucy, and all was settled. Esther slipped upstairs to get dressed. She was about to put on the clothes she usually wore when she went to Marion's, when a thought struck her. Malcolm was a very decided man. He had repeated several times that God had definitely spoken to him that she was to be his wife. He wouldn't give that up easily. He was probably going to lay down some ultimatums—tell her she must promise never to repeat last night's performance again. If she ever became his wife, all that sort of thing would be gone forever.

Esther frowned. She hated confrontations with a passion. Her family knew that only too well. Then, too, she often found the arguments of good people very persuasive, and Malcolm and Marion were very good people.

A smile flitted across her lips as she reached into the closet. Maybe talking wouldn't be necessary. She pulled out a bright pink short sleeved blouse and put it on. It was very modest, but not what she usually wore to the Morgans'. Then she chose a long, floral skirt, slipped on a pair of white sandals, and began to brush her hair. She was tying it back as she had done for several years now, when she shook her head. She knew that Malcolm had only seen one side of Esther Popescu apart from his vision of her on the television the night before. If he were to be her future husband, he had to see the other side, within reason that is.

She suddenly realized that she had been trying to act what she wasn't inside. She had always liked pretty things, colorful things; she always wanted to look her best and she had stultified all these desires, stamped on them, but it had been no use. Her vanity wouldn't be handled that way or the Velvet Curtain either, she thought. There was surely a better way, though she hadn't found it yet. Esther gave her long raven locks a vigorous brush, then let them cascade in waves around her shoulders.

"Mr. Malcolm, here I come, for better or for worse," she told her image. Then she stopped short. What was she trying to do? Charm and shock the good man at the same time? That wasn't worthy of her! She turned back to the mirror and with a few deft twists of her hair, she had piled it up in loose coils on top of her head just as it had been the night before. Then she reached for her favorite Romanian clasp and placed it carefully in her thick locks. "There," she thought, "apart from the roses and the long gown, I look just like I did last night."

She grabbed her white purse and made for the door; she knew what she had to do. She could never, ever, be Malcolm Morgan's wife. She could never make the promises he wanted her to make. She had no idea what God was fully trying to tell her through that concert last night. Her heart still longed for Romania, but she wouldn't make a loveless marriage the price she must pay for the privilege of living safely in her beloved land once more. It wouldn't be fair to Malcolm, to his motherless children, or to herself. And Gabby? She remembered the look on her sister's face when she had told Esther that she would miss her if she lived in Romania. That had been a year ago. Gabby had changed a lot in twelve months. Still, maybe she would need her big sister around when she got back from Europe.

Mary thought Esther looked very much like the girl she had first met as she tripped down the stairs and announced cheerily, "I'm ready. Will I do?"

Her aunt smiled and kissed her on the cheek. "Let's get going," was all she said.

In the two-hour drive to Silver Springs, Esther told her companion everything, or nearly. "You would have been in a mess if the mail had come, Esther," her aunt commented when her niece had finished.

Esther grinned, then sobered. "But all isn't over yet," she remarked.

Mary patted the girl's hand. "God will give you all you need. Just trust Him, Esther."

Aunt Lucy had a wonderful meal waiting for them when they arrived. She was overjoyed to see her great niece once more. Esther excused herself before the others had finished eating. "I promised to be at Morgans' by three o'clock, Aunt Lucy."

"Watch yourself!" Lucy told her as she saw her to the door. "I don't know what you're up to. You're either trying to shock Malcolm Morgan or charm him." The old lady paused a moment and peered at Esther over her spectacles. "Has that man proposed to you?" she asked sharply.

"Yes, Aunt. He has."

"And have you given him your answer?"

"Not yet. That's what I'm going to do now." Esther ran to the car. She had said all she was going to say.

"Don't do anything you'll regret, Esther," Miss Lucy called after her. "And drive carefully. It's the Fourth. There'll be a lot of crazy drivers around today."

Marion was on the front porch to meet Esther as she made her way up the familiar dirt path. She slowly climbed the rather rickety wooden steps. The two girls stood for a few moments, facing each other. Then Esther stepped forward and gave her friend a hug.

"Take a seat, Esther. Malcolm will be here in a few moments." Marion's voice was very matter-of-fact and rather too business-like for Esther's liking.

While her friend went to make her some iced tea, Malcolm's two little girls peeked at her shyly from a corner of the porch. Esther had never succeeded in becoming very close to them. She didn't have Gabby's way with kids. Her sister seemed like a magnet to nearly all the boys and girls she met—in the store, in the park, on the plane, or wherever.

Marion soon reappeared with the tea and some homemade cookies. The two friends slowly sipped their drink and talked of the weather, the children, and how the farm was doing. The minutes ticked by and still no Malcolm. Esther grew nervous. Finally she heard the sound of his car in the drive and the next minute he was climbing the porch steps. She looked at him in his dark blue dungarees and work boots. She saw his care-worn face, his horny hands, roughened from farm work and more than all that, she caught a glimpse of the pain in his eyes as he looked at her. She dreaded what was coming. How could she face hurting this man? True, he was stern and demanding but that was his type of piety. And Marion! She couldn't bear to see her look so troubled. There was a shadow between them that had never been there before.

Malcolm took a seat beside his sister. He stared at Esther for several minutes in disbelief. Then he turned his head away and let out a long, drawn-out sigh. When he finally turned to face her again, Esther couldn't quite figure out if he pitied or admired her, if he was angry with her or simply embarrassed. She was a little surprised. She had not thought him so complex.

"Thanks for coming so promptly, Esther." Malcolm stroked his beard and scrutinized her from top to toe. She squirmed. She felt like a juvenile delinquent now. "We won't need to keep you for long. I don't think much discussion will be necessary."

Esther looked at him inquiringly. "I mean," he stammered, "I've seen all I need to see. The question's been decided for me."

"I'm not quite sure what you're trying to say, Malcolm," she faltered, turning to Marion for help. But her friend shook her head and said nothing.

"You don't?" Malcolm sounded incredulous. "Well, then, that makes it even worse. I thought you'd at least have a conscience."

Esther's large dark eyes flashed dangerously. Malcolm couldn't meet her gaze. "Don't you realize how you looked last night?" he muttered, gazing at his boots. Then he raised his eyes to hers. "And haven't you got a clue what signals you're sending out by the way you look right now, as you sit there opposite me?" There was frustration in his voice now and even a little contempt. Esther still said nothing. Malcolm dug his hands deep in the pockets of his coveralls. This woman wasn't making it easy for him. He rather thought she would have burst into tears by now and begged his forgiveness.

"Well," he began again, "didn't you hear the applause last night? I mean you looked like a…" He couldn't find the right word. Still Esther refused to come to his aid. She sat demurely, hands on lap, waiting for whatever was coming next. Malcolm's frustration had reached its limits. He rose from his chair and took a step or two nearer. He opened his mouth again but nothing came out. He glanced helplessly towards Marion and motioned for her to speak.

"Esther," her gentle voice was a little sharper than usual, but just a little, "we couldn't believe our eyes when we saw you up on the stage in your long, white gown and we can't believe what we're seeing today, either. I think my brother is totally taken aback by your appearance. I mean, you're giving us a completely different picture from the girl we thought we knew. After all, you had indicated, to me at least, that you had left that type of life well behind you."

Esther found it easier to talk to Marion. "You mean my singing career? I thought so too, Marion," she replied in a low voice. "For three whole years, I've refused to sing over here in America," her voice grew firmer now, "and then out of the blue, I was asked to go to the concert in Knoxville. I had been so confused for weeks about what I should answer your brother that I had asked for some sign from God. The invitation to the concert came right after that. It seemed to be the sign I was asking for, but I wasn't sure which way it was pointing. In the end, however, I went, and I really did feel blessed singing once again of God and of His love."

"You're not the only one who asked for a sign," Malcolm had found his tongue again. "After I saw you last night, I went through a real conflict." He paused.

"I'm very sorry," Esther said in a low voice.

Malcolm looked at the girl in the chair opposite him. Her eyes were fixed on her lap. It was just as well, he thought. Those large, speaking eyes always unmanned him. She was indeed the most beautiful creature he had ever met and, if he handled her rightly, she might still become his wife.

Esther felt his eyes upon her and stirred awkwardly in her chair. He turned back to his seat. Clearing his throat he began again, "I thought when I saw you on TV that you might just be having a last fling. I wondered if you thought it was a way to earn some money for your trip to Romania, or that maybe you had simply given in to pressure. I know you're not that strong and can be rather easily influenced."

"I'm strong enough to resist your pressure, Mr. Morgan." Esther was getting annoyed now.

Malcolm flushed. "Well, I wanted to give you the benefit of the doubt, so I asked you to come over today so that I could see…" His words failed again.

"He asked that, if God meant you for him, you would be the same plain Esther we knew and loved in Romania," Marion explained. "But…"

"But I've put on a bright blouse, and a white skirt and sandals. That's all."

Malcolm turned to face her. "But look at your hair! It's…" He paused trying to find the right words. "It's just so worldly!"

Esther stared at him. She had done her best to accommodate his principles that morning and what thanks did she get! "Worldly? It's done up on my head just like Marion's. What can you mean?"

Marion came and put a hand on her friend's shoulder. She reckoned it was time to come to her brother's rescue. "I think you understand what Malcolm means." Her voice was gentle but firm. "And you know very well that you've not done your hair up like mine."

Esther looked for a moment at her friend. Her long, blonde locks were pulled back tightly on top of her head. Not a wave was allowed to escape the pins that held it firmly in place. Esther blushed and hung her head, feeling once more like a naughty child.

"You deliberately wore your hair like that today, didn't you?" Esther noticed that her friend's tone was a little sharper now. "Why did you do it?"

Esther rose from her chair. She'd had quite enough. As Gabby had remarked several times, it took Heaven and earth to rouse her sister, but once roused, you had better run for shelter. Her eyes were flashing now and her chest heaving. She put up her hands to her hair. With a few deft movements of her fingers and a shake of her head, her long, thick, raven tresses came cascading down over her slim shoulders. Marion stared at her friend in total disbelief while her brother grasped his chair for support. Then he turned his head away. He couldn't look at the girl.

Esther saw their discomfiture and gave her head a final toss as she exclaimed heatedly, "There, now I've shocked you both good and proper. Now you see the real Esther Popescu. I was going to come like this in the first place, but out of respect for you both, I put my hair up in a respectable fashion. And what did I get for my pains? Nothing but reproaches! Well, now you see me just as God made me."

She paused, but the others still had not found their tongues. "I really do want God to deal with my vanity," she went on a little slower now, "but I've discovered that it doesn't come by plastering my hair back like I did in Romania." She caught Marion's reproachful glance and went on hastily, "Oh, I don't mean that He doesn't ask some to do that. I'm sure it's God's will for you, Marion, for example. But doesn't God love variety? Do you think He expects the lily to look like the rose, or vice versa? And what about the Body of Christ? I think Paul got the idea better than most of us have gotten it." Esther had run out of breath. She stopped abruptly, face flaming, eyes flashing, hands clenched.

"I'm so glad this has all happened," she went on, her voice calmer now. "It has set me free to be the creature God made me, to find His will for me—Esther Lydia Popescu. And it has shown me that you live your lives smothered by a Curtain just the same as I do. You try to escape the twentieth century world, but you create another in its place, with its own iron-clad rules, its unbending demands, and its biased judgments."

"Have you had your say?" Malcolm asked coolly, when the girl had finished her tirade. He had gained his composure now. He watched the children play for a few moments and then continued, as he adjusted the strap of his overall, "Esther, no wonder you've never achieved the peace my sister has. You are playing with both worlds."

"I'm not playing with anything," she retorted indignantly. Then her voice changed. "Look, Malcolm, I greatly respect you, and as for Marion," she glanced fondly at her friend who was shifting uneasily in her seat, "I've come to really love her as a sister. I greatly admire her and her devotion to God. But I've been trying to imitate that devotion, thinking it would bring me the same serenity she has. Marion told me herself once that God had a different path for everyone. I'm going to take the path that God seems to be pointing out for me to take."

"Esther," Malcolm's voice was commanding, "look at my sister over there for a moment, will you?" Esther stared at him in surprise.

"Now, what do you think of her?"

"Please, Malcolm," Marion pleaded, tears in her eyes. But her brother would not be stopped.

"I'm asking you, what does she look like?"

Esther stared at her friend for a few moments, then said softly, "She's pure and beautiful, like an angel from Heaven."

Malcolm's face softened. It was very clear that the girl really did love his sister. "Well then," he cleared his throat, "she may be a lily and you a rose as you suggested a few minutes ago, and she's also beautiful just like you are," he blushed scarlet as he said this. "Yet she has chosen to be subject to her Maker, and to her father, and to me, as the men in her life. As a sign of her submission, she dresses as she does. This is Biblical, and I don't think a Christian woman has any other option but to follow my sister's example. You are subject to no one, and I'm warning you that you are on a dangerous path. I hate to think what God may have to bring into your life before you learn your lesson." Esther felt again like a guilty child. She lowered her eyes and stood looking at the ground.

"And," he continued, "your beauty, or rather the way you used your beauty, entrapped me. I mistook God's voice for my own fleshly desire. I have confessed that to God and He has forgiven me."

This was too much for Esther. She raised her eyes to Malcolm's again and took a step nearer as she began, "I never once used any beauty I have to entrap you, Mr. Morgan, and you know it. You have never loved me or you wouldn't talk so coldly to me. You wanted a wife to rear your children; you were desperate for a companion in your mission to Romania. I arrived at the right time. I happened to be a native Romanian who was young and not that bad looking into the bargain. Well, I can understand your thinking up to that point. What I can't understand is," her words were coming faster now and she had to pause for breath, "why you need to make me into someone other than I am, though I suppose I'm partly to blame in that. I dressed like you wished, acted like you wanted, and that was a bit deceptive, I admit. Actually, if you want to know the truth," her face was flaming now, "I wrote you a letter of acceptance last night."

Marion gasped, and Malcolm's mouth fell open. "But I had forgotten it was a holiday today, so the mail didn't go," Esther went on, avoiding their eyes and trying in vain to keep the joy out of her voice. "I had written because I was afraid I'd miss God's will for my life, but at the same time, I was also reluctant to marry someone I did not love."

She saw the expression on Malcolm's face and went on hastily, "I respected you very much and reasoned that maybe I could marry first and fall in love later. But, as I wrote the letter, I asked God to intervene if this was not what He wanted for my life. Yet even when I took the envelope out of the mailbox this morning, I was still afraid to take this as God's intervention. Then the phone rang and it was you. And, well, you know the rest. But," and she looked from brother to sister as she spoke, "you both ought to know that I really did think that your simple way of life might be an answer to my problems with the Velvet Curtain, I really did. But now I know it isn't, at least, not for me. I'm positive of that now."

"But it is, Esther!" Malcolm almost shouted. "It is! Can't you see that we're in the world but not of it? We've found the answer, and you can too!"

His eagerness made Esther realize he had cared at least a little for her. She looked at him sadly and shook her head. "It might be an answer for you. It seems to be for Marion, at any rate, but it is not for me. It's just another type of curtain, closing me in. I…"

It was now Malcolm's turn to let vent. "That's enough, Esther Popescu! May God in His mercy keep you from being a snare to other men as you've been to me. God knows how I've been tempted to make exceptions for you I make for no one else. What compromise you have nearly brought me to, but I've seen the light, thank the Lord! But beware of rejecting His light; it's very, very dangerous."

Esther knew it was time to go. She turned to face both brother and sister. Taking a deep breath, she said slowly and deliberately, "Then it's Goodbye." Esther held out her hand, but Malcolm turned away.

Esther blinked back the tears. Then she ran up to Marion and threw her arms around her. "Please forgive me for any unhappiness I've caused either of you and remember I still love you like a sister. You've been a good friend to me. Please, let it stay that way."

Marion said nothing. She couldn't. Esther saw her face and turned abruptly away. She had thought that at least Marion would understand.

Grabbing her bag, she shook back her hair, squared her shoulders, and made for the porch steps. Then she almost ran to the car without one backward look, her long raven tresses flowing behind her.

Malcolm stared after her and then sat down heavily in his seat and turned to his sister. "There, it's all over. I've gone and done it now. I've lost her forever."

Marion came over and put her arm round her disconsolate brother. "You did it for the best, Malcolm. I'm very sorry, too, of course. I had so wanted her to be my sister-in-law, for I'm very fond of her."

Malcolm sat up in his chair. He was regaining his composure fast. "We must put her out of our minds forever, Marion."

Marion drew away from him a little. "I can't do that," she said flatly. She already regretted her coldness to her friend. "I'm going to keep in touch with her. There's no prohibition to that, is there? She is my sister in the Lord. And, Malcolm," she took his hand and sat down beside him, "please listen to me. I think we've been a bit hard on her. She's right in a way. God has a different path for each of us. Esther is seeking to find that path, and so are you. You are not suited, the two of you, and would never have been happy together."

Malcolm put his hands to his ears. "Don't talk about her any more, please. The subject's closed once and for all."

Marion looked at him pityingly. "Poor Malcolm!" she muttered half to herself. "Poor dear brother! But you'll soon get over it. You weren't bitten that badly."

"How do you know?"

"From experience," his sister told him sadly. "No, I kind of think you'll go and marry some woman quite soon, a quiet, plain little woman whom you can handle without any problem, but she'll adore you and be a good wife and mother, and you'll be quite happy and content. But Esther? I don't know what she'll do. I don't know how God will lead her."

"Through chastisement, that's how," muttered her brother. "And what about you?"

"Me?" Marion turned to gather the empty glasses lying on the old glass-topped table so Malcolm could not see the tear drops gathering in her clear blue eyes. "When you marry, it'll be Africa for me. I'll go there and not come back. And I'll be happy, very, in His will." She dried her eyes and disappeared into the kitchen.

"I've a saint for a sister," muttered her brother as he rose to follow her. "A real saint! How she puts up with such a sinner as me, I'll never ever know!"

Just then, he heard the police siren in the distance. A few moments later it raced past his house, followed not long afterwards by an ambulance and fire truck. Marion came back out onto the verandah.

"Some bad accident, I'm afraid," Malcolm told her.

"Sounds like they were in an awful hurry," commented his sister. "Wonder if it happened near here." Then her face blanched, "Malcolm, you don't think it could be Esther?"

Malcolm stared at her. "I mean," his sister went on hurriedly, "she was terribly upset when she left us. If it was Esther, I'll never forgive myself." She sat down heavily on a chair and stared out at the distant hills.

"Well, even if it is Esther," Malcolm tried to speak calmly, "it's not our fault, is it? I mean, I did warn her that…"

Marion put up her hand. "Don't say it, Malcolm Morgan, don't you dare say it. If that girl's had an accident it's probably because she was so upset, not because God rained down judgment on her for letting her hair down or singing in that concert."

She rose from her chair and literally stomped into the house. Her brother didn't try to follow her and had no idea that she was ringing Miss Lucy's number. But the line was busy.

Marion went up to her bedroom and got down on her knees. "Oh Lord," she prayed, "I am so sorry for my attitude to Esther today. Please forgive me and give me a chance to ask her forgiveness. And please, wherever she is right now, put Your loving arms around her and give her peace, Amen."

# Chapter Twenty-Two

## *Len Comes to Tiny Gap*

Len Atwood turned up the narrow lane that led to Hugh Gardner's chalet. After winding steeply up the mountain for a mile at least, the road ended abruptly in front of a log house. Braking to a halt, Len got out of the car and inhaled a long, deep breath. The air felt fresh and invigorating. He turned and gazed out over the mountains. This was surely God's own country, he thought, and in a place like this, maybe he would hear God's voice and receive direction for his life.

Conscious of eyes upon him, Len glanced towards the front porch of the quaint, wooden house. A man of about seventy-five was coming down the steps to meet him.

"Welcome to Tiny Gap, Len." Hugh Gardner's voice was hearty as he held out his hand. "Come in and make yourself at home. You must be thirsty. Here, let me make you a cool drink, and then let's sit where we can gaze at the mountains and have our spirits refreshed."

"I need that, Mr. Gardner."

"Don't we all!" Hugh smiled as he led the way to the screened-in porch where he spent much of his time.

The two men said little as they sipped their grape juice. Len felt a little awkward. After all, he had never met his host before and had come that day on his cousin's recommendation. Hugh Gardner, Ron had told him, could help him if anyone could.

He put his glass on the table by his chair and let his eyes feast on the panorama that spread out before him. "You have a breathtaking view here," Len commented, as he turned to face his host.

"Yes. It's the envy of all my neighbors," Hugh told him proudly.

Len cleared his throat. "You must be wondering why I've intruded on you like this," he remarked.

Hugh shook his head. "You're not intruding. To tell you the truth, I get very lonely at times. My grandson is spending most of his spare time with his parents these days. They're home on furlough for a year.

I miss him. He's such good company for an old man like me. So you're very welcome, Len."

"Thanks. Ron told me you were very hospitable."

"Ron?" Hugh repeated thoughtfully. "I only met him once, three years ago."

"Yes, he said that. He also said that you were a great help to him and his friends at that time."

Hugh smiled. "Well, it's good to hear that. Ron Atwood has often been in my prayers. But now, go ahead and tell me about yourself. I'm a good listener. Have to be with a grandson as talkative as Aaron around."

Len stretched his legs and leaned back in his chair. He was feeling so very much at home already, that it didn't seem as difficult as he thought it would be to open up to his new friend. As he had driven up to the mountains that morning, he had wondered just why he was making the six hour trip to a man he did not know.

He had spent a difficult year since he had left Pine Grove Evangelical Church. He had not tried to find another position as youth pastor. He felt he needed the time to rediscover himself. The news that he was not the true son of Steve Atwood had taken months to sink in although, in reality, he and his step-dad were closer than they had ever been. But both of them were struggling with their grief. It was hard to adjust to life without the one who had been the center of their lives. As they told each other quite often, neither was in a state to help the other out of their sorrow and depression.

But it was the sense of utter failure that was Len's biggest problem. It haunted him day and night. He had made a mess of his vocation, and the future looked bleak and hopeless. At times, slight rays of light would glimmer through his darkness but they were fleeting. He needed some strong and powerful light, such as St. Paul had seen on the Damascus road, to show him the path ahead. And that was why he had come that July Fourth to Tiny Gap.

Hugh had heard of Len from Connie and Esther, and what he had heard had not been exactly complimentary. But looking into his companion's dark eyes that afternoon, Hugh glimpsed despair. Whatever Len's past had been, it was obvious that he needed help to regain hope and direction.

"I'm really pretty desperate, Mr. Hugh," Len's voice broke into his reverie. He looked pleadingly into the older man's face. "I've given up preaching," he paused and gave a short and rather bitter laugh. "Well, that's not quite correct. My actions pretty much put me out of the pastorate. And I don't know what to do with my life. I still don't have peace."

"Tell me about it."

Len gulped. "It's not a very pretty story."

"I didn't think it was." Hugh gave a smile. "Otherwise you wouldn't be here, would you?"

It was Len's turn to smile. This man, he felt, would at least try to understand him. He was someone whom he could truly trust.

For at least half an hour, Len shared his heart with "the old man of the mountain" as Hugh was called by many locals. He even told him about his illegitimate birth. Up until that day, he had kept his secret to himself. But there was something about Hugh Gardner that inspired trust.

"So here I am," Len concluded. "I've shut myself away for twelve whole months, doing nothing but teaching a few students piano from time to time, occasionally filling in for the organist at dad's church, and helping him keep up the house. But this relative seclusion hasn't helped me a bit. So, Mr. Hugh, what do I do? How can I begin again?"

Hugh put a hand on the younger man's shoulder. "I've tried seclusion too, Len," he admitted. Then he began to speak of his own dilemma, of how, even as a more mature Christian, he was finding it almost impossible to be in this world yet not of it, of how he had felt recently that he should not lead such an isolated life, that it was a selfish way round the problem. He needed to be down in the valley where the battle was going on. He needed to demonstrate to younger men like Len that with God's help, one could still live a simple life with God—a life above church politics, and gimmicks, and competitions.

Len's tired face lit up with a smile. "So you're going back into the ministry?"

"Just for two years, while a friend of mine takes a break abroad. And I've been praying for an assistant. It's not a big church, but I'll be seventy-six in September. There are quite a few young people in the congregation." He paused a moment and gave Len a peculiar smile. "So, you see, that's where you'd come in."

"But..." Len gasped.

"Well, maybe God sent you."

"But you don't know me. You've only just heard my story."

"Exactly, and hearing it made me feel that you could just be the right man for the job."

Len was shocked. "But you'd need good references. And those," Len gave a wry smile, "might be hard to come by. Maybe you should talk to Esther Popescu or Connie Frith. They'll give you my true pedigree." Hugh thought Len's smile was a little bitter.

"I can't go by Esther right now. She's very confused."

"So are we all," Len sighed.

"And Connie has already told me all about you. She came here a year ago and poured out her heart to me."

Len rose from his chair. "I'm sorry to have wasted your time, Mr. Hugh. Why didn't you tell me you knew all about me before I spilled out my story?" Len was embarrassed and annoyed now.

"I wanted to hear your side of the story," Hugh told him.

"And?"

Hugh put an arm on the young man's shoulder. "And you painted yourself blacker than Connie did, by a long shot. That's what made me feel I could trust you as my assistant."

Len stared at his new friend in stunned silence. "Well, let's both think about it," Hugh went on. "It wouldn't be till after Christmas. And no one knows of this just yet, so keep what I've told you in confidence. Let's tell the Lord about it," Hugh suggested.

Len nodded. He remembered his cousin's words, "I've forgotten most of what Hugh told me that day, but I've never forgotten his prayer. I could recite it to you now, if you like."

And as the old man poured out his heart to God, Len understood Ron's words. Hugh prayed as if God were sitting there on that porch with them. And he prayed as if he expected an answer.

When Hugh had finished, Len tried to speak but his voice was choked with emotion. "I need to be off now," Len told him finally, as he made for the porch steps.

"Are you going back to Cincinnati tonight?" Hugh asked, surprised. "It's a long way, and the roads will be very busy."

"No, I'll stay in a motel somewhere. I wondered if you could spare me some time tomorrow, Mr. Hugh. Just being with you and hearing you pray is a tonic."

Hugh's face lit up in a radiant smile. "Of course I can spare the time. That's what my life is all about. But be my guest. I've a spare bedroom. Aaron's away and I'm lonely."

"That's awfully kind of you."

"Not at all. In fact, stay a few days if you like. I'll really be able to get to know you then."

"Maybe that's not a good idea." Len dropped his eyes as he spoke, "I've been…" He paused, not knowing how to go on.

"You've already told me what you've been."

"But I'll never get away from my past." And Len let out a long, mournful sigh.

"Well then, let God take it. He's the only one Who has the capacity to really forget."

Len smiled a little. "Thanks for the encouragement. Trouble is, I don't feel at home with the new Len Atwood. I mean, I'm trying so hard to be different but it just doesn't seem really me."

"You're probably trying too hard," Hugh told him gently. Then he got up from his chair and asked rather abruptly, "Now, how about a little visit to our mutual friends?"

"Meaning?"

"Meaning Esther and her aunt, of course."

Len's face clouded. "I don't know any of Esther's family very well. Oh, I've met Rachel, I think. And I knew Ramona." He felt sick at the remembrance of what he had done to Ramona. "Anyway," he went on, "I'm not sure Esther will want to see me. I spoke to her last night on the phone."

"You did?"

"Yes. I saw her on TV. She was singing at a concert in Knoxville."

Hugh gasped in surprise. "But she hasn't sung in public since her illness."

"I know. But there she was, dressed in white and looking and sounding like an angel from Heaven."

"Do you know Esther well?" Hugh asked after he had digested what Len had just told him.

Len gave a short laugh. "I knew her pretty well at one time. I don't think she'll be keen to see me, Mr. Hugh, really I don't."

"Well, even if Esther doesn't make you welcome, Mary certainly will. She's one of the most motherly women I know, apart from Marjorie Porteous. You must meet her, too. But come on, let's go. You can't be this near and not drop in."

When they arrived at Mary Popescu's white-boarded house it looked as if no one were at home. "Mary's car's here," Hugh told Len, after he had rung the bell three times, "but Esther's isn't. They're both out, that's obvious. Let's drive to my friend Marjorie's. She keeps a guest house up the road. She may know where they are."

Marjorie was very glad to see them. Rachel was up in Velours, she told them. And Gabby was in Indianapolis and due to leave that very day for Europe. But she couldn't figure out where the others had gone.

"Oh well, we'll try again tomorrow," Hugh said as he got into the car. "It's the Fourth after all, Len. Had you forgotten?"

Len smiled. "Yes, I had, actually. But look, there's a police car turning up Mary's driveway."

"Better turn in, too, and find out what's wrong," Hugh suggested anxiously.

"Hope it isn't Esther," muttered Len.

"Or Gabby, or Rachel, or Mary," put in Hugh.

They weren't kept in suspense for long. The tall, broad-shouldered police officer got out of his car and was going up to the door when Len shouted to him, "There's no one in. We've just tried."

"Better make sure. That's our job," the man told him, as he pressed the bell and waited. When he had become convinced that no one was at home, he turned to the two men standing just behind him. "Are either of you related to Esther Popescu?" he asked.

"No," Hugh told the man, "just good friends."

"Well," he said, avoiding their eyes, "Esther has been in a bad accident." Hugh and Len looked at one another in shocked silence. "She collided with a truck head on," the man went on.

"She's still alive?" Hugh managed to get out.

"Yes, but barely. Her injuries are very serious."

"Where is she now?"

"She's been taken to Knoxville General Hospital."

"Knoxville? But where did the accident take place?" Hugh asked, sitting down to steady himself in one of the chairs on Mary's front porch.

"The accident took place near Silver Springs. It's only forty minutes from Knoxville. The hospital there is better able to cope with her injuries than any other in the area. Now, how do I get word to her nearest of kin?" the policeman asked. "Problem is, this is the only address we found on the accident victim."

Len shuddered at the idea of Esther being a victim of anything or anyone. He glanced at Hugh who was breathing a silent prayer.

"Well, if the accident occurred near Silver Springs, then she's probably visiting her great aunt," he told the police officer. "Was she alone in the car?"

"Yes."

"Strange. Mary's gone too. Look," and Hugh turned to the waiting policeman, "I don't have her Aunt Lucy's number here on me. I can look it up in the phone book. I think Marjorie might remember her surname."

"Marjorie?" The man was getting impatient.

"Yes. She lives nearby and is a close friend of the family. I'll call Esther's aunt from there."

"Sorry, but I'll have to speak myself to the girl's next of kin." Hugh nodded. The policeman was only doing his duty.

It wasn't long before Marjorie located Lucy Farthington's number. Esther's great aunt answered but was so shocked at the news that she tottered and would have fallen had not Rita held her up. Mary took the receiver.

"What? An accident? But Esther's just gone down the road. About five miles."

"Accidents can happen in five miles, you know. Was the girl upset about something?"

Mary paused. She could imagine that Esther had been very upset before she had finished talking with Malcolm. "I wasn't with her, but yes, she could well have been very upset."

"All I can say is that whatever caused her to collide with the truck like that at the junction with the I-40 I don't know. A passenger in the car behind said it seemed like the girl simply didn't seem to see it coming."

"Was it really a bad accident?" Mary had a hard job to control her voice.

"Yes, very bad. She's in Knoxville General Hospital, and I'd advise you to get down there right away. And I mean right away. You are her aunt?"

"Yes, by marriage."

"Her parents are living?"

"No."

"I see. Any siblings?"

"She has a sister who has left for Europe today. We'll try to get in touch with her as soon as we can. And we'll phone her uncle and two cousins immediately."

"Good! They need to know. And, please, get down to the hospital immediately. There's no time to lose."

"I will." Mary sounded calm, but her heart was pounding violently. "And now can I speak to Marjorie, please?" The policeman handed the receiver to Marjorie, nodded to the men and was off. Marjorie soon motioned to Hugh to come to the phone.

"Mary," his voice sounded so soothing to the distraught woman, "I'll drive down immediately and be with you tonight." Len motioned that he would go with him. "And Len Atwood, Ron's cousin is here. He'll be with me, he says."

"Great!" Mary sounded very relieved.

"God's watching over Esther at this very moment," Hugh reassured her. "And over you, too. Now, God bless. See you soon."

"Bye."

Mary turned to Lucy who was sitting with her eyes closed. "Esther of all people," Lucy muttered. "And I was just beginning to love someone again." Tears were trickling down her withered cheeks as she spoke.

Mary stooped down and kissed her gently. "Who doesn't love our sweet Esther?" she said softly. "But she's in God's hands, Aunt Lucy."

Mary turned to the phone again. She didn't feel like it, but she'd have to break the news to John and Rachel. Her daughter answered, and it was all her mother could do to get the words out.

"I'll leave for Knoxville as soon as Dad gets back," Rachel managed to say. "I'm almost sure that he'll come down with me. He's gone out for an hour or two, but Ron's here. I'll tell him too. What? Len and Hugh are going there? Len Atwood, did you say? That's strange. But I'm glad you'll have moral support tonight. Bye, Mom. Take care."

Rachel's voice was breaking as she turned to face Ron who was standing close behind her. He had obviously overheard some of the conversation.

"It's Esther?" he asked breathlessly.

"Yes. She's had a terrible accident. It might be fatal. They don't know yet."

Ron gripped the chair by the table to steady himself. "Esther, my Esther," he muttered. "And what about Gabby? Is she with her?"

"She's gone off this morning with Larry and Andrea and some other friends to spend a month in Europe," she told him. "We'll have to trace her as soon as we can," Rachel went on in a matter-of-fact tone that belied her true feelings. "I'll get Dad to phone Dr. Porter."

"Do you think it would be terribly out of place if I drove down to Knoxville?" Ron asked hesitatingly. "I mean, I'm not next of kin or a relative or even…" His voice broke and he could not go on.

Rachel came over to where he was standing and looked up at him. Her eyes reminded him painfully of Esther's. "Look, Ron, Len and

Hugh are there and they've not been as close to her as you've been. So many people love Esther," and Rachel's whole frame shook as she tried to control her emotion.

Rachel's pain made him forget his own for just a moment. He took her hand in his and squeezed it. "I know you love her too, Rachel. You've been very close. She'll need you now that her sister's away."

"Yes, I know. And she may need you as well."

Ron shook his head. "I doubt it. But I've got to see her. I mean…it might be my last…" He couldn't go on. He turned on his heel and left the kitchen.

Rachel eventually got through to her dad's cell phone. He was in the city, but in no time at all she heard his car racing up the drive. A few moments later, the car door banged shut, and John burst into the house followed by a very subdued looking Diane. He had soon gotten the gist of the story from his daughter. In no time at all, he was calling Larry's dad who informed him that he had no address at all by which he could contact his son. Larry had said he would call home in a week or so and let them know their whereabouts. John grunted in disgust as he put down the receiver, but what more could he do?

He picked up the phone again and dialed Ramona and Claude. They were away in Florida for two weeks and he told them not to interrupt their vacation just yet. He'd go down and see the situation, and if the worse came to the worst, he'd phone Ramona to come up to Knoxville immediately. Ramona had not seen much of Esther during the last few years and had never been as close to her as her sister had been. But she had a big heart. John could hear the sob in her voice as she exclaimed, "Poor Esther! How awful!"

Rachel was too shaken to drive so Ron drove her car and she went with her dad. Meanwhile, Hugh and Len were speeding towards Knoxville as fast as Len's car would take them.

"You're a godsend," Hugh told the young man as they swung onto I-40.

Len smiled weakly. "I hope so," he said. "It's about time I did some good on this earth. But this terrible accident! What a tragedy!"

"Yes, though God can turn tragedy into triumph."

"I know He can. He *can* do anything. Problem is, *will* He?"

"He always does if we let Him. Even death can be turned into triumph. God's will be done, Len."

Len gripped the wheel tightly. "Amen," he said softly. "God's will be done."

## Chapter Twenty-Three

## *At the Hospital*

"You may go in, Mr. Atwood, but only for a few moments." Ron scarcely heard what the nurse was saying. He seemed to be a part of some drama that had no end. During the long drive down to Knoxville, he had envisaged this moment over and over again. Sometimes it had seemed like the climax of some Shakespearean tragedy, sometimes the bizarre ending of a twentieth-century romance, but he and Esther were always the main actors. Everyone and everything else were secondary—even the doctor's verdict seemed to appear less important than their love for one another.

As he had cruised down the interstate, Ron could visualize it all—he would rush in and clasp the delicate little hand he had held so often in his own, and the tears would drop down on the bedclothes just as they had done those three long years ago. The girl in the bed would look up at him from under those long, curling eyelashes and give a feeble smile; their eyes would meet, and their hearts would be one. There would be no more lifting of curtains, for there was surely none to lift now. And his vibrant love, his comforting presence, his voice, his touch—they'd bring her back from the brink of the grave if anything could.

But now, as he stepped into the small room which had become Esther's temporary home, he came face to face with reality. It had been difficult to persuade the head nurse to let him in. The patient, he was reminded, was in intensive care and critically ill, and after all, he was not family. But the desperate look in his eyes told it all. This young man was in love with the girl in the bed in room 301. Nurse Gadger had seen that look before, and she knew she had to respect it.

Ron took a few steps forward. He told himself that there must be a figure in the bed, though all he was aware of, at first, were the crisscrossing of tubes and the clicking of monitors. And the bandages! They were everywhere—round her head, her arms, her chest. His throat turned dry. Why had no one warned him it would be like this? But of course they had. Mary had grabbed his arm just before he had gone to Esther and whispered in his ear, "Remember, she's had a head-on collision, Ron. She's in terrible shape."

He stood a moment to regain his equilibrium. Then he drew another step nearer. He reached out his hand just as he had envisaged he would do, but what would he touch? Where were her hands, her arms, her neck? She was like some Egyptian mummy. He gave a shudder. Was she even alive? The heart monitor told him she was, but barely.

He took another step forward. "Esther, it's Ron." His voice was gravelly and awkward. There was no sign of recognition in those slits of eyes between the ghastly white bandages. He clutched the bedrail and tried again. "I love you," he murmured, but it seemed that his words rebounded from the bedclothes. He stood a few moments as if glued to the floor, staring blankly at what he kept telling himself was his beloved girl. The silence in the room was suffocating. He glanced once more at the figure in the bed. "Oh, God!" he moaned, putting his face in his hands. "Oh, dear God!" If only he could cry, he thought, but not a tear would come. His soul felt dry and shriveled. He took his hands from his face, gave one last look, then turned and fled the room.

"Sorry," he muttered, as he nearly collided with Rachel in the corridor. "Got to get some air."

He bolted into the nearest escalator. Rachel watched as the door closed on him. She made her way back into the waiting room and flopped into the dark brown leather chair in the corner. She picked up a magazine and stared unseeingly at the cover page. There was a dead silence in the room. Len and Hugh had gone to a motel for some sleep, but Mary had insisted on staying through the night.

Soon it was John's turn to go in. He knew from Rachel's silence and from the look on her face that Esther must be in pretty bad shape. He gritted his teeth, took a deep breath, and made for room 301. Five minutes later Mary saw him reenter the waiting room. She glanced at his ashen face. "You all need to go and get some sleep. There's nothing really we can do but wait."

"I couldn't sleep if I tried, Mom," Rachel said softly.

Mary shook her head. "But I'm afraid there'll be more than one night of waiting. You've had a long journey, all of you. Len and Hugh will be back at seven, so…"

"I couldn't sleep, not for worlds," John told her.

"Nor could I," echoed Rachel.

John gazed intently at Mary for a few moments. He didn't think he could stay all night there, watching and waiting, with this woman who had once been his wife. "Maybe you're right," he told her rather abruptly. "I'm not much good to anyone as I am now. I'll come back at noon tomorrow, how's that? If there's not many here tonight, you and Rachel can stretch out on the sofa over there and get a few winks, maybe." Mary nodded, greatly relieved.

John found Ron sitting in the car, staring blankly out into the summer's night. He put his hands on the young man's shoulder. "Come on, let's go and get a bit of rest. We've had a long journey."

He expected Ron to protest but instead, he put the keys into the ignition and motioned to John to get in beside him.

"Are you fit to drive?" John asked compassionately. "You look simply awful!"

These words seemed to stab Ron back into consciousness. He put his foot on the accelerator. "I'm fine," he said, trying to sound firm but not succeeding very well. "I've had a bit of a shock just like you have. It'll take me a while to get over it, but I'll probably feel a whole lot better tomorrow. Let's go."

The night seemed endless to Mary as she sat and watched her daughter sleep the hours away. The doctor arrived early the next morning and informed them that Esther was in a coma, and no one could say when, if ever, she would awake. At present, all they could do was wait. Nurse Gadger seemed especially concerned with her new patient. And when Ron returned to the hospital later that day, she accosted him in the hallway.

"Young man," her voice was abrupt but her eyes kind, "are you a special friend of my patient in there?" and she pointed to Esther's room.

Ron dropped his eyes. "I was engaged to her," he told the nurse in a low voice.

"I see." Nurse Gadger read between the lines. She was very good at doing that. "Well, I don't want to interfere in your personal lives, but that young lady may never wake up, you know."

The nurse wanted to startle him and she succeeded. Ron put his head in his hands and said nothing. "So we're looking for ways to rouse her," she went on in her matter-of-fact way. "She may have lost all desire to live. In other words, she may be choosing not to waken. That's just a theory, but if it is correct, then," she paused and put her arm on Ron's shoulder, "you ought to try your best to waken her. Maybe your voice will stir memories."

Ron shook off her arm. "No, I can't do it. I might stir the wrong sort of memories. I've already told her I loved her several times and that is the truth. But it's all over between us and has been for three years now. I mean, it would just be..."

"I'll say no more. It was just a thought, that's all." Nurse Gadger turned and sped down the corridor. She didn't want Ron to see the disappointment written all over her kindly face.

Ron peeked in at the patient several times that afternoon but only stayed a moment or two. He greeted Len and Hugh briefly when they came back from a snack in the cafeteria, but it was obvious he was in no mood for conversation. Hugh went in to see the patient later that morning. He knelt by her bed and offered a brief prayer for her, but there was no response.

The atmosphere was tense in the waiting room. Mary and Rachel had gone off for a rest, leaving the four men on duty. Len had absented himself some of the time, feeling rather redundant. The nurse had told them that only relatives and very close friends were allowed in periodically to see the sick girl. He could only imagine from the faces of his companions how very ill she must be.

That evening, after supper, Ron asked to see Esther once more. There was another nurse on duty, but she let him in. He took a seat by the bed. He would bring her back into their world again, or at least he would try. If he succeeded, he would leave it to providence to determine what happened next. He'd just take the first step. He reminded himself that there, in that mummified body beside him, was his beloved Esther—his beautiful angel, his former sweetheart, and his one and only true love.

He put his hand on the bandages and began in a low voice, "Esther. Can you hear me? If you can, then listen to me, please." His voice was mechanical. He didn't have faith this was going to work.

"It's Ron," he began again. "I'm here beside you. I love you. I want you to get better. Come back to us, Esther. Please!"

There was no sign of recognition in the one eye that was discernible. None at all. Not a muscle twitched. It was all stillness, deathly stillness.

He tried again and again. For half an hour, he repeated the same words. Finally, the nurse tiptoed into the room and tapped him on the shoulder. "Your time's up," she whispered. He breathed a sigh of relief and followed her out of the room.

"I tried it," he confided in Nurse Gadger the next morning. "It didn't work."

"Try it again," she urged, "and again, and again."

"I can't," he almost shouted. "You don't understand. I just can't."

He made for the waiting room and threw himself onto the sofa. The room was empty except for Rachel. After a few minutes of silence, he glanced up at her. "I can't go on like this," he said, his tone desperate. "I want to wait here till she wakens, but I can't stand it. They expect me to be the one who brings her to. But it's no use. It's just no use."

Rachel forgot her shyness for once and came over and sat down beside him. She put her hand on his arm. "Ron," she began, she didn't really know what to say but she sensed she had to say something, "neither of us have eaten properly today. I'm feeling just rotten. I don't seem to have it in me to cope with all this," and she waved her hand in the direction of the corridor and Esther's room. "We're just human after all. Now will you take me for something to eat or will I have to take you?" She wondered afterwards why she was saying these words. He must think she was crazy, or bold, or just simply out of her mind.

At first, Ron made no response. She said nothing more but just sat there, waiting. She heard her father's voice in the corridor. Then Ron rose from his chair and gave a weak smile. "Come on, Rachel. You're right. We can't vegetate here in this room. We'll go out and eat, and not in the cafeteria either."

Half an hour later they were facing each other in a nearby restaurant. Both were finding it hard to swallow the food in front of them. Suddenly, Ron pushed his plate away and put his head on the table. Soon Rachel saw his whole frame shaking with sobs. After what seemed an age, he raised his head. "Sorry," he murmured. "I'm not much company."

"Neither am I," she told him. "But I think we need to talk it all out. I feel if I don't, I'll burst."

He stared at her. She was usually the reserved one. "Yes," she went on, "I know you're thinking that I'm acting out of character. But maybe we all are. It's been so awful, Ron. I mean, I've loved Esther as a sister. I don't know what I'd have been if she hadn't come to Velours."

"Stop it," he said almost fiercely. "Don't talk about her."

Rachel leaned across the table and grabbed both his wrists. "We've got to talk, or we'll go mad. We can't bottle it all up. We've got to face it. Esther's in a coma and may never wake up. We may lose her forever."

Ron raised his bloodshot eyes to her face. He started. It was as if Esther were staring back at him. Then he looked again. There was real sympathy in those great dark orbs, and understanding. This quiet, detached girl seemed to know how he felt.

He let out a sob as his hands fastened on hers with a grip that made her wince. "Yes, we may lose her," he repeated. "And oh, Rachel, I can't reach her, not even with my love—the love I thought was so deep, so everlasting," he gave a bitter laugh. "But what or who did I really love? I loved the beautiful girl with the olive skin, glowing eyes, gorgeous figure, silky raven hair—the girl with the voice of an angel. I loved to take her in my arms, to kiss her, to hold her tight. I loved to buy her jewelry, dresses, purses, shoes. I loved to take her to town, to know I was the envy of all the guys around. Sound's selfish, doesn't it?"

Then his grip tightened. "But can you blame me?" he asked with a sob, "she was so perfect, so sweet, so…"

He put his head on the table again. Rachel got out a Kleenex and wiped her eyes. When he sat up again she offered him one.

"Thanks," he muttered. "You're kind to listen to me."

"Go on, if it helps," she told him.

"It does a bit," he admitted with a faint smile. "Problem is, Rachel, that as I look at that figure in the bed, I wonder who she really is. Do I really know her? Did I ever really know her? I guess I won't know the answer to that question till she comes to, if she ever does. I thought that my love was so strong, but it can't seem to bear up under the strain. And it can't even get through to her. And tomorrow I've got an important appointment in Nashville. I'll have to go away for at least a few days."

Rachel nodded. "There's not much any of us can do right now but wait. You go and we'll keep you posted. And," she said with a smile, "don't judge yourself so harshly. If she does come round and can communicate with you, you'll find it'll be different."

He looked at her with the dawning of hope in his eyes. "Think so?"

She nodded comfortingly as they both rose to go. "Well," he told her, looking brighter than he had for several days, "I'll go then. But take care of yourself, Rachel. You and your mother are taking the full brunt of it all."

"Mother's a wonder, Ron."

"Yes. She seems to cope the best of us all. I wonder why."

"I know what she'd say."

"That her faith sustains her?"

Rachel nodded again. "Yes. She spends a lot of time praying these days. She says it's the only way she can keep going."

"Wish I could pray," Ron muttered. "But I can't."

"Same here."

He grinned slightly. "We're a pair of heathens, aren't we?" The girl said nothing as she followed him to the car. After all, what could she say?

The next morning Ron slipped into room 301 to take one last look and then he was off. Len and Hugh had already left for Tiny Gap, but John insisted on staying longer in Knoxville, for another week at least. Knowing that it was very awkward for both himself and Mary to be so much together, he suggested that they take shifts. After all, he was Esther's closest blood relative apart from Gabby. Mary saw the wisdom of this suggestion. Her strength was giving way, and who knew what was in store for them during the next months? The three girls had rented their apartment for another year, so she and Rachel were spared the expense of a motel.

The days seemed to drag by in unending succession. There was still no word from Europe. Dr. Porter told John that he was waiting for a phone call from his son.

"But why on earth didn't they leave contact numbers in case of emergencies?" John's voice was irritable. "I mean, it was very irresponsible."

"They had their reasons," Dr. Porter told him abruptly. What he didn't say was that he had urged Larry to give some addresses, or phone numbers, but he had flat out refused. This was to be a vacation of a lifetime, especially for Gabby, he had told his dad. He didn't want her folks bothering her while she was abroad, or that Aaron guy trying to look them up. He was lumbering around Europe somewhere, and you never knew what he might be up to. So that was that.

John hung up feeling very angry. But there was nothing he could do, nothing at all. Just wait.

Finally the day came when he had to leave. "Phone me any time, day or night, if there's any news at all, please," he begged his daughter, as he said goodbye in the parking lot. "Even a flicker of an eyelid, or the slight movement of a muscle—that would be wonderful news to me."

"Of course I'll tell you right away, Dad, if anything like that happens," she assured him.

Hugh, meanwhile, was enjoying Len's company in Tiny Gap. The young man had decided to stay in Tennessee for a while longer. He prized the daily seasons of prayer with his new friend and drew strength from their long conversations together. He would sit for hours on the deck, his Bible on his knee, looking out over the mountains. Just letting the atmosphere of peace that enveloped the place invade his whole being, seemed to dispel, at least temporarily, the gloom and despair which had dogged him for months. But sometimes the old restlessness would steal over him. Hugh would urge him to get out a bit, visit friends, take a quick trip home. But Len would shake his head.

"I've come up here to find out God's will," he said. "I don't want to go back till I know the next step to take."

Not wanting to be idle, Len tried his best to help out in the garden, to cook an occasional meal, or paint the back porch. But he liked it best of all when he would hear his host say, "Play me something." Then he would slip upstairs for his guitar, perch on an old stool on the porch, and sing his heart out. It seemed that he was singing out his desire to God, singing away his frustration with his life, and through his song, finding little by little a new purpose to living.

Hugh phoned the hospital almost daily only to be told the same news. Esther's condition had not changed. He sensed that Rachel and her mother were becoming very wearied. The others had gone, and they had been alone for a few days. On the tenth day after Esther's accident, Hugh told Mary they would be down that afternoon to give them some relief.

Hugh was just locking up when a thought struck him. "Have you forgotten your guitar, Len?" he called.

"My guitar?"

"Yes. You seldom go anywhere without it, do you?"

"But," Len stammered, "it'll be no use where we're going, will it?"

Hugh walked up to the car and laid his hand on the young man's arm. "I've been thinking," he said thoughtfully, "that maybe it's music that'll bring our Esther round again."

Len stared at him. "But she's in intensive care. I mean, they wouldn't let me take this in there. I'm not a relative or even a close friend."

Hugh looked into his friend's dark eyes. "I know, but you have an extraordinary gift of music. And so does Esther. I think the nursing staff would be glad of any experiment to try to bring her back to consciousness."

Len shook his head. "No, I can't do it. I'm nothing to Esther. She wouldn't want to open her eyes for the first time in days and see me there. You can't know what I've been, Mr. Hugh."

"You've told me often enough," Hugh said, his eyes twinkling just a little.

"I know. But I don't think Esther or any other girl has a scrap of respect left for me."

"Look," Hugh sounded a little stern now. "Esther's life is hanging in the balance. We have to consider anything that might help, so at least put that instrument of yours in the car. I can't force you to do what you don't want to do, but have it handy in case you change your mind."

Len went back into the house and returned with his guitar. He put it in the back seat very reluctantly. He considered this was a wild scheme of Hugh's which might only do harm.

When they got to the hospital, they lost no time in making sure that Rachel and Mary got at least twenty-four hours' rest. They'd phone their apartment if there was the slightest change in Esther's condition, they reassured them.

"By the way, I asked Len to bring his guitar," Hugh told Rachel and Mary as they made for the escalator. "I thought maybe music would help to bring Esther round. What do you think?"

The two women stared at him in surprise. "The nurse asked Ron to talk to her and call her name," Mary told Hugh, "but it didn't do any good. And if he failed, I doubt if Len could succeed."

"But it won't be Len," Hugh reminded her. "It will be the music which is a link to her past. Len is very reluctant, but I think he should try it. Do I have your permission?"

"Of course," Mary told him. Rachel said nothing. She was still very wary of Len Atwood. He was very subdued these days but he was still Len. She noticed the nurses making eyes at him from time to time, though she had to admit that he did little to encourage them. But he had something about him. He was just Len Atwood, that was all. He wasn't and never would be Ron. Rachel sighed. Why had God permitted another tragedy to happen to her beautiful cousin? And maybe she wouldn't be beautiful any more even if she did make it. Rachel shuddered. What would Esther be like without her beauty, she wondered?

# Chapter Twenty-Four

## *Esther Awakes*

"Amazing Grace, how sweet the sound," Len began softly. His fingers were trembling, and he could hardly find the right strings to pluck. Nurse Gadger listened unobserved in the corridor. At first, when Hugh had begged permission for Len to try playing to the sick girl, she had thought it was a very strange request. If that other young man who was in love with her patient hadn't succeeded in awakening her to reality, then how could anyone else succeed?

"But Esther was a singer," Hugh had explained. "Len used to accompany her in her concerts and knows some of the songs she would sing. He's very reluctant and embarrassed to do this, but I've begged him to give it a try. It can't do any harm, can it?"

"No," Nurse Gadger had agreed. "It's a question of life and death. Tell him to go right ahead."

Len hadn't seen Esther up until that day. As he gazed at her motionless form, he felt, as Ron had done, that the girl he had once known was not really there. However could he sing? Here was a young woman whose life had been wrecked in one moment. He was no match for such a tragedy. He, Len Atwood, with a reputation as a charmer, how could he ever do one solitary thing to help anyone, let alone this angel of a girl? Hugh's idea was preposterous. But then he remembered something that Hugh was constantly telling him. He was being transformed by God's grace, day by day, little by little. It seemed so slow a process sometimes, but he knew he was changing, and others knew it too.

"That saved a wretch like me," he went on, his voice choked with emotion. Nurse Gadger fished in her pocket for a Kleenex. "I once was lost, but now am found, was blind but now I see." Len stopped abruptly. He couldn't sing any more. But he could at least play.

The minutes ticked by. Nurse Gadger slipped up to the bed and looked at the monitor. She stared in disbelief. The heart signals were stronger, definitely stronger. There was still no sign of recognition in the eyes, or movement in the muscles, but that might come later, or again, it might not.

"That's enough for today," the nurse told Len. He rose to go.

"It's not done any good," he said mournfully, glancing at the form in the bed. "I didn't think it would."

"Look at that," the nurse told him, pointing to the monitor. "Her heart is beating more regularly and stronger, quite a bit stronger."

"Did the playing do that?" he asked incredulously.

"Looks like it," Nurse Gadger said, patting him on the arm. "Keep it up. I'm not promising that it'll really do the trick but let's give it a few more tries. Come back tomorrow morning and play and sing again. You have a voice the angels would envy."

Len reddened. "OK," he told her, "I'll try to find the words of her favorite Romanian hymn by tomorrow."

"Great. Now you'd better go."

Len left Hugh at the hospital that night and went over to Mary's apartment for her key. He had told her by phone that he wanted the words to *Numai Harul*.

"They're in Esther's Romanian hymn book," she told him. "The book is in the piano stool in our living-room."

"I'll spend the night at your house, if that's all right with you," he told Hugh on the phone. "I'm fetching Esther's Romanian hymn book. The nurse wants me to try singing, and maybe something in Romanian might be more effective, not that my accent will be any good." Hugh was excited. He felt they were on the right track.

Len was back by nine the next morning. Nothing more had happened, Hugh told him, but the doctor had remarked that Esther's heartbeat was consistently stronger. He refused to attribute the improvement to Len's playing. He was much more skeptical than Nurse Gadger had been about the possibility that music might bring Esther out of her coma, but he said that at least it would do no harm.

So after the nurses had cleaned the room and seen to the patient, Len took his place again by the bed. He stared at the face swathed in bandages, and gave a long sigh. Then he propped Esther's hymn book on the dresser by the bed, put the strap of the guitar over his shoulder, and sat down. He had practiced much of the night. He was glad he had heard Esther sing in Romanian more than once and tried hard to remember how she had pronounced the words those many months ago. It was good, he told himself, that he wasn't attempting to sing in Russian or Chinese. Even so, he wasn't sure if the song would sound right coming from someone who knew no Romanian, but he'd give it a try.

Nurse Gadger came into the room to keep an eye on the patient while Len sang. At first, Len found her presence disconcerting. The nurse saw his nervousness and gave him a broad smile of encouragement. With a quick prayer for the stamina to go through with this, for he felt an utter fool, Len began in a low voice, *"Numai Harul, Numai Harul."* By the second verse, his voice had gained strength. The plaintive melody began to fill the room. He tried to focus on the image of a white-robed figure, her dark hair piled high on her head, her large dark eyes shining like an angel's, pouring out her heart in song. He closed his eyes. If he kept that image of Esther before him, he could sing better. By the third stanza, he had almost forgotten where he was.

Then he began to repeat the chorus again and again, sometimes changing the key slightly, sometimes just playing, sometimes just singing. Suddenly, Nurse Gadger let out an exclamation of astonishment and joy. Len stopped abruptly.

"I think, but I might be mistaken, that her eyelid fluttered just a tiny bit," the nurse told him. "Go on. Keep it up for a while longer."

For another half an hour, Len repeated the same song over and over again. Just when he felt he could not even sing one line more, the nurse came over to where he was sitting, bent over him and whispered, her voice tense with emotion, "Her one eye opened and looked at me then closed again."

Len almost dropped the guitar. "Are you sure?"

"I'm positive. Try it just once more. This time he kept his eyes fixed on Esther's face. It was one of the most thrilling moments of his entire life when he saw her right eyelid open and close. The nurse saw it too, and tears began to pour down her lined cheeks.

Soon Hugh had been told the news and Rachel and Mary had heard it, while they were eating their breakfast. And John heard it in Velours and immediately passed on the good news to Ron.

"You there, Ron?" John asked, when he had told his stepson the wonderful news. He had expected some sort of response, but it seemed an eternity before he heard Ron's voice at the other end. "Thanks for telling me, John," was all he said. The receiver clicked and the line went dead.

John stared at Diane in silence. "He's hung up on me," he told her.

Diane nodded. "He's too emotional to speak, John. Give him time. I mean, this'll be wonderful for him."

John stared down at the carpet. Something in the young man's voice sounded strange. Was he glad, or wasn't he?

That was the same question that Ron asked himself as he poured a glass of Pepsi a few moments later. What actually had been his reaction? Of course he was glad Esther had shown the first sign of life in days, but…?

He sat down in the recliner and sipped his drink. Deep down, he knew he was eaten up with jealousy. He also felt dreadfully confused and frustrated. His cousin, his good-for-nothing cousin, the guy who had to leave his church because he had played with girls' affections, had gone and stolen the show again. He had done what the faithful lover, the knight in shining armor, the wonderful, honorable Ron Atwood, had failed to do.

"The music did it," John had told him. Ron shook his head as he drained the last drop in his glass. No, his cousin had done it. He'd used his musical talent to charm the girl back to life. Now who would she be eternally grateful to? Then he gasped. What was he doing? Esther's life still hung in the balance, and here he was letting some insidious monster take over his soul when he needed to be back up there, by his love's side. He grabbed the phone and was soon sharing his plans and his hopes with his mother. An hour later, his red sports car was speeding its way down the interstate.

Meanwhile, Len was finding it difficult to cope. He was exhausted as well as deeply embarrassed by everyone's thanks and praise, well, not quite everyone's. Rachel had been unusually quiet over it all, though it was obvious that she was glad her cousin was waking from her long and frightening sleep.

As Len flopped on his bed in the motel later that morning, he found that the tears would flow. He wasn't weeping just for joy that Esther might, after all, be on the mend, or even that he had been at least partially responsible for it. He was overwhelmed by a deep sense of fulfillment he had never felt before. He realized, lying there staring up at the white ceiling tiles above him, that he had to take his hands off his life from then on. He must let God do with him what He would. Len turned over in his bed, gave a long sigh of contentment, and then fell into a dreamless sleep.

## Chapter Twenty-Five

### *Gabby Gets the News*

If she had not been so weary after arguing with Larry for an hour at least, Gabby would have found the train journey to Ploieşti very amusing. At first, she had refused to take him to her aunt's, knowing how tongues would wag, and how upset her aunt would be to see her trailing around Europe with a young man who, even with the greatest stretch of the imagination, could not be called Christian. But he had won the argument as usual with his persuasive reasoning and newly protective air that he had assumed since the plane had touched down in Bucharest earlier that day.

She had chosen to travel second class, partly out of habit and partly out of mischief. Gabby smiled to herself as she saw her companion pull out a snowy white handkerchief and put it to his nose with one hand, while he clutched the window strap with the other to prevent his falling on top of the old man in the ragged jacket beside him, who kept staring into his face as if he had seen a ghost. It was obvious that tourists weren't that plentiful yet, Gabby thought, though she had seen quite a few Westerners in the airport and at the hotel. But she guessed they didn't travel second class, at least not in Romanian trains.

Aunt Ana did not know they were coming. She still had no phone, and her niece's decision to come to Romania had been very sudden. Gabby felt so strange being in her native land again. Larry's presence made her conscious of how much her life had changed since she had slipped across the border to Poland three long years ago. She was no longer the innocent little Romanian girl who had kissed her aunt goodbye at the train station. She remembered how she had arrived in Velours that memorable night and found a transformed Esther. She had wondered if this Velvet Curtain her sister talked about, would affect her too. But of late, Gabby had come to identify this Curtain with liberty and freedom. She admitted that it had influenced her in many ways. That was why she had consented to leave the others in Frankfurt and agree to spend a week traveling with Larry. She knew quite well what it would probably entail. But that, she figured, was all a part of her new life.

Gabby glanced around the train compartment. There didn't seem to be any Velvet Curtain here, even though Romania now claimed to be a free country. The dirt and grime seemed even worse than before. And there were still beggars everywhere.

She peered through the grimy window and saw, in the distance, the flames from the oil refineries. That meant that they were nearing Ploieşti. She nudged Larry. "We'd better get our bags ready. The train only stops for two or three minutes, so we'll have to be quick."

Soon they were steaming into Gara de Sud. "We've arrived," she announced as she pushed her way down the narrow corridor. She felt rather pleased to be Larry's guide for once. He was so masterful in everything, but in Romania she had the advantage, for some of the time, at least.

Half an hour later, they were climbing up five flights of dingy stone steps to her aunt's apartment. They had discovered that the lift was broken. Gabby remembered that that was nothing new. Her heart was beating dreadfully fast as she put her hand to the little knocker on the familiar door. Number thirty-six was painted in faded white letters. She could hear her aunt talking to someone as she approached the door.

"She's got visitors," she whispered to Larry. "That's maybe just as well. She won't say so much in front of them." Larry said nothing. He was in a daze. He had never imagined Romania to be like this.

The door opened slowly. As Gabby stepped forward, her aunt stared in disbelief. "It can't be! It isn't…"

Gabby threw herself into Aunt Ana's arms. "Yes, it is, Aunt. It's your own Gabby."

Larry thought they would never stop hugging each other. He coughed slightly. Gabby broke away from her aunt's embrace. "Aunt, this is Larry Porter, a good friend of mine. He wanted to see what Romania is like," she said in Romanian. Then she switched to English. "Larry, this is my Aunt Ana."

Larry held out his hand as Gabby beckoned him to step inside. Ana took it in her thin, bony hands and said in Romanian, "Welcome to Romania, Larry." That was all she said. Her eyes seemed to bore holes in him, he told Gabby later, as he followed her into the hallway. Ana looked from Gabby to Larry in confusion. She glanced at Gabby's hand.

"He's just a very good friend, Aunt," Gabby stammered, blushing to the roots of her hair, as she took off her shoes and put them neatly by several other pairs lined up by the door. Then she stopped. Next to her aunt's was a pair of men's Nike shoes, which looked very American.

Ana followed her gaze and her whole expression changed. She grabbed Gabby by the arm and began in a very distressed tone, "Seeing you put everything out of my head. But Gabby, there's someone you know in the living room, and he's brought very bad news."

Larry didn't understand what the woman was saying but he saw Gabby's face blanch. "Bad news," she repeated. "Is it...?"

"Let him tell you himself. You'll get it more exactly from him."

Ana took Gabby's arm and led her into the small living room that also served as a bedroom when she had guests. She had forgotten completely about Larry. He followed Gabby and stopped stock still. There, sitting on the old green sofa, sat Aaron Gardner from Tiny Gap.

"Aaron!" Gabby gasped, "what news did you bring? Tell me quick!"

Aaron rose from his seat. He had heard Gabby's voice in the hallway, so was at least somewhat prepared. "Sit down first, then I'll tell you." His tone was unusually gentle. Larry helped her into the seat. Aaron nodded at him and then began, "Your sister has had a very bad accident."

Gabby stared at him unseeingly. "An accident?" she muttered almost unintelligibly.

"Yes."

"But she's alive?" The words came out from her mouth like bullets from a gun.

"Yes, but only just." Aaron was finding it hard to get it all out. "She's been in a coma for nearly two weeks. But yesterday I heard that she opened one eye several times. It is a good sign, but she's not out of the woods yet by any means."

"When did it happen?" Gabby managed to ask.

"On the Fourth, the day you left."

Gabby sprang from her seat and grabbed Aaron by the arm. "Then why, for goodness' sake," she almost shouted, "didn't anyone tell me? Didn't they think I'd care?"

Aaron waited till she had calmed down. "Gabby," his words were softly-spoken but very clear, "you didn't leave any address or phone number. They've been trying for days to get you a message."

Gabby's mouth fell open. Then she covered her face with her hands. Larry went up to Gabby and began to stroke her hair. "It's OK," he told her, "we'll get through this together, Gabby."

"I think a woman is needed at this time, young man," Aunt Ana told him curtly as she put her arms around her niece. Larry didn't understand a word but he got the message. He backed off and took a seat beside Aaron.

Gabby put her head on her aunt's shoulder and began to sob almost uncontrollably. "There now, Gabby *dragă*," Aunt Ana murmured soothingly, "God has Estera in His hands. Leave her there. Let us thank Him that she is still alive. Let us thank Him, Gabby." Gabby stopped crying. How could her aunt know that she couldn't thank Someone Whom she wasn't even sure existed?

"How did it happen?" she began, trying to focus on Aaron's face.

"She had a head-on collision with a truck. She was alone in the car at the time. She had been visiting friends in Silver Springs."

"How bad is she?"

"No one really knows yet. She's been in a coma all this time. But they're afraid she's injured for life if she recovers."

"But how did you know I'd be here?" Gabby went on, greatly puzzled.

"Well, as you know, I was in Germany all summer doing research. I had planned to come to Romania for a week or so just before I went home. Then my grandfather phoned me and told me about Esther. That was almost two weeks ago. So I came here a few days earlier than I had planned. I thought that just maybe you would visit Romania while you were in Europe. And you had given me your aunt's address, so I came straight here today. Oh Gabby, I'm so glad you've come!" Aaron's eyes filled with tears. "They've been nearly distracted trying to reach you."

"I don't think this is the time for reproaches," Larry broke in. He hated to see the look on Gabby's face when Aaron had said his last few words. "Can't you see the girl is shattered?"

Aaron turned and gave Larry one long look before he rose to his feet. "I suggest that you and I go into the town for a while and leave

Gabby alone with her aunt. She's had a real shock and I think needs a bit of mothering."

Larry's face flushed in anger. Aaron was so overbearing. He glanced at Gabby who shrugged her shoulders. She really didn't care what happened next. The news she had just heard had completely overwhelmed her.

"We'll need to talk over what we're going to do next," Larry said coolly.

"Of course, but give the girl a while to get over the shock first," Aaron advised.

Ana went up to Aaron and took him by the hand. "Listen," she said, "go back to Brother Luca's house where you're staying. I'm sure he'll keep this other young man for tonight. Sister Luca has a meal ready, she told me. You eat there and then come back and make your plans."

Aaron told Larry what Ana had suggested. He frowned and bit his lip. Their plans had gone awry again and there was nothing he could do about it.

# Chapter Twenty-Six

## *Gabby's Choice*

"This is the situation, Gabby." Larry was standing in the middle of Aunt Ana's tiny living room, looking very tired and not quite the impeccable young man Gabby was accustomed to.

"I'm waiting," Gabby told him, folding her arms and looking up at him with one of her cherubic expressions which always put him on his guard.

He and Aaron had just enjoyed a four course meal. Larry had been impressed, in spite of previous prejudices, by his first taste of both Romanian cuisine and hospitality. The dingy apartment buildings, dirty staircases, and odors which weren't very hard to define, had not prepared him for Brother Luca's immaculate, two-roomed apartment. He had stared in amazement at the antique bookcase and china cabinet, the exquisite tapestry and the colorful oriental rugs on the floor, the starched white tablecloth, sparkling crystal glasses, and shining silverware. All this had utterly confounded him. He thought he understood a little better why Gabby daily perplexed him.

After their delicious meal, Larry had found he could tolerate Aaron's company a little better. Their half mile walk to Brother Luca's had been taken in almost complete silence, but on their way back to Aunt Ana's, both their tongues were loosened. Each of them found themselves involved in the same tragic situation, and would soon have to help Gabby make some important decisions.

As they talked, however, Larry became more and more angry. He discovered that Aaron had called Gabby's aunt in the hospital, and had promised to do his best to find her niece and to bring her home as soon as possible. His assumption that he would be the one to conduct Gabby back to America infuriated Larry.

"Has it never occurred to you, Aaron, that the girl might just want to return home with me?"

Aaron's mouth fell open. He had assumed that Larry would want to finish his month's vacation. "There's no need of you to break your holiday like this," he stammered.

"No need?" Larry had stopped walking and turned to face his companion.

"Well, I'm going back anyway so…"

"You are jumping to some very hasty conclusions," Larry told him, nostrils flaring. "Has it not just occurred to you that I might decide that I have some sort of obligation to this young lady? I've become her very close friend, you know." There was something in Larry's words that sent the blood rushing into Aaron's cheeks. "And I'm not about to desert her now," Larry continued.

Aaron lifted his eyes to Larry's grey ones and said quietly, "Yes, you are one of her close friends, that's obvious, and I'm not. I do happen, though, to be more involved with her family than you are. I mean, had you intended to go to the hospital with her when you return?"

"What we decide to do is between Gabriella and me," Larry replied coldly as he began to walk again in the direction of Aunt Ana's apartment. "I tell you what," his face brightened, "let's put it to the girl and let her decide. Does she go back with you or with me?"

"Or with both of us?" Aaron couldn't help adding.

"No, it won't be with both of us. That's not a third alternative." Larry's eyes were steely as he went on, "I wouldn't like to put the poor girl into the situation of having to sit between us for hours on end."

Aaron had said nothing. And now sitting opposite Gabby, he waited patiently, arms folded, as Larry put before her the two choices. When he had finished, the girl glanced from one young man to the other. She remembered once having asked herself in Indianapolis what would she do if she had to choose which side she would take, Aaron's or Larry's. Now the moment had come. But there really was no choice at all. She had made her choice that day during Spring break. She had chosen her path. If she now decided to go home with Aaron, she would be indicating to herself and to Larry that she was taking her sister's path, and that she was certainly not ready to do.

"Of course I'll go with you, Larry," she sprung from her chair and put her hand in his.

He bent down and kissed her in front of them all, ignoring Aunt Ana's frown. Aaron turned away. Those two words, "of course" had stung him to the quick. It was as if he had never even existed as far as the girl was concerned.

Maybe Gabby had seen her aunt's expression or maybe she had felt a twinge of conscience, but the next moment she had left Larry's side and was standing in front of Aaron. She reached out her hand. "Thanks a lot for coming here and giving me news about Esther," she said, flashing him a brief smile. "I'll never forget what you did."

Aaron did not return the smile. After all, what good were words without actions? "I only did my duty," he told her abruptly.

"I'm sorry if I've upset your plans," Gabby went on hurriedly, "but I think it's best as it is."

Aaron looked at her long and hard. She desperately needed help and counsel, but he felt instinctively that he was not the one to give it, at least, not right then. "When will you leave?" he asked after a long silence.

Gabby looked at Larry. "He'll have to arrange it," she said. "I haven't got my wits about me yet. It is all such a shock."

Aaron nodded and handed her a slip of paper. "Here's the hospital phone number. You had better get in touch with them as soon as possible."

"I will." Gabby turned to Larry. "And now, I'm going to get a good sleep. I'll need it for tomorrow. Do you think if we arrived at the airport early in the morning, we'd get a seat right away? It is an emergency."

"Let's go for a short walk, Gabby. We need to talk things over," Larry suggested, taking her arm. "We'll be back in half an hour," he told Aaron as they made for the door.

They made their way down the five flights of stairs in silence. It was only when they reached the wide tree-lined avenue that led into the city that Larry began: "I know everything has come as a shock, Gabby, but we need to look at it all in a sane light."

"Meaning?"

"Meaning that I don't see the sense in rushing to the airport tomorrow morning at six o clock. We'd have to leave here at an unearthly hour. You need a good long sleep and so do I."

"I want to get back to Esther right away."

"I know. But we have to change our tickets, remember? And your sister is past the worst, isn't she? We'll call your aunt as soon as we've booked our flight. One or two days longer won't make a lot of difference."

"I suppose not," Gabby admitted reluctantly. "But we've got to go as soon as we can."

"Of course. We'll go back to Bucharest tomorrow. It's too late tonight. And we'll get the tickets changed at the airport or in an agency and hopefully get a flight for the next morning."

Gabby looked down at the pavement and then up into his face. They had booked a room together at the hotel near the airport. Larry had joked that this time, there would be no Rachel to turn up at the wrong moment.

Gabby kicked a stone with her toe. Had the Almighty stepped in again to make sure she stayed on the straight and narrow? If she insisted on going the next day, they wouldn't need to use that hotel room. She glanced up and she saw the look in Larry's eyes.

She stared at a tram which was stopping just beside them. Even though it was nine o'clock at night, there were at least twenty people waiting to get on. She watched them crowd up the steps, and heard the bell as the driver closed the doors. It slowly chugged its way up the road. That road was her road. She had chosen to take it and there was no going back for her.

She put her arm in Larry's. "I'll leave all the planning up to you now," she told him with a smile.

"That's my Gabby," he said, putting his arm around her and drawing her close.

Larry slept very well that night in spite of the springs which would stick into his ribs each time he turned, but Gabby did not. Aunt Ana had been very upset. She had pled with her niece to change her mind, to leave Larry and go with Aaron. And when her pleas seemed to fall on deaf ears, she began to warn and reproach. Gabby bore with it as best she could.

When Aunt Ana finally bade her niece good-night, Gabby's heart felt like a lump of lead. She wished her aunt had chosen other tactics that evening. She might even have relented. After all, she wasn't made of stone. She loved her family and her country, and she still cherished those memories which would flood her now and then and almost threaten to engulf her entirely. But she had questions that neither of her aunts, nor her sister, nor even Hugh Gardner could answer. She had tried their religion. It hadn't worked. So if there were no God, and if the Bible were not her standard of right and wrong, then, she was free to choose her own path without fear of the consequences.

She turned to face the wall as the clock struck two. Aunt Ana did not understand. The path she was taking would not lead to perdition; it had already proved a very pleasant path indeed. She often thought of Dr. Porter and Sally. No marriage vows held them together, yet they seemed perfectly happy and lived good, wholesome lives, as far as she could see.

Gabby put up her finger and traced the pattern on the faded wallpaper. How many times had she done that as a teenager, struggling with thoughts of bitterness against a God Who had taken her father and mother from her, leaving their two children almost alone in a cold and friendless world! And now He had let all this happen to her saintly sister, who was determined to devote her whole life to Him. Esther's accident had been the very last straw. Such a God didn't deserve her devotion.

She pushed the sheet aside. There was no air-conditioning and it was mid-July. Her hands were sticky and the back of her neck damp. She thought of the basement apartment in Indianapolis where she had been living for a month, with its private shower, plush recliner, and color TV. At that moment, she would give anything to be back where it was always cool even when the temperature soared to over a hundred outside. Maybe, she thought as she turned over again, just maybe, Romania wasn't all she had thought it to be. The clock struck three and four and when her aunt came to waken her at seven, she felt as if she had not slept a wink.

Larry arrived at eight. They wanted to be off in good time for they had to arrange for a flight the next day. Goodbyes were brief and, on Gabby's part at least, tearless. But for days afterwards, when she closed her eyes, she could see the two figures leaning over the banister—small, tiny Aunt Ana, waving a snowy white handkerchief in one worn gnarled hand, and Aaron, his thick brown locks as unruly as ever, his face solemn, his eyes sad, with one arm round the little woman by his side and the other waving them off just as if he did it every day.

## Chapter Twenty-Seven

### *Under the Bandages*

"Gabby is coming back tomorrow," Mary announced to the others as they ate lunch together in the hospital cafeteria. She had been called to the phone just before they had begun their meal.

"That's great!" Rachel said, draining her coffee cup.

"She'll be at the Knoxville airport tomorrow at ten-thirty in the evening," Mary continued. "One of us needs to go and pick her up. By the way, Larry's coming back with her."

"Isn't Aaron bringing her home?" Hugh sounded very surprised.

"No. Evidently not. The line was terrible. She was phoning from a post office and had tried three times already to get through, so we couldn't speak much."

"Well, it's a relief to know she'll be with her sister soon," Len commented. He had decided to go back to Cincinnati for a time at least. Since Esther had regained consciousness, she needed almost constant medical care. He figured he could only be in the way if he stayed on. He would drive Hugh back to his house that evening, and then make for home.

Mary got up from the table. "Have you forgotten that we're to hear the specialist's report on Esther at one this afternoon? We'd better get going."

They all looked at one another. As long as the patient had remained in a coma, it had been difficult to assess the exact extent of her injuries, but now she was undergoing several important tests. Dr. Garrington had told Mary that he would have some report to give when the specialist had been to see her that morning.

Rachel thought Dr. Garrington looked especially solemn as he greeted them a few moments later. He cleared his throat and began, "I know you are all overjoyed that Esther has come out of her coma. However," he coughed again and avoided their eyes, "the prognosis is not good."

"Tell it to us straight, Doctor," Rachel told him, gripping her chair with both hands.

"I will, young lady, though it's not going to be what you want to hear. Your cousin has had multiple injuries. It is a miracle she is alive. But she will never walk again, I'm afraid."

There were gasps all round. Mary's eyes were filled with tears as she asked in a tremulous voice, "You mean, never?"

"I'm afraid so."

"And her head injuries?" Hugh's voice sounded strange even to himself.

"Fortunately they're not too severe."

"Thank God!" Mary exclaimed.

The doctor turned and looked straight at her. "But your niece will be scarred for life, you know."

Mary stared back in dismay. She felt sick. That beautiful, extraordinarily beautiful girl marred for life. It just couldn't be!

"But what about plastic surgery?" Ron found himself asking.

"She's already had some surgery, of course. The gash was ugly and had to be taken care of right away. But the actual plastic surgery has to be done later." He saw the expression on all their faces and continued hurriedly, "Modern techniques are so advanced that amazing things can be done. But her left cheek and eye were badly hit. In fact, we're hoping she does not lose her sight in one eye. I believe she was a real beauty?"

They all nodded. Mary pulled out a picture of Esther at her last concert. Dr. Garrington took it in his hands and stared at it in silence for a few moments. "She'll never be like that again," he whispered, "never! And she'll be in a wheelchair for the rest of her life."

No one spoke for a while. "Is Esther aware of all this?" Mary asked.

"No. And when she is, she'll need all of your support. In fact, some in her situation have lost all desire to live. That's the danger."

"Our Esther won't do that," Mary said confidently. "She has faith in God and will pull through."

Hugh looked at her strangely. "But she is human, Mary. It'll be touch and go if she can accept this terrible verdict."

Len stared at his friend. Esther Popescu, that white-robed angel he saw in his imagination so often, not accept anything from the Almighty?

Hugh caught his gaze and held it. "She may need your music again, Len," he told him. The doctor had slipped out and they were left alone.

Len shook his head. "I don't think so. I think my services are finished now. And anyway," he glanced at his cousin, "Ron's here. I'm not needed any more."

Ron gave a short laugh. "Me? I doubt it. You're the hero of the show, Len."

The bitterness in his tone was unmistakable. Len colored a vivid red and bit his lip. This is just what he didn't want—another rupture between him and his cousin just when they were becoming real friends. He rose from his chair. "Look everybody, let's get this straight. It wasn't me who did anything. It was music, harmony, memories of the past. Anyone of you would have achieved the same results if you had done what I did. Anyway, it was Hugh's idea. I didn't want to do it."

"That's right," Hugh reiterated. "I had a job to persuade him. But I know it was the Lord Who put the whole idea into my head, so let's all give Him the glory."

Ron rose from his chair and slipped out of the room. Give God the glory? It was all right for the others to talk like that. He knew nothing about God or His glory and probably never would. It was good he had to be in Nashville the next morning. He had left everything and come up the day before when he had heard of Esther's coming to consciousness. Nurse Gadger had let him see her right away. But she had showed no signs of recognition when he had tried to talk to her, though he thought she could hear him by the occasional twitch of her eyelid and the slight movement of her fingers.

Ron drove mechanically to the motel, left a note that he was leaving but would keep in touch daily about Esther's condition, and then made for Nashville.

When Hugh read Ron's note later that afternoon, he shook his head. "Your cousin needs God in his life, Len," he told his companion sadly. "Neither he nor any of us can make it through times like this without His strength."

That evening, when they had arrived home safely and were sitting on the porch, watching the sun set over the mountains, Hugh startled Len by saying, "Don't leave for Cincinnati tomorrow. Stay at least one week longer. I have a feeling you may be needed again at the hospital."

Len shook his head. "I think you're wrong there," he said with a slight smile. "My part in Esther's drama is over now."

"And I think it's you who are wrong," Hugh countered. "At least, take a few more days to pray and study and think about your future. I'm going to do the same. In one week, I've got to give my final answer regarding the offer of a pastorate. And remember, if I take it, I will need an assistant whom I can trust, someone who thinks like me, at least on the important issues of life."

Len hung his head. "I'll never be suitable or trustworthy, Hugh, never."

"So you're limiting God's grace?"

"No, of course not! I'm only too aware of my ability to receive that grace."

"Then make room for more, Len, that's the secret. Emptying and filling—that's the secret."

"I know that in theory," Len said thoughtfully, "but practically, it's awfully hard."

"Don't I know it!" and Hugh let out a long sigh as he leaned back in his seat.

"And I don't think I'll ever be different."

"In what way?" Hugh wanted to know.

"Well, take for example when the nurses try to get my attention, I kind of like it. It flatters my ego."

"I saw them making eyes at you," Hugh grinned. "And I'm not sure if that'll ever change. Esther couldn't help men looking at her either."

Len's face sobered. "I'm sure she must have depended a lot on her beauty, maybe more than she realized."

Hugh nodded. "I'm almost sure she did. Tell you the truth," his voice fell to almost a whisper, "it'll be a miracle if she pulls through. I'm afraid she has lost her will to live."

"How do you know?"

"I watched her several times. I think she may be more conscious than we think. She's shutting out the world around. Someone who can handle that needs to spend a lot of time with her, and I don't know who it would be. Ron seems to be falling to pieces." Hugh wrinkled his forehead as if deep in thought.

"Who better than yourself, Hugh?"

"Me?" Hugh laughed. "Are you forgetting that I'm seventy-five? Of course, I'll always do what I can, but that won't be enough in these circumstances. Now if only Ron…" He stopped.

"Yes?"

"If only he knew the Lord, Len, and they were engaged or married, I think he just might pull Esther out of this. She'd have an incentive to live. But now, with Gabby taking her fling and worlds apart from her sister, and no parents to take care of her, it doesn't look hopeful. I know Mary will do her best, but she's not her flesh and blood." He paused and tears filled his eyes as he added, "Crippled as the girl will be and scarred as well, maybe it would be better for the Lord to take her. She'll be able to walk up there and sing, and she'll be her old beautiful self, even more so." Hugh wiped two large tears that were making their way down his weather-beaten cheek.

Len took out his Kleenex and blew his nose. Then he began slowly, "But don't you think that Ron could be the one still? I know he has searched for God during these past years."

"Then why has he not found Him?"

Len paused. "That's a question only he can answer, I suppose," he said after a few moments' thought.

"Yes, it is," Hugh agreed. "But we are sure of one thing: if we seek Him with all our heart, we will find Him. You're discovering that, aren't you Len?"

"Yes, every day."

"Then Ron will find Him, too, when he meets that condition. Now, let's have a good hot cup of English tea."

"Can I have iced tea, please?"

"You're welcome to your iced tea," Hugh said with a grin.

While the two men were sitting chatting together on Hugh's porch in Tiny Gap, Rachel had arrived at Knoxville airport and was waiting impatiently for her cousin to arrive. At last, she saw Larry's tall figure pushing the luggage cart up the long ramp that led to the swinging doors. Gabby walked at his side, slightly tanned and slimmer than ever, but looking very tired.

A moment later, and her cousin's arms were around her neck. "Oh, Rachel, I'm so glad to be back!" Gabby exclaimed. Rachel felt Gabby's tears on her face. She stroked her hair and muttered, "And we're so glad to have you back. Esther needs you." Gabby pulled away. She felt so guilty at not having come sooner.

"Where's the car?" Larry asked. He had greeted Rachel very briefly and, the girl thought, very coldly. She knew he had not forgotten that night in Florida.

Soon they were speeding towards the city. "There's a motel nearby which is very convenient," Rachel told Larry. "The others stay there when they're visiting at the hospital. There are special rates for visitors. And you're coming with us, aren't you, Gabby? To our old apartment, I mean. We've been staying there, Mom and I, for nearly three weeks now."

"She's staying with me till I go back to Indianapolis, whenever that might be," Larry told Rachel coldly. "We've decided that already, haven't we, Gabby?"

Gabby gulped, and looked out her window at the cars speeding by. "Yes. I think it's best for right now, Rachel."

"But why? I mean, you aren't…?"

"We're not married if that's what you're asking, or even engaged." Larry's tone was very sarcastic. "But we've become very close this summer and we've decided that we're not going to be kept apart any longer." Rachel's eyes blazed but she held her tongue. This wasn't the time to blow her top.

"You see, Rachel," he began again, and his tone was condescending, "you need to understand that Gabby needs me right now. I need her too, come to think of it."

Gabby saw the expression on her cousin's face and cringed. But it was only what she had expected. She had been determined not to act the hypocrite in front of her family. If she stayed with her aunt and cousin, there would be a dreadful strain. But she had come to feel at home with Larry. He had been so caring and considerate just when she was most in need of a comforter. She had no restraints with him now.

Rachel kept her eyes on the road ahead and said nothing during their drive to the hospital. She felt like giving them both a lash of her tongue. Now, while her cousin was still hovering between life and death, these two were acting like irresponsible teenagers. Then she remembered that Gabby probably did not know her sister's true condition. Once she saw that, it might be a different story.

Half an hour later, Gabby was sitting by Esther's side. Tears trickled down her cheeks and onto her sleeveless, floral top, some even making wet patches on her denim shorts as she gazed at the bandages which still swathed her sister's head and much of her face, though her arms were free now. Gabby reached up and took Esther's small, thin hand in hers. "I've come at last," she whispered.

Esther opened the one eye that was uncovered. Gabby felt her fingers twitch slightly in her hand. "You must get better; we're all missing you terribly," Gabby continued, her eyes fixed on her sister's face. That one eye seemed to stare right through her; then it closed again.

Gabby rose from the bed. It was too horrid for words. She couldn't stand it any longer. She fled the room and found herself in Larry's arms.

"This girl desperately needs a good night's rest," he told the others. "We'll be back first thing tomorrow." Gabby kissed her aunt and Rachel and they were gone.

True to their word, Gabby and Larry were back early the next morning. They insisted on relieving Rachel and her mom, who were almost at the end of their tether. For the next five hours, Gabby made frequent visits to room 301 and always with the same result. Esther would open one eye, move her fingers slightly, and then all would be still again.

That afternoon, Nurse Gadger announced that they were going to remove the bandages from Esther's face. Her eye had been operated on some days previously and now was the time to see if it had been successful. An hour later the eye specialist came in smiling. "It's successful," he said. "She won't lose that eye."

Mary, who had returned to the hospital, gave Gabby a hug as she exclaimed, "Thank God! That's the first piece of good news we've heard in three weeks."

Gabby rose from her chair. "I want to see her," she told Larry, "without the bandages."

As she entered the little room that had virtually become Esther's home now, Gabby saw for the first time the large deep scar across her sister's left cheek, just missing her eye and stretching up into the side of her forehead. The wound had been sewn very neatly and the nurse assured them that the scar would gradually fade to some extent at least, no one knew quite how much.

Gabby stared in shocked silence at her sister's face. A black eye patch covered the one eye. Her long raven locks had all been shaved, and it was only that one dark eye with the long curling lashes and the lips that curved just like they always did but which were so pale and bloodless now, that told Gabby that this was indeed her sister.

She had not realized how much the girl in the bed could comprehend until she saw her lips compress slightly. Then she detected a startled, frightened look in that one good eye as it caught Gabby's shocked expression. The head turned to one side and the eye closed. Gabby took her sister's hand. This time, tears would not come. She felt dry-eyed and heart-sick as she whispered softly, "I love you, Esther. You'll always be my own precious sister."

There was no movement of the head, no pressure of the hand, just total stillness. Gabby rose from the chair and backed out the door. "Take me away, Larry," she pleaded, as she bumped into him in the corridor. "I've got to get out of here for a while."

That evening, John and Ron arrived. The older man had questioned whether it was wise for Ron to return to the hospital. "I can't keep away," Ron admitted, as they entered the hospital foyer and made for the elevator. Mary's heart sank as she met them in the corridor. How could she prepare them for what was awaiting them?

John was the first to go into Esther's room and when he came back he looked ten years older. "I don't know if you'd better go in, Ron," he said. "The bandages are off and, well, she's terribly changed."

"I've got to face it sometime, and the sooner I get it over with the better." Ron tried to keep his tone calm as he squared his shoulders and exited the waiting-room. The others waited apprehensively; no one spoke as the minutes ticked by. When he did not appear after twenty minutes, John rose and tiptoed to the door of room 301. Ron was sitting, head in hands, shoulders heaving though no sound escaped him.

John glanced at the bed and gave a start. Esther's one large dark eye was fixed on the figure in the chair. Then as John stared, he saw her thin arm move for the first time. A sudden strength seemed to suddenly fill her frail body as she reached out a hand and pulled up the sheet which was folded over her chest and placed it over her face till it covered it completely. Ron looked up just then and saw it all. "Esther, no!" he exclaimed out loud and literally ran from the room.

Nurse Gadger appeared from nowhere and took in the situation at a glance. She went up to the sick girl. She took the sheet and folded it back again over her chest. "You mustn't do that, my dearie," she said in her thick Irish accent, "but at least you've shown strength you've not shown since you were brought in here."

She motioned for John to leave the room as she drew the curtains around the bed. Rachel met him in the corridor. "Dad, what's happened? Ron ran down the corridor to the elevator. You'd better go after him. Something's dreadfully wrong."

"Don't worry, I'll take care of him," he reassured his daughter.

Half an hour later, Nurse Gadger described in detail what had happened. "It's good and it's bad," she told Rachel and Mary. "Good, because Esther reacted more than she's done since her accident and it shows she's aware of what's going on, more than we've realized. But it's bad because it indicates that she wishes to hide herself from the world." Nurse Gadger hesitated before adding bluntly, "The girl wants to die. I know the signs. Unless another miracle happens, we'll either lose our patient after all, or she'll stay alive, but turn into a bitter, morose and unmanageable cripple. I've seen it all before." Nurse Gadger turned away and left the room.

The next day Ron had regained his courage and insisted on sitting with Esther. This time he did not weep. He was determined to master his feelings. So he took the sick girl's hand and murmured, "Esther, it's OK. I'm here. I love you." He looked into that one dark eye fixed on his face. Then the hand came up again and pulled the sheet over her face, but he was prepared and pulled it away. This happened three times. The third time Esther's lips moved. He bent over to catch her words. "I want to die," she whispered. Then again, stronger this time, "I want to die."

In spite of all his resolutions, he simply could not take it any longer. Out in the corridor, he told Nurse Gadger what had happened. She shook her head. "Keep at it, if you can. Maybe you'll get her to change her attitude," she told him.

For the next three days, Ron made frequent visits to Esther's room, but instead of things improving, they got steadily worse. His presence always seemed to harass the patient. Sometimes she'd shake her head at him; sometimes she would try to pull the sheet over her face. Once she mustered all the energy she could and exclaimed with a strength that seemed almost supernatural, "It's no use. I'm going to die. Leave me alone."

It took all Ron's strength not to turn heel and go back to Nashville immediately. He had taken a week off work but that week was coming to a close. He told Nurse Gadger that he had only a few more days. "Keep hoping for a miracle," she told him.

Then the crisis came the evening before he was due to leave. He was attempting, as he had done so many times before, to reassure Esther of his love, when she turned her head and looked at him full in the face with that one terrible eye. Then summoning all the strength she had, she half raised her head and pointed at him. "You don't love me *now*," she said very clearly. Then she lifted herself still higher in the bed as she repeated the words, "Ron, you don't love me *now*."

He tried to remonstrate, to reassure, but the words sounded tinny and unreal. He took another look at the girl whom he had so proudly shown off to all his friends, the angel who had been his guiding star—the unbelievably beautiful, perfect Esther. He tried to ignore her shaved head, her scarred face, her angry expression. But it was no use. The bitter wreck of a woman he saw before him was now the real Esther Popescu. He had to face reality.

Back in his motel room he threw himself on the bed. Did he still love her—love her, not as she had been, but as she was now? But who was she? Did he know her, really and truly? Could he still take her in his arms, kiss her scarred face and say truthfully, "I love you, my Esther"?

That night as the shadows fell and the world outside grew still, Ron Atwood came face to face with himself and he didn't like what he saw. Where was the gallant, noble knight who had three brief years ago been willing to sacrifice his own happiness in order to save his lady's life? He had been willing to forgo a future which spelled nothing but bliss for him. Where was that same courage now?

He wasn't sure of the answer. He only knew that before, there had been no alternative. Esther would have died if he had not made his sacrifice. But what would it take now to save her life? A pledge of lifelong devotion to a scarred and bitter cripple? Maybe he would find that his love was that deep. But didn't Esther need more than that? Didn't she need restoration—an injection of faith to save her from despair and even death? Didn't she need to accept her fate and bow to it? And he had no faith. He could not point her to God for he did not know the way himself.

"You don't love me," she had said.

"But I do," he shouted into the darkness. "You're wrong. I do."

"You love the Esther that was," she seemed to call back mockingly. "You loved my beauty. You admired my figure. You were allured by my lips; you were moved by my voice. But I have no beauty. My body is twisted. I have no figure to allure you now. My voice is no longer sweet as an angel's, for my spirit is bitter, and my faith buried under the wreck of my life. This is the Esther that is. And you cannot, do not love *her*."

Ron buried his head in the pillow. He remembered their conversations together. The main subject had been her beauty, her talent, her goodness, or what he could buy for her—a new dress, a pair of shoes, a pearl necklace! But Esther's soul? He did not know that, had never known that, and certainly didn't know it now. And how could he love what he didn't know?

The next morning, Ron told John he was going home. He found out that Larry was returning to Indianapolis that day. So they decided to rent a car and travel together.

Larry kissed Gabby, nodded at the others, and got behind the wheel. Ron lingered a few moments. He felt he was saying goodbye to Esther for good. He looked up at the mammoth building looming in front of him, his face ashen, his eyes sad.

Mary came over and kissed him on the cheek. "It's best if you go, Ron," she said. "You can't take this any longer. But remember, we all love you. You are a very special young man. I've always thought that, and God is looking for you. In all this tragedy, He's looking for you."

"Bye Mary, bye girls, take care of…," his voice broke, "of *her*," and he was gone.

## Chapter Twenty-Eight

*I Want to Die!*

Gabby switched on the TV. She couldn't stand the quiet. Larry had gone, and she was back in the apartment she had shared with Rachel and Andrea for the past year. She didn't like being alone. Rachel and her mother had taken a much needed break at home while Gabby held the fort. She was glad that Hugh and Len had just arrived and had offered to stay at the hospital that night. The next day they were moving Esther out of intensive care. This would mean that her friends and family could be with her as much as they wished.

Gabby's eyes misted over. No one had voiced the fears that clutched at all their hearts and tormented their minds. Just what would happen to the crippled girl? She couldn't stay in the hospital forever, though it would be a while yet before she would be transferred to a rehab center. They would start intensive physiotherapy the next day, but the specialist had told them that very afternoon that much depended on the patient's spirit. If she remained listless and unresponsive and did not cooperate with the therapist, then she might have to lie flat on her back for the rest of her life. If this happened, a nursing home would be the only alternative. A home nurse was a possibility, but that was probably financially impossible.

Gabby stared unseeingly at the TV screen. She felt miserable and very depressed. Rachel had definitely given her the cold shoulder since she had returned from Romania. Her aunt had been loving enough, but Gabby couldn't stand the look of pity mixed with reproach in those blue eyes that often seemed to rest on her face. She had been relieved at first when Larry had left. His presence was too overpowering at times. But he had not been gone two days before she wondered when he would return. The worst of it was that she scarcely knew what sort of relationship existed between them.

Gabby lay back in the recliner and closed her eyes. She felt that she was an outcast in her family now. The shrill ring of the telephone interrupted her reverie. It was Larry. Could she not come down for a week to Indianapolis? He was missing her very much, he said. She couldn't stay with Esther all the time, he told her. She needed a break. No, he wasn't coming up just yet. He felt very uneasy with her family and superfluous at the hospital.

"I'll have to stay till Aunt Mary returns with Rachel in a few days," she told him wearily. "No, I'm not alone. Len and Hugh will take turns to relieve me."

Larry groaned. That was just what he didn't want. "Well, come as soon as Mary gets back," he told her.

"I will," Gabby reassured him. She would give anything to get away from the smell of ether, the sight of bandages, the endless corridors, and the meals in the cafeteria when hardly anyone spoke and the food was horrid.

"But I'm going to be specially loving to Esther," she promised herself as she went to bed that night. "I'm her nearest and dearest after all." The prospect was not cheering. She had tried talking to her sister, telling her she loved her, kissing her, but Esther's one good eye had just kept staring at her. Even if she got angry or cross it would be better than stony silence, Gabby thought.

Hugh was thinking much the same as he sat at Esther's bed that evening. He had not been prepared for what lay under the bandages. He now understood Ron's reaction. That one eye seemed to take in every expression on his face. He had prayed with the girl, had read some verses of Scripture, had spoken soothingly to her, but there had been no response. A week had passed since they had last been at the hospital. They had come back to be with Gabby for a few days till her aunt and cousin returned.

"You may need to use your guitar again, young man," he told Len when he went back into the waiting room. "Tomorrow, she'll be moved from here and we'll be able to spend a lot of time with her. Be ready to have another try, but be prepared for what you find. You won't recognize much of the old Esther any more," and Hugh shook his head sadly. It took all the faith he had to keep hold of the promise that "All things do indeed work for good to those who love the Lord." And Esther did love the Lord, he knew that.

The next day Gabby arrived and told the men to get some sleep. She watched as they moved her sister to the floor below. She had a room to herself, and the window overlooked the quadrangle at the back of the hospital.

"You can stay with your sister as long as you like," the nurse on duty told Gabby, as she pulled the curtains from around Esther's bed and motioned to Gabby to enter. The second floor was not Nurse Gadger's domain, though she assured them that she would still try to keep an eye on the patient from time to time.

There was a seat that reclined in one corner of the room and a TV. Gabby settled into her chair, drew out a book from her bag, and tried to read. From time to time, she would speak a few reassuring words to the motionless form in the bed, or watch as the nurses came to turn the patient, or take her vital signs, or change the feeding tube. They were going to try taking it out in a day or so, the nurse had told Gabby.

Then mid-morning, Doris, the physiotherapist, and her assistant arrived. Gabby slipped out of the room, but a few moments later, she was called back in. "Can you try to persuade your sister to cooperate with us?" Doris whispered as she drew Gabby into the doorway. "She stiffens right up and refuses to even move one muscle. We suspect she can do it, for she isn't paralyzed, but we know that it must be painful. Try explaining to her that the consequences are grim indeed if she doesn't let us help her now."

Gabby swallowed hard. "I'll try," she said, but she hadn't much hope that her words would do any good. She went over to the bed and bent over her sister. The eye patch had been removed, much to Gabby's relief.

"Esther," Gabby began, "you've got to let these doctors and nurses help you get better. If you don't move your limbs even a little, you're going to be bedridden for life."

Esther's eyes remained closed but her eyelids were flickering. "I know you are hearing me, Esther," Gabby said, her tone showing just a little exasperation. "And I know you can speak when you have to. Ron told me that."

Esther's eyes opened at the mention of Ron. Her lips opened and she began to speak in a weak but fairly clear voice. "I want to die, Gabby. Let me alone. Please tell them to let me alone."

Gabby gulped hard. How did one cope with this? She couldn't, she knew that. Maybe Hugh would succeed. She gave one last try. "You're not going to die, Esther. We need you; I need you. Please do what they say. Give it a try, please."

Esther's shook her head slightly and said again. "Leave me alone. I want to die."

"It's no use," she told the physiotherapist.

"At least you got her to speak," Doris told her, patting Gabby on the shoulder. "Keep it up. Try provoking her a little, just a little. It might do some good. We'll try again later today."

Gabby did try hard to provoke her sister that day but it was hard to keep it low-keyed. "Don't be so spoiled," she found herself saying once. Esther had just stared at her and turned her head away. Gabby really felt angry with her sister. Sure, she was in a very sad and pitiable state, but she could at least show some gratitude to those around her. This was not the Esther she had grown up with. A knot tightened in her stomach. This was just another proof that God did not exist.

Gabby was more than relieved when she saw Hugh's familiar face peek in the doorway late that afternoon. "Come in, Mr. Hugh," she told him.

"Well, young lady," Hugh told the patient, as he approached the bed. "You are improving. Here you are out of intensive care at last. This is one of God's miracles!"

Esther positively frowned at him and her large dark eyes narrowed. "I want to die," she said, turning her head away.

"Please try to persuade her to cooperate with the doctors and nurses," Gabby whispered. "I've been trying all day but it's no use."

She got up glad to escape. "I'm going out for a while," she told Hugh. "I'll be back this evening."

Hugh watched her slip out of the room. He sighed and turned back towards the girl in the bed. "I want to die," the girl muttered again and again. Doris came back again but to no avail. She shrugged her shoulders after trying for half an hour to get the patient to move her toes and fingers. Hugh followed her into the corridor.

"I'll have to report this to Dr. Garrington," Doris told him. "If this goes on, it will be fatal to the girl."

Dr. Garrington told Hugh the same thing later when they removed the feeding tube. The nurse brought in some chicken broth and they both watched as Esther closed her lips firmly just as the spoon reached her mouth. The broth spilled down over the napkin lying on her chest.

"Maybe she'll take some dessert," the doctor suggested.

The nurse nodded, and in no time at all had produced some Jell-O and ice cream but it was the same story. Esther would not eat.

"We'll keep the tube out for a while," the doctor told them, "and see if she gets hungry. If not, then, it goes back in."

Tubes all her life? Hugh didn't ask the question. It would be premature, but it would have to be asked sooner or later.

In their motel room that evening, Hugh had a long talk with Len. "You're going to have to try your music tomorrow," he told him. The young man nodded. He'd try; he'd do his best, but now that the patient was conscious, it was highly unlikely she would respond to anything he would do. Esther had never liked him, he thought. And he couldn't blame her. He epitomized all that she liked least about American religious culture. To her he was an integral part of that Velvet Curtain which had nearly smothered her.

The next morning Nurse Gadger smiled when she saw him approach Esther's room with his guitar. She had just been visiting her old patient. "Good, young man. You succeeded once; you may again."

Len shook his head mournfully. "But she's conscious now."

"So?"

"She's never liked me, Nurse Gadger. So what good can I do now?"

The nurse stared at him for a few moments. "You won't do any harm, at least," she told him with a smile. "And if she gets angry with you, that's OK. An angry response is better than none at all."

Len had to repeat these words to himself during the next half hour. The minute he had entered the room, Esther's eyes had been fixed on his face. Although Hugh had warned him, it was almost impossible not to reveal his shock. Could that be Esther Popescu? But those dark black eyes were the same, and that mouth, and nose, they were all the same. That at least was a comfort, though the eyes were no longer sparkling with life, but full of frustration and anger.

Len took his guitar and began to sing and play. Esther was startled at first and shook her head quite violently at him. Then, raising herself slightly in the bed, she looked straight at him. "Leave me alone," she said very distinctly. "I'm going to die. It's no use. Leave me alone."

Len ignored her and began to play *Numai Harul*. Every word was an effort and a prayer. The perspiration stood out in beads on his forehead, but still he kept on singing. Keeping his eye on the guitar, he could continue, but he daren't look at the girl in the bed.

When he had reached the third verse, he thought he heard what sounded like a faint sigh. Cautiously, he raised his eyes and found Esther staring fixedly at his face. As she caught his gaze, her face puckered into a frown. "Your accent's terrible," she grumbled. "I don't want your music."

Len put down his guitar. He just had to leave the room. Then, from somewhere far beyond and above him, Len felt an infusion of strength racing into him. He wouldn't give in to this girl. She couldn't hurt him like she had Ron. He really had nothing to lose.

Grabbing his guitar again, he looked Esther straight in the eyes and said coolly, "Stop interrupting, Esther. I'm going to finish my song. And how can I have a good accent when no one's tried to teach me?"

He didn't wait for a response but began to sing again. When he had finished, there was complete silence in the room. He looked over at the bed. The patient's eyes were closed and her breathing was regular. He slipped out of the room. Collapsing into a chair in the waiting-room, he wiped his forehead with his Kleenex.

"What happened?" Hugh asked.

"She told me to go, of course," Len muttered with a half laugh, "but being stubborn, I kept right on."

"And?"

"I think she's asleep now."

Hugh stared at his friend but said nothing. Len's eyes were closed and he seemed utterly exhausted. A few minutes later, Nurse Gadger popped her head round the door and confirmed what Len had said. "The nurse on duty has just told me that Esther's sleeping," she told the men with a broad smile. "He's done it again," and she pointed triumphantly to Len as she spoke.

"It's not me, Nurse," Len said quietly. "She told me to go as she always does. But somehow the music gets right to her. Anyone could do what I did."

"I don't think so," she told him. "But that's beside the point. It was you who did it and it is you who must keep on doing it. Try your music again this afternoon, nurse's orders. And meanwhile get a good meal to keep up your strength. You'll sure need it."

And he did. That afternoon, that evening, the next morning, the next afternoon, and so on—for one whole week, Len visited Esther four times a day and stayed about half an hour each time. Always he took his guitar, sometimes just playing, sometimes singing.

His reception was varied. At least half the time he was ordered out of the room, and sometimes the patient's displeasure was so great that he had no choice but to go. At times like these, he told Hugh that he was going back home the next morning. Then Nurse Gadger would persuade him to keep at it. Reluctantly, he would pick up his guitar once more and try again. Sometimes he could laugh it off and persevere until he would see those great dark eyes close and hear her regular breathing. And sometimes, she would just lie and stare at him, saying nothing. The patient still refused to eat so now the feeding tube was in again. And Doris still could make little headway. Music soothed her but had not yet given her the will to live.

After the first three sessions, Len phoned Gabby in Indianapolis and asked for a list of Esther's favorite music. Gabby was skeptical, but made out a list of the songs and hymns and classical pieces that she knew Esther used to play. Len went meticulously over each one and practiced for hours in his motel room.

On the third morning, he arrived at the hospital to find Nurse Pennington, all smiles. She was Esther's main nurse now. Young and pretty, she had been only too glad to follow Nurse Gadger's advice to keep an eye on Len and encourage him with his *music therapy*, as she called it.

"Look in Esther's room, will you," the nurse told Len. "You'll get a surprise." And he did. Sitting in the corner of the room, was a keyboard, one of the latest, on a stand.

"One of Esther's friends sent it," she told the astonished Len. "That person wishes to be kept anonymous. But they thought that maybe Esther might respond even more to organ and piano music."

Len was skeptical at first. Gingerly he sat down on the stool and ran his fingers over the keys, conscious that the eyes of the girl in the bed were fixed on him.

"What shall I play, Esther?" he asked without looking round. He always dreaded looking into that pale, sad face that held only a very faint reminder of the Esther of by-gone days, and he seldom greeted her for it seemed to perturb her. Conversation annoyed her. It was only while he sang and played that she seemed to be at peace.

Now, as he expected, there was no answer from the bed by the window, so he chose the church organ mode and soon the rich strains of "Amazing Grace" were filling the room. As the last note died away, he glanced towards the bed. The girl had turned her head away so he could not see the expression on her wan face, but to his amazement and consternation, he saw her chest heaving and thought he could hear one or two stifled sobs.

He rose abruptly and made for the door. Esther turned her head and her face was tearstained. Pointing to the keyboard, she whispered, "Go on. Play some more."

Len was stunned. This was much more than he had ever dreamed of. He sat down again and for one hour, he played hymn after hymn. Then he felt Nurse Pennington's hand on his shoulder. "I think that's enough for one day," she whispered.

Len made for the door and threw one last, furtive glance at the girl in the bed. She was asleep, and for the first time since her accident, a very faint smile was playing on her lips as if her dreams were no longer of screeching brakes, clashing metal, and splintering glass, but of angels and Heaven, of days without pain, and of a body that was whole again.

That night Len dropped into bed exhausted, but the happiest he had been in months. He was of some use after all. Maybe soon he would be redundant once more, but for one night at least, he was a musician who had achieved his dream and he would make the best of it. God had used his music to give one scarred, crippled girl at least a temporary reprieve from hopelessness and despair. And that made life worth living. And maybe when he had done all he could with Esther, God would use him somewhere else. He gave a sigh of satisfaction and fell into a deep and dreamless sleep.

# Chapter Twenty-Nine

## *Len Takes a Break*

It wasn't long before Len found himself spending most of his day in the sick room. Although the patient still pouted and grumbled at him, it was obvious that she preferred his presence to anyone else's. When Doris tried therapy once more, it was Len who was called in to persuade Esther to comply. The pain was so great, however, that Len had to take her thin hand in his and squeeze it gently, while the therapist worked on her hands and feet. And it was then that he received the first sign of gratitude from the sick girl.

"Thanks, Len," she whispered as she lay back exhausted. Len said nothing, but made his way to the keyboard and began to play one of her favorite songs. It was not long before the girl's dark eyes closed and she drifted into a deep sleep.

Everyone was amazed at the way in which music had opened the door into Esther's spirit. Len had entered, of course. What else could he do? But where would it take him, he asked himself? What if he grew indispensable to the girl? He couldn't spend his whole life entertaining an invalid, could he? If he wasn't careful, he'd end up being tied to this girl for life. He had to get away before he became trapped.

Eventually, he talked it over with Mary and Hugh. "I need to get away for a while," he confessed.

They both nodded. They had seen this coming. "We'll manage just fine," Mary assured him, sounding much braver than she really felt.

That afternoon, after spending the morning with her, Len bent over the sick girl and whispered gently, "Esther, I'm rather tired. I'm going away for a little while. I need to see to some business at home. Mary, Rachel, and Hugh will take good care of you. So I'll say bye for now." He patted her hand gently and then turned to go but not before he saw the hurt in the girl's dark eyes. She said nothing, but turned her head to the wall. Len slipped from the room. He knew if he didn't make a quick exit, his sympathy would get the better of him.

"Don't stay away too long," Nurse Gadger told him as he met her in the foyer.

"I'll be back in a week or so," Len assured her. "I need a break."

Nurse Gadger shook her head as she entered the elevator and pressed the button for the third floor. She had grave doubts that anyone could quite take Len's place and she was right. From that day on, there was a marked deterioration. Everyone did their best, but it just wasn't the same. No one could sing or play or read aloud like Len Atwood. Esther grew more moody, refused to eat or take her therapy, and caused the nursing staff more concern than most of the other patients put together.

Meanwhile, back in Cincinnati, Len was doing his best to relax and enjoy himself. He went to concerts, read the books he had wanted to read for years, visited old friends, wrote several songs, and began to teach some of his former piano students once more. But the reports he received from Knoxville General Hospital were disturbing. Esther had been moved back to intensive care. "I want to die," was all she could seem to say. No one could do anything with her. Esther's uncle had wept tears at night much to his wife's distress.

They told him, too, that Ron, after much persuasion, had made another visit to the sick girl but had been unable to evoke any response and left upset and broken-hearted. A few days later, Aunt Lucy had visited her great-niece and returned home shocked and depressed. Marion had also been to the hospital and then cried all the way back to Silver Springs. Even Hugh seemed burdened down with sorrow. As for Gabby and Rachel, they forgot their differences in their mutual love for the girl "who wanted to die." And Mary's tears often wet the blanket that covered the still, lifeless form of her niece. Tubes were going in and out once more. Esther had no will to live. What would the family do?

"We need to call Len," Mary told Nurse Gadger one Monday morning. He had been gone for nearly two weeks. "I don't know why he's stayed away so long. He knows how much Esther depended on him."

Nurse Gadger gave her a knowing look. "He's afraid," she said curtly and turned on her heel.

Mary stared at Rachel in dismay. "I think she means that he's afraid to get more involved, Mom," Rachel said, with a short laugh. "I mean, what future is there in looking after an invalid like Esther? It seems so unfair." Her mother wondered at the intensity in her voice as she went on, "Here's Ron, dying to be of use to Esther and she won't let him, and there's Len who seems to be the only one whom Esther wants right now, and he's reluctant to come. Why does life work out like that sometimes?"

Her mother said nothing, but a few minutes later she was dialing Len's number. "You're needed here," she told him. "It's a question of life and death now."

"But why me?" Len almost wailed. "I can't cope with it. I don't know where it's all taking me."

"Can't you trust God with that, Len?" Mary's voice was gentle and soothing. "He opened the door. You entered and a miracle was taking place. Now, would God open a door and not lead you all the way? Trust Him."

That evening, Len Atwood faced himself fairly and squarely. What was he afraid of? He had prayed for months to be led by God and now…?

The next morning he was speeding down the interstate to Knoxville. And that afternoon as he entered Esther's room, he saw that he had come none too soon. Without saying a word, he sat down by the bed and began to sing softly, *Numai Harul.* He had left his guitar in the car but he knew he had to sing anyway.

Esther opened her eyes and stared at him. "You've had a long break, Len Atwood," she whispered faintly. "A very long break."

Len brushed back a tear. "Yes. I…I…"

"She's too weak to talk much, so don't excite her," the nurse whispered.

Len rose. Esther was too sharp for him. She read him like a book and sensed he was afraid. Then he paused. As Mary had told him, he must trust God. He wouldn't lead him down a road where there was no ending. It was his duty to help the girl who had become so dependent on him. God would have to take care of the rest.

Looking back, Len never could quite describe the days that followed. It seemed that an unseen Hand was guiding him through the fog of his own fears and doubts. Sometimes he could only see enough to take the next step. It was tough emotionally too. To be ordered around by a girl who hardly ever laughed or smiled and used you as a servant was enough to dampen anyone's ego. But then, he figured when he had sense to figure at all, that maybe that's what it was all about, and when God had humbled him enough, He would provide a way of escape.

And he wasn't the only one who was puzzled at the way things were working out. Ron had heard about Len's music and the second miracle it was working in Esther's life. A strange mixture of emotions would sweep over him. Why shouldn't his cousin do what he couldn't? Anything to save the girl's life! But why, oh why, had God used Len and not him? Len didn't love Esther. He never had. Then he would catch himself. This was not a case of romantic love. It was a case of necessity, of life and death. And at least, there was no danger of his flyaway cousin falling in love with a scarred cripple who seemed to do little else but grumble and command.

## Chapter Thirty

### *The Velvet Curtain Again*

"You know, Ken, I'm afraid Gabby isn't the same girl she was a year ago."

Dr. Porter dropped the book he was reading and looked at Sally. "Of course she isn't the same." The doctor tried to sound jocular. "No girl of her age stands still for twelve months. In my opinion, she's a lot more normal now."

"Normal?"

"Oh, come on, Sally, you know what I mean." Ken really didn't want to discuss Gabby. "She does all the things you and I do. That's what I mean by normal."

Sally glanced over again at Gabby who was sitting on a deck chair at the other end of the porch. Her top and shorts were matching; her hair had recently been given the latest cut by Sally's own hairdresser, and her sunglasses, pushed on top of her head, gave her the air of a model posing for a photograph. Her slim, lithe body glistened in the sun. The doctor followed her gaze.

"See—what more could you want in a girl?" he asked his companion with a smile.

"Oh, she's attractive enough," Sally conceded. "But look at her for a moment."

"With the greatest of pleasure!"

"Please be serious, Ken," Sally pleaded. "Look at her face. It's lost its freshness, its innocence."

"She couldn't remain a child forever," Ken protested.

"No, but she didn't need to change into a worldly-wise woman almost overnight, did she? And what about last weekend?"

"You mean Len's birthday party?"

"Yes. She got really drunk and made an utter fool of herself, remember?"

"Well, it hasn't made any difference to Larry, has it?"

"Maybe not, but he also doesn't seem as desperately keen to be with her as he used to be."

"Oh, Sally, you're a hopeless idealist."

"Me?" Sally's face looked just a little sad. "No, I lost most of my idealism long ago. But I don't want Gabby to lose hers. And, Ken?"

"Yes?" The doctor was getting a little tired of the conversation.

"Now that Gabby's giving him all he wants, do you think he'll grow tired of her?"

Ken threw Sally an angry look. "I've no idea," he said irritably. "Leave them to sort things out between them. Gabby's quite capable of standing up for herself. She's a ball of fire when she wants to be. And what's more, it's pretty obvious he's not the only one who's getting pleasure out of their relationship."

Sally got up from her chair, her tears mingling with her mascara as she made for the patio door. "I just hope that your precious son won't discard his plaything, now that he's made her like everyone else, or nearly." And Sally disappeared into the house.

Ken sat for a few moments looking at the girl in the deck chair. He was very fond of her and certainly hoped that Sally was wrong. He had joked about it, but in his heart he knew he'd give his son a piece of his mind if he treated that girl anything but decently. Just then, he saw Larry bound up the porch steps. He nodded at his father and went over to Gabby's side. She put down her book immediately, and the next moment they had gone into the house, hand in hand.

A few minutes later they were sitting side by side on the sofa in the basement apartment that had been put at their disposal for as long as they wished. Larry had his laptop on his knee. Together they were reading the latest addition to Larry's dissertation.

"What now?" Gabby asked quizzically as he closed the lid and lay back on the sofa.

"That question could be taken several ways, Gabby?"

Gabby blushed. "You know very well what I mean!"

"Aren't you quite happy with things as they are?"

Gabby's face clouded. "I don't know, Larry." She glanced around the apartment. "I mean, you're all spoiling me silly but…"

"What's wrong, Gabby?"

"Wrong? How can anything be wrong?" she gave another laugh which jarred on him a little. "I mean, here we share a plush apartment just as if we were a decently married couple."

"So that's the trouble?"

"What?"

"You're still troubled about the decency of our relationship?"

"Oh, I don't know any more," and Gabby let out a long sigh. "I don't know quite what our relationship is, Larry. That's the problem."

"Well, if you want me to marry you in the next few months…," he began sharply.

"Who's talking about marriage?"

"I thought you were."

"I've stopped thinking about marriage any more." Something in her tone made Larry take his arm from around her waist and turn round so he was gazing into her eyes.

"Look here, let's get all this straight."

"Well, we're soul mates, aren't we? And marriage might be in the picture one day but not now. I know that. And I've accepted it, I think, or I'm trying to. And anyway, I'm not sure I would want to marry you."

Larry's mouth fell open. Maybe he had tutored his girl just a little too well. "Well then," he said, trying to sound calm, "what's the problem?"

"The problem is love, Larry. Shouldn't any relationship like ours have love in it somewhere?"

"Isn't the kind of union we have the best sample of true love, Gabby? A guy doesn't need to say 'I love you' every day to prove his fidelity, does he?"

"Not every day, Larry, but you haven't ever said it."

Larry got to his feet. He was angry now. "Well, Gabriella, I didn't think you were still so naive. You're confusing romance with love. Of course I love you, but in my own way, and you'll have to be satisfied with that."

"Well, I'm not sure I love you," was her honest reply.

Larry was beet red by now. "Then why on earth…?"

"Soul mates," she said smoothly. "That's why."

For a moment, he wasn't sure whether to leave the room or take her in his arms. After a few moments of silence, he sat down again and held her close. "You're playing me at my own game, you clever little she-devil."

He thought he felt the girl shudder slightly. "Yes," she replied with what he thought might be a smothered sob, "yes, you've taught me well."

"Why, I do believe you're crying." His tone wasn't all pity, she noticed.

Gabby pushed him away. For the first time in weeks, she felt completely smothered by his presence. She stood up to get some air. What was enveloping her? Could it be the Velvet Curtain that she had come to believe was only in her sister's imagination?

She looked at the date on her watch. "You know, Larry, I've been up here two full weeks."

"So what? School begins soon, and then we won't see each other very much till Christmas."

"But my sister! I've left her all this time."

Larry stirred impatiently in his seat. "She's got Rachel and your aunt and that crazy Len guy with her, so…"

"Don't you dare call Len Atwood crazy," Gabby's eyes were literally blazing now, "though I suppose such a sample of selflessness does seem crazy to you. You probably don't have any other word for it in the text books you study."

Larry sighed and pulled her down beside him. "Calm down, you little vixen," he pleaded. "Sorry I used the wrong word, but you have to admit that spending all his time with a scarred cripple does raise some questions about his sanity."

"Please don't, Larry. She's still my beautiful angel sister to me. But Len or no Len, I'm her closest blood relative and I've been away from her too long."

"OK, have your way."

"Well, I'm not sure how much you'll miss me really, I mean me, Gabby Popescu. Oh, you'll miss what I give you, of course," she added meaningfully, "but I've noticed you don't spend as much time during the day with me as you used to."

"I'm awfully busy, Gabby. You know that. I have to get my dissertation done."

"Of course."

"Anyway, I'll drive you down for a few days."

"You know you don't want to be near my family. No, I'll go myself and stay there till school begins. I know how I'd feel if my only sister was off with a guy right when I was facing an operation. Look," she added as she saw the expression on his face, "I'll stay over the weekend and then go up on Monday. I called the hospital today and Esther's making real good progress. Aunt Mary said that she still has relapses, when Len has all he can do to hold his own with her and not turn tail, it gets so bad, but they're getting fewer and fewer. So that's a relief."

That weekend, Larry spent all his spare time with Gabby. And Gabby had determined to enjoy all the attention she was getting. Yet the more time he spent with her, the more she felt she had to get air to breathe in. She hated to admit it, but Larry Porter was too overpowering.

Gabby lay back in the deck chair and gazed up at the cloudless blue sky. She was packed and ready to go. She and Larry were spending their last few moments together on the front porch. "Let's see," she began dreamily, "I wonder what your analysis of me really is, Larry."

He looked at her sharply. "Analysis? But it's not you I've been using in my dissertation."

"I know, but you've been analyzing me all right. And you can't deny it, either. You want to see how much I can get free of my past if I'm placed in a completely new environment."

Larry grinned sheepishly. "Well, go on," he told her.

Gabby gave him a roguish look. "Let's see, you have concluded that while background has played an extremely important part in my life, the more isolated I am from my old environment, friends, and ideas, the more my new environment kicks in. So," she paused, and toyed with the bracelet he had just bought her the day before, "you conclude that a new environment affects a subject in proportion to the extent that that subject is isolated from his or her past or upbringing, especially in the case of a religious upbringing. And," she twirled her sunglasses in her fingers, "if that subject could be isolated completely, then previous teachings and inhibitions etc. etc., I can't put it in a scholarly way, you know," she apologized.

"No, of course not, but you're making a good stab at it. Go on."

"And if complete isolation could be achieved and the new environment was sufficiently challenging and provocative, then that subject could reach a state of such freedom that the inhibitive teachings and principles of the past could be completely overcome and even obliterated."

Larry stared at her in admiration. Gabby caught his gaze and blushed. She leaned over and kissed his cheek, then grabbed her small suitcase and made for her car.

"Just a moment," Larry said, following her to the car.

"Yes?" Gabby asked as she got in the driver's seat and started up the engine.

"What exactly are your plans?"

Gabby wound down the window. "Plans? Oh, the hospital for two weeks and then college, of course. I'll keep in touch." She wound up the window and turned the key in the ignition.

"Not so quick, Gabby," Larry told her. He yanked open the car door, bent over, and pulled her towards him. "I don't quite know what you're up to," he murmured as his lips met hers, "but whatever you say or whatever you do, you're mine now. You've given yourself to me, remember? And I'm not about to let you go."

Gabby didn't try to pull away. But when he finally released her, she opened her lips to speak, and then closed them again. What could she say? He was right. She *had* given herself to him. Then was she his—forever?

"Bye," she told him again, as she put her foot on the accelerator. "I'll call you from Knoxville."

Gabby glanced through the rear-view mirror as she sped down the driveway. Larry, in his immaculate white shorts and shirt, was standing stock still, watching her car until the last possible moment. Her eyes blurred. She had grown rather fond of this young man who had literally forced his way into her life.

As she turned on to the interstate she stared at the road stretching out unendingly before her. Knoxville was at the other end of it, she knew. But as for the road of life, she had no idea where it would lead eventually. That was her problem. She thought of the choices she had made during the past year. Were they irrevocable? "I'm not about to let you go," reverberated in her mind as she sped south.

At Lexington, she stopped to get gas and freshen up. As she sipped the diet Coke she had just bought (she had become very figure conscious of late), she took a deep breath. Something was different. Had she left the Velvet Curtain behind her in Indianapolis, she wondered?

# Chapter Thirty-One

## *In the Looking-Glass*

One morning, Esther suddenly interrupted Len's reading by asking for a mirror. "Why do you need one?" Len asked gently, trying not to show his dismay. She was talking a lot now, and soon he reckoned he would be able to keep up a running conversation with her.

"All women need mirrors," she said, but there was no smile on her lips this time.

"Maybe another day," he told her.

She pouted. "I want one now, Len. Now!"

Len knew that he was spoiling this girl. Everything she asked for he gave. But he figured there would be time enough for others to *unspoil* her. So now he gave in as usual.

He found a small mirror in her vanity case in the closet. His heart beat fast and his mouth felt dry as he brought it to the bed.

"Let me see it, Len." Esther's voice was surprisingly firm. He sat on the bed and held it up. She lifted her head a little and stared a long time at her reflection. Len watched her intently and his heart sank. A change was coming over her. The old look of anger and bitterness could be seen once more in that pale, sunken face.

Suddenly, in fact so suddenly that it caught him completely off guard, the girl grabbed the mirror, yanked it from his hands, and then, with what seemed supernatural strength, threw it on the floor. It smashed into a thousand pieces.

Len stared in dismay at the shattered glass. It seemed to speak of Esther's life and maybe even of his own. He looked up at the girl in the bed. Her great dark eyes were glaring at him. "Get out of here!" she yelled. "I don't want to see you ever again. You've deceived me! You made me think I wasn't so bad after all."

He stooped over her and began to speak, but she took her left hand and gave him a resounding slap on his right cheek. "There," she said, her eyes full of what he thought must be hatred, "never ever come back in here again, never!"

Len's face blanched. He had been prepared for some stormy scenes but not for this. He turned towards the door. He had been an utter fool! Then he took one more look at the bed. The girl was staring at him intently. "Get out!" she shouted again.

"All right, all right, I'm going!" Len was thoroughly roused now. "Don't worry, I won't bother you again, Esther. If I ever come back, you'll have to ask for me."

He bolted into the hallway and nearly collided with Nurse Pennington who had heard the commotion and had come to see what it was all about.

"She's told me never to come back," he said heatedly, "and I won't. Good luck with her! She's a little vixen!" And he left the astonished nurse gazing after him in utter confusion and dismay.

By the time Len reached his car, he realized more fully the gravity of what had happened. He had to tell Mary or Rachel. He went back into the foyer and dialed their apartment. "It's all over, Mary," he said. "Esther wanted a mirror and I had to give her one. She looked in it and then went into a rage, threw the mirror on the floor, slapped me on the cheek, and told me to go and never ever to see her again, and she meant it. So I'm off. She's more like an animal than a human when she's in this mood." Mary was going to remonstrate with him, but he had hung up.

Back home in Cincinnati, he was surprised that evening by a call from his cousin. "Just wanted to find out how you'd gotten on with Esther." Ron's voice was tense.

Len gulped. "Well, actually, she shouted me out of the room today."

"I thought she would." Len resented Ron's tone. It sounded just a little patronizing.

"But," Len put in hastily, "she was doing wonderfully—eating, talking, and responding to me in a way I never dreamed possible. And then," his voice broke, "she asked me for a mirror, and when she saw herself in it, she threw it on the floor, hit me on the face, and ordered me never to come back again."

There was a very long silence on the other end. Then Len heard his cousin say abruptly, "I'm sorry."

There was nothing more either could say. Ron had to admit that he was secretly glad Len had failed. If his cousin had succeeded, what would that have meant? He could hardly even frame thoughts, let alone words to describe what he felt. How could he have stood by and seen this cousin of his—the very guy he had despised most of his life, this religious prig, this self-righteous hypocrite—succeed where he had miserably failed? It would have been the humiliation of a lifetime.

Len had no idea of his cousin's emotions that evening. He only knew that he was in the deep and narrow valley of humiliation, looking wistfully up at the peaks of perfection he wished so much to scale. "But My strength is made perfect in your weakness, Len," God seemed to whisper to him as the hours dragged slowly by. "Go back to the hospital and see what My strength can do."

"No!" he almost shouted. "I can't! Esther told me never to enter her room again." He turned his face towards the wall. What man would subject himself to further humiliation from a girl who was at war with the whole world?

"But you were the hero," a Voice whispered deep inside. "You basked in Nurse Gadger's admiration, in Dr. Garrington's appreciation, and in your own sense of nobility. If you had succeeded, who would have gotten the praise and the glory?"

When Len phoned the hospital the next morning, the news was not good. Esther was not back in intensive care, that was one blessing, but she was eating barely enough to keep her alive. Mary told him that she was making life almost unbearable for all who tried to help her.

In the days which followed, Len tried in vain to put Esther Popescu out of his mind. Instead, she filled nearly every waking moment, haunted his dreams, and took away his appetite. His step father grew concerned. "Put that girl out of your head, Len," he advised.

"I've tried, Dad," he said piteously. "But it's no use. She's gotten right into my bones, and I don't know what on earth to do about it. I'm afraid to go back to her. I'll get so involved that there'll be no drawing back. And yet, it seems I can't live without her."

It had slowly dawned on Len that Esther didn't really hate him. She hated herself. She hated the image she had seen. She had relied on her beauty for twenty-four years and now she had none. And she was also nursing bitterness towards God—that was only too obvious.

He asked himself over and over again, was it pity or something more that had kept drawing him back to Esther? Maybe he didn't need to analyze his feelings. Maybe he just needed to obey the Voice that seemed to be urging him back to the hospital. But every day he reasoned that he needed more time to think and to pray and to sort himself out, and every day he became more confused and depressed than ever.

## Chapter Thirty-Two

*Love or Lunacy?*

When Ron answered the doorbell one morning and found his cousin on his doorstep, he had no idea what had brought him there that hot, dry August day. "How are things?" he asked, as he ushered his visitor into the living room. "Have you been back to the hospital since I spoke to you last?"

"No, I haven't," Len said quietly. "But I'll be there tomorrow. And that's what I want to speak to you about."

"Me?" Ron queried, raising his eyebrows. "I don't know where I figure in all this."

"I'll do my best to explain, but it won't be easy," Len replied.

Ron went to the refrigerator and took out a can of Pepsi. "Have a seat," Ron told him as he handed him the can. "Make yourself at home."

Len took his drink, placed it on the table by his chair, and looked up at his cousin. Ron thought he looked paler than usual, and nervous. He could never remember Len being nervous in the old days.

"Well," Len began slowly, "I need to recap a little to put you in the picture. As I told you before, my music really seemed to do something for the girl, and gradually she was becoming very dependent on me."

"I know," Ron said, his face grim.

"When I tried going away once before," Len went on, trying to ignore the expression on his cousin's face, "she had a relapse, so there was nothing for it but to stick by her. And she was improving fast. Then there was that whole episode with the mirror."

Ron nodded. "You seemed pretty fed up at the time and said it was all over."

"That's what I thought." Len looked down at the carpet. "For several weeks, now, I've tried to put Esther Popescu out of my mind, but it's been useless." Len took a gulp as he went on, "Life without her seemed empty. I realized I had grown awfully fond of the girl. I'm not saying it's the sort of affection that's needed for a marriage, but it might be some day."

Ron gave a start. What right had Len to sit there and even hint of marriage to his one and only love? Then he put his head in his hands. That was all in the past. He tried to concentrate on what his cousin was saying.

"Although I knew I was getting fond of her," Len went on, "I was also afraid. I felt God wanted me to go back to the hospital, but every day I put it off. I didn't know where it was all taking me." Ron nodded. He could follow his cousin so far, at least.

"Then, Ron, I had a dream the other night." Len leaned forward in his seat as he spoke. "Esther was in a wheelchair, dressed in white just as she was at her last concert, with a mike in her hand. She was singing." Len's voice shook a little. This was awful, simply awful. He daren't look at Ron's face just now. He had to go on. "And there was a man by her side. I looked closer, and it seemed to be myself." Ron had risen from his chair now.

Len kept his eyes fixed on the carpet, but he heard his cousin begin to pace the floor. He went on so hurriedly that Ron found he had to listen hard to catch all the words. "The dream vanished, but it had been so real, just as if it were happening in my very room. And then God began to talk to me almost as plainly as I'm talking now, though I can't say I heard an audible voice. I knew that my place lay with Esther. I knew that I had to go back and resume my music therapy, as Hugh calls it. I knew I had to face my feelings for her and hers for me. And," his voice shook as he spoke, "I knew that all this could lead to a lifetime of devotion to a scarred and crippled girl who will probably never regain a fraction of her former beauty and might remain morose and difficult for the rest of her life. As I fasted and prayed, I knew I should take the first step in faith, and let God lead me in the rest."

Ron had stopped pacing the floor now and was standing in front of his cousin. He bent down and grabbed Len's arm. "What are you going to do? Spit it out, for goodness' sake!"

Len raised his eyes to Ron's. He saw fear there, and anger, and desperation. He tried to speak, but the words stuck in his throat.

"Afraid to say, aren't you?" Ron's voice was almost mocking.

Len rose to his feet and looked his cousin in the eyes. "No, I'm not afraid or ashamed to say it. I have to say it. I'm going back to Knoxville and will tell Esther exactly what I've told you."

Ron gripped the table edge to support himself. "And you're willing to marry her if it comes to that?" His voice was tense and shrill.

"Yes," was the simple response. "If we find we love each other, I'll marry her, just as she is."

Ron was regaining his composure fast. This was a figment of Len's imagination. It was simply lunacy. It would pass, or Esther's behavior would soon put it out of his head. Then he noticed that his cousin's fine eyes, nearly black as coals, were glistening with tears. To Len, at least, this was no fantasy.

"So I had to come here first of all, before I went any further," Len went on. "I've told no one, so far, but you."

The muscles in Ron's face relaxed slightly. "Well, you had no obligation to tell me," he said. "I mean, I'm no longer engaged to Esther. And what happened a month or so ago showed me that there's no hope of our ever getting together again."

He saw Len was about to remonstrate, but he held up his hand. "Let me finish, please. It wasn't only the fact that she treated me as she did, or that I utterly failed to convince her of my love. It was…," his voice broke, "it was the sudden reality of the situation that struck me. In the first place, I didn't have it in me to do anything for her. I just knew that. I couldn't lift her up. I couldn't inspire her to live. I admit that it wasn't just sheer cowardice. There was something else even greater than fear that tied my hands completely. It wasn't so much that I didn't want to devote myself to her, I just couldn't do it. I couldn't bridge the gap that has always been between us. Even if I nursed Esther for the rest of my life, there would still be that gulf between us if I didn't change. I couldn't pray with her, sing hymns to her like you could. I couldn't help her get rid of her bitterness and hopelessness. All I could give was just what I, Ron Atwood, had to give, and that, I had discovered, was practically nothing."

This time Len insisted on speaking. "But you can find her God, Ron. And if you did, you'd be the ideal one to save her."

"I never will find God till I want Him for Himself, and I'll never do that as long as Esther is my chief aim in life."

Len had not expected all this from his cousin. He grabbed Ron's hand. "Thing is, you were always so much better than I was. No, don't protest. You know it's true. And Esther saw that too. She told me once that you acted more of a Christian than I did." His face was red. This was a hard admission to make. "But maybe because I'm so flawed—and everyone knows that only too well—well, maybe because of my failures not in spite of them, I was ready for God's grace. But," he cleared his throat again, "to get back to the present. I won't go any farther in this if there's any hope that you could do it. I mean…"

"No way," Ron interrupted. "I can't do it for the reasons I've told you already. I admit that if you succeed, it'll be the worst blow to my pride I've had since I was born. And it'll hurt a lot. But that girl needs a savior, and I can't be that to her. If you can, go ahead, and with my blessing. But one thing is bothering me," his face grew grim now.

"Then out with it. It's probably bothering me too."

"Well, I really thought I loved Esther but when I saw her without the bandages, I felt she was not the Esther I had known or loved. She seemed an utter stranger to me. I pitied the girl lying there but did I love her? Even now, I'm not sure if I love *that* Esther." Ron stared out the window for a moment then went on, "Don't you think that it's mostly pity on your part and a matter of necessity or a sense of indebtedness on hers that draw you to each other? And will that work?"

Len's face was deep red under his tan. "I've asked myself the same question, Ron, but look," it was his turn to pace the floor now, "I'm getting fond of the Esther that exists now, not the Esther that was. That makes it easier. And just maybe," he turned to look at Ron now and there was just a slight smile on his lips, "God is doing another Balaam trick, I mean using an ass as His messenger."

Ron gave a short laugh in spite of himself. "Well, thanks for coming today. All I can say is, good luck. Go ahead and do what you have to," he told his cousin as he made for the door.

Len went over his conversation with Ron as he sped towards Knoxville. He knew he had hit his cousin between the eyes and wondered, in the long run, what his real reaction would be. He'd have to leave that to God and trust that everything, in the end, would work for good.

When he reached the hospital the next morning, Len found that he couldn't face anyone just yet. For one whole hour he paced the parking lot. Had he been a fool? What was he letting himself in for? How would he approach Esther? He had heard that physically she was improving slightly, but that she was morose, petulant, and bitter. What had he committed himself to? "Calm down," he told himself, "and get something to eat. You'll sure need it."

After a light meal, Len made his way towards the elevator and met Nurse Gadger in the foyer. She eyed him grimly. "So you've appeared again, have you?"

"Yes, I'm like the bad penny, always turning up." Len tried to sound playful, but he didn't like the look on the nurse's face. She looked as if she was going to give him the lecture of his life. "And this time, you'll not get rid of me easily."

The nurse looked incredulous. "I'm not playing, Nurse," he said calmly. "Look at this bouquet of roses. Now, how'll that do for a start?"

It took a lot to shock Maria Gadger, but Len never forgot the look on her face as she stared at him in utter confusion. "The strange thing is, that when I went back home, I felt I couldn't face life without Esther," Len said with a broad smile. "I don't know if you could call it love yet, but it could well be, some day."

Len turned his head away for a few moments to hide his emotion and then began again, "I know it'll be tough going all the way. But she needs to know that someone will take care of her, that someone has hope in her."

Nurse Gadger put her hand on his shoulder. "Her progress is awfully slow. At this rate, it'll be months before she's released from the hospital. And her spirits are so low. She eats just barely enough to keep her alive. But at least she's not on tubes any more, that's a comfort." Then she straightened her shoulders. "Well, if you're sure you know what you're in for, then come along."

Len noticed that the room was darkened as he went in. "She insists on having it like that," the nurse told him. Then she went to the bed. "Esther, I have a special visitor for you," she whispered.

Esther opened her eyes when she heard these words. They were awfully dark and solemn, Len thought. He came over to where she could see him without turning her head and spoke just a few words. They were simple words, but they bound him irrevocably to the girl he was coming to love.

"Esther," he said in a whisper. "I'm back to stay." He bent over her and placed the roses in her hand.

Two large teardrops began to make their way down the girl's wan, emaciated face. Len reached for a Kleenex and wiped them away. "But you'll have to do as I say, or I won't sing or play for you." Len tried to sound confident.

"Now, can I have a vase, please, to put these flowers in," he asked the nurse. He went to the window to pull up the blinds. "We need some light on the scene. I won't be able to read or to play in this darkness."

He went back to the bed and bent over the sick girl. "I'm going to go and fetch two large ice cream cones," he announced with one of his special smiles. "I feel like celebrating."

Esther buried her face in the scarlet blossoms. Then she closed her eyes for a moment and asked in a tremulous voice, "Are you sure you won't go away again?"

"Positive," Len reassured her as he smoothed the blankets. "You'll have to get the police on the scene if you want me removed," he joked.

When they had finished their ice cream, Len settled down for a serious chat. "You may wonder why I came back so suddenly," he began as he smoothed her pillow and then took a seat by the bed.

Esther nodded but said nothing. Len took her little hand in his and held it tightly. "I couldn't get you out of my head, day or night," he began, his voice almost in a whisper. "And I finally concluded that I couldn't live without you." As he spoke, Esther's eyes never left his face, but he could tell from the twitching of her fingers, that she was feeling far more than she showed.

"Then," he went on, "I had a vision which really made me think." And he told her, still holding her hand, what he had told Ron the day before.

"So," he concluded, "I've decided to come back and stay back, if you'll let me. I admit that I was very hurt when you ordered me out of the room and, it seemed, out of your life. But I came to understand that it was not me you hated, but the vision of yourself that you saw in that mirror."

Esther nodded and whispered, "I thought you had deceived me. I had grown to think that you really were getting fond of me." Len noticed to his delight that she was actually blushing now. "And then, when I saw myself, I was certain that I'd been mistaken."

Len squeezed her hand. "But you were not mistaken, Esther, dear. And as the days go by, if we find that we really can't do without each other, then…" He paused and impulsively stooped down and gave her a quick kiss, but before Esther had courage to raise her eyes to his, he had fled from the room.

The next morning, Len told them to try physiotherapy again. Esther had refused to take it ever since Len had left. Doris looked at Len skeptically as she approached the bed. He saw the girl shrink back. She shook her head. "I want…" she began. He came up and put his finger on her lips. "No, Esther. You're not going to say that anymore, remember? Maybe if I stand right by and hold one hand, you can do what the lady wants."

She shook her head again. "Can I have a word with her alone?" Len asked. Doris frowned but left the room.

"Esther," Len whispered. "You've got to go through with this. The more you can move, the better it'll be for both of us. Now, I'll try to help you bear your pain, but I think God is going to do some miracles if you trust Him. Together we'll go through with this, right?"

Esther tried to lift the sheet over her face but his hand was there before hers. "No, you don't!" His voice was firm now, even sharp. "Now look here, don't you think you're being selfish? Stop having a pity party. With me beside you, you can do it."

His hand went to her head as he spoke. "You know, your hair's going to grow in again and it'll be as beautiful as ever. I can feel the fuzz already. I'll have to call you my golliwog." Esther's lips curved upwards. "So will you cooperate if I call Doris back?"

"If you'll hold my hand," she told him softly.

"Of course."

For the next few minutes, Len thought he had surely made a mistake. Esther's whole body seemed racked with pain. The sweat stood in beads on her forehead. But she was doing exactly as Doris instructed her.

"There, that's enough for today," she was told. "I don't know what this young man has done to you, but it seems like he has a charm none of the rest of us have."

Esther gave another faint smile. "Yes. He's a real charmer." Len's laugh was almost merry as he took a damp cloth and bathed the girl's forehead.

"Thank you," she told him. He gave her hand a gentle squeeze but said nothing. But then, he didn't need to. His eyes said it all.

Len had Esther to himself that day. The others were taking a well-deserved break. So he fed her some mashed potatoes and gravy for supper, and then, as the sun began to set on the horizon, he sat at the keyboard. "I'm going to give you a little evening entertainment," he announced.

She shook her head, but he shook his too, and began to play softly, *Numai Harul*. Then his voice took up the refrain. When he had finished, she motioned to him to come nearer. "You don't say it right," she said, pouting. "Your accent is terrible."

"Then correct me," Len was saying. "How do you expect me to sing it right when I've had no teacher?"

"I'll be your teacher when I'm…" She stopped abruptly and the old look came over her again. "Go away!" she almost shouted. "I want to die."

"Stop it!" he shouted back. "Just stop it! You're going to live, for my sake if for no one else's! So now, let's let the nurse give you your medicine, and I'll go away to get a bite of supper. But I'm going to stay right here all night in this recliner. When you need me, just call. OK?"

Esther's mouth relaxed into a faint smile again. "OK."

Len met Dr. Garrington in the hallway. "A word with you young man," he told him. He took him into an empty room. "Your coming back on the scene is already doing wonders, only," he paused, "I would like to warn you plainly what harm you might be doing if you don't really mean all this."

At first Len felt angry at the doctor's words. Why couldn't he trust him? Then he realized how utterly crazy his behavior must have been that day.

"I hope you've thought very seriously about the consequences of your action," Dr. Garrington went on soberly.

"I have, Dr. Garrington. I stayed away for three weeks until…," Len's voice choked with emotion, "until I couldn't stay away any longer. I don't think I can live without her. I'm not absolutely sure, neither is she, of what the future holds for us. But we're very fond of each other, so that's a start."

"Certainly is, if it's true," Dr. Garrington muttered. "But remember, don't play with her emotions. It could cost her her life, understand?"

"Yes. I do. I've thought a lot about it."

"Then why are you doing this? Did you care for the girl before she had this accident?"

"I admired her greatly but she wouldn't look at me. She was a real beauty. Nearly all the men I knew were crazy about her, just as I was. But no, I didn't love her."

"Then…" the doctor looked puzzled.

"Let's just say that God opened the door for me with my music and told me to enter. I didn't know at first what it might mean. Now I've a good idea and I won't back out unless she does."

"You're a brave man," the doctor told him, his eyes glistening. "I wish you all the best. And if you do get engaged, I want to throw a party, right here in the hospital."

"Think she'll still be here then?" Len asked in surprise.

"At the rate you two are going, of course she'll be, and," the doctor's eyes twinkled, "I want to be at the wedding, too."

"If there is one, you will be," Len assured him. "You certainly will be."

## Chapter Thirty-Three

*The Proof of Love*

"What on earth are you doing, Len?" Rachel's voice was very sharp. The day after Len's return to the hospital, she cornered him in the corridor just outside Esther's door.

"What do you mean?" Len flushed under Rachel's gaze.

"I caught you just now, flirting with my cousin. It's no joke, Len. The girl's life is in your hands."

Len knew the time had come to tell his secret. "I can't blame you in the slightest for thinking this of me," he told Rachel soberly, "but this time, I'm not flirting. I've become very fond of Esther and am willing to spend my life taking care of her."

Rachel gasped. "You can't mean that?"

"You see if I don't!" Len said with a grin. Rachel stared at him as he went back into Esther's room. Then she smiled to herself. He'd run away again the first time her cousin threw a tantrum. He'd never stick it out, never!

For the next few hours, Len was kept busy. At the patient's request, he read to her; he sang to her; he brought her juice; he bathed her brow; he fed her lunch, and then after she had a long afternoon nap, she spoke the dreaded words, "Len, bring me a mirror."

He had feared that moment, but it had to be faced. He went in search of Nurse Gadger. He knew she would give him good advice.

"She wants the mirror again," he told her disconsolately.

"Then give her one."

"But…"

"Give it to her. She has to face it and so do you." Nurse Gadger turned to Len. Her voice was stern. "You need to be dead sure if you're going through with this or not. Is your love strong enough to endure her violent mood swings?"

She saw his face redden and put her hand on his arm. "You can't fake love with that girl. She'll know it immediately. But," and her eyes were glistening as she spoke, "if you can stick it out and find it in your

257

heart to really love her just as she is, then you'll be her hero for life and," she gave him a quick peck on the cheek, "you'll be mine too."

"Here's the mirror," Len told Esther a few moments later.

He stepped over to the bed, sat down on it, and took her hand firmly in his. The fingers twitched, but he held them tightly. "Esther," he said, his voice shaking just a little, "this time, you and I are going to look into the mirror together."

She turned her head away for a moment then looked back. Her eyes showed terrible fear. He put his arms around her and raised her slightly. Then he held the mirror so that both of them were staring at her image. "I'll tell you what I see in there," his voice was gentle and soothing. "I see the girl I love. I know now that I really love this girl in the mirror. She's got a big scar down her left cheek." He felt her hand trying to pull away. He relinquished it for just moment and put his hand to her face. Gently, very gently, he traced the scar with his index finger. "We'll not be frightened, my girl and I, of this scar. It's not going to divide us again, ever."

Esther looked in wonder into his face. He was looking into the mirror again. "And she's lost her hair, but nature will have her way pretty soon. It'll come back as black and wavy as ever. We'll let it grow long as it used to be. And," his voice was dreamy now, "we'll let it hang down around her shoulders. We'll let it frame her face. Or we'll put it up on her head and she'll look just like Queen Esther of old."

He looked down at the girl beside him. She was actually smiling. He turned to the glass again and went on, "Her lips are almost white but that won't last. After I've kissed them every day for a year or so, they will be as red and soft as ever. And her cheeks are thin and sallow. But I'll feed her ice cream sundaes, and chocolate brownies, and T-bone steaks, and we'll go to the beach, and the sun will kiss those cheeks again until they'll be bronzed and glowing with health."

Len paused for breath and then continued, "I also see two beautiful eyes, just the same as they always were—big, dark, and luminous. No head-on collision could mar their beauty or their charm. Together we'll chase away the sadness in those eyes until they sparkle and dance once again." His voice broke.

"Esther," he went on, "I love you, scar and all. I love you if you never walk again. But we both have to face what you are now. You are no longer the fabulous beauty you once were." He felt her tremble. "But maybe, just maybe, you relied on your looks to get you through life. Now you can't do that. But you have God. He's still there, and you have me. And I'm terribly sorry for running away like I did. Now, will you forgive me?"

Esther put out her thin hand and gave his a slight squeeze. Then she whispered softly, "And will you forgive me?" His tears and his kiss were answer enough. Esther closed her eyes and before long fell into a deep sleep.

That evening after supper, Mary came to the hospital. She was delighted to see Len back again, but her daughter was still skeptical. "He'll spend all evening kissing Esther, and then leave her tomorrow the first time she frowns on him." Her eyes flashed dangerously. "He'll do more damage than good."

"Think so?" Mary asked with a smile. "Look in there!" She pointed through the open door. Esther was lying in a deep sleep, while Len was reclining in the chair by her bed, a smile on his lips, his dark eyes fixed on the girl's face.

He heard their voices and looked towards the door. Tiptoeing out of the room, he joined them in the corridor. "Forgive me for leaving you for a few weeks," Len apologized holding out his hand.

"How can you love my cousin and run off like that the moment she looked sideways at you?" Rachel couldn't help asking.

Len blushed, and Mary could see he was hurt. "Listen, Rachel," his voice was calm but his eyes were flashing, "one day you'll have to accept me as a member of your family. And you might as well know that I'm a very flawed person. I've got so many faults it would fill any girl's diary in no time if she tried to note them all down, and you probably would if you were Esther. Fortunately for me, the girl in the room down the hallway is in no position to see my faults at the moment. And, after all, it's her I made up my mind to devote my life to and not you." And with that he stalked back to Esther's room.

"Wow!" Rachel muttered. "Sure has some fire in him! But he's coming back. Probably not finished with me yet!"

"Rachel!" All the anger had gone out of Len's voice as he stood in front of her, his black eyes anxiously searching hers, as if pleading for forgiveness. "You were right in what you said a few moments ago."

Rachel stared at him but said nothing. "I mean," he was stammering now, "I was an utter coward and I still am. Only," he paused and his face became alight as he spoke, "I happen to be a coward saved by grace, and that makes all the difference." He turned on his heel and was gone.

Mary's eyes were moist as she took Rachel's arm. "Let's go and eat; we haven't had a decent meal for days."

Rachel nodded, but her mind was not on food at that moment. "Mom, that guy's very strange. I can't make him out."

"You mean Len?" her mother asked as they entered the elevator.

"Yes. Who else? He seems very changeable."

"You never forget, do you, Rachel?"

"What do you mean?" The girl's voice was sharp.

"I mean," her mother's voice was kind but firm, "that when someone doesn't quite come up to your standard of perfection, you store their failure away in some cubby-hole of that complicated brain of yours. Not only that, but you take it out now and then and give it a good airing."

"I do it with myself, too." Rachel's voice was very defensive now. They had reached the foyer and were making their way towards the large swinging doors.

"I know you do. Only you haven't let yourself down yet like Len has or Ron or Gabby or even Esther."

"Mom! How can you talk like that!"

"You're as moral as any mother could wish," Mary went on. "You always try to be just and fair in every situation. You never cheat. You never fritter your days away in parties. You read sensible, solid books. You're a star student and make all your professors proud. Only…"

Rachel turned to face her mother now. What had gotten into her? She had never talked like that before. "So you want me to sleep with men like Gabby's done to keep me humble?" Rachel asked contemptuously.

Mary gave an involuntary shudder. "Rachel, how can you talk like that about your cousin! Of course she's done very wrong." Her voice was a little sharp. "But your goodness seems to spring from you, not from God. And that's dangerous and can't last forever."

Rachel tossed her long hair back from her face and reached into her purse for the car keys. She gave a little smile as she said lightly, "Thanks for the lecture, Mom. I'll remember it. But let's just live one day at a time. And when my goodness does run out as you seem to think it will, it'll be a comfort to know that I've a mother who has a hotline to God." She turned and gave her mom a kiss. "Now, come on. I'm hungry as a wolf."

"So am I," Mary told her with a laugh. She knew she'd said enough for one day, maybe more than enough.

Later that evening, Gabby returned from Tiny Gap where she had spent a day or two. College was beginning the next week, and she needed to prepare her clothes and books for the coming semester. She had faithfully taken her turn with Esther since she had returned from Indianapolis, but the others had noticed a marked change in her. She was restless and unhappy. Every time Larry phoned her, she was unsettled for hours afterwards. And being with her sister did not help. She felt guilty and unable to comfort her or be of any real help.

More than that, she was secretly disappointed in Len Atwood. She had defended him to Larry and even now, could hardly blame him for staying away. She had experienced more than one of Esther's tantrums. Yet in her heart of hearts, she felt let down. Some of it, she knew, was sheer selfishness. Len's absence meant that she had to spend hours with her sister.

"I'll go to the hospital first thing in the morning," she told Rachel, as she put away her clothes in the closet. "I suppose Esther's much the same?"

"Len's come back," her cousin told her abruptly.

Gabby stared in astonishment. "Len back? I can't believe it!"

"He's back all right. He brought Esther a bouquet of red roses and told me that he's serious about her."

"What do you mean?"

"Just that it looks like they'll be engaged some day soon."

Gabby took her cousin by the shoulders and almost shook her. "What?" she shouted. "What? He's willing to devote his life to my sister? Are you standing there and telling me that Len Atwood, of all people, really loves a scarred cripple?"

"Well, that's what he said, though only time will prove it, I suppose."

Gabby gave no reply and after a few moments, she abruptly left the room. Len Atwood was either out of his mind, or the clearest sample of God's love, if there was a God, she had witnessed since she had said goodbye to her beloved father.

As the days passed by, Len and Esther would look in the mirror together and every day they would talk of the Esther that was and the Esther that was to be. Len watched with pride as he saw her gaining strength, very slowly but very surely. She could even sit for half an hour at a time, but there was one thing she would not do. She refused to listen to Len when he read the Bible to her or prayed. She would stop her ears, turn her head; then, if he continued, she'd pout, glare, and get so upset that he knew he had to desist.

After three or four attempts like this, Len had to speak his mind. "I'm surprised that you won't listen to the Bible or let me pray with you, Esther. You never used to be like that." It was out before he could stop it.

There followed another scene much like the one which had sent him packing. Only this time, he didn't get near enough to let her slap him. He just quietly slipped out the door and went into the waiting room. It was night and hardly anyone was around. He stretched out on the sofa and tried to get a few winks of sleep. But first, he would indulge in a pity party. Then it hit him. He swung his legs to the floor and sat bolt upright. It seemed he had a little glimpse into her soul. Here she was, bedridden, beauty snatched away in one brief moment, body wrecked for life, career ruined just when she had begun to sing again. Yes, that was it. She couldn't understand why God had done it all. And what would he have done in her place? Taken it all like an angel? He very much doubted it. No, he'd have to help the girl regain her faith. It might take days, weeks, even years.

Len rose from the sofa and went back to her room. Esther was not asleep. She was staring at the ceiling, her face as white as the bedclothes that covered her.

"Esther," he said softly going over to the bed.

She glared at him. "Get out!" she ordered.

"No, Esther, I'm not getting out. I'm not giving in to you this time. But I will promise one thing."

"What?" she asked, curious in spite of herself.

"That I'll never again read the Bible or pray unless you ask me to."

She stared at him with her great, dark eyes and then nodded. "OK, that's a bargain."

"And," he went on, "maybe some day you'll share with me what's going on inside you. And I'll have to tell you what's going on inside me. That's what marriage is all about, you know." She smiled faintly, and he knew the storm had passed.

Five days later, Esther went for another X-ray. Dr. Garrington told Len that an operation on her spine might just be successful enough to enable her to sit up in a wheelchair, though he doubted if she could ever walk, even on crutches. It would be a painful operation and involve weeks of recuperation. He recommended moving her to a rehab complex just outside the city. But further recovery really depended on her will to survive.

Len told Esther about the operation. At first she refused and began the old refrain, "I want to die," but Len told her that if he was willing to devote his life to her then she ought to try for his sake to get as mobile as possible. It was then that Esther broke down and cried and cried and cried. She told Len about what she remembered of her accident, about those terrible days afterwards, about Ron's visit and her feeling that she never wanted to show her face to anyone again. She told of her bitterness towards God, of Malcolm's words to her that God might have to chasten her, and how she had been convinced that she was being punished for refusing him.

"You mean that guy proposed to you?"

"Yes, he sure did!" She had to smile at Len's face. He was actually jealous.

"Yet he hasn't been in once to see you, has he?"

"His sister has. After all, would you have come to visit me if I had refused you?"

"You haven't refused me, so I can't answer that," Len laughed.

"But you don't think I'm being punished?" Esther asked very seriously.

"Of course not. You were upset when you left the Morgans. You were probably so preoccupied with what had just taken place that you didn't see the truck coming. I don't want to ever hear you talk about punishment again, Esther." He turned to her. "And talk about refusals. It's true you haven't refused me, but neither have you accepted me, because, of course, I've never actually asked you." Esther's face really went pink now, but she said nothing.

"When can I ask *the* question?"

"After the operation."

"Why then?"

"Because," she stammered, "because if I'm to lie here day and night, I can't marry you."

Len pulled back the covers and very gently but very firmly took her frail and crippled form in his arms. He held her to him for a few moments. He could see that she winced in pain but he also saw the biggest smile on her face he had seen since her accident.

He laid her gently down again and covered her with the blanket. "There, that's to prove that I'll still find ways to love you even if you lie flat all your days." Esther hid her face in the pillow.

"Crying?"

"Yes, for joy." She looked up at him and he noticed teardrops in her long eyelashes. "But, seriously, Len," Esther began again after she had regained her composure, "how can we know, you and I, that you aren't wanting to marry me just out of pity and that I am accepting you because there's no other alternative for me?"

Len's face was as serious as hers now. That had been a question he had mulled over day after day. He certainly felt love for her, but to say he didn't pity her at all would be a lie. "Esther," he began slowly, "I know I still feel some pity for you, but every day it gets less and my love gets stronger. I'm sure before long, love will swallow up all pity."

"And every day," Esther replied, "I become more certain that I'd marry you if my looks were given back to me and if I found myself walking again."

"Oh, my darling niece," Mary exclaimed one morning as she bent down to kiss her, "how happy I am to see you so much better!"

"It's Len, Aunt," and Esther pointed towards the figure in the chair by her side. "He's been so forward that I had to get better to defend myself."

Len put his book down. "What did you say? Defend yourself? I like that. But yes, I fuss over you a lot because I love you a lot and because I'm trying to bring back the red into your cheeks."

Mary smiled through her tears. "Where's Gabby?" Esther asked suddenly. "She hasn't been to see me today."

"She'll be here later," Mary reassured her niece. She did not tell her that ever since her sister had heard about Len's return, she had acted strangely.

"I worry abut her," Esther said slowly. The pain in her eyes was so great Len couldn't stand it.

"But you mustn't, Esther. Worry doesn't help you right now."

Esther put her thin hands to her face and began to sob. "But I made her go astray. I didn't show love to her. I was hard on her."

It was in vain that Mary tried to comfort her. Len gave her a knowing look and she tiptoed out of the room.

"Esther, both you and I have some repenting to do."

"You, Len?"

"Oh, come on," he laughed a little. "Don't pretend you have forgotten how I acted when you first knew me."

Esther nodded. "I remember. How can I forget?"

"And yet you'll still have me?"

"I'll have to keep you safe from all those nurses who make eyes at you."

Len blushed. "So you notice?" His voice was pensive. This was a sore spot with him.

"Yes. But I know you can't help that any more than," she gulped, "than I could help men looking at me when I…," she stammered, "when I was beautiful."

"So we're two of a pair. God knew what He was doing when He brought us together, didn't He?"

"Yes."

Len opened his mouth to remind her who he really was, but closed it again. He had already told her all about his mother's letter, and she had assured him that it made no difference to her. "You are God's true son, Len," she had whispered, "and that's all that matters to me."

Now, looking into those wonderful eyes of hers, he knew everything was all right. "Well then," Len announced with a broad smile, "I'll go and buy the ring when you want me to. Shall it be tomorrow?"

"Wait till I've had the operation," she said. "Please."

Len groaned inwardly but agreed, and he thought that she gave him the most beautiful smile he had ever seen. Then Esther yawned. "I'm tired. Sing to me, please, one of your own songs, Len."

"On one condition."

"Yes?"

"That, one day when you've had your operation and can sit up straight, you'll sing, too?"

She flopped back in the bed. "Oh no, Len. I'll never sing again. It always brings me trouble. Please don't make me."

"I'll never ever force you, dearest. But you must promise me that if you ever have the urge to sing with me, you won't suppress it."

"I promise," she said.

Len opened his Bible at Psalm ninety-one. He was meditating on the first few verses when he heard a very small voice from the bed asking, "Read me a few verses, please, Len. Just a few."

Len's face was a pleasure to see as he began in his soft, musical voice: "He that dwelleth in the secret place of the most high shall abide under the shadow of the almighty."

When he had finished the psalm, he looked over at the patient. She was sleeping again as she often did these days. "Under His shadow," he breathed, as he closed the Bible. "Lord, keep us under Your shadow, Esther and me. And I thank you Lord, that the shadow of the Almighty must be more than big enough to cover both of us. For where she is, Lord, where Esther is, there I'll be for the rest of my life."

## Chapter Thirty-Four

*Aunt Lucy Drops a Bombshell!*

"Len, you need to get a few decent nights' rest." Gabby had crept into Esther's room. Her sister was fast asleep, but Len was in his chair as usual, his eyes fixed on the girl in the bed beside him.

"Do I? I hadn't noticed," Len replied.

Esther stirred and opened her eyes. Gabby went over to the bed. "Do you mind if I relieve Len tonight?" she asked. "He looks very tired. Those chairs aren't that comfortable, you know."

"No, I'm used to having Len," her sister told her with a pout.

Gabby's face darkened, but then, what could she expect? She had deserted Esther when she needed her most. She felt simply rotten about it. Still, Len's complacent smile got on her nerves, even though she thought he was just about the most courageous person on earth.

Gabby's eyes flashed dangerously as she saw him lean back in his chair. He was there for the duration, that was obvious. She knew she had to be careful not to disturb the patient too much so she said quietly, "Well, I'm going to stay all night with you, whether Len's here or not. That young man of yours won't push me quite out of your life, sister dear. I'm going to find another chair," and she made for the door.

"It'll be too crowded," Len protested.

"Yes, far too crowded," echoed Esther. "And I want Len to stay tonight." The patient's voice was persistent. "After all, where were you when I needed you most?"

The florescent light was shining full on Gabby's face now. Len studied it for a moment. There was some look there that betrayed an emotion he had struggled with himself for months. Guilt, that was it, and shame, and something else. He looked again. Gabby was standing gazing down at her sister. Her green-grey eyes seemed to look past the bed, the hospital, to some distant horizon. What was she seeing? Her past? Her future?

Esther was obviously totally unaware of her sister's mood. She only knew she wanted Len, no one else, to stay with her that night. "You ran away, Gabby," she said accusingly. "But he…"

Len stood up. "I ran away, too. Remember?" His voice was sharp and made Esther start. "So stop being so hard on your sister. You don't need to rub it in like that. Can't you see she feels sorry for what she's done? What would you and I be today without forgiveness?"

"I do forgive her," Esther said, trying to sound meek, "but I'll never sleep tonight if you're not here with me. And you know I need sleep. The doctor said…"

"The doctor said not to spoil you as much as I've been doing," Len said calmly. And it was true. Dr. Garrington had taken him aside just that morning and warned him. "Esther's becoming a very selfish girl," he said. "You're her little lackey. If that's how you want to begin marriage…"

"But," Len had stammered, "she's so handicapped and needs so much care and love."

Dr. Garrington had placed a fatherly hand on the young man's shoulder. "Yes, she needs all that, I admit. But we have to help her return to at least some state of normalcy. Would you, for example, allow any other girl to order you around like Esther does?"

Len had gotten the message, but he thought the doctor too severe. "He doesn't understand the situation," he had muttered to himself as he left the doctor's office. "How can he?"

But now, as he looked at Esther's face, he changed his mind. Her bottom lip was hanging down in a plain, spoiled pout. He looked into her eyes. He always liked to do that. He had never seen finer eyes in all his life, but there was still a defiance lurking in their depths that bothered him.

"Esther, you and I will have a private talk about some things tomorrow, but tonight I'm leaving you with Gabby. I think she needs some sisterly counsel."

"I'll stop eating again if you go, Len Atwood. And they'll put me on tubes and take me back to intensive care and…"

"Listen," Gabby said gently, bending over her sister. She had never fully realized till then how much she had missed her. She ran her finger gently over the scarred face and squeezed Esther's thin hand. "Look at Len for a moment and tell me what you see. Now, take a good long look."

Esther pouted again but obeyed. Her eyes soon began to mist over. "Why, Len Atwood," she exclaimed, "you look simply horrific!"

"Me, horrific?" he said in mock surprise.

"Yes. I know it's a terrible blow to your ego, but it's the truth. There are huge, dark circles round your eyes; your cheeks are nearly as sallow as mine, and you've lost a lot of weight. It doesn't suit you at all. I've wondered why the nurses simply ignore you these days. Now I understand. And, besides," her voice choked, "we need at least one good-looker in the family."

Gabby grabbed a Kleenex and wiped her eyes. Then she smiled. Her plan had worked. Esther wasn't as selfish as she seemed. And what would she be like in her place? She'd become a spoiled brat within twenty-four hours.

"Get a good night's rest, Len," Esther went on very gently now. "Come and say goodbye tomorrow morning and then get a break from me for at least three or four days."

"A break from you? I…"

"You'll do as I say, Len Atwood." Esther tried to sound severe but her tears belied her tone. "I've got to learn to do without you from time to time," she said.

"OK, I'll go if you order it," he said resignedly. He turned to the girl standing opposite him. Her tears were falling fast on the white bedspread. "I'll be in to check up on you tomorrow. Now, don't talk all night. I know what girls are."

"Promise," Gabby managed to say. Len slipped out of the room, but not before he heard the girl say between sobs, "Oh Esther, you're absolutely right. I've been mean, selfish, unthoughtful, and worse than that. Oh, you'll never know how bad I've been, how bad I still am. And if Len really knew, he wouldn't want to leave you with me tonight." Len hurried out of earshot. It was time he got out of the way. He just hoped Esther wouldn't be too worn out the next morning.

That night was a memorable one for the two sisters. Gabby told Esther nearly everything and when she had finished, the invalid beckoned her to the bed. Gabby felt her thin arms trying to go round her and felt her scarred face close to hers. Their tears mingled freely, for it wasn't just Gabby who needed to apologize.

When they had finished their talk, Esther was exhausted but happy, and fell asleep long before Gabby. She scarcely slept at all. She was glad Esther had forgiven her. But God? She still wasn't sure about Him. There were still many unanswered questions. But maybe being reconciled to her family was the first step in the right direction. She certainly hoped so.

When Len came in the next morning and looked at the two sisters, he knew he could take a few days' break with a light heart. He made it a point to call Ron as soon as he got home and let him know Esther's progress. There was a long silence at the other end of the phone line, and then he heard his cousin say slowly and with some effort, "Congratulations! I am really glad that it's working out for you after all. Just as I said, I'm green with envy, but at the same time, I'm thrilled to see something taking place before my eyes that I thought only happened in story books."

When Len got back to Knoxville a few days later, Esther told him that Gabby had been a wonderful nurse, but she whispered into his ear when her sister had left the room, "No one can feed me or sing to me or…," she paused, "or kiss me like you can."

Len beamed on her. He had missed her terribly, though he had needed the break. He had gone to bed when he had arrived home and slept for nearly twenty hours straight.

The girls had received quite a few visitors in his absence: Marion had come to visit and stayed at least an hour. Malcolm was back in Romania, she told Esther. Then Ramona and Claude had spent two whole days in Knoxville and had come several times to the hospital. Betty and Keith Cripps, too, had paid Esther a long visit, and Uncle John had come and stayed one whole day. Esther had enjoyed seeing her friends, but visiting still exhausted her and left her petulant and demanding.

"My sister's needs seem never-ending," Gabby told Len when they were alone. "Orange juice, water, reading, you name it, she wants it and wants it now. And some things she tells me only you can do." She grinned. "You know, Len, Esther's crazy about you."

Len blushed crimson. "So you think it's not just because…?"

Gabby stopped him. "She's falling in love with you! Anyone could see it who had eyes." Gabby smiled as she walked to the elevator. Esther had asked almost the same thing the day before. "Len dotes on you," she had told her sister. Esther had looked up into Gabby's face questioningly. "You don't think it's just because…?"

And Gabby had replied gently, "He's madly in love with you, sister dear. I've never seen any man use his eyes as that guy does when he's anywhere near you."

When Gabby left the hospital the morning of Len's return, her mind was in a turmoil. There were only a few days before term began, just enough time to… To what, she asked herself as she started up the ignition? To go to Indianapolis to thank them all for their kindness and hospitality; to see Sue and suggest that she come and work in Marjorie's guest house; and, last but not least, to have a much-needed talk with Larry?

This is certainly what she had planned to do once Len came back and relieved her at the hospital. But now, Gabby wasn't too sure what she would say if she did have that talk with Larry. Was she willing to part with him? Was she ready to change her life style? Was she now so sure that there was a God that she would devote her life to serving Him as her parents had done? These were questions she could not yet answer. She and Larry had spoken together on the phone at least once a week, and their conversations always left Gabby depressed. He confused and overpowered her.

Right at that moment, she wished she could put her life into neutral for at least a few months, hoping for some providence to come along which would take decision-making out of her hands. Then she gave a start, turned off the ignition, and leaned back in her car seat. Did she really need further signs from providence? What about Esther's accident, about Len's extraordinary devotion? Weren't these signs enough?

She leaned forward again. Yes, she would go to Indianapolis and finish it all with Larry. She couldn't continue to live as she had done. But the thought of Larry Porter made her uncertain again. Rachel had said he was too much for her and he was. Was she certain enough of her course to push him out of her life forever and did she really want to?

She gave a yawn. All this reasoning was tiring. And after those days alone with her invalid sister she was exhausted. She would postpone her trip north for the time being. She was too weary to confront anyone, let alone someone like Larry.

Gabby had just reached the main road when she recognized her great aunt's car. She peered closer and saw Rita at the wheel. She hoped they wouldn't see her. She couldn't face Aunt Lucy right then.

Later that evening, Rachel burst into their apartment with exciting news. Miss Lucy had been to the hospital and had just announced to Esther that she had left everything to her in her will. Not only that, but she was arranging for most of the income which she received quarterly from some inheritance, to be put at Esther's disposal as soon as possible. This would mean that the invalid could have a permanent nurse to take care of her when she was discharged from the hospital.

"I suppose my sister was overjoyed," Gabby commented as Rachel made herself a drink of hot chocolate.

"I suppose so but she was in such a state of shock that the nurse had to be called. She nearly fainted. This made Len hopping mad with Aunt Lucy who had to make a quick exit."

Rachel sipped her chocolate for a few moments and then went on, "Why your aunt had to announce it in such a dramatic fashion, I've no idea. It wasn't thoughtful of Esther though it is wonderful news!"

### Aunt Lucy Drops a Bombshell! 271

"Yes, it is," Gabby agreed. "It'll mean that she won't need to stay in a nursing home forever."

"And it will also mean that Len doesn't need to spend his life devoted to an invalid."

"Yes, I suppose it will relieve him somewhat. He couldn't have done it all himself, could he?"

Rachel gave an impatient toss of her head. "Sometimes, Gabby, you are unbelievably naïve. Don't you see that the guy is let off the hook now?"

Gabby stared at her cousin in surprise. "So you don't think he really loves Esther—that he's just doing all this because he feels obligated—that she might die if he didn't?"

"Well, don't you think that's just what he is doing?"

"No, I don't," Gabby replied slowly. "I think he's devoted to her. But I suppose the next few days and weeks will give us a more definite answer to your question."

Rachel gave a short laugh. "I think we'll know by tomorrow. So be ready!"

With Rachel and her aunt back from their vacation by the sea, and with Len once more ensconced at Esther's bedside, Gabby had planned not go near the hospital the next day, but curiosity drew her there like a magnet first thing the next morning. Len met her at the door of Esther's room and held up his hand. "Your sister's still asleep," he told her.

Len stepped out into the corridor so that he could talk. "Rachel told you, didn't she?"

"Yes."

"Then why are you looking so solemn?"

Gabby flushed but said nothing. Len studied her intently for a few moments. "Why, you don't think," he stammered, "you can't think this will make any difference to me, do you?"

"I really didn't," Gabby began, "but..."

Len didn't let her finish her sentence. "Miss Lucy thought that her news would let me off the hook. I told her in front of Esther that as far as I am concerned, it makes no difference except, of course, it has come as an answer to prayer. I know I couldn't have coped alone."

"And Esther?"

"Esther?" Len repeated. "Well, she was too weak to say much after her aunt left, but I told her what I felt. She gave me one of her wonderful smiles and reached out her thin little hand and squeezed mine. 'I love you, Len Atwood,' was all she said. And that was enough for me."

## Chapter Thirty-Five

### *Duets*

"Esther Popescu, will you be my wife?" Len was kneeling by Esther's wheelchair. This was the second time she had sat in it since her operation a few weeks previously. She buried her face in the beautiful bouquet of flowers Len had placed in her hands. Then she raised her head and her eyes met his.

Len met her gaze and held it steadily. He was not afraid of what she might see. His faults were open to all the world, so he was not afraid for Esther to discover them. He hoped that they would be covered by his love, budding love maybe, but love sure and steady, blossoming deep in his soul. Sometimes, when he remembered for a fleeting moment the Esther that had been, deep pity for the invalid girl would indeed sweep over him. But mostly, as now, when he looked into those wonderful eyes, it was not pity that made him want to kiss her, or hold her close, or buy her pretty things, or sing to her.

It seemed that they looked at one another in silence for a very long time. Esther was conscious that she, too, was far from perfect. She smiled a little as she remembered Jean's words those long months ago, "The trouble with you is you're too good to be true." She wasn't like that any more. She had become a spoiled girl, who pouted to get her way. And she still fought with bitterness, especially when she mulled over what the specialist had told her—that there was no hope of her ever walking again. Then she would think of others who were worse off than she was, and remind herself that she had so much to be grateful for.

So what did those great black eyes see, staring into hers? Could Len read her soul as she seemed to read his? In case he couldn't, she reckoned she'd better tell him right away to put him out of his suspense. "I'll be your wife, Len Atwood," she said very softly but clearly, focusing now on the roses in her lap, "if you'll assure me you know what you're doing."

"*I* do, Esther. And what about *you*?"

"Ever since Dr. Garrington spoke to us together in his own forthright way a few weeks ago, I've thought a lot over what it will mean."

"And?"

"I think God knew what He was doing when He picked out you to be my husband. So, Len, if you'll take me as I am, I'm yours for life."

In a moment, he had lifted her from the chair and cradling her in his arms, he began waltzing round the hospital room. She laughed and clung to his neck. "Put me down before the nurse catches you acting like this with one of her patients," she ordered.

Len placed her carefully in the chair once more, then he reached in his pocket. Esther's heart beat fast as she watched him take out a ring with one pearl upon it and gently, almost reverently, put it on her finger. Her hands were so thin, he thought, but the ring was small and fit perfectly. But before he had slipped it on all the way, he paused.

"I just have to make sure about one thing, Esther," he said in a low voice, "and then I won't ever mention it again as long as I live. I know you've had a ring, much more beautiful and expensive than this one, placed on this very finger before."

Esther blushed. She remembered that day only too well. "Now," he went on, "I've told you, I think, that I've talked to Ron about my intentions to marry you. And he wishes me all the best. But…"

"It's all right, Len," Esther whispered softly. "That's in the past. It was a wonderful memory in many ways, but I don't think Ron and I were made for each other. He's so intense, so serious, that he couldn't have coped with me as I am now. I need someone who laughs and is silly at times when I get into one of my disagreeable moods—someone who can sing and play like an angel. And besides," she was in deadly earnest now, "he didn't understand the spiritual side of me."

"No," Len agreed, "but I think Ron is realizing at last that he needs God, and that's the first step on the way to finding Him. You know, Esther, my cousin always was much more of a gentleman than I was."

She laughed merrily. "I told you that, didn't I?"

"You certainly did."

"I just didn't know how to handle you, Len. And besides, you've changed an awful lot."

"So have you," he retorted with a grin. "But, now that Ron is well on the way to being a real Christian, I want you to be sure…"

Esther put a finger to his lips. "Maybe you didn't know, but I talked with Dr. Garrington yesterday when you weren't around, and he said very few men could cope with marrying someone like myself. Very few!

He says that your temperament plus your love for me and for God will carry you through. And it's different with you. You didn't begin to love me till I was crippled and scarred. Ron loved the girl I used to be so he found it very hard to transfer that love to the girl I really am now."

"Little philosopher!" Len teased as he pushed the ring over her knuckle.

"It's beautiful," she breathed as she gazed at the pure white stone.

"I thought that the pearl suited you perfectly. It stands for purity, and," he added blinking back the tears, "for beauty that comes through suffering. You know how the pearl is formed?" Esther nodded. He didn't need to say any more.

Len stood up. He could never be serious for long. "Now for a celebration," he announced. "I'll be back in about half an hour. Nurse Gadger will take care of you till I come back, won't you, Nurse?" he asked, as he nearly collided into that good lady in the doorway.

Nurse Gadger came up to Esther's chair and stooped to kiss her. "Congratulations!" she told her, looking from the roses to the ring on her finger. "I'm not sure that this room has ever hosted an engagement party before."

"A what?" the girl gasped.

"Enough said!" Nurse Gadger put a hand to her lips. Len had sworn her to secrecy. Soon another nurse had come to help her push the bed into the corner, wheel out the dresser, and bring in as many chairs as they could squeeze into the room.

"Sitting up? Well, what a change!" a voice exclaimed at Esther's elbow. She looked up.

"Aunt Lucy!" she exlcaimed. "I've not had much chance to thank you for all you're doing for me."

"That's nothing, child. Nothing! I'm just so happy that everything has turned out as it has! God is very good!" Miss Lucy turned away. She could say no more.

"What a wonderful surprise to see you looking so well, Esther!" a soft voice exclaimed in her ear. Esther gave a start. It was Marion.

Her friend bent down as she took the invalid's hand in hers, "Forgive me, dear Esther," she whispered, tears in her blue eyes, "for what happened the day of your accident. I find it so hard to forgive myself."

There were other guests waiting in line to shake hands, so Esther only had time to whisper back, "I'm learning that everything works for good to those who love God, Marion."

Marion glanced at her friend's scarred face and crippled body. Then her eyes fell on Len who had just entered the room, his eyes full of tenderness and love as he gazed at his fiancée. "Yes, all things certainly have worked for good," she murmured as she let go her friend's hand.

"How well you look, Esther!" said another very familiar voice.

"Yes, doesn't she, Mr. Hugh, and look at her hair. It's grown in a mass of shiny black curls, to match Len's. They make a fine pair, don't they?" It was Gabby speaking now.

"They certainly do!" That was Aunt Mary's voice. Esther would know it anywhere.

Esther looked from one to the other. She saw Rachel was coming in the door just then and another figure behind her. It was Aaron. He came up and shook her hand. Then he began to greet her in Romanian. Esther leaned back in her chair. "How did you all know?"

"I told them," Len exclaimed, pushing his way to her through what seemed to Esther crowds of people though really it was only a few of her closest friends and family. "They had official invitations."

"But what if I'd said 'No'"?

Len didn't answer. He had received at least a score of "yesses" in the past weeks. This was just an official confirmation to what each had already known in their hearts and spoken with their eyes.

"So that's why the nurse dressed me up today!" Esther exclaimed. It was the first time she had put on her clothes since her accident.

"Yes. This is going to be a real party. It can't go on for too long, though; Dr. Garrington said you've not to get over-excited. He's coming too. Oh, there he is."

The doctor came in just then and beamed on them all. Then a nurse wheeled a trolley into the room. Esther gasped. There were all sorts of goodies on it, and Len was acting the host as if he did it every day.

When they had all eaten and congratulated the happy pair, someone asked Len to sing. He looked over to Esther but she shook her head.

Len reached for his guitar which he always kept handy, and sang several songs he had composed himself. When he had finished, Gabby's voice called out, "What about *Numai Harul*, Len? You learned that, you know."

"Yes," Len said, "I learned it one night under very stressful circumstances." He saw Esther's eyes fill with tears. "Now I can sing it in this same room but with joy and gladness. It is truly 'only grace' that has brought Esther and me together. So it's very fitting that I sing it at our engagement party."

He was so busy positioning his guitar that he didn't see Esther's face, but Rachel said afterwards that she had noticed a very strange expression come over it. It seemed there was a terrible battle going on inside her cousin. Then as Len struck the first note, a wonderful peace had stolen over the invalid's thin features, making her much more like the Esther everyone had known and loved in Velours.

"*Numai Harul*," Len began.

"You don't say it right," Esther interrupted.

Len put down the guitar and pretended to be offended. "Well, I've told you several times that I needed a teacher and you said…"

"That I'd teach you when I was better." Her voice choked, and her friends standing around held their breath. "And though I'm not all better yet, I've come a long way. Now, Len," and she pretended to be stern, "you don't make that *r* liquid enough."

"Liquid?"

"Like this," and she rolled her *r* until they all laughed.

Len tried again but she stopped him for the second time. "No. It's just not right." She paused. Then Len's heart nearly stopped beating as he saw her raise herself in her wheelchair. "Oh dear," she muttered, "I'll have to show you. Give me the note, please," she ordered imperiously.

Len's fingers could hardly find the strings as he tried to pluck the opening chord. Then to their utter amazement, the invalid girl, her eyes fixed on Len, began to sing her favorite hymn. At first her voice faltered a little. Her fiancé was beaming at her and nodding encouragingly. He knew the ordeal it must be and the memories which would be flooding her at that moment.

Nurse Gadger handed around the box of Kleenex. Len heard sniffles coming from the door and taking his eyes off the singer for one brief moment, he was amazed to see the corridor filled with nurses.

Esther sang all the verses without a pause. Her voice might not have been quite as strong as it had been, but it was just as sweet and pure and true. When she had finished, Len was about to speak when she stopped him. "Let's give them a duet this time," she suggested smiling. "How about *Amazing Grace?*"

Len couldn't speak. He certainly hoped he wouldn't break down completely. He and Esther had never sung a duet before, but it was a day he had dreamed about for weeks. Sometimes it had seemed as if the sick girl would never ever sing again. But the vision he had had that night in Cincinnati would rise before him as it did now. He looked over at Esther. The scar was still there all right, but he had almost ceased to notice it now, and her hair would be simply gorgeous in six months or so. If this was not the complete fulfillment of his vision, it was certainly a sweet foretaste of things to come.

Then Len realized they were all waiting for him to begin. "You'll have to excuse us. We've had no practice," he apologized, as he changed the key and played a few opening bars. He looked at the girl in the wheelchair and nodded.

It was all impromptu, nothing planned, but it didn't need to be. Len found it easy to blend his tenor with Esther's bell-like soprano. And how better to celebrate their engagement than by singing together about God's grace that was doing so much in their lives right at that very moment!

Gabby looked wistfully at her sister. She put her hand up to her face and felt her own clear, smooth skin. She dangled her legs over the windowsill where she was perched. She could run and swim and play tennis as well if not better than most of her peers. She could offer a man a flawless face and figure, and a lithe and graceful body which her sister could no longer do. She thought of the jealousy she used to feel as she saw Esther admired and praised wherever she went. Now the roles were reversed. She wasn't the beauty her sister had been, perhaps, but she had grown into an extremely attractive young woman who never lacked for compliments wherever she went.

Gabby glanced again at her sister. Esther might be marred and scarred in body but she was pure as a lily in her soul. She gave a slight shudder. Any young man she would want for a husband now, would never look at a girl who had done what she had done, would he? And she hadn't just been a poor, deceived soul who had been seduced by some conniving villain. She thought of Romania and her aunt's little sitting room where she had made her choice to go back to the hotel room that fateful day. Well, she was paying the price now. Try as she might, she couldn't feel quite at home in her family any more. She felt a sort of outcast, even though they were very forgiving, surprisingly so, all except Rachel, perhaps.

As she listened to the singers, Gabby's mind went to John Newton. He had tasted nearly every form of evil and yet he had written that song! Could God forgive her just as He'd forgiven Newton? Theoretically she knew He could. That's what she'd been taught all her life, but practically, it was hard to believe. But if and when she did find God's true forgiveness, then she'd love Him and serve Him the rest of her days. She would get her degree, then leave America with its Velvet Curtain and its Larry Porters. She'd make a clean start in her native land where she could forget her past sins and mistakes and become a new Gabby Popescu.

Sitting on that windowsill, listening to the two singers, Gabby knew exactly what she had to do. A few months previously, she hadn't been so sure. But now she had no question. Not all the Larrys in the world could persuade her to live like she had been living that summer. God's grace was tugging strongly at her heart. She must respond while she was still young and free.

Watching the girl's expressive face from across the room, Aaron Gardner wondered what she was thinking. Gabby caught his eye for a moment but dropped hers almost immediately. Aaron's face clouded and he turned his head away. Why did the girl always avoid him? Why couldn't he simply be friends with her? That's all he wanted now, nothing more. He had a girlfriend in Romania whom he thought simply adorable and who seemed to worship the ground he trod on. He basked in this adoration, even though his granddad remained skeptical about the whole affair. "No wonder she adores you!" had been his comment. "She probably sees you as a passport to the West." But passport or no passport, it felt mighty wonderful to be adored instead of shunned by girls like Gabby Popescu.

"Come back to earth, Aaron," Hugh whispered in his ear. Aaron started. They were all clapping now.

"This has been a truly memorable occasion," Dr. Garrington said, when the applause had ceased. "But I think my patient is exhausted and needs her rest." Len looked anxiously at Esther. She did look very pale.

She caught his eye, and, looking round the crowded room, she said with a radiant smile, "Thank you, everyone. I'll never forget this day as long as I live."

Gabby was filing out of the room with the others when she felt a bony hand on her shoulder. "I want a few words with you, Gabriella. Somewhere quiet." Gabby stared at her great aunt in astonishment. She had never spoken to her since that fateful Christmas nearly two years previously.

"Come into the waiting room. There's no one in it at present," Gabby told her aunt.

When the old lady had seated herself she cleared her throat. "I think we need to be reconciled, you and I, Gabriella. I don't know how long I have in this world and I certainly don't want to go into the next and have to admit to my Maker that I wasn't on speaking terms with one of my few remaining relatives." Gabby smiled in spite of herself. Great Aunt Lucy did have a unique way of putting things.

"I'm glad to take this chance to apologize to you, Aunt. I was very rude to you and..."

"That's all forgotten, child. You reminded me so much of myself at your age, that was the problem. It brought back memories." Gabby stared at her aunt in astonishment.

"Yes, I was stubborn, rebellious, and wayward," Aunt Lucy continued. Gabby winced at such a graphic description of herself.

"But you don't know how bad I've been this past year, Aunt," Gabby interrupted.

"Maybe I don't know exactly, but I can guess." Aunt Lucy peered at her great niece over her spectacles. She seemed to be reading more than her face, Gabby thought. "You don't know how bad I was either." The old lady gave a faint smile as she went on, "I had one son, you know." Gabby nodded; she knew that already.

Lucy cleared her throat. "But what you don't know was that I wasn't married when I had him."

Gabby gasped. Looking at her prim relative in her long black skirt and high-necked white blouse, she couldn't believe her ears.

"Yes," Lucy went on with a sigh. "And in those days it was an absolute disgrace to have a child out of wedlock. The father wouldn't own me or the child, but I later met a man, God bless him, who took me and my boy into his heart and home." Lucy got out her snow-white, lace-trimmed handkerchief and wiped her eyes. "I don't really know why I'm telling you this," she continued, "except that watching your face in the room there, and seeing it look so sad, I thought maybe what I was saying would encourage you to realize that there is forgiveness with the Lord. I've discovered that from personal experience."

Gabby was still in shock. Why was her aunt really telling her all this? But Miss Lucy hadn't finished. "And I want you to know that keeping my boy was the best thing I ever did. My family wanted me to have him adopted. But I wouldn't and I'm sure glad I didn't. And remember," she bent over and looked deep into Gabby's green-grey eyes, "that there are still noble young men in this world who will have you, just as you are. Remember that. Such a man may be hard to find, but wait for him. He does exist."

Gabby couldn't quite analyze her emotions as she helped her aunt out of her seat and walked with her along the familiar corridor to the elevator. When they reached the foyer, Lucy took her great niece by the arm and whispered in her ear. "One more thing, Gabriella. I've made out most of my estate to your sister. She sure will need all she can get." Gabby nodded and beamed on the old lady. "But I've not forgotten you. You may need all you can get, too."

Gabby's mouth fell open. "Yes," Miss Lucy whispered again, "I'm arranging for you to have five hundred dollars per month from the estate beginning as soon as it can be settled legally. I'm sorry it isn't more but..."

Gabby flung her arms round the old lady's neck. "Aunt Lucy, you don't know what this means to me. I'm going back to Romania next year, when I've finished college. Wages over there are pitiful, but this amount of money will more than keep me. I'll have extra besides to give to my aunt and friends and orphans and..."

But her aunt had slipped from her embrace and was gone. Gabby stared after her retreating figure. Then suddenly she felt tired and sick. She had felt that way quite often lately. But she also felt the happiest she had felt for months. God was working everything out for her, even though she didn't deserve it.

She slipped upstairs to say goodbye to her sister, but the scene that met her eye made her turn quietly away. Tears filled her eyes as she made her way to the car. Had her Aunt Lucy spoken the truth that afternoon? Would any Christian young man look at her the way Len was looking now at her sister? She thought over her acquaintances and stopped short. What was she doing? She was going to Romania to start anew. Maybe there would be someone waiting for her over there.

While Gabby was driving back to her apartment, her sister was enjoying a few moments of privacy with her fiancé. "I hope you've not overdone, darling," Len said anxiously.

Esther smiled. "I feel utterly exhausted, but it's been worth it all. Do you know that those first two words *Numai Harul* were the hardest words to get out. It seemed like my lips were shut fast by a clamp. But as I opened them and the first notes rang out, the last vestige of bitterness seemed to evaporate. You see," she said very softly, "I had told God I'd never ever sing again. But I knew, when I heard you strum those opening bars, that it was now or never. What kind of a marriage would it be if I entered it with this kind of rebellion in my heart?"

"I think *Only Grace*, is hard for us all to sing," Len said thoughtfully. "But as Newton says, "its grace that's brought us safe thus far."

"And grace will lead us home."

Len patted the hand that wore his ring. "Get some sleep and rest," he told her. "We're officially betrothed now, you know."

"Yes. And Len?"

"What?"

"Will you promise me something?"

"If I possibly can, dear."

"That you'll take me back to Romania, for a visit I mean. I want to show you a land where there is no Velvet Curtain."

"That would be like Heaven."

"No, it won't be like Heaven. There's too much poverty and disease and dirt for it to be anything like Heaven will be. But," and she smiled up at the man who was giving up so much to be her husband, "for me, it's as near Heaven as this earth can be."

"Then let's go," he said, "maybe for our honeymoon."

Esther's face clouded just a little. "Len, you know…"

"I know," he said stroking her face gently. "I'm marrying an invalid and it's going to be different. But," and his eyes twinkled, "I like a challenge."

"So I've seen. And I'll be the biggest challenge you've ever known, Len Atwood. I really will."

"No, you won't, Esther." He was serious now. "To conquer my own nature is my biggest challenge. To let God change me—the…"

He felt a finger on his lips. "No. Not tonight you won't. You've cataloged your failings so many times in the past weeks that I know them all by heart. Tonight is a night of praise and rejoicing. It's one of the happiest nights in my life."

Esther clasped her hands together and began to sing softly, "How great is the God we adore, our faithful unchangeable Friend, Whose Grace is as great as His power, and knows neither measure nor end."

Len swallowed hard and joined in: "'Tis Jesus the First and the Last, Whose Presence will guide us safe Home. We'll praise Him for all that is past…"

They both stopped spontaneously and looked deep into each other's eyes. Len clasped Esther's small white hand in his and bowed his head. Esther did the same. They had pledged each other their troth that day but now they were putting their hands into the Almighty's. "And trust Him for all that's to come," they concluded in unison.

Nurse Gadger couldn't help peeking in just then. "Amen," she said in her loudest and most Irish of voices.

"Amen," Dr. Garrington echoed from behind her.

"Amen," Esther's clear girlish voice took up the refrain.

"And Amen," Len concluded.

## Chapter Thirty-Six

### *Gabby in Shock*

"Gabby? Are you all right?" Mary's voice sounded anxious. Why on earth should her niece phone her at six in the morning? She waited for a response, but all she could hear was a muffled sob at the other end of the line. "Gabby," she repeated, "what's happened?"

"I'm pregnant, Aunt Mary." Only four words but they turned Mary's world upside down.

"No one else knows." Gabby sounded like a scared child. "I've suspected it for a month or so now, but didn't have the courage to really find out if I was or not. But this morning, I tried one of those home tests and…" Her voice trailed off.

"Those tests aren't foolproof, Gabby. You need to see a doctor." Mary tried to sound reassuring.

"I will, Aunt. But I've been sick for weeks now."

"How far along do you think you are?" It was hard to keep her voice normal, but Mary knew she had to stay calm.

"I don't know exactly, but about eleven weeks, probably. It's past the middle of October now, so the baby should be due the end of April or beginning of May. Oh, Aunt, I don't know why this has happened. I mean, I took every precaution, or so I thought. But…"

"Gabby, dear," Mary's voice was soothing now, "leave it in God's hands. Your life is His now. He's forgiven the past but, and I don't mean to sound trite, we do reap what we sow."

"I know, Aunt Mary. I'm discovering that nearly every day. Question is, what do I do now?"

"Do?" Mary sounded as if she didn't quite understand the question.

"Yes. I'll have to tell Larry, won't I?"

Mary took a long gulp before answering, "Of course you will. But I'd get a confirmation from your doctor first. No use telling him and then finding it's all a mistake."

"But I don't want to marry him," Gabby wailed. "Please don't make me marry him."

Mary thought privately that Larry wouldn't even consider that an option, but she only said quietly, "Nobody's going to make you do anything, dear. Let's take a step at a time. Now, first things first. Call the doctor immediately and get this confirmed."

"But I'm so ashamed, Aunt. To think that I let this happen after all I've been taught."

Her aunt said nothing and her niece went on, "Can I come over and see you this weekend?"

"Of course. You know you're always welcome."

"It's just that I have to talk everything out."

"Then come, dear. I'm alone right now. By the way, how's Esther?"

"I saw her yesterday. Rehab is so different from the hospital and a lot more challenging. But Len's always there, every day."

"Is he working?"

"He's moved into an apartment the other side of the city from us, nearer Cherry Place where Esther is. And he's got a few piano students. He's afraid to get too many and then have to cancel them when he gets married and they move somewhere else." Gabby laughed in spite of herself as she went on, "You should see them together. It's really comical. But he does Esther the world of good—lightens her up, and she sure needs that at times. She gets really depressed and still fights bitterness. If it weren't for Len…" Gabby paused.

"If it weren't for Len, Esther wouldn't still be with us, Gabby."

"I know that. And his pure unselfishness did more to bring me back to my senses than anything else. Even now, he has to have oceans of patience. My sister's not easy to handle these days."

"I know," Mary's voice was grave. "She often acts like a spoiled child. But each time I see her, there seems to be an improvement."

"Definitely! Well, I'd better get ready for college."

"You'll be in my prayers all day long, Gabby. Stick in there! God can make good come even of this, if you trust Him."

"Think so?"

"Know so! Now, bye! See you in a few days' time."

Gabby sighed softly as she hung up the receiver. Her Aunt Mary was a real mother to her.

She never knew how she got through the next few days. The doctor confirmed her fears. She was pregnant all right. That Friday evening, Gabby discussed it all with her aunt. She would tell Larry that very night. She felt better calling him from Tiny Gap with her aunt there for support.

"Now, Gabby," Mary advised, as her niece went to the phone after they had had a prayer together, "remember, don't commit yourself to anything right away. Just tell him the facts and then say you'll contact him again in a few days when he's had time to think it over. Remember, it'll come as a shock to him as well. What do you think his reaction will be?"

"Have an abortion right away so he can wipe his hands of me."

"Then why were you afraid you'd have to marry him?"

"I don't know. Larry's strange. You never know which way his reasoning will take him. Now," she gritted her teeth, "here goes." Gabby dialed the familiar number, but it was a very unfamiliar voice that answered at the other end—a young woman's voice with a strong southern drawl.

"You want Larry? Just a minute. Who did you say was speaking?"

"Gabby. Gabby Popescu."

Soon Gabby heard Larry's cool, clipped voice saying, "Gabby? This is a pleasant surprise!"

Gabby gripped the phone tighter. "I really need to speak to you when you're alone, Larry."

There was a silence on the other end and then, "I'll call you back in an hour. You're at your aunt's, right?"

"Right."

"OK. Speak to you later."

Larry put down the receiver and gave a low whistle. "That's odd."

"An old flame, eh?" the girl by his side taunted, as she laid her head on his shoulder.

"Let's say close friend," Larry said with a laugh, though the girl noticed the flush on his face and snuggled closer.

"Like me?"

Larry turned abruptly to face her. "No," he said sharply. "Not a bit like you. No two people could be more unlike each other."

The girl laughed. "Oh, I know she couldn't be a patch on me for looks. I was talking about our relationship."

Larry got up from the sofa. "Look here, Charlene, my relationship with Gabby Popescu is none of your business. I've invited you here for the weekend because I was lonely. I wanted a bit of distraction."

"Oh, did you now? What you really mean is that you wanted me as a sort of substitute for your precious Gabby." The young woman grabbed her sweater and made for the door. "Well, I could have any guy I wanted. I'm not used to being regarded as a substitute. *Adieu*, it's been nice knowing you."

The door slammed behind her and she was gone. Larry leaned back on the sofa and let out a long sigh. Nothing had gone right since Gabby had left. He had missed her more than he could say. Charlene might be the local Varsity Beauty Queen but she couldn't make up for Gabby. No one could or ever would.

He picked up the receiver and dialed Gabby's number. "Hi! I got free sooner than I thought. My visitor left so we can speak now."

Gabby wondered how many girl visitors he had had since she left but said nothing. "I've got something to tell you, Larry."

"Fire away then. Gabby, I've sure missed you."

Gabby gripped the receiver tighter. She wasn't expecting this reception. "Thanks." She cleared her throat. "I've been to the doctor this week and, well, I'm pregnant!"

There was a long silence, and then she heard him say calmly, "Then we'll need to get together soon, won't we? We've a lot to talk over."

"I suppose we have," Gabby replied. "I'm eleven weeks along already."

"Then it is urgent that we sort something out, isn't it?"

"Yes."

"I suppose there are only two alternatives open to us."

Gabby's heart beat faster as she repeated, "Two alternatives?"

"Yes. Abortion, of course, or marriage."

"There is a third alternative," Gabby suggested in a small voice.

"Really? What?"

"I could keep the baby myself, or have it adopted."

"So that makes four alternatives, doesn't it, if my math is correct?"

Gabby winced. "Yes. It does make four."

"Now," Larry went on meditatively, "I'm sure that you have decided already that abortion is out of the question."

"Of course!" Gabby shuddered. To think she would even be discussing these things with a young man, the *father* of her child! "Abortion is not an alternative for my child, Larry."

"It's *our* child, remember?" Larry reminded her. "It takes two, Gabby, like it or not. And I'm not sure I would consider abortion either."

"No?" Gabby couldn't believe her ears.

"No, I think I'd prefer marriage. And it is more traditional, you know, more up your street, I'd have thought."

Gabby's face turned white. She grabbed the table for support. Mary came up to her and patted her gently on the shoulder. This helped the girl to gain her composure. "Is that a proposal?" she heard herself asking.

"Could be," Larry replied with a short laugh. There was a long pause and then he said softly, "Maybe this baby's a blessing in disguise. But look, we need time to think this over. We'll have to talk face to face about this. Can you come up here?"

"I'd rather not. I'm feeling sick most of the time these days and it's a long trip to Indianapolis."

"Then I'll come to you. How about tomorrow? I'll stay in a motel overnight."

"OK. See you tomorrow."

"Bye, Larry."

"Bye, Gabby!"

The next afternoon just as the sun was setting, Larry knocked on Mary Popescu's door. She didn't exactly give him a warm welcome, but was civil enough and had prepared an excellent meal. Then, when the dishes were cleared away, she excused herself and slipped upstairs to her bedroom.

Larry took Gabby's arm and led her to the sofa. She noticed from the beginning that his whole attitude seemed to have changed. Holding her hand in his, he began more tenderly than she had ever heard him speak before, "Gabriella Popescu, will you marry me?"

Gabby pulled away her hand and jumped to her feet. "You can't mean that, Larry Porter. You really can't. I mean, you avoided talking marriage all the time we were together and now…"

"You weren't ready to consider marriage with me, and you know that," he told her reproachfully. "But I think you might just be ready now," he said softly, pulling her down beside him. "And I want you to know that I never found out till yesterday how much I really do love you. And we have always had so much in common, Gabby. You know how we felt in Florida last Christmas. We discovered that we were more than just friends—that we were soul mates. Remember?"

Gabby raised her eyes to his. She knew the moment of truth had come. "Yes, we did feel that, Larry. But we can't be soul mates any longer. We might pledge ourselves to be man and wife, but soul mates? That's impossible now."

"Why?"

"I've become a Christian."

Larry's eyes dilated wide and he turned white as a sheet. "Well then, it's…" he began heatedly, getting up from his chair. Then he stopped short. It was obvious to Gabby that he had mastered his first reaction to her announcement.

"I know this is a bit of a shock to you, Larry, but my life from now on is going to be devoted to serving Christ, because He has forgiven my sins and given me a peace I never knew existed."

"Look, you can love God if you want," Larry's smile was somewhat sickly as he spoke, "as long as you have some love left over for me. We'll strike a compromise. But," and he grabbed her hand with a force that made her wince, "I *must* have you. I love you passionately; without you, I'm in a desert; I worship your body, your mind, your soul. You've already given yourself to me. In God's sight we're already married. We've become one flesh. And the new life begun in you is a proof of our union."

Gabby stared at him in a dazed sort of way. She felt so confused. Right and wrong seemed so intermingled in Larry's presence that she couldn't think her way out of the muddle. Larry leaned towards her and looked deep into her eyes. He was just about to give her a long and passionate kiss when the door opened. Larry straightened and faced the intruder, eyes blazing.

Mary came up to the sofa and bent over her niece. "Gabby," she said gently, touching her on the shoulder, "can I help in any way?"

For a moment the girl stared at her blankly. Larry began stroking the girl's cheeks. "Gabby, darling," he whispered tenderly, "don't let anyone separate us any more. I'm here to look after you and the baby. Why don't you come with me to the motel. We can talk it all out, once and for all."

Gabby stared at him in disbelief. Didn't he understand that she was done with that type of thing? "Have you forgotten, Larry. I'm a Christian now."

"Yes, yes, I know," he said soothingly as if talking to a child. "But that doesn't stop me loving you. OK, I'll go and leave you in peace, but I'll be back tomorrow to talk more about our situation." He bent down and kissed her. "Get a good sleep," he whispered, and before Mary could say a word, she heard the front door click behind him.

She sat down beside her niece. Gabby sat there, staring at the door. "He's gone," she muttered.

"Yes," her aunt replied grimly. "He's gone all right. Now you need to get to bed. Here, I'll help you upstairs."

Gabby seemed to fall asleep the moment her head hit the pillow. Mary decided to sleep in Esther's bed that night, just in case Gabby woke and needed her. She longed to make a phone call or two but was sworn to secrecy. It was her niece's task, not hers, to break the news to the rest of the family.

About two that morning, Gabby woke with a start. She had been dreaming about Larry. It was their wedding day and she was putting on her wedding dress when he burst into her room and took her in his arms. "You won't escape me again, little bride," he told her, kissing her passionately. "This time, I'll bind you to me forever." Then he put her down and began to bind her with white silken cords. "Matches your dress," he had told her with a charming smile. She had begged him to loosen her, but he had just taken her in his arms again and kissed her. She had fought against her captor, but he had been too strong.

At last, however, she awoke. She had never been so happy to awaken from a dream. She lay and stared at the wall opposite for what seemed hours. What was God trying to say to her? Larry binding her? As the hours ticked by, Gabby slowly came to a conclusion. Larry had planned the whole thing from the start. A baby, he figured, would bind the girl to him—for life.

"Are you awake, Gabby?" she heard her aunt ask as the clock struck four.

Gabby sat bolt upright in bed. "I had a dream which set me thinking, Aunt Mary."

"Yes? Want to share it with me, dear?"

"Yes, Aunt. I've been very puzzled why Larry didn't seem surprised about my pregnancy."

"He wasn't surprised at all?"

"Well, it seemed to me that he was trying to act surprised but his first reaction was not at all what I thought it would be."

"So?"

Gabby blushed scarlet. "It's awfully hard for me to come out with this, Aunt Mary, but I need to face facts and they are cruel sometimes. Thing is, I was more surprised than he was."

Mary said nothing. She began to see where Gabby was taking her. "So," the girl continued, "I began to think over the time I spent with him. We were very careful you know," she blushed again. "Neither of us was necessarily committed to a long-term relationship, so we didn't plan for a baby to come on the scene, at least *I* didn't. But it seems that *he* did."

Mary stared at her niece. "Then you mean…"

"I mean he planned it all out," Gabby interrupted. "When I spent those two weeks in Indianapolis after I had returned from Europe, I was very depressed at times—about Esther of course, and I was also flooded with guilt much of the time. I tried to hide it, but I think Larry became afraid I would up and leave him for good."

"He loves you so much?" Mary tried not to sound sarcastic.

"I don't know. I just don't know!" Gabby said in frustration. "But on his birthday, he invited friends to our basement apartment. We had a feast, of course. Sally and Ken were there for the first few hours and then they left when the music got a bit loud. Well, we danced well past midnight and we drank. There was plenty of alcohol around and I got tipsy." Gabby hung her head. "No, I've been tipsy before. This was different. I got really drunk and made a fool of myself. Larry dismissed our guests and put me to bed."

"When was that, did you say?"

"Late July."

"And you're eleven weeks pregnant?"

"Yes, Aunt." Gabby's voice sounded far away.

"Had you never been drunk before?" Mary felt she needed to be sure she was understanding correctly.

"No."

"Then why that night?"

Gabby thought a moment. "Well, I was wanting to forget my depression and my guilt," she confessed, but I never would have drunk so much if…" She stopped abruptly.

"If what?"

"If Larry hadn't kept encouraging me to drink more wine. It didn't seem like him. I mean, he always drinks in moderation and looks down on those who can't do the same." Gabby stopped again. Mary was looking at her very strangely.

"You mean that he did this deliberately, so he could get you pregnant?"

"Yes, Aunt Mary," Gabby replied quietly. "I mean just that. He must have figured that if a baby came along, then I'd be bound to him, maybe forever!"

In reply, Mary knelt down by her niece's bed and brought everything to their Heavenly Father. When she was finished, Gabby knew God had answered, and as her aunt had said, He would work good out of this mess in His time and in His own way.

The next morning Larry came again and was as charming and persuasive as ever. Mary was afraid to leave Gabby alone with him, but her niece had smiled and said softly that she would be all right. God was right beside her now.

Mary never knew exactly all that passed between her niece and Larry Porter that Sunday morning. She only knew that it was noon before Larry left, and by the way he slammed the front door shut, she gathered that the outcome of his visit had not been at all to his liking.

She found her niece, sitting in the recliner, tears rolling down her cheeks, but a peace on her expressive features that Mary had never seen there before.

"It's all settled, Aunt," Gabby said softly. "We covered a lot of ground," she went on. "I faced him with what I told you last night and he admitted that he had wanted a baby to bind me to him. But it was my newfound love for Christ that really got under his skin. He tries to hide it and says that he will be tolerant and all that. But the more we talked, the more convinced I became that the Bible is right. "How can two walk together except they be agreed?" I know I haven't heard the last of Larry. He made that clear. He might, he said, be forced to give me up, but he was the father of the child, and that was something he would never let me forget."

Gabby was right. She had not heard the last of Larry Porter. A week passed, and then a letter arrived in the mail. In it, Larry said how sorry he was that Gabby had decided as she had, but that he had finally come to terms with her decision. Gabby breathed a sigh of relief, but then caught her breath as she read on. "But the baby's a different matter. I will *not* relinquish my rights to the child, and as a father, I will never cease to exert my influence on him or her as long as I live."

"Read that," the girl muttered, handing Mary the letter. It took her aunt only a moment to scan the page in front of her. Her face darkened. Then she turned the page.

"I don't think you've read to the end, dear," she said gently.

"Read it aloud, please."

"However," Mary's clear voice began, "I don't want to be unreasonable. As I'm not much good with babies, I won't insist on my rights till the child is older—say three or four years old? Once the baby is born, I'll see that some legal settlement is drawn up. I'll do it before you make off for Romania or wherever you intend to go. I'm going to insist legally on eventually having the child as much as the law will allow me. Remember that in three or four years' time, I haven't decided exactly how long yet, I will insist on you living where I can have visitation rights. I know that you could just disappear somewhere if I let you go out of my sight now. But I trust you, Gabby. I know you are a fair and just sort of person and won't deny me what I've every right to have. And, of course, once we draw up the settlement, I'll send child support every month. You may not want to receive it. Well, that's up to you. And you might as well take it, because whether you do or not, won't alter in the slightest my determination to be as much of a father as I possibly can to our child. I will keep a copy of each check, so no one will be able to say I haven't tried to send you support."

Gabby had looked up as her aunt was reading, a new hope dawning in her face. "There are just a few lines more," Mary told her. "Just hold up a bit longer, dear."

Mary cleared her throat as she started again: "I'm sorry that it has to be like this. We could have been married and together given the child a good home if you hadn't been so stubborn. Now you'll be a single mom. And I don't suppose any of your Christian guys will take a second look at you now. Maybe, just maybe, you'll come back to me in the end. You're too smart to swallow all this religious jargon forever.

"Bye, Gabriella. It's been great knowing you. And, believe it or not, I do love you, Larry."

"P.S. I do want to see the baby when he or she is born. And we'll decide together what we'll call the child."

"That guy thinks about everything," Mary said as she folded the letter and put it back in the envelope. "Better keep all your correspondence, Gabby. You might need to refer to it some day."

"I'm not taking a cent of his child support," Gabby said sticking her chin in the air.

"I'm not sure that's wise, dear."

"But with Aunt Lucy's money beginning to come next month I'll make out fine."

"We need legal help on all this, Gabby."

"Maybe," the girl conceded reluctantly. "Anyway, I'll have to give up college, of course. I'm not putting the baby in day care, that's for sure." Gabby paused and her face brightened. "A lot can happen in three or four years, Aunt. I can take the child to Romania away from Larry at least for a while and from the Velvet Curtain. And," Gabby's eyes shone as she spoke, "I'll have that time to train my baby. I don't believe Larry's influence is so strong that it can undo mine so easily or quickly."

Gabby's eyes were shining as she spoke. Motherhood was already softening her features and making her beautiful, Mary thought. "Yes, a lot can happen, Gabby," she said softly. "And you may be married to a good man by the time Larry comes on the scene again."

The girl tossed back her hair as she rose from her seat. "And make this 'good man' have to deal with Larry all our married lives? No, Aunt, Larry's right of course; no decent Christian guy will look at me now."

"Don't you think Len Atwood's actions have shown what a young man given to God can do, Gabby?"

"But that's quite different. Esther was deformed in body but not in soul."

"And neither are you, dear," Mary reassured her as she took her in her arms. Gabby's whole frame shook as sobs racked her body. "You've been transformed. God has plunged your sins in the sea of His forgetfulness as the Bible tells us."

"God may have done that, Aunt, but it's hard for us humans to do it."

"I know," Mary said softly as she stroked Gabby's thick wavy locks. She was only too aware of the tragedy of Gabby's situation. "But the closer we are to God, the easier it is to forget a person's past. But come, we've talked enough for one day. That baby of yours needs nourishment. Now drink this glass of milk while we discuss some practical plans."

"Such as?" Gabby asked mechanically.

"Well, you'll have to take time off from college, won't you?"

"Yes. I'm stopping at Christmas."

"And the baby's due the end of April?"

"Yes."

"I also got a surprise letter in the mail today," Mary told her niece with a smile. She reached into her pocket and pulled out an envelope. Then, she drew out a piece of paper, unfolded it and held up a check. "Look at that!" Mary told her.

Gabby bent forward and examined the figures written on the check. "Two hundred thousand dollars!" she gasped.

"John has sent my part of our settlement at last," Mary breathed. "And he's been generous. They've been prospering these years, so he said this is only what I'm due with a bit of interest thrown in."

"Wonderful, Aunt Mary! That means you can buy a house."

"Maybe, or maybe not, Gabby."

Her niece looked up wonderingly into her aunt's face. Mary looked radiant. "This money will come in so handy, Gabby," she said stooping to kiss the girl's upturned face, "when I go to Romania with you."

Gabby nearly fell off her chair. "But what about Rachel and Ramona?" she stammered.

"Ramona and Claude will be in Romania by then. As for Rachel, she doesn't need me right now like you do. And we can only stay in Romania a few years, right? I'll put some money by for the future when I come back here some day. So don't argue. You'll need a nursemaid for that child of yours. I'm teaching just one more semester."

"What will they do without you at the school? You've become Jeff Garnet's star teacher, Aunt Mary."

Mary blushed. "I've been there long enough, Gabby," she said quietly. "It's time for a change." Mary liked her principal and they had become good friends, but recently he had begun to expect more than ordinary friendship. There had been only one love in her life and besides, John hadn't been unfaithful to her while they were married. So scripturally, she wasn't sure she had the right to marry again.

Gabby wondered a little at her aunt's embarrassment but said nothing. She only knew that this gentle lady with the blonde hair and sky blue eyes was willing to change countries and careers, to say nothing of spending her well-deserved money, just to be sure that her flighty niece and her baby would have all the loving care and counsel they would need in the coming years.

Gabby rose and threw her arms round her aunt. They held each other close for a few moments, and then Mary gently disentangled herself. "Now drink up that milk, child," she commanded in a matter of fact tone. "Your baby will have to be a real strapper if he or she is going to gallivant half way round the world with the two of us."

Gabby took the glass in her hand and held it to her lips. "Three or four years, Aunt! We've got three or four years!"

"They'll be glorious years," repeated Mary, reaching over for a Kleenex as she spoke. "What you and I won't do with that child during those years is nobody's business."

"Not even Larry Porter's," Gabby muttered as she drained her glass.

# Chapter Thirty-Seven

## *Dr. Garrington's Prescription*

"Sit down, sit down," Dr. Garrington told Len as he shook his hand warmly. "Well, well, you're looking a bit under the weather, young man. Is your fiancée giving you a hard time?"

"Esther's a wonderful girl," Len replied, his eyes glistening a little as he spoke, "but she can be pretty demanding and, yes, I am a bit worn out. It seems as if she's not made much progress since she arrived at Rehab."

"That's true. Everyone at Cherry Grove is concerned about this, so as an old friend, I was asked to have a word with you."

"I'm glad, Dr. Garrington. What do you think is the reason for her lack of progress, and what can we do about it?"

The doctor could see that Len was desperately worried. That was good. It meant that his love hadn't worn off. He bent over his desk and looked into the young man's dark eyes. He thought he detected traces of tears there. "You want to know what the reason is?" he repeated slowly. "You are the reason!"

Len jumped up from his chair. "Me?" he almost shouted. "What on earth do you mean?" He was edgy these days.

The doctor rose and laid a comforting hand on his shoulder. "I simply mean that you aren't following the advice I gave you in this very office some months ago."

Len sat down again and put his head in his hands. "Remember I warned you not to spoil her?" Dr. Garrington went on in a gentler voice. "Well, that's exactly what you are doing, and it's keeping my patient from progressing. Now," he went on, not giving the young man opposite him a chance to protest, "I've got a prescription for her which you are to fill. Don't bother taking it to a pharmacy. They don't have the right medicine there, but you have it, inside of you. Now read it out to me to make sure you understand it."

Len took the piece of paper from the doctor's hand and began to read slowly and distinctly:
**Prescription to happiness and health for Esther Popescu**
1. Len is to find a job immediately at least fifty miles from Cherry Grove.
2. The lady who will eventually become Esther's home help once she is discharged, is to take Len's place while he is away.
3. Len is to visit Esther no more than once a week. Visits are to last no more than eight hours. He is to spend no nights in the nursing home unless a real crisis arises.
4. He is to find living accommodations near his work and fix it up for an invalid even though it may only be a temporary residence.
5. Len and Esther are to set their wedding date no later than three months from today i.e. on or before May 30th.

Len put down the paper in disgust. "You call this a prescription for health and happiness? It'll destroy our relationship, Dr. Garrington."

"OK, then give me your objections, one by one, Len," the doctor said calmly, folding his arms.

"Well, point number one is impossible."

"Why, can't you find a job? Have you tried?"

Len reddened. "Actually," he stammered, "I've a good job waiting but it's impossible."

"Where is the job and with whom?"

"It's in Lexington, in a church there. I'd be youth pastor and choir director."

"Well, sounds wonderful to me. What's wrong with the job? Aren't you qualified enough for it? Is it so poorly paid?"

Len's mouth twitched a little. "It's just my type of job and the pay isn't bad and actually, Hugh Gardner, the senior pastor, is a good friend of mine."

Dr. Garrington leaned back in his chair. "All objections to number one removed. Go on to the next."

"But wait, Dr. Garrington," Len objected. "It's in Lexington and…"

"Perfect. It's to be at least fifty miles from Knoxville, so it fits the bill."

"But I can't be that far away from Esther."

"You *must* be that far away from Esther," the doctor countered sternly. "You're with her far too much. You need to treat her more normally. She has to get used to someone else taking care of her at least part of the time. Now lets move on."

"But," Len's voice was tense, "sometimes I have to sing to her at night to soothe her. No one else would do that, would they?"

"The girl's taking advantage of you and you can't see it!" Dr. Garrington purposely avoided Len's eyes as he said this. "Go away for a week and see what happens. Then come back and renew your objections if you still have them. So we've covered number three. Now for the next."

"Well, that'd be no problem. My friend says there's a house waiting for me."

"Great. Now for the last one. This should be the easiest of all to two young lovers waiting to be united."

Dr. Garrington looked closely at Len as he said these words. He noticed the young man's face had clouded and he was biting his lip. "Well?" he persisted.

"Esther's not ready for marriage yet. She insists that she have plastic surgery first."

"And what do you think?"

"I'd marry her tomorrow, just like she is. She's grown beautiful to me." Len's eyes were dreamy as he spoke.

The doctor nodded. "Exactly as I thought. It's Esther who's stalling. Doesn't she love you?"

Len flushed angrily. "She dotes on me, Dr. Garrington."

"Then she'll marry you as soon as you wish."

"But, you don't understand! It's not as simple as you're making it out to be."

Dr. Garrington got up from his chair and placed his hand on the young man's shoulder. "You've got to realize, Len, that Esther's afraid of marriage. She's afraid she will disappoint you. And as long as she has you all the time, she's quite content. She's been nearly eight months now inside an institution. She can't face life outside. That's quite normal. You've got to make her want to get married soon. So absent yourself. And be firm—very! If you are, you'll see that she'll begin to make quick progress all of a sudden."

A week later, Len headed for Lexington, leaving behind a very tearful Esther. The past seven days had been like a nightmare. As he had anticipated, Esther had fought every step of the way and had even reverted to her old refrain, "I want to die." But he had stood his ground.

For the next few days, he called her daily from his little house in Lexington, and every day she had threatened to break off the engagement if he didn't come back immediately.

"You don't love me," she pouted. "You want a break from me. That's all!" And every night for that first week, Len cried himself to sleep. Esther was refusing to eat, to sleep, and to take her therapy. He knew he had only one course of action left to him.

One day when she began the old refrain, he grabbed the receiver with both hands and shouted, "Stop it, you foolish girl. If you don't eat your meal tonight, or get a few hours sleep, or do your therapy tomorrow, I'm not coming to see you this week at all."

Esther did not believe him, so that week, Len refused to take the three hour trip to Knoxville to see his fiancée. She had taken off her ring and put it in the drawer, and refused to speak to him that evening. But the next day, she ate a decent meal for the first time in days, took her therapy, and that night, slept for hours on end.

The next Saturday, Len spent the day with his beloved girl. Then came another crisis. Len insisted on setting the date for their wedding, three months later. This meant she would have to complete her course of therapy by that time if she were to be discharged from the center. Esther refused. She couldn't make quicker progress than she was making, she protested, and she must have plastic surgery first. And so it went on.

Half choked with tears, Len told her it was now or never. They would have a quiet wedding with just a few family members and close friends present. There would be no photographer or fancy reception. And finally, three weeks after Len had moved to Lexington, Esther gave in.

After that, even Dr. Garrington was amazed at the patient's progress. Every second weekend, Len would take her to Tiny Gap. Aunt Mary had fitted special invalid bars in the bathroom and in her own bedroom downstairs which she had temporarily vacated.

The first weekend wasn't easy. Jean, Esther's new helper, had gone along too. Esther's uncle had recommended her. She already knew Esther and had become very attached to the Popescu family. It wasn't long before she became very devoted to the girl she had once dubbed

"Miss Perfect," so much so that Len had even shown a little jealousy of Esther's dependence on her. It was obvious to everyone that she had indeed grown indispensable to them both.

"You'll have to get used to me being around, young man," Jean told Len grimly as they drove back to Rehab one Sunday evening.

Len grimaced. "Well, I'm determined to become such a good nurse that you won't always need to be around, Jean."

Esther smiled up at him. "But you're needed for different things," she whispered to her fiancé. "I'll want you to play and sing with me all day long you know, and bring me flowers, and kiss me of course so…"

Len put one finger to her lips. "You want me for your humble servant. Well," and his eyes grew so misty he could hardly see the sign for Knoxville looming ahead, "I'm your servant for ever, Queen Esther. I can't say 'humble servant' because you're always telling me what wonderful eyes I have, and hair, and smile and voice and…"

"I'll keep you two down to earth, don't you worry," came a voice from the back. "And heaven knows you'll sure need it. What with singing and playing and roses and poetry—life isn't all romance you know." Jean stopped short and gave a gasp. What had she said?

Len glanced into the rear vision mirror and saw the good lady was wiping her eyes and sniffing into her handkerchief. He then glanced at Esther, huddled in the front seat, propped up with pillows and looking very pale after her weekend jaunt. Her eyes were closed, and he wasn't even sure if she had heard Jean's comment. But after a moment or two, she caught his gaze and gave one of her smiles that always transformed her scarred face and made it truly beautiful once more.

"Not all romance?" she repeated, eyes dancing. "Well, maybe not quite. But if anyone can make it that way it's the charming Len Atwood. So yes, Jean, it's good we have you to keep our feet on earth though at this very moment I feel very nearly as if I'm in the seventh heaven." She thought she heard a decided sniff coming from the back seat. "You OK, Jean?" she asked, her own voice trembling a little as she spoke.

"OK? How can I be, when your young man is going nearly eighty miles an hour!"

"Sorry, Jean."

"Apology accepted. Now, will you two sing me a song, please?"

## Chapter Thirty-Eight

*Wedding of the Century!*

"You may now kiss the bride," Pastor Cripps told Len. The couple had taken their vows, and everyone present thought that the words they were repeating seemed to have special meaning that day.

Margaret, who was the maid of honor, turned the wheelchair round so that the bride faced the groom. Esther had dreaded this moment. Len had told her that he would either kiss her through her veil, for it was rather thin, or they could omit this part of the procedure. But she had replied softly that they had to begin marriage the way they meant to continue it—in truth and honesty. "You have a scarred bride," she had said with a slight sob, "and neither you nor I can hide that fact from ourselves or from our friends."

So now, as Len stooped over her, she put up a small gloved hand and slowly drew aside her veil. Long and lovingly, the groom gazed into the bride's eyes before he implanted a kiss right on the ugly scar that ran down her right cheek. There was scarcely a dry eye in the church as Keith Cripps stepped forward and said in his strident voice, "Ladies and Gentlemen, I present to you, Mr. and Mrs. Len Atwood!"

The guests erupted into cheers. Dr. Garrington turned to Nurse Gadger and muttered thickly, "I told you it would be the wedding of the century."

Esther had not wanted an official photographer present, but had given permission for friends to bring along their cameras. "Keep everything low-keyed," Mary had begged Hugh. "Esther is still very weak." Yes, it was low-keyed all right, Ron thought to himself, as he followed the others out into the May sunshine. He couldn't help comparing the event to the lavish wedding he had planned those four long years ago.

Ron had surprised everyone by accepting the invitation to the wedding. "I have to get on with my life and this is one way back to normalcy," he had told John Popescu, as they drove to Lexington that afternoon, but as he stood in the line waiting to greet the newly weds, his heart was thumping almost uncontrollably. Gabby, watching him, thought that maybe he had made a big mistake to try this. And, she sincerely hoped that he wouldn't upset Esther by his presence.

"Congratulations!" Ron found himself saying almost mechanically to his cousin as he held out his hand.

"Thanks, Ron. It means a lot to have you here."

Then Ron approached the wheelchair. Esther had lifted her veil, much to her husband's surprise. He knew what that was costing her, especially now, as his cousin reached down and took her hand.

"Congratulations, Esther!" Ron repeated. "I'm very happy for you both."

Mary had made her a simple but elegant white dress and a circlet of roses nestled in her thick, glossy black curls now almost reaching her shoulders. Ron saw in an instant what a long way she had come in the past nine months, but he saw, too, that the girl in the wheelchair was a very different Esther Popescu from the one who had graced Ramona's wedding two years previous.

"I'm glad you came, Ron. It means a lot to both of us," the new bride told him. Ron noted that her voice had not changed one iota, or her smile, or her large dark eyes.

"I had to keep an eye on my cousin here," Ron joked. "Blessings on you, Len," he told him with a slight catch in his voice. "And on you, Esther," he turned again to the girl in the wheelchair.

Len was about to say something, but Ron had vanished. He looked down at his wife, wondering if the emotion of meeting his cousin had been too much for her. She smiled up into his face. Then she reached over and squeezed his hand reassuringly. "It's all right," she said softly. "I just hope that one day your cousin may be as happy as we are today. He deserves to be."

"Yes, he does," her husband replied. "But you're tired out. It's time to go home now. Ready?"

"More than ready!" Esther assured him with a radiant smile.

Gabby watched the groom as he hovered over his bride. It was so beautiful. Sure, it wasn't the stunning wedding she had thought her beautiful sister would have, but Gabby felt very grateful to God that Saturday afternoon. She had needed Him those last six months; it had been hard to cope with stares and raised eyebrows. Her family had been very supportive, but she could never forget that she had disappointed them terribly.

She heard a faint cry from the crib by her side and turned in her seat. Her son had wakened and would need feeding soon. She pulled back the blanket.

"David's awake, Gabby?" Mary asked, as she came up to where her niece was sitting. Gabby had refused to be an attendant, and though Esther was disappointed, she understood her sister's feelings.

"He's grown a lot in a month," Mary murmured, looking down at the bundle in Gabby's arms.

"Yes, hasn't he!" Gabby said proudly. Just four weeks before, she had given birth to a nine pound baby boy. Larry had visited the hospital just after the birth and had seemed very pleased with the newborn. They had decided to call him David. Larry had tried to make up to Gabby. He brought her flowers and taking her hand in his, he had murmured, "I miss you still, Gabriella," as he stooped to kiss her cheek.

"Even with Charlene to keep you company?" she had asked sweetly, the phone conversation of two days previous still ringing in her ears.

"Larry's coming up to see the baby," Sally had told her. "Maybe it would help you to handle him better if you knew that he has his blonde Charlene with him in the basement most nights now." Gabby had been angry and glad at the same time—angry that a guy could have so little principle and glad because it made it easier for her to feel she had no obligation to him whatsoever, except, of course as her child's father, and that, she thought with a pang, was obligation enough.

"What a fine baby, Gabby!" These words jolted her back to the present in an instant. The moment she had dreaded had arrived. She had not seen Aaron Gardner since Christmas, when no one except her immediate family had known of her pregnancy.

"He certainly is!" Mary agreed, coming to Gabby's rescue.

"He's got your eyes," Aaron said, stooping over the baby and taking its small fingers in his.

Gabby nodded. Yes, he had her eyes, but she remembered the nurse's comment in the hospital when Larry had first taken the baby in his arms. "He's the image of his father!" she had exclaimed. Larry had given a smug smile when he had heard those words and muttered as if to himself, though Gabby had heard every word, "I wonder whether the Porter genes will predominate or the Popescu? Maybe it won't matter, and then again, maybe it just might make a difference to the way things work out. Preacher? Politician? Playboy? There'll be a lot of options."

Aaron saw that Gabby was miles away. "I hear you and Mary are going to Romania soon," he remarked, thinking it best to change the subject. He felt very awkward in Gabby's presence now.

"Yes. We're leaving next month," Gabby told him with a smile that lit up her face and reminded him more of the girl he had known that summer in Indianapolis.

"I'll be over there, too," he told her. "Maybe we'll meet."

"Maybe," Gabby answered, keeping her eyes on the baby in her arms. "I believe you've made some friends in my old church in Ploieşti." Her voice had just a touch of sarcasm in it.

Aaron reddened a little; then he squared his shoulders. "Yes, I have actually," he said rather coolly. "I write to Lena Colescu. I believe she's an old friend of yours."

Gabby's face darkened slightly. "Well, I went to school with her so I know her pretty well."

Aaron raised his eyebrows. He could see that Gabby did not consider Lena as a close friend and he was right. If Hugh Gardner's grandson had to choose a Romanian girl, and after all, Aaron was partly Romanian himself, then Gabby wished he had chosen someone other than Lena. The two girls had never gotten on well. They had seemed opposites in every sense of the word. She wondered what Aaron had seen in her, apart from her beauty, of course. But then, she remembered that men, even Christian men like Aaron, were drawn like bees to a flower by a girl's smooth skin, rosy lips, and slim figure. And Lena was a beauty, there was no denying the fact. She and Esther had been considered the most attractive girls in the whole church.

Just then it was announced that the bride and groom were leaving. Aaron gave Gabby and the baby one last look as he turned away. They made a picture—Gabby slim and frail in her long, pale green gown, her thick, light brown hair held back loosely in a bow to match her dress, smiling down at the tiny infant in her arms, his eyes fixed on her face and one tiny finger entwined round his mother's finger, the finger that should have worn a ring. Aaron's eyes met hers for one brief moment, but the girl looked quickly away.

"Why does she avoid me like that?" he muttered, as he followed the bridal pair outside. "It must be that I'm just not her type." Then a vision of his Lena rose before him, and he gave a smile. When he married, it would be an innocent girl, pure as a lily and sweet as an angel, with long dark hair, olive skin, and large, dark, luminous eyes.

Len had rented a special van for the weekend to accommodate his bride. As he wheeled Esther up the ramp and closed the door, a cheer went up from their friends watching on the sidewalk. Len got behind the driver's wheel and waved goodbye.

"God bless them both," Jean said fervently.

"Amen," said a voice at her elbow. She glanced up. It was Ron Atwood. She put her hand on his arm. "You're a brave man to come here, Ron," she told him. "Never you mind! One day I'll be saying 'Amen' at your wedding. I'm expecting an invitation, you know."

Ron laughed nervously. "Not much likelihood of that for a good long while at least, Jean."

"No? Well, just remember that there are a lot of wonderful young women out there." She saw Ron's face and added wisely, "Oh I know what you're going to say, but I think you can't see the forest for the trees?"

"What?"

"Oh, never mind. You'd think me plain crazy if I explained what I meant." The van had turned the corner now and the crowd was dispersing. "It's just that you need to remember that sometimes the best flowers grow in clumps. Where you found one, look for another."

Ron went to answer, but Jean had gone. He was still thinking about her words as he made for his car a few moments later. "For a long, long time," he murmured to himself as he turned on his ignition, "I'm not going to think of any woman. I'm going to get to know the God I've so neglected and give Him all my heart."

Meanwhile, the bridal van had drawn up in front of 50 Ash Ave. Esther watched as Len went up the short path to the front door and put the key in the lock. She still couldn't believe she was married.

"Ready, Mrs. Atwood?" he asked, as he came back to the van. She held out her hands. He lifted her tenderly and carried her towards the house. "Happy?" he whispered.

"Terrified," she whispered back. But she was smiling through her tears.

"No more than I am."

"You're not afraid of anything, Len Atwood."

"No? Then feel my heart. See how it's thumping?" Esther put her small white hand to Len's chest. He held her close.

"For better or for worse," he murmured.

"In sickness or in health," Esther's voice was trembling.

"Till death do us part," they both said spontaneously.

"Well, here goes," Len told her as he stepped over the threshold. Esther gasped as she glanced around the room. Loving hands had been very busy, that was obvious.

"It's wonderful, Len," she gasped, "and it's our very first home!"

"Our very first," he repeated as he laid her gently on the sofa. "Now, let's dedicate our lives together. Our marriage will be full of music," Len said softly as he opened the lid of the grand piano which nearly filled the little living room. "So let's start it with a song."

"The piano's beautiful!" Esther exclaimed.

"Yes. It's my mother's. Now," and he ran his fingers softly over the keys, "what shall I play?"

"*Numai Harul.*"

"I can't sing it right."

"But I can. You play; I'll sing. Lift me up a little Len, please." He came over to the sofa and propped her up with pillows. Then he went back to the piano.

Len thought Esther had never sung as beautifully as she did that evening. And when she had finished, he came over to the sofa and knelt down.

"Pray, please, Len. Pray for our marriage."

Len reached for her small, delicate hand and took it in his. "Dear God," he began huskily, "Esther and I are beginning a new life. Please," his voice choked with emotion. Esther patted his hand encouragingly as he went on, "Please bless our lives together. It's going to be 'only by grace' all the way." He paused again, and this time his wife took up where he had left off: "Yes, Lord, I especially need your grace to wash away all the bitterness, to give me patience, to make me a wife that Len can live with. And," she added, and here Len couldn't help opening his eyes. Esther's face was transformed. Yes, the scar was still there, and the pallor, and the weakness, but there was that angelic beauty there once more, and peace. "And," she was concluding, "please show us how to keep safe from the Velvet Curtain. Amen."

"Amen," Len echoed as he gave his wife a long kiss.

"Where's Jean?" Esther murmured.

"Of all questions!" Len retorted, pretending to be annoyed. "I've given her a week off, of course."

"But how will you manage? I mean…"

"*Numai Harul*, Esther, isn't it?"

His wife smiled contentedly as she leaned back on the cushions and closed her eyes. "Yes," she replied and her voice was low and tremulous, "It's *Numai Harul* all the way."